D0947462

OPEN CITY

OPEN CITY

Seven Writers in Postwar Rome

Ignazio Silone ✦ Giorgio Bassani
Alberto Moravia ✦ Elsa Morante
Natalia Ginzburg ✦ Carlo Levi
Carlo Emilio Gadda

EDITED WITH AN INTRODUCTION BY

WILLIAM WEAVER

WITH THE EDITORIAL ASSISTANCE OF

KRISTINA OLSON

STEERFORTH ITALIA
AN IMPRINT OF STEERFORTH PRESS · SOUTH ROYALTON, VERMONT

ATHENS REGIONAL LIBRARY
2025 BAXTER STREET
ATHENS, GA 30606

Introduction copyright © 1999 by William Weaver

ALL RIGHTS RESERVED

For information about permission to
reproduce selections from this book, write to:
Steerforth Press, P.O. Box 70,
South Royalton, Vermont 05068

"The Nameless One," from *The House of Liars* by Elsa Morante, translated by Adrienne Foulke with the editorial assistance of Andrew Chiappe. First published in the United States in 1951 by Harcourt, Brace and Company, Inc.

Excerpt from *Bread and Wine* by Ignazio Silone, translated by Eric Mosbacher, translation copyright © 1986 Darina Silone, English translation.
Used by permission of Dutton Signet, a division of Penguin Putnam, Inc.

"Valentino," by Natalia Ginzburg: Copyright © 1951 by
Guilio Einaudi editori s.p.a. Translation copyright © 1987 by Avril Bardoni
First published in the United States in 1988 by Seaver Books, New York, NY.

"Agostino," from *Two Adolescents* by Alberto Moravia, translated by Beryl de Zoete. Copyright © 1950 by Valentino Bompiani & Co., S.A. First published in the United states by Farrar, Straus and Company in 1950.

Excerpt from *That Awful Mess on Via Merulana* by Carlo Emilio Gadda, translated by William Weaver, English translation copyright © 1965 by George Braziller, Inc., reprinted by permission of George Braziller, Inc.

Excerpt from *The Garden of the Finzi-Continis* by Giorgio Bassani, copyright © 1962 by Giulio Einaudi editore s.p.a., English translation by William Weaver, copyright © 1977 by Harcourt Brace & Company, reprinted by permission of Harcourt Brace & Company.

Excerpt from *The Watch* by Carlo Levi. Translation copyright © 1951 by Marianne Ceconi and John Farrar. Translation copyright renewed © 1979 by Margaret Farrar. Reprinted by permission of Farrar, Straus & Giroux, Inc.

Library of Congress Cataloging-in-Publication Data

Open city: seven writers in postwar Rome / Ignazio Silone . . . [et al.] ;
edited with an introduction by William Weaver,
with the editorial assistance of Kristina Olson.
p. cm.
Originally published in Italian
The nameless one, from House of liars / Elsa Morante —
from Bread and wine / Ignazio Silone — Valentino / Natalia Ginzburg —
Agostino / Alberto Moravia — from That awful mess on Via
Merulana / Carlo Emilio Gadda — from The garden of Finzi-Continis /
Giorgio Bassani — from The watch / Carlo Levi.
ISBN 1-883642-82-5 (alk. paper)
1. Italian fiction—20th century—Translations into English. 2. World War, 1935–1945—Fiction. I. Silone, Ignazio, 1900—1978. II. Weaver, William, 1923– . Olson, Kristina.
PQ4257.E5064 1999
853'.91408—dc21 99-15666
CIP

Manufactured in the United States of America

SECOND PRINTING

To three friends who have enriched my life after Rome:
Andrew Porter, Umberto Eco, and Leon Botstein.

TABLE OF CONTENTS

Introduction

THIS ANTHOLOGY TAKES ITS TITLE from the great film of Roberto Rossellini, originally called *Roma città aperta*, which was shot in the Italian capital within months of that city's liberation, despite every sort of difficulty: economic, bureaucratic, temperamental. The result, a triumph of artistry and determination, was an immediate, world-wide success, and a historic achievement for Italian culture.

For two decades before the making of that movie, Italy had been a Fascist country, and while its artists — film-makers, writers, painters, and musicians — continued to produce, their product appeared in the shadow of the regime, which, along with its other bad qualities, was also xenophobic. In effect, creative Italy had, for a generation, been cut off from the rest of the world.

From the moment Rossellini's film opened in New York, at a little movie-house near Times Square, it caused excitement, sparked discussion, and quickly created a cult following. I saw the film half-a-dozen times, usually taking friends along to admire it with me. For us it was not just a movie, it was convincing evidence that the Italian spirit — the country's vital creativity — was once more ablaze. The movies that soon followed — Rossellini's *Paisan*, De Sica's *Shoeshine* and *Bicycle Thief* — gloriously confirmed this first impression.

Soon afterwards, there was further testimony to Italian vitality in other fields: translations of Carlo Levi's moving autobiographical narrative, *Christ Stopped at Eboli*, and Alberto Moravia's *The Woman of Rome* introduced English-language readers to contemporary Italian literature, brilliantly proving that Fascism had been unable to keep great writers from writing. Exhibitions presented the new painters and sculptors, and also — memorably — the new Italian industrial designers. The sleek Olivetti Lettera 22 was proudly, and rightfully, displayed at the Museum of Modern Art.

Now, half a century later, that thrilling postwar explosion of the Italian genius has inevitably been muted by time and by subsequent Italian excitements, from Fellini to Eco. But the validity of that first, postwar discovery is beyond question; and this anthology hopes to recapture some of the varied, urgent spirit of that time. This is very much a personal selection, for it derives from my own experience as a wide-eyed witness.

In the late winter of 1944 I drove an ambulance in Southern Italy. For the most part I traveled in a limited area between Naples and Monte Cassino, along bumpy, pocked dirt roads, through sodden, depressed little towns, past makeshift army field stations or British-occupied Italian hospitals. As many veterans have pointed out, war may be hell, but it is more often boring.

I was frustrated. I had been in Italy for more than six months, and the only cities I had seen were Naples and (a fleeting glimpse) Salerno. The weather was vile. The front line — though "line" gives a misleading sense of precision — seemed eternal, set in cement. What's the point of a war if you don't capture anything?

The roads all looked alike, and I established few landmarks — a shattered tree, a stable with a stenciled, now-ridiculous Fascist slogan — but there was one recognizable intersection that I slowly came to hate. It was a T-junction where, coming from the east, I was stopped by two arrows pointing in opposite directions, one north and one south. The first said ROMA; the second said NAPOLI. I was not being presented with a choice, for I could turn only southwards. Rome and much of the countryside between me and it were still firmly in German hands. The northern arrow seemed put there to taunt me. Me, personally, not the whole Allied forces, though they were in my same position.

Rome, that unattainable Rome, became a legend, the stuff of my constant, frustrated daydreams. Unlike Naples, Rome — the imagined Rome of my obsession — was tidy, clean, brightly-lighted, sunny; there were bookshops with books in English, newspapers, theater, music. There were dinner-parties and smart cafés — there was the Europe I had yearned all my brief life to visit. It was the supreme, evil jest that now I was actually there, in Europe, and I spent a lot of my time hating it. Rome, Rome. . .if only. . .

I never got there. Not that time, anyway. In May — only weeks before the Allied break-through and the liberation of Rome — I was sent back to the States. But before I left Naples, many things had happened to change my attitude, to dispel my gloom, to feed my lifelong passion for Europe. By a lucky chance, I met a group of young Neapolitans my age, who shared my interests and my ambitions. My first Italian friends, they introduced me to their favorite writers, to their city, to their lives. The dream of Rome remained with me, but became less troubled. I began to discover the city around me, elusive, deceptive, rewarding Naples; I began to love its very untidiness, the disorder that was really a healthy contempt for order. That spring of 1944, when I finally boarded the Liberty ship that would take me back to the United States, I could not entirely share the raucous bliss of my American companions.

And the unfulfilled yearning for Rome remained with me through the next few years, during which I took my degree, got a job, saved my money, and finally had accumulated enough, I calculated, to support me for one year abroad.

I sailed, now a pampered passenger, on the Vulcania. Even in cabin class (my parents, bravely suppressing their fond, xenophobe possessiveness, had generously stumped up the fare), vestiges of pre-war luxury evoked the sophisticated travel of the golden days. Then, after a restorative stay in Naples, in the affectionate comfort and baroque decay of Palazzo Donn'Anna, I set off for Rome, the fabled, the perfect, the ideal answer to every dream.

It was raining when we arrived, and the rickety bus finally emptied us — me and my Neapolitan friend Raffaele — into a small, dark square near the Borsa. This was Rome? True, there were some scarred ancient columns along a street-front, but they were grimy with soot. I had imagined a city of snowy white, elegant classical forms, resembling perhaps the columned Citizens National Bank in Front Royal, Virginia, my childhood paragon of fine architecture. Rome, I saw, in shock, was different from the black-and-white Alinari photographs of art history courses; it was orange, yellow; rust-color; there were even a few neon signs blinking on baroque facades in the early winter dusk.

From the Piazza di Pietra we went to our pensione. Again, with reminiscences of E.M. Forster in my head, I imagined a place of relaxed conversation and, of course, a room with a view. The Pensione Sieben had once been a solid, spacious, middle-class apartment. Now the Siebens (he was an elderly German, a retired translator) lived in the kitchen and in a crammed bedroom next to it. An old lady, Herr Sieben's mother, occupied the next bedroom. In the front of the apartment, my friends Peppino and Mario shared the former salon, a once-splendid room now almost empty save for two cots, a desk, and a wood-burning stove, jutting from what was a formerly decorative fireplace.

Across the vestibule was a much smaller room, where I was to sleep. It also contained two cots, but the few square meters could not accommodate even a small desk. The cot farther from the door was occupied by Achille, another Neapolitan friend, an actor just getting his first small roles in a repertory company specializing in new Italian plays (they were not usually very good, so the bill changed often; Achille was building a large, useless repertory). Until the previous week, my cot had been occupied by yet another Neapolitan, Francesco Rosi, an aspiring film-maker; now he had landed an enviable job, as assistant to Luchino Visconti, and had just gone off to Sicily to join the director in working on what was to prove an enduring masterpiece, *La terra trema*. The room's single window gave on an air-shaft and a blank wall.

Achille was a trying roommate. Unless he had a rehearsal, he slept until midday (so I had to dress in the dark). Afternoons, he received his lovely and long-suffering girl-friend, and I was expected to go out for an extended walk — it was a rainy winter — and stay out until dark. He was a hypochondriac, and when he discovered my super-giant family-size bottle of aspirin — calculated to last me for my whole Italian stay — he began happily popping pills; the aspirin level in the big jar descended at an alarming rate. He was also fascinated by my clothes, ordinary as they were, and constantly borrowed them, with or without asking me first. He particularly liked to wear them on stage; so I became used to seeing my Princeton sweatshirt or my favorite striped pyjamas turn up on a set representing an Italian living room.

After a few days in Rome, I dutifully made my way to the University, planning to enroll in some courses, to justify and, presumably, enrich my Italian stay. My first real tangle with Italian bureaucracy ensued: a nightmare of waiting in the wrong line, lacking this or that document, failing to understand angry, shouted directions from the grouchy staff behind the windows or the confusing attempts at help from equally beleaguered Italian students.

I gave up (two years later, thanks to a Fulbright, I actually enrolled at the University and attended a few classes), and determined to dedicate myself to my other Roman project: the novel I expected to write. Having published two stories in national magazines (*Harper's Bazaar* and *Mademoiselle*, which had published stories of Truman Capote and other rising stars), I — and my friends — assumed that a novel was the next step. There was just one difficulty: I had nothing I particularly wanted to write about. But I didn't let that stop me. Mornings, when Peppino had gone off to his job at the RAI, the Italian State Radio, and Mario to his classes at the Accademia di arte drammatica, I moved into the former salon, sat at their desk, opened my copious notebooks (a Gide fan, I could not contemplate writing a novel without keeping journals, *cahiers*), and tried to work. I had never been successfully self-critical. But even permissive me soon had to concede that the novel was a dud.

If the rain let up, I soon found an excuse to go out. The excuse was always the same: my determination to get to know Rome. It was not a matter of visiting churches, studying frescoes, deciphering inscriptions. I wanted to gulp down real Roman coffee in the morning, eat real Roman pasta at lunch, drink all the real Roman wine I could afford. I wanted to read the newspapers, see the movies and the plays, hear the music.

I was perfectly situated. Dreary as the Pensione Sieben looked at first, it turned out to be a hive of cultural, and social activity; a center of fun. The big salon of Peppino and Mario served as a gathering-place for a host of young people from the Accademia, writers from the RAI, and other newly-arrived Neapolitans aiming to break into film or journalism.

And I had a trump-card of my own. I was an American, and to the Italians — whatever their ages or degree of fame — that nationality inspired endless curiosity. For many I was the first American they had encountered, except perhaps for a stray GI a few years earlier. And so I was consulted as the expert on everything American: my opinion on William Wyler was seriously pondered. I was asked whether I would place Gershwin in the mainstream of white jazz or in the area of classical music (the question, for me, was unanswerable, as I knew far more about Puccini than about my popular compatriot). I was invited to contribute to nascent literary magazines, some of them born only to die after the first issue, which perhaps included my little piece on Karl Shapiro or John O'Hara.

Through a visiting American I met the Italian painter and writer Dario Cecchi, a few years my senior, scion of an Italian literary/artistic family with ramifications extending into every area of Italy's cultural life. Dario's father was the eminent and powerful critic Emilio Cecchi; his sister was Suso Cecchi d'Amico, the script-writer of Visconti and others, and her husband, Fedele d'Amico, was a brilliant, polemical music critic and polymath, eventually to become a treasured friend and colleague.

The chain of acquaintances grew, link by link, creating degrees not of separation but of connection. And some of these connections soon became hubs, branching off in one direction after another. It was Dario who took me first to meet Princess Marguerite Caetani. He told me little about her beyond the fact that she was American- born (a Chapin from Connecticut), a patron of the arts who had lived for many years in France, but had returned to Italy with her musician husband before the second world war and had remained in Rome. In Palazzo Caetani she edited an international literary review, *Botteghe Oscure*, after the name of the street where the Palazzo had stood for many centuries. The fact that Communist Party Headquarters now stood in that same street, making its name a synonym for the PCI, was a minor nuisance that the Principessa airily dismissed.

We stepped into the dark courtyard of the great, grim palace, took an elevator to the piano nobile, and were shown into a huge, high-ceilinged hall, hung with dusty portraits (I looked around for Boniface VIII, the Caetani pope pilloried by Dante, but I couldn't identify him): then Dario, who knew his way around the palace, led me to a modern corkscrew staircase in a corner of the room. We climbed it and, passing through a plain little door at its top, stepped into a large, but cozy, New England living room: sofas covered in beige monkscloth, low tables, a fire in the fireplace, French windows revealing a broad terrace beyond. A large tea-pot stood on one table, and plates of sandwiches circulated.

The Principessa, in heather tweeds, only a few wisps of her gray hair out of place (to hint at her artistic side?), welcomed me warmly. And the welcome was equally warm from other guests, all clearly frequenters of the house. They were not many, and I remember almost all of them, as they all became friends of mine very soon: Elena Croce, the daughter of the philosopher but with a lively mind of her own; Umberto Morra, an aristocratic anti-Fascist and old friend of Bernard Berenson; Ignazio Silone — whose works I had read in translation — with his beautiful, ebullient Irish wife Darina, whom I had already met for a fleeting moment. And Giorgio Bassani, titular editor of *Botteghe Oscure*, though Marguerite clearly made all the operative decisions, while encouraging Bassani to propose new writers, especially for the Italian section of the magazine. At that time, Bassani was known, if he was known at all, as a poet; he had just published the first of what were to become the now classic *Five Stories of Ferrara*.

After that first visit, I returned to Palazzo Caetani countless times, and each visit was memorable, especially those when I was alone with Marguerite, who soon discovered — and exploited — my boarding-school experience as a proofreader. The Italian printers, excellent artisans, inevitably made gibberish of some of the magazine's English and French texts, and complaining authors drove Marguerite to despair ("Alfred Chester called me this morning from Paris, he cried all last night because of the mistakes in his story.") My work was unpaid — and I put in long hours — but I had ample occasion to appreciate Marguerite's real generosity. Not only did she soon publish my work: she also invited me to any number of meals. Food at the Caetani table was plain, but as I lived from day to day, a steak gained was a steak earned.

And the company! For foreign literary visitors of a certain level, Palazzo Caetani was an obligatory stop. One week there would be a tea-party for "Cousin Tom" (known to me as T.S. Eliot), in Rome to give a reading at the British Council, but also to enjoy a honeymoon with his new wife Valerie. The great poet's radiant happiness was evident, irrepressible. For much of the party he and his wife sat side-by-side on one of Marguerite's comfortable low sofas, and he could not refrain from touching her, patting her hand, pressing her arm, like an enamored schoolboy. Standing not far away, I pointed out Eliot's enraptured behavior to Alberto Moravia. "Senile sexuality," the novelist commented tartly. I remembered this remark some decades later when Moravia himself, by then close to eighty, married Carmen Llera, forty-odd years his junior.

Between the world wars, Marguerite had lived much of the time in Paris, where her house just outside the city was also an intellectual gathering place (Berenson's letters tell of visits there from the Armistice meetings, which he was attending). So the Palazzo in Rome welcomed many French visitors, among them René Char, Francis Ponge, Henri Sauguet. And there were also musicians, partly because of Prince Roffredo's background as a composer (he was Liszt's godson and had known the Wagners); in the Caetani salon I first heard Gian Carlo Menotti and Tommy Schippers discuss a festival they were beginning to think about, a place for young artists in some Umbrian town, perhaps Todi, or perhaps Spoleto.

Umberto Morra, a Piedmontese count, whose family had been close to the royal family (Umberto's father, a general, had served as the Savoys' ambassador to the court of the Czar), lived in a single room in Rome, in the apartment of some old friends. But he led an intense social life, and he particularly enjoyed entertaining new arrivals to Rome, arranging introductions. Often he would invite a new acquaintance, with perhaps one or at most two old friends, to tea at Babington's tea rooms in Piazza di Spagna. The atmosphere at Babington's certainly belonged to another world, but what world was it? I suppose the unpretentious setting was meant to evoke pre-war England (pre-*first* war, that is), and the motherly old ladies with their starched frilly caps who brought the tea and scones and cake looked like Margaret Rutherford stand-ins, imported directly from some Staffordshire village. But then you realized they spoke little English, and that smattering came out with a thick Italian accent.

In any case, the tea was authentic and delicious, the scones came with homemade jams; and the company was always stimulating.

Whether at Babington or, for grander luncheons, at the Stanze dell'Eliseo, a quirkish private club, with Morra you were always sure to meet someone who was not just interesting but was actually a person you were eager to know: Jimmy Merrill was a Morra gift to me, and so — in Florence — was Bernard Berenson. Later, when Morra headed the Italian Institute in London, he introduced me to the great Maurice Bowra, to the equally legendary Judge Learned Hand. His was a mobile salon. When you came to know him really well, he would invite you for a weekend at his comfortable, slightly shabby villa in Tuscany (Moravia "stole" the villa to use as the setting of his novel *Conjugal Love*). Again the house party was always varied, relaxed, unexpected. Even the occasional bore — the garrulous widow of a distinguished anti-fascist friend, for example — was, somehow, a bore you were glad to meet.

Morra seemed to be a friend of every Italian I encountered. But I soon realized he was unusual, if not unique in his pan-amicability. By some of my new literary acquaintances, the Cecchi family was considered tainted. For, while never an aggressive Fascist, Cecchi had been something of a social and political opportunist, not above putting his pen to the regime's service, while not compromising his high literary standards or marring the beauty of his jeweled prose. Still, his name appeared on the scenario of the absurdly, blatantly racist film *Harlem*, and his biased book *America amara* was virtually a gift to the anti-USA dictatorship. So at the Cecchis', while you might meet important writers, including the art historian Cesare Brandi or the once-notorious, feminist poet Sibilla Aleramo, you would not find Silone or Moravia. Hence my young Neapolitan friends, and their Roman acquaintances, looked somewhat askance at my association with the Cecchis, though my friendship was with the Cecchi son and daughter rather than the writer himself.

When I first arrived in Italy, in the fall of 1943, I knew the name of only one living Italian writer: Ignazio Silone, and that name was one I had learned only a few months earlier. For my generation — I was born in July 1923 — my knowledge of Italian culture was, I should think, typical. Though a couple of Alberto Moravia's books had been translated before the war, they had not attracted much attention, had not established him as the literary leader he had long been in Italy. A few Americans perhaps knew of the poems of Montale and Ungaretti, but I was not one of them.

I had discovered Silone's works in the Western Desert, in Libya. Isolated with the other thirty-odd members of my company, idle, I spent all my time reading. But books were scarce, and so there was a constant trading. I even read *Winnie the Pooh* for the first time (my father's stern literary standards would not allow the coy Milne in our house, and, after reading him, I agreed with my father). Then a fellow-driver — I forget who it was — lent me the Penguin edition of *Fontamara*, the stark title printed on a white band between two orange ones; when I had read that, the same friend handed me the Harper first US edition of *Bread and Wine*. When I came across a copy of that same edition recently in the Bard College library, it was like running into a long-lost wartime buddy; I could almost feel grains of Libyan sand between the pages.

Silone represented much more than simply my introduction to contemporary Italian fiction; those first two novels of his served also as a political primer. Though I was involved in a great war against Fascism, I had only a vague notion of what the word meant. Silone's fiction led me beyond the headlines, newsreel parades and balcony histrionics to the human facts, the meaning of Fascism in terms of daily bread and loss of freedom.

In Rome, three years later, shortly before I met Silone at Palazzo Caetani, I met — for an unforgettable instant — his beautiful, captivating Irish wife Darina. I had had a drink at the Caffè Greco with Stephen Spender (whom I had met in New York through Chester Kallman and Auden — another of the radial paths of my cultural landscape). He was on his way to a dinner party at the nearby Palazzo Torlonia, at the residence of the Irish ambassador, the elegant poet Denis Devlin. I walked Stephen to the door of the Palazzo; as we were saying good night, a taxi squealed to a stop, and from it, in breathless haste, a tall, blonde Viking of a woman descended, her face half-covered by a light veil. I was introduced, and I heard her soft, melodious accent for the first of many times.

Of course, I was envious. I wished with all my heart that I had been invited to Denis Devlin's party, and I imagined all sorts of beautiful and brilliant guests, as I saw Stephen and Darina disappear inside the massive portal. A moment later, when I was alone in the Via Bocca di Leone, I grasped the irony of seeing a Silone enter the palace of the Torlonia family, the landlords of southern Italy, who are the ultimate villains of Silone's peasant world.

I met Darina soon again at Marguerite's, and at the same time I met Silone. At a first encounter, he was a forbidding presence, taciturn and — this was my impression — disapproving. This impression persisted after I had been invited to several dinners and parties at the Silone apartment, in an anonymous, outlying part of the city near Piazza Bologna. The foreign visitors who gravitated there were often different from the Botteghe Oscure salon. At the Silones, in addition to a small group of left-wing dissidents, among them Nicola Chiaramonte and his delightful American wife Miriam, you might encounter *Partisan Review* people, Philip Rahv, William Phillips or Dwight Macdonald, or (separately) Edmund Wilson or Mary McCarthy.

One day, after I had been there several times, never exchanging more than a few formal remarks with my host, Darina called with another dinner invitation. Unfortunately I was already engaged for that evening, and so expressed my regrets. "What a pity!" Darina exclaimed. "Silone always enjoys himself so much when you're here."

I was dumfounded. True, at the Silones', as elsewhere, I liked to talk (and also listen): I told stories, asked questions, ventured opinions, sometimes shaky ones. And then, more often than not, the next morning, if I didn't have an out-and-out hangover, I had the nagging suspicion that I had talked too much and maybe even made a fool of myself. Remembered, Silone's stern silence took on an accusatory quality. But now I could slough off those qualms, and speak to the admired writer more easily. At about this time I made another parallel discovery. Reading a book about anti-Fascists in exile, I found a reference to Silone's humor, which kept his companions' spirits up, making the table in some humble Swiss beer-hall rock with laughter.

Incredulous, I asked Morra about this Silone, so different from the one I knew. "Oh, yes," Umberto confirmed. "Silone has a wonderful, quick wit. He can be very funny indeed."

Eventually, I came to appreciate this side of him (I should have sensed it also from his novels, rich in sly irony). After some years of our acquaintance, he asked me to translate a book of his, an old work, *The School for Dictators*, written in exile and first published in 1938, in German. Darina, herself a first-rate translator, had been responsible for some English versions of his works; but for personal reasons about which she remained vague, she preferred to pass the assignment on to me.

I set to work happily, although the text — a Platonic dialogue on the subject of power, rule, authority — was not the sort of thing I had translated thus far. But both Darina and Silone were separately helpful. I went a number of times to the Piazza Bologna apartment and, over tea, discussed my problems. When I had almost finished a last revision, Darina had to go off to London, and I began to see Silone alone.

Often between a translator and the author a kind of subtle conflict can grow up. (In some cases, as with Italo Calvino, it was not all that subtle). That competitiveness did not develop with Silone, but, all the same, I was a bit pleased with myself when I uncovered a couple of minor factual errors in the Italian text (Hitler's birthplace was given as Brunau, which I corrected to Braunau). I was also smugly amused to discover that a book by Napoleon III, which Silone referred to as *Rêveries poetiques*, was, in reality, entitled *Rêveries politiques*, a more plausible but less entertaining title. I pointed out Silone's mistake tactfully; he thanked me for the information and, in an apologetic tone, he murmured. "You see, I didn't have any libraries at hand." Ashamed of myself, I realized he had written the book in exile, perhaps in the Davos sanatorium or even in prison, under conditions that other writers would consider heroic.

But that same evening, as we went out to dinner, I had a glimpse of Silone's humorous side; in fact, I provoked it, insisting that he be my guest. To convince him to accept my invitation, I used a Jesuitical argument, explaining that paying the bill would be an excellent spiritual exercise for me. In the past, I had always considered myself poor, but recently I had been awarded a Fulbright fellowship, so I should stop thinking of myself as needy. And anyway I wanted to repay — or, at least, make a gesture of gratitude — after months of Silone's hospitality.

"Ah, but paying would be a splendid spiritual exercise for me, too," Silone, said, immediately picking up the spirit of the discussion. And, as he really had been educated by Jesuits (I, by mere Franciscans), his arguments were much more dazzling and elaborate — and funny — than mine. And, to cap them, as we finished the meal, he added: "And besides, this is an Abruzzese restaurant; they'd never let a guest pay." Actually, I'm not even sure they let him pay. I didn't see a bill.

When I settled into the Pensione Sieben where I stayed most of the winter of '47-'48, Alberto Moravia and Elsa Morante had only recently moved nearby, into the apartment that was to be their home for the rest of their marriage (and Elsa's chief residence, after the separation, almost until her death). It was in Via dell'Oca, an oddly broad, but short street, running the two or three blocks from Piazza del Popolo to the embankment at the Tiber. Though they had been married for over five years (and had been together for some time before the marriage), Alberto and Elsa had never had a proper house of their own. Now thanks to Alberto's foreign royalties and the film work he continued to do, they were able to fit out the house comfortably, with many sofas and easy chairs in white or cream slipcovers, with paintings on the walls (at this time largely by Moravia's sister Adriana Pincherle, later by Elsa's tragic infatuation Bill Morrow), and with a varying number of Siamese cats, long ruled over by the imperious Gatto Tit.

For Elsa, who had grown up in grimly respectable poverty, the Via dell'Oca house represented luxury; and, to crown this elegance, she engaged a cook. Thus — probably for the first time in her life — she gave dinner parties. For the rest, Alberto and Elsa almost never ate alone, even in earlier times, when they went every evening to some trattoria. Then, if you called up during the day to ask Alberto for supper, his characteristic reply was "come by around eight and we'll go out somewhere."

Sometimes — but very rarely — I'd be able to go out to dinner with just Alberto and Elsa. More often, I would find other friends with them, or indeed I would find strangers, anybody who had called either him or her in the course of the day to ask what they were doing for dinner. When that evening's group had collected, there would be a discussion, sometimes heated, about where to go. La Campana? Too crowded. Trastevere? Too noisy. Another trattoria was regularly rejected because, according to Elsa, the proprietor treated his cat badly. Sometimes we would end up at La Carbonara, in Campo de' fiori, not because anyone was particularly fond of the place, but because there was always room. I remember those big impromptu dinners with mixed emotions. Moravia's circle of acquaintance included a few inevitable hangers-on, whom he treated, I felt, with more consideration than they deserved, especially since some of them — trying to assert a factitious independence — openly criticized him and belittled him. One particularly aggressive Communist art critic I found insufferable, and ill-luck sometimes placed me beside or opposite him at the long table, with Elsa and Moravia at separate, unbreachable distance from me.

But once in a while it would be just the three of us. Still, these more intimate nights were also fraught with risk. Speaking of Elsa once, some time after her death, Moravia — who continued to refer to her with affection and understanding long after their separation — said, "Elsa was profoundly *ingiusta*." "Unfair" is too mild a translation, and "unjust" sounds too juridical. What Moravia meant, I think, was "Elsa liked to deal low blows." And I have to agree with him. She could also be impulsive, and the blows could hit the innocent.

To make matters worse, Elsa — at least, in certain frequent moods — loved to quarrel, and to cast blame, almost always on Alberto: if the chosen restaurant happened to be closed, or the service was poor, or if a special dish was absent from that night's menu, the fault was somehow Alberto's. Elsa had a piercing voice that could cut, knife-like, through normal restaurant hum. Whether or not the deafness that later affected Alberto was already incipient in those days, he also tended to speak in a louder voice in restaurants. So their debates were, willy-nilly, overheard by fellow diners.

There is one restaurant in Rome — Romolo at Porta Settimiana — that I still enter with hesitation, though the embarrassing argument must have taken place fifty years ago. Unlikely as it now seems, the argument, as I recall, was about motherhood or perhaps about Southern Italian peasants. What I indelibly remember is Elsa's culminating retort: "Don't talk nonsense, Alberto, in the south peasant mothers masturbate their children to put them to sleep at night." The crucial verb was uttered in a shrill, loud cry, which seemed to echo interminably beneath the low vaults of the restaurant ceiling. The other diners had long since suspended their conversations in order to listen to ours. We ate the rest of our meal surrounded by silence and by the total attention of everyone in the place, customer or waiter or host. Only Elsa remained supremely unaffected.

Often I saw Alberto and Elsa separately, as did all their friends (for that matter, each also had separate friends, whom they saw on their own). It was easy to run into Alberto on the street, not only because Rome was small in those days and we lived in the same neighborhood, but also because Alberto was an indefatigable walker, his lame, rollicking gait recognizable blocks off. For a long period, when he was suffering from some form of sciatica, he took long, therapeutic walks for hours every afternoon on doctor's orders. When you encountered him, he would invariably ask you to accompany him for a while, as walking seemed to stimulate his conversation (not that it needed stimulation: it flowed naturally, with fascinating shifts and turns, unexpected aperçus).

In those immediate post-war years, Rome was a walker's paradise. There was barely any traffic, and the cluttering crowds of tourists were yet to return. At that time, American tourists were still afraid of drinking the water or of running out of toilet-paper.

Often, in the course of that first winter, when I went to see the Sistine ceiling or the Caravaggios in San Luigi dei Francesi, I would find myself totally alone.

Taking walks was also a recognized convivial activity. At lunchtime, on a fine day, a friend might call up and suggest a walk later in the afternoon, as he or she might invite you for tea or a cocktail. One particularly enjoyable walking companion was Elena Croce, whose quirkish conversation (never a received idea) and irreverent opinions made the walks such fun that often I remained unaware of the streets we passed, the monuments, the genre scenes that are still an integral part of Roman outdoor life.

For one season, while she was at the American Academy, I went on walks with Eleanor Clark. Either I would take a bus up to the Janiculum and we would stroll among Risorgimento memories, the places where Bixio and Manara fought, perhaps where Jessie White or Margaret Fuller tended the wounded. Or we would walk downhill, to follow the curving alleys of Trastevere. But these walks were never aimless, and our attention never flagged. Eleanor had a list of things to be seen that day, and she ticked off the palazzo or the church or the historic spot. Later, when I first read *Rome and a Villa*, I recognized some of the ticked-off places, now caught in a double light: the illumination of Eleanor's recorded perceptions and the warm recollection of sharing with her the external experience if not necessarily also her intellectual epiphany.

I don't remember ever sight-seeing with Elsa, though any reader of her novel *History* will realize that she knew her native city stone by stone. But, in the early years of our friendship, I remember many occasions where I saw her alone — or, rather, without Moravia. For a time, around 1950, I was lent an elegant apartment near Piazza di Spagna, and there I also could do some entertaining at last.

I quickly learned the protocol to adopt in inviting Elsa. The important thing NOT to do was issue a double invitation. You were never to say, "Could you and Alberto come — ?" Even the use of the plural *voi* was a grave infraction of Elsa's personal rules. Sometimes Elsa's reply would be a simple no. More often she would say curtly, "Ah, you want Alberto? Call him at —" And she would supply the number of his studio.

The proper course was to invite Elsa: Can you — *tu* — come for dinner on Thursday? Almost invariably Elsa would accept, and set a time. In later years, she would perhaps inform you of the restrictions of her diet, never the same on successive occasions. Then, when all was agreed, you could venture, in as offhand a tone as possible: "If Alberto's free, tell him to join us.' "I'll tell him," she would reply, audibly dubious. But then Alberto never failed to show up; or, if he really couldn't come, he would telephone separately and explain.

Elsa, socially, had a low boredom threshold. One evening, in my elegant borrowed apartment, she discovered a complete run of *Connaissance des Arts* in a living-room bookcase. For the entire evening, without a word to any of the other guests (or to me), she sat on the floor in a corner and, with almost scholarly attention, went through one number of the review after another, dutifully reading the texts as well as studying the illustrations.

But, on another occasion in the same apartment, when boredom threatened, she reacted in an entirely different way. She took charge of the guests — most of them old friends — and invented a series of guessing games, *bouts rimés*, the anti-social game of the tower, enjoying herself hugely but also inspiring the others. I had a moment of overweening pride when a verse of mine won her praise. There was this childish side of Elsa, rarely allowed to shine forth, yet irresistible when given free rein.

The child-Elsa could also be naughty; and like other naughty children, she liked to cause discomfiture. For this the tower game was ideal: the game consisted simply of obliging the player to imagine him (or her) self on a high tower with two people one of whom he had to push off. Elsa would insist on dreadful choices (herself? or Alberto?), always among people present at the table; and she would become truly angry at any waffling on the part of her victim.

At one of her dinners, she had invited Marco Visconti, a younger cousin of Luchino's, with his fiancée, the only other woman present, who was meeting Elsa for the first time. Wilfully, Elsa directed the conversation to sex and, specifically, to Lesbianism.

"I know, I know," she said, "some people say that I'm attracted to members of my own sex. Absolutely false. I do not like women. What's more, I don't like men who like women."

The three or four male guests exchanged impassive looks and tried hard not to glance at Moravia, the most impassive of all.

Elsa answered the unasked question. "Yes, even Alberto. Though I know he hasn't had any such experience. . . still he would have a strong tendency."

Moravia's blank astonishment made all of us laugh, and enabled someone to change the subject.

When I first met Elsa I knew her simply as Moravia's wife (fortunately she was unaware of this ignorance). Someone did tell me then, I believe, that she was herself a writer. But I hadn't read a word of hers. Then, during that first year in Rome, her great, vast first novel appeared: *Menzogna e sortilegio* (much later it came out in a heavily-cut English version, unhappily entitled *House of Liars*). I bought the thick Einaudi volume, but — as my Italian was still a work in progress — I set it aside, waiting until I could summon the nerve to tackle those densely printed pages.

Still, since it was much discussed at the Moravia dinner table, I felt it might be a good idea to let her know that I at least owned a copy. So one night I took it along to dinner and asked her to sign it for me. To be on the safe side — I knew her diabolical instinct for vulnerable spots — I confessed at once that I hadn't yet read it. And I braced myself for her ire. Of course, Elsa surprised me.

"Oh, how I envy you!" she said with immediate, genuine enthusiasm. "How I wish I could read my book with a fresh mind! What a wonderful experience you have in store for you! You're really lucky!"

Her love for her book was, in its way, also childish, innocent, pure and complete. Later, as I gradually learned the story of how that book was written, and how she risked her life to rescue the manuscript from Nazi-occupied Rome, I better understood the way *Menzogna e sortilegio* was her beloved first-born. True, she loved her other books possessively, too (creating problems for her translator, as I was to discover when she chose me to turn *La storia* into English); but *Menzogna e sortilegio* occupied a unique place in her life, and today, if I pick it up and leaf through it, I feel her passion — and sense of ownership — in its pages.

Moravia, even when his personal relations with Elsa were troubled, was steadfast in his high estimate of her talent. But then, as I often had occasion to observe, he was always honest and generous in his judgement of colleagues. Though he sometimes made fun of Carlo Levi's notorious vanity, he referred to Levi as "solare", a sunny person; and Levi, as I recall, always came into a room with a beaming smile on his face. Since, along with Rossellini, he was an artist I had deeply admired — I considered, and still consider *Christ Stopped at Eboli* one of the great Italian books of this century —, I sought him out. Seeing him at a large party, I went up to him and more or less invited myself to his studio. His reaction was cordial, but the meeting itself did not turn out well. He had little to say to me, and, after repeating my enthusiastic words about his book, I found that I, too, had run out of conversation. Afterwards we met again, here and there, but we never got beyond a cordial formality. I may have been held back by my lack of appreciation for his paintings (which dominated the studio and were his great pride); I was also out of sympathy with what seemed to me his over-zealous Communism. And, to make matters worse, I couldn't seem to like his then companion, Linuccia Saba, daughter of the Triestine poet.

Later, I regretted not having tried harder, for Levi's next book, *The Watch*, was a colorful and penetrating portrayal of the very Rome that he and I had then been living in.

I met Giorgio Bassani at about this same time, but I have no memory of seeing him together with Moravia or Elsa or with Levi, though he naturally knew them all. Usually I found him at Palazzo Caetani, or — if I was on proofreading duty — we met at De Luca's printing establishment, out near the University (where I was at last, theoretically, enrolled).

But Bassani also had a regular teaching job — in Italy, teaching is in effect a part of the civil service — and he was a professor of (I believe) art history in a Liceo in Naples. This position required him to make regular trips to the Southern city, usually spending a night there. Naples had remained my Italian home town, and my adopted family, the congenitally hospitable LaCaprias, always had a bed for me in their helter-skelter apartment in Palazzo Donn'Anna. I made frequent trips there, to go to the San Carlo, to see Neapolitan friends, or simply to eat Rosaria's cooking. And sometimes I would arrange to spend a Neapolitan evening with Bassani.

These, too, were great walks, but very different from my Roman strolls. After a simple meal somewhere in the dark, shifty Spaccanapoli area — pasta, fried fish, bottles of murky red Gragnano or amber Ischia — we would venture into the narrow, noisy streets, along rows of *bassi*, the characteristic one-room dwellings, occupied largely by multiple beds, while the large double door, wide-opened, allowed house and street to merge into a single space as filled with activity as an 18th century Neapolitan *presepe*, where old women roast chestnuts over a brazier as the Magi approach from the opposite direction.

At any hour, one or more members of the family would be eating — a meal much like the one Giorgio and I had just finished — a radio would be blaring, perhaps some commerce (in contraband cigarettes, the priceless penicillin, or some less respectable merchandise) would be in progress. One evening, I remember we passed a wake: the feet of the corpse, in white stockings, pointed straight at me, the jaw bound by a white handkerchief, a rosary in the stiff, folded hands, and Ave Maria's being wailed in rapid succession, the words compressed into a clotted, meaningless lament.

I don't know what Bassani was like as a teacher in the Liceo classroom, but he was a wonderful peripatetic instructor in Italian and in Italian culture. We talked about writers — ones we both knew and ones that, to me, were strangers — and he tried to make me share his enthusiasm for certain dialect poets, Giacomo Noventa for one, whom he had managed to impose on the Principessa. He was also devoted then to Mario Soldati (they had a clamorous quarrel some years later), whose elegant Italian I could appreciate but whose much-praised gift as a teller or tales I found less impressive. To me, the stories always seemed contrived: often engaging beginnings, with irresistible lures, then degenerated into unconvincing trick endings.

For Bassani, in any case, Soldati had the great virtue of being a cosmopolite, a man of the world; and such men — or women — in the still-confined panorama of Italian cultural life were few. Bassani was, like all his work, firmly rooted in the provinces, in Ferrara and the surrounding country, but he had cosmopolite aspirations, and so he was in his element at the Palazzo Caetani.

He had settled in Rome after the war, begun teaching, found an apartment large enough for his family (he had a wife and two young children). But he seemed to keep his marriage separate from his life as a writer-editor. He wife sometimes appeared at gatherings, but more often did not; and only very occasionally would there be a luncheon or a gathering at their house. I remember only one with any clarity: some other writers were present (the poet Attilio Bertolucci, I believe, with perhaps Giorgio Caproni, and Elena Croce). After the meal, we sat, somewhat crowded, in Bassani's study, as he read the opening pages of a story, a puzzling but haunting episode, an introduction — but to what? It was not clear, and I don't believe Bassani himself knew then the title of the work. Years later, when I read *The Garden of the Finzi-Continis*, I recognized the words I had heard in Bassani's voice that Sunday. Curiously, in his everyday speech, Bassani had a slight stammer; but when he read aloud — an activity he much enjoyed — that defect vanished, he read with fluent confidence, in a soft, musical, appealing voice.

Am I giving the impression that my first months in Rome were nothing but a dazzling succession of literary gatherings, cultural events, glamorous encounters? Not so. Much of the time I spent with my coeval Italian friends, and with their friends, observing the rituals of youth, giving no thought to the fame of others but eagerly (and, in some cases, accurately) looking forward to our own.

Of course, we were all movie-lovers; and almost every night we went religiously to a film (having arrived at a choice after long, sometimes heated discussion), preferably American or French. Fan of Rossellini and De Sica, I had imagined an enlightened Italian film industry, producing one masterpiece after another. I was thus ill-prepared for some of the dogs that appeared that winter: an Italian re-make of *Les Misérables* in two parts, a light comedy with the great tenor Beniamino Gigli playing a taxi-driver. My Italian friends adamantly refused to waste time and money on what they considered unworthy trash, so I would go off by myself in the afternoon to see these rejects, convinced that they were good for my Italian. And, on the same pretext, I went to see dubbed American films: *Addio Mr. Chips*, *Il postino suona sempre due volte* (with Lana Turner miraculously speaking in a low, sultry Italian voice instead of her familiar baby whimper).

But the real ritual was observed at midday Sunday. No, we didn't attend noon Mass at a Roman church. Instead, like every other person of culture in Rome, we headed straight for the Cinema Barberini, at the foot of the Via Veneto. Closed at that hour to the paying public, the theater — vast as a hangar — was reserved for the Rome Cineclub, in which all of us were enrolled.

Though there were no restrictions on membership, the Cineclub was, in its way, exclusive: it seemed to attract only true enthusiasts, most of them young and left-wing. There were many students, but mainly the Sunday showings were frequented by people like us: graduates now embarking on a career, apprentice directors, debutant actors and actresses, writers with one script in their pocket and another taking shape in their mind. Older film addicts were often there, too: Moravia (not yet an active film critic, but long an inveterate moviegoer) and Morante, and professionals: Visconti could occasionally be spotted, surrounded by his court of bright and beautiful young men, or the tall, silver-haired De Sica, resembling the ambassador from some small but distinguished country.

The club's direction, like its membership, was solidly leftist, so our Sunday fare often had a people's-republic flavor. We got more than an eyeful of muddy Sovcolor, and even today if I want to make my eyes glaze over in self-induced boredom, I have only to think of *Mitchurin or Life in Blossom*, a biopic about the Soviet scientist who proved — to the Party's satisfaction — that Mendel's law was erroneous and — according to the film — somehow made a fool of Luther Burbank. The narration consisted largely of endless pans over gently waving fruit trees or uniform acres of blooming vegetables, to music of Shostakovich worthy of a better fate.

There was some uncertainty always about the programs. Almost every showing was preceded by an announcement: the scheduled film had arrived but the cans were still in customs, or perhaps some of the cans had been delivered, but the last reel was still in customs. The projection would begin, in the hope that the conclusion of the movie would reach the Barberini in time.

On occasion the film failed to arrive altogether, and it would be replaced by some threadbare classic — *Un carnet de bal* or *La kermesse heroïque* — announced to a chorus of impatient groans from the assembled cinéastes. After the delayed start, the program would often last until two PM or later, when, faint with hunger, I joined the others in the inevitable Sunday stroll up the Via Veneto, past the tables of Café de Paris or Rosati or Doney, where we could ogle the visiting American stars (an Anita Ekberg sighting? Was that Vincente Minelli?) and wave proudly to the few Doney customers we knew personally.

I must not make Rome in the late '40's sound too idyllic. The war, the horrors of the *Open City* days, the nagging everyday shortages and hardships were — for most of the people I met — a recent, painful memory. There were still unhealed wounds. And that winter of 1947-48 was a time of political turmoil; after two decades of the Fascist regime, and the earthquake of the war, Italy was suffering some after-shocks, the quakes of *assestamento*. In my peculiar position, the token American most of the time, I was the target — or perhaps the butt — of conflicting propaganda.

My friends, the little band — Peppino, Mario, Achille, Franco, and aggregates like Nora and Antonella — were mostly Communists, or at least left-wing Socialists. This was true also of many of the writers I was meeting, as well as the film-directors. I was aware of other groups — it was impossible to ignore them — but I tended to view them from my friends' critical point of view.

In the weeks before the now notorious elections of 18 April 1948, the campaigning was intense. Some evenings, after the last, late movie, we would stroll to Piazza Colonna and the Galleria, where clusters of people, mostly young, mostly men, would have gathered to argue political issues. Though I grew up in an active, politicking Southern Democrat family and had seen campaigning from my infancy, I had never witnessed anything quite like this. It was as if the Galleria were filled with miniature debating societies, of shifting composition, as, say, a Communist, having spoken with passion to one little group of four or five anti-Communists, would move on to expound his ideas to another group.

I tactfully kept my mouth shut most of the time. But one evening, after I had been listening to an eloquent young man for a few minutes, it dawned on me that he was indulging in what was officially called "apologia del regime," a crime: he was defending Mussolini.

Without thinking, I blurted: "Why then, you're a Fascist?!"

Caught off guard by my blunt assertion, he stammered in reply: "No, no. . .I just don't deny the past, and I think we have to recognize the achievements —"

These were words I had heard before and would hear again. But, for the most part, I met only Communists and Socialists, and I assumed they would win, and the wonderful Italy that my friends wanted would be created.

The American government also intervened with a heavy hand in the campaign. One particularly foolish poster showed, in splendid full color, a beautiful crusty loaf of bread, roughly broken open to reveal its craggy-crumbed, snow-white interior. The legend said, more or less: Don't vote against those who are giving you your daily bread (i.e. the USA and its allied Democrazia Cristiana).

One consideration, however, made the poster ineffectual: there was no white bread in Italy. Even in the good restaurants you ate rolls that were a pale gray. Not unpleasant to taste, but nothing like the USIA propaganda. Heaven also weighed in, with several apparitions of the Madonna. One took place in Assisi, a few days before I arrived there to visit an American friend at the nearby Università degli Stranieri. Having read about the miraculously moving statue crowning the facade of the otherwise uninteresting church of Santa Maria degli Angeli, I wanted to take a look, and made my reluctant friend accompany me. Perversely, by the time we got there, the image had stopped moving her arms. All we found were disappointed visitors and mobile ice-cream stands. Still, according to the press, hundreds of torn-up Communist party cards littered churchyards all over the country.

As usual, on the night of 18 April, we went to the movies. We may have gone to the Barberini, because I remember that, coming out of the show — it was about 1 AM — we walked down the Via del Tritone until we came to a café, surprisingly open. The radio was broadcasting the returns, incomplete but already totally clear. An overwhelming landslide for the Christian Democrats, for the party of film censorship, of reaction, of former Fascists slightly whitewashed over — that is how we saw them then, and how they would seem for the next twenty years, until, like the Communists, they eventually fell apart.

Something went out of Roman life after the election; a kind of dull resignation set in. It was as if almost everyone I knew had belonged to a single, widespread, defeated party of opposition. At the RAI, Peppino rose to a position of authority and (literary) power, but his immediate superior was an affable mediocre playwright of confirmed political reliability and guaranteed lack of daring. The cinema, too, was moving from its period of incisive attack to a safer area of light comedy, of *neo-realismo rosa*, the same slums, the same characters perhaps as the earlier, stronger, realistic films, seen now through rose-colored glasses, with forced optimism and humor.

But the past was not dead, nor could the new masters cover all with whitewash. Among the most disturbing books that appeared then was a collection of letters, whose title described the content: *Letters of those Sentenced to Death in the Resistance*, published by the Turin firm of Giulio Einaudi.

One of the most affecting — and the best-written from a literary point of view, though literature was of small importance here — was written by the young scholar Leone Ginzburg to his wife Natalia. Here is most of the letter, its impact inescapably dulled by translation.

> Natalia cara, amore mio,
>
> every time, before setting out, or at similar moments, I hope I am not writing you the last letter; and so it is also today. Inside, I feel still, even after almost a whole day has gone by, the happy excitement aroused in me by your news and by the tangible proof that you love me so much [. . .]
>
> We must go on hoping that we will finally see each other again, and all these emotions will be composed and extinguished in our memory, forming a whole that becomes bearable and coherent. But let's change the subject. One of the things that saddens me most is the ease with which the people around me (and sometimes I myself) lose their taste for general problems in the face of personal danger. Consequently I will try to talk not about myself but about you. My hope is that you will normalize your existence, as soon as it's possible, you must work and write and be useful to others. This advice will seem facile and irritating: but it is the finest fruit of my tenderness and my sense of responsibility. Through artistic creation you will be freed of the too many tears that choke you; through social activity, whatever its nature, you will remain close to the world of other people, to whom I was so often your only connection. In any case, having the children will mean you have another great source of strength at your disposal. I would like Andrea to remember me, if he were not to see me again. I think of them constantly, but I try not to dwell on the thought of them, so as not to be weakened by melancholy.

> The thought of you, on the contrary, I do not try to dispel, and it almost always has a strengthening effect on me. Seeing friends' faces again, in these days, greatly stimulated me at first, as you can imagine [. . .] I must stop now, because I was late starting to write, trusting in the light of my bulb, which, instead, is particularly weak this evening, besides being very high above me. I will go on writing, blindly, without the hope of rereading this[. . .]. Ciao, my love, my tenderness. In a few days it will be the sixth anniversary of our marriage. Where and in what state will I be on that day? What mood will you be in then? I have been thinking, lately, of our life together. Our only enemy (I have concluded) was my fear. [. . .] If and when we are together again, I will be freed from fear, and not even these clouded areas will remain in the life we share. How I love you, my dear. If I were to lose you, I would gladly die. (This is another conclusion I have reached lately).
>
> [. . .] Kiss the children. I bless all four of you, and I thank you for being in the world. I love you, I kiss you, my love. [. . .] Don't worry too much about me. Imagine that I am a prisoner of war, there are so many, especially in this war, and the great majority of them will come home. We must hope that we belong to the majority, mustn't we, Natalia?
>
> I kiss you again and again and again. Be brave.

The letter was written early in 1944 (Leone Ginzburg died on 5 February). When I read it, in 1952, I realized, with shock, that during this very period , not many miles to the south, I was looking at the ROMA arrow and creating, in my fantasy, a magic city of order and grace and amusement. But this, this had been the reality, the Rome of the Germans and the Fascists, of torture and death, the Rome I had already come to know through Rossellini's *Open City*. Leone Ginzburg's letter imposed reality on me.

By a jarring coincidence, only a few evenings after I read that letter, I met Natalia at Elena Croce's. Typically, Elena did not introduce us. Hospitable and generous as she was, Elena was a terrible hostess: she could rarely find a decent cook, she would set out bottles then forget to offer anyone a drink, and she would become so absorbed in a conversation that she let her guests, most of them accustomed to her eccentric hospitality, fend for themselves.

Natalia arrived with Gabriele Baldini, a young man two or three years older than I, a friend of Dario Cecchi, and a fanatical opera-lover. Like Dario, Gabriele was the son of a once famous writer, his reputation now faded. Gabriele himself was at the beginning of a stellar academic career, and had already published some translations. Later he would produce a complete Shakespeare in Italian, but he also wrote charmingly and perceptively about opera and the theater, and, briefly, he appeared in Pasolini's film *Hawks and Sparrows*, playing an eccentric scholar who likes to conduct recordings (as he did in real life).

It was Gabriele then who actually introduced me to Natalia. I had read little of her work, and felt unusually shy in her presence, as I had with Silone. I knew of her dauntless personal heroism, her life with three small children in *confino* (forced residence in a remote locality where surveillance was easy for her Fascist minders), while her husband was in prison or in hiding. After the "racial laws" of 1938 they both were further oppressed by the restrictions on Jews. Also that letter from her husband, which I had just read, acted as an emotional barrier. I felt I had intruded unforgivably into the most private and sacred part of her life.

Gabriele and Natalia were married shortly thereafter, and they moved to London; so I got to know them only much later. In a delightful essay ("He and I") Natalia has written amusingly about their superficially incongruous marriage, about Gabriele's attempts to opera-ize her. It was not unusual to see the distinguished novelist blissfully dozing in her orchestra seat, while the Shakespearean scholar followed every word and note of the Verdi or Mozart performance. Sometimes, leaving Natalia at home, he would appear in a box at the Saturday matinée with the Ginzburg children.

Memory is a collage. The events, the people, the associations I am describing here did not occur in any neat order. Often they overlapped, and I may be recalling them anti-chronologically. How much time passed between my first cup of tea with the Principessa Caetani and my meeting with Natalia at Elena Croce's? In between those two encounters, I believe, came my trip to Florence and the beginning of my friendship with Berenson — but that is not part of this story. Well, in a way it is: Berenson read my Naples diary in *Botteghe Oscure*, complimented me on it, and recommended me for a fellowship (which I didn't get, though my other recommenders were Robert Lowell and Norman Mailer. So much for the clout of big names).

And, though I avoided seeing Americans in my first Roman months, I knew some of the fellows at the American Academy; and I made friends among other Americans living in the city, chief among them the art historian (later successful business man), Richard Miller, my companion in arduous sightseeing excursions and in economic eating. It was Richard who discovered the ONARMO "restaurants", a series of soup kitchens for the destitute middle class, sponsored by the Vatican. Richard, a genius at saving money, not only found this clean place where you could have a nutritious, bland meal for a couple of hundred lire. He also discovered that if you gave up the bread, you saved thirty lire; and if you bought your own fruit at a stall outside, refusing the usually tasteless ONARMO apple, another fifty lire was knocked off the bill.

Often, after our meal with the destitute — highly proper destitute they were, the gentlemen in threadbare jackets and ties, the ladies with long-outmoded hats and darned gloves — we would walk to nearby Piazza di Spagna, wash our fruit under a jet of the Barcaccia fountain, and sit on Bernini's steps, eating grapes or plums and watching the passing swarms of tourists.

Passersby saw us, too; and one day Richard was somewhat surprised to see me nod and wave to an elegant American woman in the back of a US Embassy limousine. I explained she was a family friend, wife of our naval attaché, and the previous evening I had been to a black-tie dinner at her immense apartment in Palazzo Ruspoli.

Also in these years — around the end of the fifties or the early sixties — an older, more stable Anglo-American colony was forming. My closest friends were John and Virginia Becker, he a writer, she a painter, whose means allowed them to take almost an entire floor of the Palazzo Caetani, where they gave the best parties in the city. They soon became friends with the Reuters correspondent Patrick Crosse and his wife Jenny Nicholson (Robert Graves' daughter) and Jenny's cousin, the Tallulah-like actress Diana Graves. By this time I was sure enough of my adopted-Italian status to indulge, without fear of contamination, in excesses of Anglophone entertainment. Once in a while, some Italian writers or artists would turn up at a party, but they rarely seemed at home. Fellini once appeared at the Beckers, sat on a sofa the whole evening in silence, then left without comment. Later one of Virginia's pictures was visible in *8 1/2*, of which Virginia commented: "The movie reminded me of that night at our party: he didn't have anything to say and he didn't know when to go home." Much as I came to like Fellini personally, I felt the same way about that film.

So I, too, led a double life, alternating borrowed luxury, Italian or American, with self-imposed poverty. A year after my arrival in Rome, I was awarded a Fulbright grant, and my standard of living soared. Richard received a similar grant, and as a symbolic first action we went — separately — to custom tailors and ordered new suits (mine was a snappy gray sharkskin). When they were ready, we made an appointment for lunch and met at Passetto's — the restaurant that for us signified affluence. Previously we had only been there when invited by some well-to-do visiting relative or friend.

Rome, at the end of the 'forties, had acquired the fame of being the Paris of the 'twenties reborn. A foolish notion, since periods can perhaps be revived, by artificial respiration, but not repeated. Rome was Rome. But many young — and not so young — American writers and artists duly came, hoping to bathe in some invisible spring of inspiration.

And as I now had the status of an old Roman hand, sometimes they arrived with my phone number or with a note of introduction. So I found myself spending more and more time with visiting Americans. Some — like Francis Steegmuller, whom I met at lunch with Moravia — became life-long friends. Others became transient, one-story memories, postage stamps in the collage: Frederick Prokosch, Truman Capote, Tennessee Williams.

In a celebrated essay on Williams, Gore Vidal describes a party at the playwright's apartment in Via Aurora. Naturally, in Vidal's highly personal account it becomes a fascinating occasion. I remember it as being dull and its dullness seemed to me typical. Most of the Americans who came to Rome made little or no effort to learn the language, meet the local writers (except Moravia, whose English was fluent and whose curiosity and hospitality were great). So these occasional gatherings had a transient, touristic quality, like a shipboard gathering.

There were exceptions. One was Bill Demby, who eventually married an Italian and remained in Italy forever. Bill's future wife was the sister-in-law of the painter and writer Toti Scialoja; and they were the initial point of another network, through whom I met a number of artists and critics.

As my Italian grew fluent, I began to make a living — I was hired (on the basis of no experience) as music critic of a new Italian weekly — and I worried less about becoming a part of Rome. Sipping the coffee, drinking the wine, eating the cuisine had quite simply become my life. I was as close to being a Roman as I was ever going to get. And, as for that part of me that remained American, I came to cherish it. I enjoyed my hybrid position, which gave me a special detachment, a capacity for seeing both Italy and America with a critical eye, belonging to both and to neither.

The anthology that follows is meant as a kind of extension of the memoir that precedes it, and thus its table of contents reflects the contents of my memory. Some important writers are not here:

Cesare Pavese, for example, is absent as he was largely absent from Rome then. Of course, I was aware of his work, but Pavese the man was not a part of my Rome (I believe I saw him once, at a distance, at a crowded party, perhaps one of the lethally boring Sunday afternoons at the Belloncis). Calvino, who was to become very important in my life, is also not included in this volume, because in my Roman years he lived almost entirely in Turin or Paris. I would have liked to have Pier Paolo Pasolini in this anthology, but he, too, was a relative latecomer to Rome; and though we became good friends, I always felt — in Roman terms — his senior.

Sadly, too, my oldest Italian friend, the now distinguished novelist and essayist Raffaele LaCapria, will not fit into a Roman context. Now he has lived in Rome for decades, but in the late forties, he was still lingering in Naples, in the maternal comfort of romantic Palazzo Donn'Anna, writing and re-writing the first novel that was to launch his career (and mine, as it was my first translation) and, at the same time, enjoying the "belle giornate", the beautiful Neapolitan days of sun and sea and pensive idleness that he was to make his own special, unmistakable trademark.

Carlo Emilio Gadda is included in this volume, though I hardly knew him in the period I have written about. At that time he was approaching retirement age and had been given a position at the RAI (the Italian Radio, whatever its defects, supported a whole army of writers, including several of Italy's best). I must sometimes have passed the tall, slightly bent, quiet and courtly gentleman, whose duties were vague, but whose presence at the office was scrupulous; but I didn't recognize him at that time.

Gadda's presence on the Roman literary scene was also profoundly felt, even if he was not often found at official receptions or smart parties. If Moravia was, through no fault of his own, Italian literature's spokesman and official greeter; Gadda, also through no fault of his own, was Italian literature's best-kept secret. It was not until 1957, when his great, forever-unfinished novel *Quer pasticciaccio bruto de Via Merulana* appeared, that his name was known beyond a select circle of admirers, including many writers and artists. That novel did nothing to diminish the aura of difficulty that surrounded his work; and I have to confess that, though I heard much about him, I had read nothing of his until, in 1963, John Ashbery wrote me from Paris, asking me to translate a Gadda story, "The Fire in Via Keplero", for a new review, *Art and Literature*. I did, and in the process I came to know Gadda. At almost the same time, George Braziller asked me to take on *That Awful Mess on Via Merulana* (as it became in English), and — emboldened by my completion of the short story translation — I did.

For the next several years, I saw Gadda frequently, always in the company of his friend and future biographer, the critic and editor Gian Carlo Roscioni. Though I think Gadda liked me, we never became friends; and yet there were moments when I felt close to him, in what seemed his raw vulnerability and his narrowed life, confined by manias and codes all his own.

By the time I got to know him, he had retired from the RAI and was living alone in a tidy, anonymous apartment in a colorless, middle middle-class street, Via Blumenstijl, in a newly-developed quarter beyond Monte Mario. He had a daily woman, of uncertain but not young age, but she left before dark, because Gadda feared neighbors might gossip if she stayed on. He had a telephone but never answered it; for communication, the protocol was this: you telephoned his concierge, she gave him the message with his mail when he went out for his late-morning walk, and then he returned your call after the walk.

The first time I went to see him, shortly after I had signed the contract with Braziller, Gadda offered me a cup of tea. When I accepted, I saw a look of profound dismay come over his face. He excused himself, then I heard him in the kitchen conferring with the maid. She appeared and removed some books and papers from the table where we were sitting, a cloth was spread — but only over the part of the table directly in front of me — and, after a considerable pause, one cup filled with tea was set on the cloth, with a sugar bowl and a little jug of milk. I drank the tea, under Gadda's scrutiny, with the feeling that I was taking some medicine. Neither Gadda nor Roscioni joined me.

Meanwhile the conversation proceeded, in a —to me— mysterious fashion. Gadda, with deferential circumlocution, apologized for the difficulty of his prose, as if its complexity were some terrible burden laid upon him. Afraid that he felt my grasp of his language might be inadequate, I made a special effort to speak my most erudite Italian, a pyrotechnical display of conditionals and past subjunctives and arcane vocabulary. But we seemed to be talking at cross-purposes, until finally, taking advantage of another visit of Gadda's to the kitchen, Roscioni explained to me in a whisper that Gadda was afraid I was not being paid enough and, with extreme delicacy, he was trying to tell me that he would like to give me a contribution.

Exaggerating Braziller's munificence — and with as much subtlety as I could muster — I gently rejected Gadda's touching offer (I later learned that some of his other translators had accepted it, perhaps unaware of Gadda's straitened situation). After that meeting at his house, we usually met at a restaurant, often the particularly pleasant, high-ceilinged Romagnolo, behind the Pantheon, now a fast-food place.

It was anything but fast in those days, and our dinners tended to be protracted events, for Gadda was discreetly greedy, and besides enjoying an abundant meal he particularly looked forward to the desserts. As a diabetic, I have long learned to live without cakes and pies, but (acting on Roscioni's instructions) I always ordered some rich, creamy cake, then feigned a sudden loss of appetite, urging Gadda to eat it in my stead. I soon learned what his favorite sweets were and managed always to order the right ones for him.

Stories of Gadda's eccentricities circulated in Rome like tales of Auden's carpet slippers and his martinis in New York. But, when you were with him, even though comical episodes almost always occurred, you could not escape the sense of profound melancholy that seemed to accompany him. He spoke always as if from beyond some inner suffering, as an ill person will bravely speak of commonplaces on his hospital bed.

As I began dealing with Gadda's prose, I also began a separation from Rome. In the summer of 1965, when I had signed the contract with Braziller and was at work on *Il pasticciaccio*, I decided I had to get out of the city and find some peace; Virginia Becker lent me a strange, spacious but primitive apartment at the edge of Sperlonga, then still an unspoiled fishing-village on the coast below Terracina. With my friend Pippo Greghi (who nobly took care of cooking and shopping), I went there for a month and finished the first draft of the novel. And I started thinking of somehow finding a Sperlonga of my own, not on the sea but in the country. Though I had little money, I investigated a few possible areas — Palestrina, Anagni, Cuma, Tivoli — but none seemed quite right. Until a friend told me about a house his father wanted to sell, in Tuscany, near Monte San Savino. I drove up and saw it. Then, on 23 November 1963, I drove up again, to show it to my mother, who was in Italy on a visit. In the village — famous for its fine butchers — we bought grand steaks and brought them back to Rome for dinner. Shortly after we arrived, the phone rang: it was a friend, calling to tell us that President Kennedy had been shot. For some reason, this national and international tragedy, associated now forever with burned steaks, confirmed my desire to get to the country, away from people. The next morning, I called the owner of the Tuscan property and told him my intention to buy it.

More than a year went by before I actually moved to Tuscany; and even after the move, I kept an apartment in Rome. But my Roman life was over. Several of my American acquaintances also moved away, some died. I continued translating some of my writer-friends, and began translating others: Calvino, then Eco. But Rome was now a place I visited. Sadly, from my detachment, I saw it change: Rampoldi's café became a haberdashery, my favorite neighborhood trattoria turned into a tourist trap, where parties of visiting Germans linked arms and swayed to the sound of their own voices singing *Ein Prosit! Ein Prosit!* and *Lilì Marlen* (a song I have hated for over half-a-century), conductors disappeared from buses, as bus-tickets were invented and cancelling machines installed.

For a little while I thought I hated Rome, but then as our new relationship developed, I realized that I still loved *a* Rome, but it was a city that no longer existed. Gradually, I learned to — if not love, at least like — the new replacement-city. At the same time, in daydreams, I sometimes revisit the old Rome; in memory I walk along those traffic-free streets, I breathe the purer air, I hear the cries of street vendors, and I smell roasting chestnuts. And I hold imaginary conversations with Alberto and Elsa and Elena and other friends now gone. This anthology is meant as a memoir of my lost, open city, and of its wonderful welcoming citizens. Here I have counted my blessings.

William Weaver
Monte San Savino/Annandale-on-Hudson

ELSA MORANTE

The Nameless One

FROM *House of Liars*

Elsa Morante on her terrace, Rome, 1950s.

I

Pock Face Appears On The Stage.
The First Of His Swaggering Scenes.

THE DARK YOUNG STRANGER was the first visitor Edoardo received after his illness. Some days earlier he had moved from his bed to an easy chair where he lay most of the day half reclining. Occasionally his fever-wasted hands played absently with his curly hair or he would slowly swing his slippered foot but even these simple motions tired him. Several times he had tried to get up and had dragged himself as far as his mirror to stare at the gaunt face and the deeply circled, haunted eyes that seemed hardly to be his own. But his strength ebbed quickly and he fell back in his chair overcome by dizziness and nausea. The lethargy of convalescence alternated with a nervous eagerness to be active and up and about; and this brought about capricious, unpredictable moods. Oppressed by boredom, he sometimes insisted that his mother or sister sit with him until he would suddenly wish to be alone and abruptly order them away. He would ask them to read aloud to him and then would rudely interrupt the reader, saying her voice was monotonous or the book dull. Sometimes his heart swelled with the joy of knowing that he was well, his thoughts turned to the outside world, to travel and adventure and all that life and health have to offer to a young man of his class. He was swept with impatience to tear himself from that chair and that room, but his impetuous desire soon subsided into exasperated self-pity.

For the first time in his short life he felt weak and imprisoned; his will was no longer absolute. He was likely to pass from a light-hearted mood into a passionate frenzy in which he would behave violently toward the nurse or members of the family who were attending him. He might be about to break into an affectionate laugh full of all his old fervor when his emaciated face would darken and for no reason he would shout insultingly at his companion: "Why are you always here? Leave me in peace! Get out! Get out!" To amuse him, his mother had had his piano moved into the bedroom and his sister often played his favorite music to him. Sometimes it soothed him, sometimes it only increased his irritability and anxiety. Music did not always free his thoughts from the burden, of reality or desire but instead filled his brooding imagination with visions of the activity and freedom still forbidden him. Instead of thanking poor Augusta, he mockingly criticized her style and accused her of playing as colorlessly as a boarding-school girl. He longed to play himself but had not the strength; and he sometimes thought of writing a poem or a song, or of painting as he had before he was ill; but weakness had killed the impulse and he had to give up in disgust. Fearing that he would tire, the doctors still forbade him to receive visitors except for the family; but he had no wish to see any of his old friends. The summer of his illness seemed in memory like a dark, fiery journey through shadowy images and incoherent voices. He felt as if he had buried his past, all his adolescence in this dark valley; he wanted new, unknown things and spurned the people who had once been dear, as though they were characters in a play who are no longer interesting because one knows the plot by heart. During his illness strange figures born of his fever but full of independent life and pain, had flashed across his vision. Now it seemed to him that these figures roamed the squares and streets of the city waiting to meet him, while he grew better all too slowly. But he missed their rendezvous and they scattered to other cities, created also by his fever. A stormy, dramatic light illuminated these phantoms, and rendered them rare and desirable. Fabulous mistresses moved before him in this light, docile opulent girls who bowed their heads that he might gather their heavy hair in his hands. What wonderful golden hair! No woman he had ever known could compete with the beauties of his fancy.

Thus he spent the days of his convalescence, torn between contempt for his past life and the desire to live again, never satisfied with the solitary pleasures of imagination but sensing that reality could never match his languid dreams in richness.

This afternoon Edoardo was more talkative than usual. His health had improved considerably; after lunching with a good appetite, he had been able to walk around his room a little and had ventured as far as the terrace which looked out over the garden. This had brought back to his joy a faith in his own strength. He imagined love affairs, travels, parties such as he had never known; as he talked about the future he glanced with vengeful triumph at the bed in which he had raved and suffered. "I am no longer your prisoner," he seemed to be saying to the hated bed. "I have been tied to you for so long but now the spell is broken, I am well, I'm free!"

Concetta, faithful attendant of his recovery, shared his happiness. But her son's tremendous pride frightened her; for she was sure his recovery was due to her prayers. Not one day had passed during his illness that she had not arisen at five to hurry to early Mass. She had sacrificed her richest jewels on the altars. In every church in the city the candles she had offered were burning, masses for the health of her beloved son had been celebrated everywhere, and everywhere *Te Deums* were being sung in thanks for his recovery. Without telling him, she had sewed little squares of lace painted by the Sisters with holy images in his mattress, under his pillows and even in the hems of his blankets and shirts. She had slipped around his thin, feverish throat the gold chain with his baptismal medal which with precocious impiety he had refused to wear as a child. The most powerful and illustrious saints of the heavenly hierarchy had received Concetta's homage and supplications. And now, her prayers having been granted and she herself been freed from her day-and-night vigil by the invalid's bedside, she allowed herself daily pilgrimages to the dwellings of her Holy Ones. Proud of performing her sacred duties, she had herself driven to this or that church, bowing in casual acknowledgment of the respectful greetings of the townspeople along the way. She passed through the rich chambers, the dim naves of the sacred buildings and approached the High Altars, disdaining to glance at the humble worshippers kneeling here and there; so the king's favorite might make his way to the throne through the throng of envious courtiers. If someone had arrived before her and was already kneeling before the High Altar, the maid who always accompanied Concetta would hurry over to the daring soul, whisper the illustrious name of her mistress and the intruder would hastily remove himself. Then, on her knees, as prescribed by the ceremony of the heavenly court, Concetta was finally face to face with the Throne. A sense of power, of regal confidence and privilege, would fill her heart. Her burning eyes, coal black in her white nun's face, regarded the candles that flamed on the altar in her name, the golden offerings emblazoned with her coat of arms, the precious chalices and the embroidered cloths, all offered by her. By virtue of her rank and her gifts she felt certain she deserved the place of honor in those beautiful, holy places. But like the faithful wife who avails herself of the king's friendship to beg a favor for her husband, Concetta prayed not for herself but for Edoardo. For though she trembled at her son's irreverence she felt she might redeem him by her own devotion.

Edoardo had scarcely regained consciousness before he took off the little baptismal chain and gave it back to his mother with a mocking smile, saying that he could not bear the weight of it. She crossed herself and, kissing the holy medal, put it around her own throat and prayed that she might thus win forgiveness for her son's sacrilege. Edoardo had not noticed the little images which she had sewn in his mattress and pillow while he slept or was delirious and his mother congratulated herself on her foresight, thanks to which her unsuspecting son would still receive divine protection.

That afternoon as Edoardo was boasting about his plans for the future, Concetta's joy was overshadowed by pious apprehension. With burning zeal she urged her son not to forget the gratitude he owed the Saints who had brought about his recovery. But in the self-confident tone his mother had encouraged in him from childhood, Edoardo laughed at her for her crazy ideas. Warming to the sport, he began to tease her and make fun of her revered saints and their illustrious names. She was horrified by his impiety and begged him to be still; this only excited him to greater irreverence. He went so far as to hurl his defiance at the whole heavenly hierarchy: "I don't believe in you!" he cried, looking up at the invisible spirits, "I swear that I have got well because I wanted to! Let me see you, if you dare! Show yourselves and contradict me! What? Does no one come? Are you afraid?" And he laughed gaily as if it were all a game, although he knew how scandalized and terrified his mother was. She was finally moved to anger and with a heavy sigh bitterly reproached him. His face darkened and he told her to go to her saints and leave him alone; scenes like this tired him, he said, and brought back his fever. As he spoke, he took a mirror from the table beside him and studied the marks of illness on his face, to which a healthier color was slowly returning. Fearing to upset him further, his mother grew quiet and hiding her rosary in her ample sleeves, she sat secretly telling her beads. Edoardo was downcast to see how thin his face was and what deep shadows ringed his eyes. "How ugly I've become," he said. To his mother these words sounded no less impious than his blasphemies of a few minutes earlier. "Ugly!" she exclaimed heatedly, in a voice still unsteady with tears. Shaking her head, she added: "You're handsomer than before, my Edoardo. Believe your mother." She wanted to convey to him with this her loving intention of making peace and her dark, tear-filled eyes regarded her son with the same expression they had in church, when she contemplated the ciborium. "Ugly!" she repeated, with a fresh, youthful laugh as if to confute such a heresy by uttering it with her own lips. She went to him and in the soft, singing voice in which the women of the South speak of love, she began to praise his beauty; calling him the delight of all women, his mother's own treasure, the handsomest man in the city. Then, impetuously pressing his cheeks between her palms, she kissed his lips and exclaimed rapturously: "He's well again, the prince of the house is well again, my beautiful man, my angel, my baby, my little one!" Edoardo reminded her laughingly that he was no longer a baby but a grown man now; even as he contradicted her, he submitted willingly to her compliments and kisses. He was demonstrative by nature and now, weakened by illness, he longed all the more to be made much of. While he laughed at his mother, he held her tight in his arms and covered her faded face with kisses and then playfully he began to remove her hairpins one by one. This childish game had once made her angry but as her beautiful gray hair fell about her shoulders now, she sighed with pleasure. While he was delirious, she had suddenly remembered this old trick of his; her heart had grown sick with remorse for having scolded him so for it and today she felt it a miraculous privilege to submit to his old, affectionate teasing. She pretended to threaten him but then broke into a happy laugh, lavishing the most tender names on her beloved one. As he let his mother's hair ripple through his fingers, he repeated: "What beautiful hair the lady has. What a beautiful, little, silver head."

The bell for vespers rang at that moment and she hastily did up her hair in front of the tall mirror. From the door she turned and in a voice of passionate authority reminded her son of the various medicines he was to take and what he was and was not to do while she was out. But already weary of her attentions, he interrupted her brusquely: "Good-bye, Concetta." From childhood he had occasionally amused himself by calling her by name, knowing that it displeased her. This time, however, she answered her son's farewell with a laughing nod and disappeared.

As she went down to her carriage, she turned over in her heart a thought common to all mothers, high or low; that for a mother, a son is always a baby. During the summer now almost over, Edoardo had been hers as he had been years ago, even though she had had to contend with Death for possession of him. If she left his bedside for a moment, the invalid had sought her even in the grip of delirium and she ran back to him, triumphant in the midst of her anguish. Weak and uncertain, he gave himself over entirely into his mother's hands; in his room she was mistress and queen. It was she who received his mail and she who answered his letters. No one could contest her right. And the other women outside, Edoardo's friends, had to come to his mother to have news of him; they presented themselves, curtseyed with humble trepidation, commiserated with her if he was worse, rejoiced with her if he had improved. They were grateful to her for her condescension, knowing that he belonged only to her. Ah, now that the danger was over, she thought back on that painful summer and had to confess that it had not been without its moments of glory!

Lost in such thoughts, she drove along in her carriage; it was then that the wheels almost brushed the skirts of her enemy, Anna, the rival she most hated, the only one who had not dared appear before Edoardo's mother to ask for news of him. Concetta, however, did not notice Anna. A few minutes later the girl received Edoardo's letter from the servant.

Her cousin had written the letter a few days earlier and when he had sealed it, he handed it to the servant with instructions to give it to the young lady the next time she came. He was aware that his cousin had come to ask for him more than once; and he knew she could never have borne the anguish of not knowing about his health, in spite of the many reasons which closed the doors of his home to her. Edoardo learned of her visits with complete indifference. As he thought back on it, his passion for his cousin seemed to him a little like places we knew in childhood which then appeared to us vast and endless but which, when we revisit them as adults, turn out to be quite small and narrow, so that we say to ourselves in amazement: "Was it really like this?" His love for her, like so many other things, belonged to another age: he repudiated it entirely. It seemed strange to him that his cousin should not understand how much he had changed and when he decided to write to her, he wrote purposely in that cold, merciless style. "She must be convinced," he thought, "that everything is over, my letter must hurt her to the quick." The letter was sent accordingly on its mission but Edoardo immediately began to think of Anna with a curiosity and an ardor free of any remorse. The letter would be delivered, it did not occur to him to take it back; it was an instrument of Fate, and he was Fate. The thought even now gave him a profound pleasure; not a frivolous, but a grave, mysterious pleasure such as a tyrant might feel as he disposed of the lives of his subjects according to his own will. He pictured his cousin's proud face when she received his cold message from the servant; he saw her small teeth bite her lips to hold back the tears, saw her tall, slender figure hurry away, watched her choose the less busy streets, seeking to hide herself and her humiliation. With his love, all traces of jealousy had also vanished from Edoardo's heart: he no longer doubted that his cousin loved him to the exclusion of anything or anyone else in the world. He knew he held her fate in his hands so completely that, for example, he could if he wished transform the girl's present despair into unlooked-for happiness. He imagined how, once he was better, he might climb up to the squalid little apartment where she was eating out her heart. She would come to the door herself, as usual; he would say that he had come to warn her in person, to impress firmly on her mind what his letter might not have explained clearly enough. Now: she was to make very sure never to come to the palace again for any reason whatsoever; she must know how unwelcome and useless such visits were. Furthermore, everything was over between them, he had come to tell her this for the last time. He would advise her never to try to reach him again in any way; she must convince herself that he no longer existed for her. All of this he would say in a dry, hostile voice; he would watch her sink down, pale and wordless, and then suddenly he would catch her to him and kiss her furiously. Even now he could feel the taste of her tears on his tongue, he could see those enchanted, questioning eyes: "But none of this will ever be," he told himself, "for I do not love her."

As he lay daydreaming, the servant boy brought him a visiting card; the card itself was quite ordinary but the printing was most elaborate and pretentious. The young gentleman of the card wished to know, explained the servant, when the master could receive him and was awaiting a reply in the antechamber. He said *young gentleman* but in a rather scornful tone and it was quite evident that in his opinion young gentlemen were of a very different breed from this one. On the card was engraved the name *Baron Francesco de Salvi*, surmounted with a tiny coronet. Edoardo did not know this baron and had never heard of his family. However, his impulsive curiosity had revived since his illness and persuaded him to receive the stranger at once.

Since the autumn twilight was falling fast, the servant who accompanied the visitor brought a lamp and placed it on the table near Edoardo. The latter rose slightly from his armchair and glancing at his caller with pleased curiosity, excused himself for having to receive him in his bedroom. He held out his hand which the other shook timidly.

The visitor was a robust young man who could not have been much more than twenty. His features were handsome and regular but his face was corroded and pitted by the deep scars of smallpox. In this face, with its high forehead and dusky pallor, his intelligent, melancholy eyes gleamed darkly. His hair, as we said before, was curly and very black. He wore a faded, rather worn suit which was if anything too sharply creased. The clumsiness of its cut betrayed the country tailor and his cheap but brilliantly colored cravat revealed, in addition to bad taste, the desire for elegant effect. It was secured by a pin of some ordinary metal worked into the form of a capital "R" and set with imitation pearls.

His velvet eyes, shadowed by long, soft lashes, glanced surreptitiously at the rich appointments of the room and in that glance there was a suggestion of insult or defiance. In an almost belligerent voice the young man hastened to explain the reason for his visit. He wanted, he said, to have news or at least to learn the present whereabouts of *a certain* Nicola Monaco who had at one time given him this address. He asked to be excused, he added, for the intrusion but he had preferred to speak to the master of the house rather than get his information from the servants, since his visit was in connection with a private matter.

He had said *a certain Nicola Monaco* but it was clear that this person held a high place in his estimation. When he said *a certain*, it was obviously only to conceal behind a feigned disdain the high opinion he had of the man, an opinion that he must have supposed was shared by many. Also, in spite of his rather aggressive manner he was careful to speak with deliberate precision and not without a slight ostentation. But even in the course of his simple remarks, he became confused and stammered more than once; this seemed to annoy him and his eyes grew dark and gloomy.

The visitor whom chance had brought to Edoardo, made one think of a wild bird borne by the wind into some city room where a sickly boy lies languishing. Full of wonder, the boy takes the proud, winged creature in. But the bird is not used to being confined and beats its wings clumsily against the walls and tries to escape while, at the same time, it is grateful to be sheltered from the storm. The boy, for his part, looks upon it with envy because it is free and can fly. Its awkward struggling seems ridiculous to him and yet it also wounds him; but above all, he wants to capture his unexpected guest to keep as a pet, and he starts at once to consider how he may catch him and clip his wings.

Having heard the young man's request, Edoardo looked at him appraisingly; after thinking for a moment, he replied that he did indeed remember that a certain Nicola Monaco had served his family as administrator until five or six years before. Here Edoardo paused to ask the other if Monaco was by chance a relative or a friend of his since, he explained hastily, the last news of him was not exactly pleasant. To this question the other responded in a precipitous, ironic manner and with a rather insulting laugh begged him to have no scruples and to speak frankly. With *that* man he had nothing but business connections.

As he listened to the stranger, Edoardo's heart began to beat quickly; he was like a man on the verge of a dangerous, harrowing adventure which, for just those reasons, he finds fascinating. His sense of malice helped him to see that the young man had lied, that Nicola Monaco must hold a very different place in his heart from that which he, whether because of pride or stubbornness or for some other mysterious reason, wished to suggest. The young man's reply opened the way for Edoardo to enter freely into this delicate region of the feelings, and to trample it or turn it upside down as he liked. On such a tedious afternoon the prospect offered our malicious cousin the foretaste of a delightful, wicked pleasure, such as he felt when he blasphemed the saints dear to Concetta. Strange as it may seem, such pleasure does not spring only from cruelty but is also mixed with a kind of tender compassion and love. In fact, is not one of the first pleasures of love perhaps the permission, whether granted or forced, to invade and even to lay waste forbidden, mysterious and holy places? And have you ever noticed with what an air of defiance and at the same time of perdition a boy will take pleasure in destroying some object dear to his small brother, if the child out of pride insists on telling him: "I don't care"? Of such mixed kinds, alas, are the few pleasures bequeathed to us by our father Adam.

And so there was a note of excitement in Edoardo's quiet, insidious voice when, not from any scruple of conscience but to prolong his own pleasure, he persisted gently: "But . . . excuse me, has it been a long time since you have heard of this gentleman?" As he spoke, he looked at the man with a rather sad, subtle solicitude, as if to say: "Give yourself up and I'll be good to you."

"Not for more than ten years," the other replied quickly but apparently annoyed to have said this much, as if it were some jealously guarded secret, he added brusquely: "But I only asked for an address, not for any personal news."

"Excuse me, but you began by asking me for news and I warned you that what you would hear would be unpleasant," Edoardo retorted. The young man grew completely confused and stammered his apologies. Striving to regain his self-possession, he said crudely: "Well, tell me what you have to say. And speak plainly." Glancing at him obliquely and speaking in the detached, neutral tone in which employers refer to their servants, Edoardo told him what he knew of Nicola Monaco. And how, after serving the family for many years, he had been dismissed because of certain irregularities in his management of the estates.

"What irregularities?" Francesco demanded abruptly. "Well," replied Edoardo, "if you want me to use the exact term for it, I will tell you that our Monaco was a thief."

As if this were a personal offense, Francesco reddened violently but he said nothing. The other continued, explaining how after such a discovery, naturally, all connections between Nicola and the Cerentanos were severed. Nothing more had been heard of Nicola until about a year ago when word had spread among the household servants of the misfortune which befell him. Before describing this misfortune, Edoardo interrupted himself again; leaning his head a little to one side, he said he was reluctant to tell what he knew; it would be unwelcome, perhaps, to the other's ear. But again Francesco protested and as if offended by Edoardo's doubts, he declared that he had nothing in common with Nicola beyond a matter of business. He laughed again the same ironic, rude laugh as before, but this time it was muffled and tremulous; then abruptly he stated that Monaco owed him money.

"Ah, if that is it," Edoardo said, with smiling eyes, "I am afraid your money is lost and you will have to give up the hope of recovering it." He explained then that according to the servants, although, Nicola lost his post with the Cerentanos, he did not lose his vices with it, unfortunately. He had finished, as was to be expected, in jail, where he had died a year ago.

Francesco turned pale. "What! Oh, yes," he said, and he smiled gently, revealing imperfect, broken, almost childish teeth. He rose from his chair quickly and glanced around him with a grim, miserable expression as if he were seeking some sign, having momentarily lost his way. "Well, thank you, then," he went on in his violent, impulsive manner. "Thank you, I shan't disturb you further. I have found out what I wanted to know," he concluded, forcing his childish grimace of a moment ago into a smile. "The address I was looking for is the cemetery. Thank you." And with this sarcastic jest, he turned hurriedly toward the door.

"What are you doing? Are you leaving so soon? Wait!" exclaimed Edoardo in alarm, half rising from his chair. As the other stood stock still in confusion by the door, he continued with restless urgency: "Stay a bit longer, I beg of you! Sit down again, please do, I ask it as a favor. Today is the first time," he went on with an embarrassed, humble little smile, "today is the first time that I have had anyone to talk to since I fell sick. I've been sick for more than two months and alone all the time. I would so like to talk to someone . . . you would be doing me a real favor." He accompanied these remarks with an urbane smile but he was so afraid the other might refuse that his eyes had grown clouded and his voice did not so much ask as command. He brightened when he saw that Francesco was intimidated and did not dare refuse; as he thanked him, a slight flush spread over his cheeks.

Then, whether out of gratitude or to win somehow his guest's consent and persuade him to stay, he began to talk about Nicola Monaco again, but in quite a different way. We saw before how Nicola had seemed at one time a most attractive, colorful person to his little master. Now Edoardo tried to recreate that shadowy figure in his memory, to piece together a kind of funeral, eulogy. Enriched and enlivened by his desire to please, his words evoked the administrator in heroic proportions. He praised the dead man's good looks, his blond beard and his infectious laugh. He celebrated his operatic gifts and his skill at the piano when he had played dance tunes for them as children, while they leaped about the room in time with his music. He recalled funny stories that Nicola Monaco had told him and which made him laugh even now when he remembered them; he was delighted to see that Francesco laughed with him. Francesco's eyes brightened at every fresh compliment to Nicola; apparently the praise awoke some secret, nostalgic memory. He was no longer the aggressive person of some moments before but seemed almost defenseless; an ill-concealed shyness, an almost harsh modesty controlled his movements. If he sat down, he sat on the edge of his chair as if he were holding himself in readiness for the first sign of dismissal from his host; to express his satisfaction he dared do no more than mutter hurried little phrases like: "Yes, he had a good voice" or "Yes, he was rather tall." But in spite of his efforts, his stiff reserve was as unavailing as a thin veil thrown over the splendor of a king's treasure. It betrayed such helpless involvement or, rather, such an absurd devotion that Edoardo was again moved by his temptation to malice. The style of his remarks changed from the complimentary and even heroic to a lighter tone and gradually his voice reacquired the dispassionate haughty note of the master speaking of his servant. Little by little, the traits in Nicola that had just received his praise became the butt of mocking ridicule. Nicola talked about Art as if Art were a woman who had given the key of her room only to him, while actually the noble lady distributed her favors to a very different sort than Nicola who, even to see her, had to climb the servants' stairs and peek at her through the keyhole. To hear him, however, it was the fault of his family, especially his wife, for having kept him from an artist's life. He went about telling whoever would listen to him what an artist he was, what a misunderstood man, what a gentleman, no less! And the day when his trickery came to light, he said that he was *highly astonished* (he used to use expressions like that) and began to swear on the heads of his children and the holy memory of the dead, as if his children or the dead counted for more than a rotten apple to a type like him! "Yes," Edoardo concluded, "I never saw such a liar, perjurer and clown! But I liked him," he added and broke into a spontaneous, provocative laugh, which his listener forced himself to echo.

"Do you want to know how I feel about it?" Edoardo went on, assuming a careless, skeptical tone and looking at the other's face to see the effect of his words. "I will tell you. It's a shame that I was still a boy when the man was thrown out. Because if I had been the master here, he would still be our manager today. The fact is I liked our old Nicola and what do I care whether he stole or not? My father felt the same way I do, but unfortunately he died too soon and the house fell into the hands of the women, and women spoil everything; they, have no imagination, they like to scratch and scrape in the fields but they understand nothing about a garden. Look at their religion; every morning they're off, all dressed up, to deposit their *Ave Marias*, prayers, genuflections, their *little flowers*, the way you deposit savings in a bank. They count on amassing a capital of blessings sufficient to live on their income in Heaven forever; they are not capable of taking in another thought.

"But to go back to our manager: you see, I come from a noble family; I am rich and as I see it, the first advantage of being rich is that you needn't bother about money; otherwise the rich would be slaves, of money no less than the poor. For example, today I ate a chicken, very well prepared, from a hand-painted porcelain dish, and I ate it with pleasure, without caring to know how it was killed, plucked or cooked, otherwise its taste would have been revolting. I don't want to know anything about the kitchen; that's the cook's business. My job is to keep myself nourished and at the same time to enjoy my food. The same goes for everything else, the managing of the estate and so on. They bring me a certain Nicola, a nice enough looking man, pleasant, who amuses me, knows how to sing, and they tell me: 'This man will look after your money, take care of all the tiresome messy business matters for you, leaving you only the duty of spending your income. But he steals! 'Let him steal,' I say to them, 'and don't bother me any more with your boring chatter. In olden times did not gentlemen allow themselves the luxury of keeping a dwarf? Well, I want the luxury of keeping a thief. He may be a thief but he knows how to play my fool and keep me amused better than any of you.' There, that would have been my answer when they accused Signor Monaco."

During Edoardo's speech Francesco had not said a single word; his silence made him seem ill at ease and he tried to hide it with forcedly casual gestures. For example, he pulled his trousers up slightly so that the crease would not be spoiled or he fingered his cravat, pretending to adjust the knot. But Edoardo's eyes rested for a moment on those coarse, red hands with wrists like a farmer's and Francesco noticed the look. A deep, mottled flush covered his face and immediately he dropped his hands and tried to hide them; but as he did so, a sudden anger made him turn pale. Jumping unexpectedly to his feet and clenching his fists threateningly, he said in a choked voice:

"I won't allow . . . I won't allow anyone to talk about him like that. . . . I forbid you to insult him. . . . Respect . . . have some respect for the dead!"

At this outburst Edoardo grew pale in a flash of anger that surprised him, since he had provoked and had even longed for the visitor's outburst. "How dare you . . . in my own house!" he exclaimed and, supporting his trembling arms on the arms of the chair, he tried to rise but this simple defensive gesture shook him so that sweat broke out on his forehead.

His desire for revenge was mixed with astonishment at seeing how weak he was, how helpless before this stranger. With an angry sigh he fell back in his chair as he searched wildly for some way to punish Francesco and then his eye fell on the visiting card the servant had brought, which still lay on the table beside him. His lips curled in a little sneer and he said: "Excuse me, *Baron*, I thought there was nothing in common between you and Signor Monaco."

This was enough to bring a flush again to Francesco's face. "What do you mean?" he said, in confusion. "Naturally . . . in fact . . . I have nothing to do with . . . I told you so already. I told you," he repeated, arming himself with a simulated boldness, "and I repeat it! What connection is there between the two questions? I am speaking out of general principle, not out of any regard for that man. What could he have meant to me, that . . . individual?"

Then, thinking he detected a slight smile on Edoardo's lips, he was overcome by anger again: "You," he continued, with angry emphasis, "you have no right to judge him. You're rich, you live in a princely house, lying in your armchair, with everyone bowing and scraping to you, you can't judge someone who worked all his life, a poor devil. . . . Do you know for sure how you would have behaved in his place? I am talking in a general way, about a sacred principle, a right. . . ."

The guest's fresh impertinences might have provoked another haughty reply from Edoardo but at that point a bell sounded from below; in the Cerentano household this was a signal that dinner would be served in another quarter of an hour. As if the sound were the signal for his dismissal and meant You *are in the way*, Francesco was upset when he heard it, and interrupted his sermon, murmuring in a stunned voice: "I am disturbing you . . . I am going . . . Excuse me . . ." and he turned once more to the door.

"Wait a minute!" Edoardo called him back once more with a sudden expression of pain and displeasure on his bloodless face. "You are going away," he went on bitterly, "without even giving me your hand." He held out his hand to his guest with a smile in which there was nothing if not liking, even a gentle affection, and he added: "It is you who must excuse me, the fault is all mine. I am weak and nervous from my illness. I beg your pardon. Won't you forgive me? *I beg your pardon,*" he insisted with warmth. At that, the other, who had heavily retraced his steps, thrust out his hand in a shamefaced, awkward gesture, standing before the invalid with his head bent, his forehead creased in a frown under his heavy black curls. He cast a fleeting, sidelong glance at Edoardo and murmured in embarrassment: "Thanks . . . thanks . . . it's time for me to be going. . . ." But Edoardo held his hand, pressing it between his thin fingers so it could not escape and with anxious impatience, he said: "One thing more before you leave. Would you be displeased if we became friends? Wouldn't you like to be my friend?"

Francesco stammered I don't know what in reply and glanced quickly at Edoardo with a timid, humble smile. Looking at him, he seemed only now to notice the pallor and the restlessness of that thin face and he was filled with pity. "You have been sick," he observed, remorseful and almost paternally protective. "I shouldn't have come." In reply, Edoardo laughed affectionately and contentedly; then, with impetuous haste he said to his visitor: "Listen, you live here in town, don't you? But your address is not on your card. Write it down for me, please, here is a pen, write it down and as soon as I am better, I shall come to see you. I'll come to see you the first day I can go out. Perhaps in a week I'll be able to go out, perhaps even the day after tomorrow. I shall come to you at once, at once." He waited anxiously for the other to write. But his visitor hesitated, held back by a strange reluctance. "Look," he said finally, with an effort, "if you don't mind, it would be better for me to come back here," and he spoke vaguely of a family that lived far away, certain complicated studies, the lack of a fixed address . . . and so on.

Edoardo's face grew long, darkened by suspicion and disappointment. "A moment ago," he said, frowning, "you said your address was here in town and now you deny it. . . . Why don't you want me to come? Perhaps you find me hateful, and you don't want to be my friend? And now you promise me to come back, but probably you will never come and I will wait for you day after day. . . ." Edoardo's lips twitched and with a nervous little laugh, he continued: "But I can see in your eyes that you are lying when you say you have no address." In a willful, wheedling voice, as if to have that address were the supreme goal of his life, he begged. "Write it down! Do! Write it for me!"

Francesco could only give in. Murmuring that it was a provisional address, a temporary lodging, that for certain reasons, and so on, and so on, he wrote with trembling fingers on his own card, under the printed *Francesco de Salvi* (he now drew a little line modestly through the Baron): in care of Consoli, Vico Sottoporta 88. His face beaming with pleasure, Edoardo was standing near Francesco with his elbows on the table and one knee on the arm of his chair; leaning over the other's shoulder, he watched him write the address. Then he repeated the words over to himself, drew a long sigh and taking possession of the card, he put it carefully in his pocket.

A clock in the hallway struck the hour; the door opened and Concetta, wearing a black felt hat, appeared in the doorway. She asked her son if the servant could bring his dinner tray but then, seeing the stranger, she added: "Ah, excuse me, I didn't know you had visitors," and she went out immediately, leaving the door ajar, however. That apparition robbed Francesco of any remaining shred of composure. "I am going . . . thanks . . . excuse me . . ." he stammered while he looked for his hat, quite forgetting that he had left it downstairs with a servant. "I'll see you soon," Edoardo told him, holding his hand with a friendly, meaningful smile. When the other was already on the threshold, he added: "Meantime, while you wait for my visit, come back and see me here. I'll be waiting for you. Come back tomorrow!" But this invitation received no reply from Francesco who scarcely heard it for he was already out of the room and down the hall where he almost collided with the servant bringing the dinner tray.

Although he did not really count on his visit (sensing that out of shyness he would not appear), Edoardo was disappointed and piqued the next day when Francesco did not come. He waited in vain during the days that followed and such futile waiting sharpened his desire to see him again. He began to suspect that the address his visitor had given him might be false and he dispatched Carmine to Vico Sottoporta, 88. The coachman returned to report that a Francesco de Salvi, student, lived at that address in a furnished room, in the house of a cabdriver. This pacified Edoardo somewhat; and no sooner was he able to leave the house than he went to visit Francesco de Salvi, as he had promised.

2

The Two Young Men Become Friends, Rosaria Torn Between Decency And Dishonor.

Carmine's information was correct. Young De Salvi was living alone and far from home in order to continue his studies and he had rented a little room with the family of a cab-driver. At the time of which I am speaking he was twenty-one, he had just finished preparatory school after which, according to plan, he would have enrolled in the School of Law at the University; but although admissions for the year were about to close he was still unable to enroll because his parents had encountered serious difficulties and could not give him the necessary fees. The news from Edoardo about Nicola Monaco had destroyed his last hope, far-fetched as it was, of obtaining the money; but as you will see later, this was not the only cause of the angry, despairing sobs to which the young student abandoned himself when he returned to his solitary little room from the Cerentano palace. From his broken, contradictory exclamations it would have been hard to understand his real feelings for he seemed at one and the same time to be accusing someone, sneering at him, adoring him, weeping for him. At one point he burst into a bitter, painful laugh which had a strange ring of satisfaction; perhaps someone who knew more of his heredity would have detected a significantly melodramatic note, a kind of atavistic, childish imitation of the laugh which echoes in the prologue of *Pagliacci*. With clenched fists he rubbed the eyes which had refused to weep, with towering rage he bit the hand which had accepted the friendly clasp of one who had insulted Nicola Monaco. After some moments of such gesticulations, he threw himself on his little bed and gave way to innocent, heartbroken tears.

However, a few days later when the detractor of Nicola Monaco, that is to say Edoardo, came in person to the cabdriver's house, Francesco did not refuse to give him his hand; on the contrary, he was embarrassed to offer such a vulgar, rough hand as his own to so genteel a clasp. His first reaction when Edoardo entered his little room was one of shame for the poverty of his surroundings; he hastened to explain that he always lived in poor houses or districts, not because he was obliged to (he came, he said, from a family of wealthy landowners) but for definite reasons of his own — with such direct, personal experience he planned to enrich the social studies to which he had devoted himself for years. As he spoke, he indicated various books on philosophy, sociology and politics which were piled up on his table and he confided to his guest that these texts contained the ideas on which the future would be built. He gave the young princeling who had come to visit him in the cabdriver's house to understand that beneath its modest appearance, that little room was in reality a mysterious smithy where the destinies of the universal society were being thrown in the crucible to be refashioned into forms as yet undreamed of.

Naturally, he concealed from young Cerentano his own financial difficulties and his fear of having to interrupt his studies; he claimed he was a student at the University, enrolled for the first year of law. He added that he was a little behind his companions because a serious illness had forced him to leave school for a time when he was a child. This was the truth and the illness he referred to was smallpox which he had had when he was eleven or twelve; he did not name the illness but when he alluded to it, he blushed violently.

The fact is that ever since his illness Francesco had worn his pock-marked face not as if it were his own natural, normal face but as if it were a kind of disgraceful mask from which he could not free himself. Never or very rarely was he able to forget that mask; but still, while he himself could not forget it, he indulged in the absurd hope that others would not notice his disfiguration. In the same way he cherished the illusion that in his one worn suit and his miserable little room in Vico Sottoporta, he was able to hide his poverty from the world.

There were rare occasions, however, when he forgot that he was pock-marked, that he was poor and in other ways most unfortunate; and that was when he drank. At their third meeting, having invited his new friend to have a liqueur at a bar, Edoardo noticed the happy transformation which alcohol brought about in him and from then on, he arranged always to meet him in bars or taverns where the two of them would sit almost every evening drinking and talking long into the night. Under the influence of wine, Francesco's lively passions, his vast enthusiasms and ambitions which normally he was not able to express without great effort, were unloosed and our rough young man became an eloquent, spirited orator of deep feeling. Often he would begin to sing in a fine baritone which rattled the windowpanes and other patrons of the taverns the two friends frequented (poor workers, for the most part) would gather around their table, enjoying these free concerts vastly. Francesco's favorite pieces were operatic arias, especially those which expressed revolt, anger, denunciation or tragic conflict. These he sang ringingly and with a true voluptuousness of despair, except for the tenor parts which he preferred but which were not adapted to his voice; he would have to break off at the high notes and in his annoyance he would thump the table with his fists.

During these evenings our student expounded at length the famous ideas of which he had told Edoardo he was the student and disciple. In the solemn, moving tones of the pulpit, he preached the advent of a prodigious, quite improbable civilization of which he was not only the herald and paladin, but one of the future pillars. He glared about him severely and declared with great heat that the present organization of the world was based on the ignorance of the many and the will of the few (among which, it goes without saying, he included not only Edoardo Cerentano and all his clan, but himself and his own ancient and wealthy house). But those who like himself knew the truth were duty-bound to shout it to the unthinking multitudes, to preach it in the market places, until the day came when mankind would ask itself in amazement how for so many centuries it could have remained buried alive in such a ridiculous bondage. He quoted liberally from his favorite prophet; for example, *Property is theft*, or he would announce in an exalted voice that *the day will come when the possession of a bit of land will seem no less impious and absurd than the once legitimate possession of a slave seems to us today*. "On that day," he announced to the young princeling at his side and to the ragged outcasts who surrounded their table listening intently, "on that day all men will be free, for the law which I preach will free not only the slaves but the masters from the burden of property which today holds them chained to the land. Wealth, once it becomes common property, will no longer be a shameful, sterile burden, no longer an end in itself, but the means to an end! Like water, like air, it will be spontaneously, naturally consumed by everyone for the sole purpose of nourishing the physical body of human society. And men will think no more of it than, today, they think of the air they breathe. Labor equally divided among all will no longer create wealth for the few but it, too, will sustain society as a whole. When labor is equally shared, man will be freed to devote his time and energy to his true destiny, his spiritual destiny. Science will have performed its great function and will have reduced the physical task of man to a minimum. Freed of Adam's curse, man will come to recognize in woman not an object of desire and jealous passion, but an angelic helpmeet destined to share with him the noble task of perpetuating the human race. When every motive for rivalry, struggle and war will have vanished, what great works will be accomplished, what great truths will be discovered, what unhoped-for destinies will be revealed to the mind! Beautiful or ugly, corrupt or honest, intelligent or stupid: these will be the bases for judgment. No consideration of class or rank will becloud justice, for even family names will be suppressed. Men will have no names other than the first names which their mothers give them, and they will talk to each other as equals and their one title will be Comrade!"

A discourse such as this moved not a few of his listeners; some applauded and others, looking at Francesco de Salvi with shining eyes, came up to shake his hand and rejoice with him. Their response had little to do with the merit of his ideas which remained quite cloudy to their benighted minds, but had much to do with the effectiveness of his resonant, grandiloquent words which soothed them like a song. Some, however, enjoying his songs more than his sermons, would move off the moment they heard him begin to talk and return discreetly to their tables to take up their interrupted games.

Edoardo enjoyed his friend's orations hugely, particularly for the natural fire and the ingenuous enthusiasm which animated them. The extravagances Francesco preached were such as Edoardo had never heard the like of, and they amused him like so many stories or fancies his friend might have invented in the glow of wine. The stern gravity with which Francesco sometimes invited him to consider or to discuss his famous projected legislation touched Edoardo as a further sign of his friend's simplicity while at the same time he found it absurd that anyone should be interested in such things. He considered privilege a right. One is born rich, as one is born handsome, or intelligent or strong. Why call a natural law an injustice? Furthermore, since this law had favored him, it seemed all the more a heresy to Edoardo to dispute it. And then, to worry about shaping and improving the future seemed to him as vain and silly as it would have been to attempt to alter the past. Past and future are two foggy, indistinct regions which the living can explore only in imagination or in memory; but perhaps memory and imagination are only instruments of illusion, perhaps it is only a misleading game for man to believe that the past stands at his shoulder, that the future lies before him. In reality, he moves over an immobile sphere, complete from the beginning, in which the past and the future are one. What use is there in exploring this realm of death? The mere effort to sound its depths causes anxiety and nausea, as if one leaned too far over a precipice.

And so Edoardo listened to Francesco de Salvi's discourses in the same spirit in which he listened to the servants in the country when they related with earnest credulity the folk tales of their villages; he enjoyed listening to him, because in such moments his friend's voice became warm and resonant, his eyes sparkled and his large hands, usually so ashamed of their vulgar ugliness, gestured freely and continually like dancers intent on redundantly tracing in the air the forms of his every word. Edoardo liked to tease him by opposing jokes and heresies to his enthusiasms. He would tell him, for example, that men are born and die slaves, that with the advent of their much heralded liberty, they would be no happier and no freer than when they were in chains. Furthermore, many of them would refuse to be liberated; for many of them slavery is the one end, the one pleasure in life; they much prefer to obey a master, good or bad, to possessing a freedom they do not know what to do with. "Exactly, they must be educated for freedom!" Francesco would exclaim. "But why, if they're happier as they are?" demanded Edoardo. "Nobody wants them to be happy, they must be men!" Francesco replied. "Men! Men! Why not angels, then?" Edoardo sneered. "It is a curious presumption in man, this idea that man is the end and law of creation! Why not educate horses or dogs to be men, then? Many mothers' sons do not want to be men in the sense in which you mean it and if forced to, they would finish by crawling around on four legs and howling to regain their lost dogs' souls. That's enough, Francesco, you're drunk. And you're a bore! And in the last analysis, you're a clown. Look here, would you be willing to be part of your great future era just as a simple member of the herd, a Comrade, as you say, and not a Leader? Oh, admit it, what you really want is a crown, nothing less than a king's crown. You, the great liberator! You, suppressor of the masters! It's that you long to be *the* master, the master of the whole world, that's the real secret. Deep down, though, you would not be too dissatisfied to be a tenor instead. That evening when we went to the theater, you were carried away by the music and the applause and you admitted to me that when a crowd applauds, it makes you want to cry. What joy, what glory for a man, you said, to be the source of a thousand joys, the idol of everyone. Come now, don't deny it, at that moment you wanted to be on the stage dressed like a tyrant with papier-mâché armor and a painted, made-up face! Clown!"

Francesco grew pale; he would have liked to hurl himself on his insulting companion but he did not dare strike that pale, gentle face which still showed traces of illness. Those beautiful, chestnut eyes, so full of malice and pride, were deeply circled with black, the pale lips trembled slightly, and the veins in those delicate temples throbbed in a touching, pathetic way. Edoardo's curls had grown faded and dull and , in contrast to Francesco's vigorous frame, his shoulders were a little stooped. But even in that sickly condition, Edoardo's beauty shone out so triumphantly that it seemed somehow to transform even his unkindest words into courtesy and in his mocking laugh there was such a youthful, affectionate note that it drove away any bitterness. Moreover, Francesco did not dare answer Edoardo's insults in kind for fear of ruining a friendship which, in this short time, had become dear or even holy to him. The appearance of Edoardo in his life had been like the sudden rising of an exotic, comforting, cheerful star. The elegance and wealth of his handsome friend, his name, his position in society, overwhelmed Francesco with amazement and pride and he felt a kind of exasperation rather than anger at his friend's jibes, seeing how little he was valued by the person for whom, before all others, he would have wished to appear clothed with dignity, if not with glory. So he did not reply to the other's insults but retired into himself and sat gloomy and depressed until Edoardo decided to win him back with friendly flattery. Just as he liked to humiliate him, he would sometimes excite Francesco with excessive praise. On evenings when he felt tired and nervous, he would say: "Sing something for me, Francesco, I want to listen to that fine voice of yours. Let's see, what will you sing for me? I'd like to hear *L'Aurora di bianco vestita*." He would sit down at the piano and accompany his friend and at the end of the song, he would exclaim with admiring excitement: "Someday, perhaps, I will be just one of the public in some great opera house, in some great capital of Europe, and you will be on the stage, like a hero, deafened with applause. . . ." But he was not slow to add with a little laugh: "Or perhaps you will be singing songs in some fourth-rate cabaret, for tips. . . ."

At other times, instead of encouraging him to take up a singing career, he advised Francesco not to indulge his passion for music, reminding him of the serious duties for which he had been born. Insisting that he recognized in him a man of exceptional gifts, of genius even, he prophesied for him the destiny of one after whom his very century is named, in whose name ideas are proclaimed, wars waged, nations tremble! I cannot say that Edoardo was fully convinced of the accuracy of all this, but I can unhesitatingly say that he was sincere in wishing to please his friend with his praise and to give him self-confidence. But when he saw Francesco's face shine at these visions, he was consumed by jealousy for fear the other dreamed of a future from which he himself was excluded. His friend's happiness seemed to him a guilty joy because it was not shared and immediately he longed to destroy it. He gave up his praises of a moment before for skeptical and sarcastic remarks and he was pleased only when he saw the joy on Francesco's face give way to anxiety and discouragement. Then he would propose a common future, trips together all over the world. And how much they would drink and sing and talk, and what marvelous pleasures they would know, what love affairs!

In addition to wine and visions of utopia, beauty and art also stirred Francesco deeply, but his taste in the arts was, to tell the truth, rather confused. In general, like children and uncultivated people, he considered anything sumptuous and vivid to be elegant and magnificent. Vulgar music could give him the keenest pleasure and he would contemplate an inferior, garish painting with ecstasy. Of course, being ignorant of his errors, he thought he was viewing world-renowned masterpieces and he felt the same sincere exaltation as if the paintings had been in fact great. Although he noticed his friend's errors of taste, Edoardo made no attempt to correct them. For Edoardo, Francesco's greatest charm was his very uncouthness and he preferred to leave his friend in his savage state, even though this might be to his disadvantage, in order to satisfy his own caprice and not spoil the pleasure he took in him.

Edoardo guessed correctly that he owed a great part of the fascination he exerted over Francesco to his social position. Therefore, jealous in friendship as in love, he avoided having him meet any of the young men he knew. He wanted to have his own splendor appear in his friend's eyes as something rare and inimitable and with jealous zeal he eliminated any possibility of such meetings. One evening a young gentleman happened by chance to meet Francesco at Edoardo's home and invited him to come the next day to visit him. But Edoardo drew him aside and, in tones of annoyance, enjoined him not to steal away his friends who belonged to him, to him alone, and not to the first comer. Not wishing to antagonize Edoardo the embarrassed young man found some excuse to withdraw the invitation and a few moments later left precipitately.

For that matter, Francesco went very rarely to Edoardo's home, and never on the occasion of any party or reception. It was Edoardo who went to Francesco's little room or, more often, they met in little cafés and taverns on the outskirts of town where they were not likely to meet the rich friends of the Cerentanos. Edoardo's jealous precautions, it should be added, were perhaps superfluous for it was very rarely that anyone sought out Francesco's friendship. There were some among the young students or workers who admired him when they heard him talk with such fervor under the influence of wine but if, the next morning, they sought out their spirited prophet, they found instead a reserved, dour young man who was more easily moved to irritation than to friendliness. And in spite of his deep need for sympathy,

Francesco fled from companionship for two motives which, although they are opposed in nature are often joined in ferocious league: pride and shyness.

There was one person, however, with whom Francesco felt quite free of shyness, or pride, or any unnatural restraint. Even his famous mask of pock-marks lost its oppressiveness thanks to this person and became a trifling thing, a vague, even an attractive shadow. Not that she pretended to ignore it. On the contrary, chattering in lover's talk in her native dialect (the only language she knew), she would call Francesco by little pet names like "walnut face" or "rough bark," and so on. As she stroked his pitted cheeks, she asked gently: "Who was the nasty worm that nibbled this lovely face?" Such easy familiarity dispelled Francesco's anguish, much as the famous ghost who terrified an entire city vanished forever when a young girl called it by its name.

It was, of course, a girl who exorcised Francesco's ghosts; she was two or three years younger than he, and her name was Rosaria. When he met Edoardo, he had known her less than two months (they had met on the street) and from the first he had been on terms of the greatest intimacy with her, but it was many days before he brought himself to tell Edoardo that he had a mistress. He was too jealous by temperament to have his gallant companion meet her so he contented himself with talking about her endlessly, for he was too much infatuated to keep still. She was, he explained, a prostitute, or rather, she had been one until a few months before but Francesco has made her realize how shameful her profession was. She had been drawn into it only because she was simple and like all women longed for luxury. But love had transformed her; she had renounced her shameless ways and had taken up a life of decent poverty and work. Although she herself did not dream of any such thing, Francesco had secretly decided to marry her when he had finished his University course, and he confided this plan to Edoardo. It is true, he added, that matrimony would be abolished in the ideal society of the future, in which a mutual declaration of affection and intention would be sufficient to bind two free lovers together without need of contracts and ceremonies. But since modern society considered matrimony to be the only respectable and legitimate tie between a man and a woman, how could one better show one's scorn for such a convention than by marrying a woman of the streets?

In his conversations with Edoardo, he described Rosaria as a great courtesan who had renounced palaces, carriages and jewels for love of him. Actually, in spite of her irregularities, Rosaria had been living in very straitened circumstances, if not in real poverty when she met Francesco. She was little more than a girl, she had only recently entered upon her life of adventure and was still quite unschooled in the ways of the world. Born a peasant's daughter, she had hated the heavy work in the fields and had preferred to come to the city to live with an elderly kinswoman who had a little hat shop. The hat shop, connecting with dark, small living quarters, was in one of the poorest sections of the city inhabited for the most part by working women who did not wear hats. And so customers were few — broken-down old gentlewomen, for the most part, or lower middle-class women who liked to pass as ladies, and the less successful prostitutes. The shop was narrow and dusty, and the entire stock consisted of a few faded moth-eaten felts, limp feathers and an assortment of tawdry ornaments. But coming from the country, Rosaria found in the shop an abundance of treasures to satisfy her vanity. In exchange for her food and lodging, she was supposed to sweep the shop, run errands and learn the trade of modiste. But she was so scatterbrained and lacking in ambition that she spent hours doing nothing; and if she went out in the morning on an errand she would not come back before night. She did learn her trade as well as she could, but only to adorn herself; if left alone in the shop, she never wearied of fashioning the most amazing, extravagant creations which she then tried on, studying herself in the mirror for hours. Since her kinswoman forbade such exercises in vanity, she gave them up in the shop where she could be surprised at any moment, but she learned to steal old felts, ribbons and artificial flowers with which, in the homes of some friends, she would make hats for herself and for them. Of all the clients who came to the shop she preferred the women of easy virtue; they were the only ones who shared her own taste in hats and besides they were the gayest, and they did not treat her as if she were an inferior but were kind to her and taught her how she should dress. Several of them became good friends of hers; the long hours she was away from the shop she spent in their homes, gossiping about love affairs and trivialities, or she went out with them and their men friends. In short, it was not long before she strayed.

In the shop she flirted outrageously with every man who happened by; laughing loudly at any foolishness, turning her gay, curly little head from side to side, she thrust out her breasts and swayed her hips invitingly. No one could understand where, since she had always lived in the country, she had learned such tricks. She made up little jokes to appear witty; and even if she only spoke in her own dialect, she had a sweet, melodious voice. Naturally, her speech betrayed the ignorance of a farm girl but it had an imaginative and strange quality; at times she spoke like a poet. If the old woman scolded her she answered back, often with obscene words for she was hot-headed, and if she was struck, she cried a little but soon she forgot blows and tears and was gay again.

She was a tall girl, not yet heavy, but large-boned and with a high color. In spite of her freckles her skin was luminous and fresh and covered with a delicate golden down. Her hair was short, thick and curly, of a chestnut color bordering on red; she had a wide, red, laughing mouth, and little white teeth, and plump cheeks. Her arms and legs were rather heavy and thick but there was something warm, even touching about their lack of grace. But the most beautiful feature of her beautiful body was her eyes, which were as gentle as a young calf's, and warm and glowing. She was curious but not gossipy, lazy and rather gluttonous. She was greedy, even avaricious in the sense that she like to accumulate things, but at the same time she liked to spend money and was quite unable to resist any pleasure. Although selfish, she was capable of impulsive self-sacrifice.

Two temptations Rosaria did not know how to resist. The first was a caress. It was not true, as Francesco thought, that she had been led astray because of inexperience and poverty. Like a trusting pet animal, she instinctively abandoned herself to caresses and gratefully encouraged them. Does a pet, in the simplicity of his heart, realize that the person who strokes him is ugly, wicked, or despicable? Does he distinguish the poor man from the rich, the young man from the old? Certainly not. It is enough for such a voluptuary that the kiss and the blandishment be kind. Rosaria was like that and anywhere, without discrimination, she took her pleasure.

The second temptation she could not resist was a gift. Since her vices were many — vanity, gluttony, wantonness — her desires were without number and it was quite easy to seduce her with gifts. The glamour of even a modest gift was enough to make her yield, but not infrequently she have herself for nothing.

When she discovered the thefts in the shop, the old woman drove Rosaria out. A little group of curious onlookers, drawn by her loud denunciations, witnessed the scene as Rosaria, all in tears, he lovely hair disheveled, walked by them unabashed. She was without a hat (alas!) and owning no other costume, she was wearing the usual skirt and blouse of a countrywoman, which she had adorned with some black lace. Bitter and defiant, crying like a child, Rosaria ran to take refuge with one of her new friends. The woman comforted her and found her a little furnished room in the house of a landlady who permitted her boarders to receive visitors but required six months' advance on the rent. It was a traveling salesman who, softened by Rosaria's tears, paid the first six months' rent and added an additional small sum for Rosaria to buy what she wanted for herself. Then Rosaria was serene again; there were many things she wanted but astutely she decided to send the extra money home to her family. She did not know how to write but a friend composed a fine letter for her, explaining that she had left the hat shop to take a better-paying job, that she was well, and that she enclosed a part of her salary. The enclosure was more persuasive, as far as her family was concerned, than the curt postcard from her erstwhile employer which they received by the same post, accusing their daughter of being a shameless hussy and a thief, and the unexpected windfall was stowed away in a chest without too many questions as to how it had been earned.

Thus Rosaria began her life of shame. At first the men she met were traveling salesmen of little account, workers, policemen, or clerks. Sometimes she gave herself for her supper or for a pair of shoes or an imitation pearl necklace. She still knew nothing of luxury, of carriage rides and elegant living but her poor little pleasures and trinkets seemed splendid and wonderful to her. A tiny glass of brandy was enough to make her tipsy and then she would sing and laugh and take off her clothes like a café dancer. And in her musical dialect she would murmur strange coarse endearments to her lovers. These passing lovers she liked, although she did not love them. With all of them she was passionate and affectionate, but few of them lasted more than an evening. It was as if she had a single lover whose name was Desire. It was her desire for kisses, for pleasure, and folly that took shape now in one and now in another of those brief loves.

She had reached this point in her life, not more than two months after leaving the shop when, like an archangel, Francesco appeared. He presented himself with the title of baron and besides he was a young and cultivated man, a student; in short, the first gentleman she had ever known. No one had yet loved her with such passion and with such gallant courtesy. The scars which disfigured his face helped make her love him, since they made accessible to her compassion and maternal feelings a man who otherwise would have seemed far above her. And thanks to her humble position and her trust in him, Francesco was freed of his timidity and proud reserve. When they were together he felt the natural self-confidence that comes from knowing one is admired and adored and the relaxation that is born of a happy accord in pleasure. Not because she was stupid, but because she was ignorant and because she worshiped him, she believed his every word. She listened in wide-eyed astonishment as he told her of the great estates, forests and stables which the De Salvi possessed and which he would one day inherit. He told her of stag hunts, of coats of arms displaying lions in a golden field, of legendary ancestors. And since she could not read, he pointed out to her the coronet which he had had printed over his name: Francesco de Salvi. She studied that little crown as if it were mysterious and irrefutable proof that he came from another world. But despite the prestige which made him grand in her eyes, she did not give up her familiar ways for him. For it was her nature to feel at one with her lover, even had he been the king himself.

From the very first Francesco set about turning her against her way of life. With the eloquence that came to him spontaneously when he could give way to his feelings, he looked at her with his tender compassionate eyes and explained to her how she was a victim of bourgeois society which fed like a monster on creatures like herself, and then cast them off. He did not hesitate to use arguments which he himself did not accept. He told her severely that she was living in sin, that she was condemning her soul to death and perdition, and that she would surely go to hell. Rosaria was not devout; her religion was confined to a superstitious cult of some sacred images and symbols and a blind faith in fortune-telling and cards. But every word of Francesco's was revelation and dogma to her; the warm, melodious voice of her young preacher, the glowing light of his black eyes and his learned, poetic expressions moved her profoundly. She was proud to learn that she was a victim and she pitied herself heartily; the threat of hell filled her with terror and she burst into tears and sobs. She seized Francesco's hands and covered them with kisses and promised him that she would live as he wished from that day forward. Francesco covered her with kisses in return and her sobs died away into gentle sighs.

Then driven by enthusiasm and love, she did change her life entirely. Her lack of money forced her to stay on in the little room which was already paid in advance, but no one except Francesco was now admitted there. It was not hard for her to put off her other men since her connections with them were only ephemeral, but it gave her a scornful satisfaction to sacrifice all his unworthy rivals without regret on the altar of Francesco. It was more difficult for her to give up her frivolous friends but since Francesco demanded this also, she wished to show that she was obedient. The little cage with the robin redbreast which she hung outside her door to signal to her friends that she was engaged was now never removed, but her three or four intimates were not long in discovering that it hung there now in token of true love. The news that Rosaria was giving up her friends for love did not make them antagonistic or even envious, for after all she was a poor girl and still very simple. Sentimental by disposition, they became her accomplices, as it were, in this romantic love, and were careful not to disturb it by their presence.

But the dearest of all her friends, the one who had taken her in the day she left the shop, who had found her the room and written the letter to her family, was away during this period, having gone to visit her mother in a nearby city. When she returned, she heard the news of Rosaria but felt sure that she was not included in the general ban. On the evenings when both girls were free it was her habit to spend the night with Rosaria in one or the other of their rooms. She was afraid of ghosts and did not dare sleep alone. The evening of her return she went to Rosaria's room and found her getting ready for bed. Rosaria seemed upset to see her. She did not embrace her, did not say she was glad to see her back and answered her questions unwillingly, protesting that she wanted to go to bed. When finally her friend proposed that they spend the night together, as they had done so many times, she dropped her eyes and murmured that she could not. "But why not?' asked her friend. Then Rosaria, no longer proud and arrogant as she had been with her other friends, but trembling and confused, said she would have to give up her friendship. This was the wish of the man she loved, a great gentleman, a saint, who had released her from her erring ways and taught her the path to Paradise. Unless her friend would also renounce her sinful ways, they could never see each other again.

During this speech the friend said not a word, but she grew red and her chin trembled. Finally she could contain herself no longer and, throwing herself into a chair beside the bed, she burst into tears. Sobbing and biting her handkerchief nearly to shreds, she cried that Rosaria was a cruel, ungrateful girl. She had forgotten what the other had done for her, acting like a sister to her, introducing her to this person and that, and even lending her her own ball dress. And, the day she went away, had Rosaria not had four *lire* from her to buy a pair of shoes with French heels? Rosaria's response to this was to frown and to say yes, and had she not offered security for the loan in the form of her crocheted counterpane? Her friend sobbed harder still. "Here, ungrateful wretch!" she cried, pointing to a bundle she had brought with her, "here is your counterpane. I brought it back, fool that I am, because I did not want any pledge from you!" She ripped the bundle open in a fury and threw the coverlet on the bed; as it opened, a quantity of figs and cakes fell out and scattered over the floor. Rosaria bent over wordlessly to recover these delicacies but the woman, with a violent gesture, stopped her. "Leave everything on the floor!" she cried, in a real spasm of tears. "They were figs with almonds and sweet biscuits that my mother made. I brought them so we could eat them together in bed while we talked, but I don't even want to taste them! You eat them, you eat them with your lover, and damn you both! Good-bye!" With this, she got up, dried her tears, blew her nose on the hem of her skirt and rushed to the door. But Rosaria who felt her heart breaking within her, was at her side in one bound and bursting into tears in her turn, she clasped her friend to her.

"Are you leaving like this?" she stammered. "You're the one who wants it that way!" said the other. "I? Oh, Anita, dear Anita, don't go away, let's talk a little." They lapsed quickly into the most tender endearments and blandishments. "Dear little hands! My little chick!" said Rosaria and kissed her friend's fingers, one by one. "My little redhead, my rose!" said the other, pulling her hair gently and playfully. And Rosaria, stroking the other's face: "My dearest dear, my berry!" In the same way they teased each other lovingly about their faults and defects. Soon they were laughing and joking together with occasional bursts of tears until Rosaria, drying her friend's cheeks, murmured: "Doesn't my little chicken-heart want to spend the night with her Rosaria?" "And my Rosaria," the other replied, "is my little streetwalker going to chase poor Anita away?" They finally decided to spend one more night together; after they had gathered up the scattered sweets, as a special token of regard they undressed each other, except for the underwear they wore even at night. And as they undressed, they continued to praise each other's secret charms.

Once in bed, they fell to chattering as they ate the dried figs and cakes with gluttonous pleasure. They went back over the proofs of their friendship, as for example, when Anita was sick with a severe cold and no one wanted to go near her for fear of catching it, the more so since the affliction made one's eyes swell, one's nose redden and one's voice grow hoarse. Such inconveniences were particularly unwelcome to girls like them, but defying danger, Rosaria had spent all her days in her friend's room. They recalled their fine projects for the future, the most ambitious of which was to put aside a lot of money so that they could rent and furnish a beautiful apartment in the center of town. They would sublet rooms to desirable young men, students or officials, and with the help of a servant would also see to their meals. What good food, what gay parties, what a comfortable, ladylike, tranquil life! "But now, everything is over," Anita concluded. "Yes, everything is over," Rosaria agreed not without a sigh.

Then came the moment for Rosaria to confide the details of her love affair, of which she could never talk enough. And what better listener than this dear friend, so ready to understand? Anita listened, full of emotion and jealous interest, but all hostility disappeared in the pleasure of confidence. Like Rosaria's other friends, she disapproved of Francesco's poverty and told Rosaria she was foolish to accept a man of such limited means; for Anita, as for all her friends, their lovers' greatest virtue was their ability to give them gifts. But Rosaria declared: "Love comes first," and Anita looked at her admiringly, the way one admires a child who enjoys playing by himself, although one also finds him a little peculiar.

They were growing sleepy, so they agreed to continue to see each other secretly and without Francesco's knowledge. At his instigation Rosaria had decided to take up her work as a milliner again and if she went out with her hatbox under her arm, on the pretext of visiting a customer for a fitting, she would be able to visit her friend frequently. And she began to do so in the days that followed.

She did not find many customers and those few were quickly dissatisfied with her work. For Rosaria was rather like a painter who paints only self-portraits; she was unable to resist the temptation of modeling her hats for herself rather than for her clients. She composed them on her own head before a mirror, endlessly modifying, adding and embellishing according to the inspiration of the moment, Naturally, no hat ever came out as the client or even Rosaria had intended. She herself would marvel at the results with a hearty laugh. An austere brown felt intended to cover the gray head of some elderly strait-laced lady would become a swashbuckling creation, complete with green feathery plumes. A demure little cap to be fastened under the chin of a young bride came out covered with ribbons and bows which would have been in bad taste even for a café singer.

Francesco was not able to add to Rosaria's small earnings, for the allowance he received monthly from his father was very small and had to cover all his expenses. He did divide his food with her, which he bought himself for a few pennies. But for the rest, without his even suspecting the need for it, Rosaria had soon to begin borrowing from her old friends. While Francesco deluded himself that she was devoting herself to her work, she was in fact spending the time during which she was not with him in idleness. Above all else, she loved to be idle, to sleep late, and to lie in bed, chattering and eating sweets. She also enjoyed playing cards and although she could not read, she was quick at numbers and was a shrewd player. With the excuse that she had customers to visit, she slipped into the habit of visiting Anita, where her recently repudiated friends usually met, and there a reconciliation was quickly brought about. Sometimes she met men there. But her passion for

Francesco was stronger than their inducements. Her childish imagination was still under Francesco's dominion even when he was absent and his loving, warning voice was stronger than the seductive advice and temptations of her friends. In spite of her poverty and her frivolity, Rosaria was able to resist this evil; and as to her small deceptions, what harm was there, she asked herself every day, in just chatting with friends, or playing cards, and telling the necessary little lies? That certainly was no sin and Francesco would have been unfair to say it was. Her friends supported these opinions quite naturally and, true to their adventurous, deceitful natures, became her accomplices in deceiving Francesco. They were also very kind and generous with her and she could never have managed without their little gifts. And besides, that autumn Francesco was obliged to relax his jealous watch over Rosaria. In spite of his fears, he finally was able to enroll at the University and from then on he dedicated the greater part of the day to his studies.

3

The Baroness Arrives In Town.

THE MOMENT HAS COME to explain that Francesco's title of baron, his great estates and the antiquity of his family were the purest inventions. In reality Damiano de Salvi, Francesco's lawful father, was a simple farmer. His property amounted to a few little fields, so small that, so long as his strength allowed, Damiano cultivated them himself with the help of his wife, Alessandra, and a hired hand or two. At this point in our story, Damiano was over eighty and the farm was worked by two helpers who were hired by the day.

Alessandra was Damiano's second wife; she had been a hired hand on the farm and when he was left a widower, some twenty-five years before, he had married her. She was young enough to have been his daughter and Damiano's feelings for her were mixed with paternal longings for together with his first wife, his two young daughters had been killed in the earthquake which had devastated that part of the country a few years before.

Francesco, his only living heir, was born about five years after his marriage to Alessandra, and Damiano lived and worked only for love of the boy. Seeing from the time the child began to talk that he was more intelligent than his companions, he cherished the ambition to have him educated. He invested all his hard-earned savings and all the slender profits from his farm in this project of love. Before he was twelve, Francesco had to live far away from his family for the sake of his schooling. The separation was painful for Damiano and Alessandra, for they lived only for the boy. Francesco suffered especially in being away from his mother to whom he had been passionately attached from the very beginning with almost a husband's devotion. But ambition was already strong in him; the city, his success at school, his hopes for the future and his secret ideals conspired to make him betray his childish love.

The monthly allowance which his parents sent Francesco was certainly not a large one but in order to afford it the couple economized almost to the point of hunger. Francesco did not realize this nor had he any idea that to keep him in school Damiano had exhausted his resources. During his vacation at home before his first term at the University, Francesco asked for money for his entrance fee and in confusion and humiliation, Damiano had to confess that he had been unable to get it together, although he had tried every means in his power. This unexpected news was a hard blow for Francesco. The close of the registration period was drawing near. It was then that in a secret conversation with his mother, he made the famous decision to seek out Nicola Monaco (why he felt the man would help him will be clear later) since no other solution seemed possible. To Damiano he said merely that he would ask for a loan from a friend in the city and he left home at once.

Five or six days later his parents had a letter from him which Damiano read aloud as usual, since Alessandra could not read. The letter said, without further explanation, that his friend had not been able to lend him the money but that nevertheless he preferred to stay in the city, hoping to find there some employment which would allow him to continue his studies. While waiting what he hoped would be a short time until he could find work, he had to ask his parents to continue to make the sacrifice of sending him, if they could, the usual small allowance. He was already looking for private lessons but they would not bring him enough to live on. As for his enrollment at the University, he would have to give it up for the time being.

All this was expressed in a style that betrayed his anger and disappointment. But only on the third or fourth reading did his parents gather the full significance of the letter. When at last there was no possible doubt as to its unpleasant contents, Alessandra's eyes glittered rebelliously. She paid no attention to the mysterious, private meaning that certain allusions in the letter could have for her and her alone, but she rebelled at the blow fate had dealt her son and she resolved secretly that Francesco must, at any cost, be enrolled regularly at the University.

This time Alessandra understood clearly that her son could count only on her and the knowledge helped her to make an extreme sacrifice. Like most countrywomen, she possessed a heavy gold chain, the traditional gift to the bride from her mother-in-law, and a pair of chased gold earrings, a wedding present from Damiano. These possessions were dearer to her than can easily be imagined because, quite apart from their beauty, they are for every bride a symbol of pride and position in the eyes of other women. She had always refused to sacrifice them for that reason and because she was miserly by nature. However, after hearing Francesco's letter, she resolved to sell them. When she lifted them from the safety of the chest (they were worn only on great occasions) her profound pain was mixed with pride; thus Abraham may have felt as he stood ready to sacrifice Isaac to the will of Heaven.

She did not want to sell her jewelry in the country, both because she feared she would be cheated on the price and because she wanted to avoid humiliation before her acquaintances. On the other hand, she did not trust the mails or any person who might take them to the city for her. Damiano was too old and feeble to make the trip and she therefore decided to go alone to the city and deliver her gold into Francesco's hands, so that he could see to the sale himself.

Since she reached this decision just at the beginning of the olive harvest, she put off her departure for a few days; she knew that the registration period did not close until the end of the month. Meanwhile, she did not inform Francesco of her decision nor of the time of her arrival, enjoying the thought of the surprise she would give him.

Francesco's friendship with Edoardo had begun at about this time and the morning of Alessandra's arrival, Edoardo had come in his carriage to take his friend for a drive. Carmine had gone upstairs to summon Francesco while his young master leaned comfortably back on the cushions, looking through the window at the movement on the poor street. As he was waiting, a thin countrywoman, quick and graceful in her movements and carrying a covered basket on her arm, appeared at the corner of the little alley. She must have been over forty but, a rare thing in the South, she still preserved a wild distinctive beauty. Her eyes, in particular, were deep and as shining as a child's, so beautiful in their black brilliance that her head seemed encircled by a diadem.

She was dressed like a peasant woman, in a full skirt which revealed her ankle and the lower calf of her leg, a short black bodice and a fustian blouse with a round neck and short sleeves ending below the elbows, over which she wore a shawl. She was not wearing the multicolored kerchief that was customary in the country but went bareheaded. Her erect head and her thin, rather hard features made one think of a bird of prey, but the graceful movements of her body made her resemble rather a swan.

Uncertain but neither ashamed or awkward, she paused in the middle of the street as if looking for someone from whom she might ask directions. No one was passing by at the moment; at the corner where the alley crossed a wider street stood only the rich carriage from which Edoardo was watching. The woman hesitated, a little intimidated by the splendid equipage but then, taking courage, she went over and handed the young man a soiled scrap of paper, asking in her rustic dialect: "Excellency, is this the street which is written there?" He glanced at the paper which bore no name but only the address, Vico Sottoporta 88, and replied yes, that the address was correct and motioned toward the doorway. The woman blushed and with a proud, unrestrained laugh, she explained that she was looking for a young University professor who was her son. "He is my son," she repeated seriously, as if to impress this prodigious fact on her listener's mind. "I kiss your hands," she added in the traditional, respectful greeting of the humble to the great, and walked toward the door.

At that moment Francesco appeared in the doorway, followed by the liveried Carmine, hat in hand. When she saw him, she called in a voice of profound joy: "Francesco!" and she ran to him and clasped him close in her arms. Francesco was quite agitated, although not with pleasure at seeing her, for other and stronger emotions destroyed his natural joy. He grew pale and then, as the woman held him close, he grew red with embarrassment; he hastily freed himself and threw a confused glance toward Edoardo's carriage. "Wait for me here," he ordered Alessandra in a dry, almost venomous voice. He moved toward the carriage as toward an ominous mirage; still blushing and uncertain, he explained to his friend that the very demonstrative peasant was a family servant who had know him from birth. Doubtless she was bringing news from him and therefore he would have to give up the drive and his friend's company for today; but if Edoardo would allow him, he would come toward evening to the Cerentano palace. Edoardo agreed, veiling a glance of knowing malice, and with a lazy nod he ordered Carmine to drive on.

A feeling of unjust anger and shame possessed Francesco for some minutes. Instead of welcoming Alessandra, he was secretly in agony for fear Edoardo had discovered the truth, that the humble countrywoman was his mother, not a servant, as he wanted Edoardo to believe. And that he was not a landowner, but the son of poor parents. To find an outlet for his anger and at the same time to explain his reception, Francesco scolded Alessandra as they went up the stairs, saying sharply that in the city such expansive gestures of affection were out of place in public. Although she was disappointed in her son's welcome which she had expected to be quite different, Alessandra was too simple a soul to suspect his real motives and furthermore, she never doubted that Francesco must be happy to see her. Eager to accept her son's every word as gospel truth and to submit humbly to his mysterious wishes, she begged his pardon, reminding him that she was not used to city ways since she had always lived in the country. Meanwhile, with passionate curiosity she studied the house where Francesco lived, eager to know this and that about his life and friends, and who the handsome young man in the carriage was.

When they were alone in his room, he told her of the death of Nicola Monaco; the woman was quite impassive, almost as if the event did not concern her in the least. Francesco had not expected from her the wild tears and gesticulations with which our Southern women usually lament the dead but he was astonished to see that she did not even shed one tear or say one kind word. He did not reveal the shame of Nicola's death in prison, and she did not ask for any explanation. There was only one god in her life now, and he was Francesco; also, she may have been restrained from asking questions by a feeling of mingled fear and modesty. "Fortune willed it so," she said finally, severely, and then almost as if to signify that the unhappy event was regrettable chiefly as a blow to their hopes, she added: "But don't worry. Your mother has taken care of everything."

As she spoke, pride made her cheeks glow and her eyes shine. Slipping a soiled, knotted handkerchief from inside her blouse, she took out the gold chain and earrings and explained the purpose of her trip. This revelation threw Francesco's feelings into the greatest disorder; he felt gratitude and remorse, joy at being able to continue his studies, and reluctance to accept such a sacrifice. Suddenly a tender, exultant passion seized him, releasing him from every fear and worry: "Oh, my darling, lovely mama!" he exclaimed and catching his mother by the waist, he lifted her high, high in his arms, as he might have done with a young mistress, saying over and over: "Oh, my good fairy, my little queen, my wonderful, wonderful girl!" Alessandra threw back her head and laughed with simple abandon. "Let me down, let me down," she cried and when he had set her down and began to kiss her feet and her hands, she spoke to him in a strong, almost dolorous voice: "Oh, my fine professor, my handsome professor!"

Then, with many a sidelong, diffident glance about her, she recommended under her breath that her son hide the jewelry in a safe place and take care to sell it for a good price. And she was not content until, having raised them to her lips for one last miser's kiss, she herself had placed them in a chest and Francesco had pocketed the key. She had also brought in her basket a roasted chicken, some little sweet cakes and some eggs (and she had not forgotten to bring a gift for the family of the cabdriver, for whom she had brought a big cake). Mother and son ate together and what was left Francesco put aside, thinking he would share it later with Rosaria. Meanwhile, Alessandra talked to him about farm affairs which, among country people, are the principal if the only subject of conversation.

As they talked in Francesco's little room, the hours passed and it was soon afternoon. The anxiety of the morning returned to torment Francesco; he was afraid that Edoardo or even Rosaria might come to look for him at his home if he did not appear at theirs, and would surprise him in conversation with this mother whom he denied. Also, ashamed to be seen with Alessandra, he refused to accompany her on a walk through the city, as she longed for him to do. She had promised herself a triumphant promenade on her son's arm; by his side her timidity would have vanished entirely and she would have felt truly the mistress of the city. Her face darkened with disappointment but a still more bitter refusal awaited her. She had warned Damiano that she might be away for two days and had looked forward to spending one night in town with her son. She had examined the bed in his room and discovered that it had two mattresses, one of wool and one of horse-hair. she proposed stretching the horse-hair mattress on the floor and sleeping there, while Francesco slept on the bed. What was wrong with such a plan? She stared stubbornly before her as she listened in silence to the many reasons Francesco offered for her returning that same day, but his improvised, fictitious reasons were not calculated to persuade her and in the monotonous, rather mournful accent peculiar to her dialect, she said over and over: "But for one night, for one night! . . ." In the end she had to give in to him. He consulted the train schedule and then accompanied her to the station, which was not far away. Grave and frowning, she walked at his side with her graceful undulating step, her empty basket on her arm, while he chose the less frequented streets, like a thief, for fear of being seen in her company.

They had a long wait and when the train finally came, it was almost empty. With the folds of her skirt falling richly about her, she sat on the wooden seat with the majestic dignity farm women often possess. Now that the danger of meeting people was past, Francesco recovered his affectionate good humor; he showered his mother with small attentions as if she were a great lady, partly to win her forgiveness but mostly to still his own feeling of guilt at having put her off. Alessandra was proud and radiant but then the whistle for departure sounded and while she was whispering for the last time instructions about the jewelry, Francesco had already leapt out of the carriage. As the train drew away, a sharp anxiety began to twist at his heart.

He went immediately to Edoardo's but his friend was not at home. In his growing distress, this insignificant fact seemed almost a catastrophe to Francesco. He would have gone on to visit Rosaria but he felt a strange repugnance at the thought of going to her, as if this would be to betray his mother. So he went home and lighting the lamp, since it was already dark, he began to picture to himself what he had given up. He imagined the hair mattress spread on the floor and his mother as gay as a girl over the novelty of it; he imagined her amazed delight at the strange city and all her curious questions and his own pleasant answers. And then he would have had supper with her from the provisions in her basket, and gone to sleep at his mother's side as he used to do when he was a child, pleased at seeing her half-awake beside him. All this seemed to him so charming and delightful that not even the most brilliant evening could have matched it; why then had he refused it? He had never noticed how sordid his little room was until Alessandra's presence had briefly lighted and transfigured it. He took out the jewelry which had shone so richly on her bosom and gleamed in her little brown ears. And he kissed the cold pieces of gold, murmuring bitter, hopeless words, as if he were speaking not to Alessandra but to an unfaithful wife who had abandoned him.

Francesco finished his evening at Rosaria's. Edoardo appeared the next morning with carriage and coachman to invite him again for a ride, an invitation which today he could accept freely. Edoardo now knew from what kind of aristocratic stock his baron had sprung but although he was sometimes cruelly frank with Francesco, he never revealed his discovery to him or to anyone else and always pretended to believe Francesco's boasts about his family. Edoardo sensed that if he had behaved differently, he would have broken his ties with his friend irrevocably. His own sense of social superiority helped along their friendship, and Francesco's lies spared the young nobody the humiliation he would otherwise have been unable to escape in the company of his young gentleman friend. Friendship was not the only thing for which Francesco's lies served as a shield. I do not know, for example, if Francesco could have defended his ideal republic with such boldness if he had been unable to strike this attitude: "Look, I am not one of the outcasts I defend, I am a nobleman, a landed gentleman!"

But it is useless to cavil. To return to Edoardo, we shall see that even the most treacherous friend does not dare be completely, perfectly treacherous any more than the most sincere lover dares be completely and perfectly sincere. In every love relationship, even the most passionate and impulsive, some blows must be held back; I mean, some words must not be spoken, some thoughts must not be expressed, some questions must not be asked. In the relationship which concerns us, that of Francesco and Edoardo, there were two or three matters on which Edoardo's heart counseled silence or acquiescence. One was the question of Francesco's noble birth; another was the person of Nicola Monaco, to whom (although he did not know just why his friend was so sensitive on this subject) he never alluded again even by name after that famous first conversation. Edoardo's discretion was such that he instinctively forbore investigating such questions. Although as secrets they aroused an idle curiosity in him, what interested him was not Francesco's origins or his past, but Francesco in person, in the present. In this realm he did not permit his friend to have secrets from him — as we shall now see.

4

The Ring Changes Hands.

When Francesco talked about Rosaria to Edoardo, he described her, we know, as a great courtesan who had renounced her life of luxury for the sake of her redemption; what would Edoardo think if, instead of that much vaunted lady, he saw a little country girl? Although he was not schooled in elegance, Francesco could not help realizing how greatly Rosaria differed from the splendid, glittering *kept women* who rolled along the Corso in their carriages. Accordingly he took pains to avoid any meeting between them, although he had little hope of being able to keep up his subterfuge for long. The mystery of the concealed mistress excited Edoardo's curiosity. Who could she be, he asked his friend maliciously, this famous courtesan whom no one ever mentioned? The circle of these attractive ladies was quite well known to him and the conversion of any one of them would soon have reached his ears. But Francesco replied that she came from a city in the North and was absolutely unknown here. But why, poor thing, should she be kept so isolated? Not to expose her to temptation. "But then," Edoardo exclaimed spitefully, "if you consider me a tempter, it means you do not think I am your friend and if you are so afraid she will fall again, it means her conversion is not sincere." Francesco could not answer these objections. Edoardo was urged on by something even stronger than curiosity, and this was jealousy of his friendship: How could a man like Edoardo bear the thought that his friend should have a secret life from which he himself was excluded? How could Francesco reserve for others, whom Edoardo did not even know, the most personal, intimate feelings of his heart, and so many hours of his time? To persuade Francesco to reveal the mystery of his love affair, Edoardo resorted to various devices: sometimes he would deliberately pretend to be skeptical about Rosaria's beauty, or he would remain maliciously silent when Francesco brought up the one topic on which he longed to talk incessantly, and quickly change the subject. At other times, irritated and tired of pretending, Edoardo threatened to follow his friend secretly and in spite of him to unearth the courtesan in her retreat. And undoubtedly he would have carried out his threat had not chance come to his aid in another fashion.

Francesco's cabdriver landlord did not permit his tenants to receive ladies; Francesco had warned Rosaria of this and dissuaded her from visiting him. This privation depressed him at first but after he had come to know Edoardo, he was not displeased with an arrangement which permitted him to keep Rosaria out of his friend's way. Rosaria had always obeyed the injunction until one day a friend of hers hinted that Francesco was using this as a pretext to conceal a rival. Immediately suspicious, Rosaria dressed in her best finery and ran to Francesco's house to catch him unawares.

She found him at home alone (it was Sunday and the cabdriver's family had gone out for a walk) and busy studying. He scolded her sharply for her disobedience but she, seeing that her suspicions were groundless, grew wildly gay and affectionate. Francesco forgave her this once but hurried to take her away since he expected Edoardo toward the end of the afternoon. And, just as the lovers were going down the stairs together, they heard Edoardo's voice from the entrance, calling Francesco. So the two met.

Edoardo's eyes sparkled with surprise; he bowed, as he would have to a lady, and kissed Rosaria's hand. Since no one had ever saluted her so grandly, she laughed at the gesture. But Francesco, irritated and embarrassed at the meeting, was not displeased with the courtesy: Edoardo's gesture showed that he considered Rosaria a lady of high society.

Actually, Edoardo had noticed instantly that the hand he kissed was coarse and a little dirty. And as for Rosaria's appearance, we know that it combined a display of poverty and the most vulgar taste. Her hat that evening was one of the most fantastic she had ever thought up. And the jacket that protected her from the cold, of velvet trimmed with rather weary cat-fur, was a discard from a friend's wardrobe, which had been given to her for remodeling a hat.

But precisely because she was herself, and so different from the Rosaria described by Francesco, this pathetic carnival-queen attracted Edoardo greatly.

Rosaria, for her part, was struck with admiration for the handsome young gallant, although she found him a little pale for her taste, and she marveled silently at his elegance. Then Edoardo proposed that all three of them go to an expensive café where there was an orchestra. It was the first time Rosaria had set foot in such a fine place and she behaved with reserve and gravity at first. But then liqueurs were brought and she soon recovered her gaiety.

I certainly do not want to try my readers with a recital of the nonsense which she chattered so loudly in her mountain dialect. People at the nearby tables turned to look at her and Francesco longed to make her behave with some dignity; but Edoardo who was dressed and bore himself like a king in the midst of that crowed, showed no signs of embarrassment; in fact, he seemed unusually gay. There was no reason, then, for Francesco to be ashamed, particularly since jealously had already driven all other feelings from his heart.

The drinks and the heat of the room had brought color to Edoardo's cheeks and his beautiful eyes shone. He had removed his overcoat and sat by the table in his light, soft suit; made happy by the wine, he joked and laughed with Rosaria, who preened herself in her shabby clothes and chattered on at the top of her voice, nodding her head (and her monstrous hat) with great animation. Again, I should like to spare my readers the thousand absurdities, the familiar, would-be witticisms exchanged in little more than half an hour between these two, at each of which Francesco felt the same surprise and dismay that a poor prisoner in the dock might experience as he watches new and ever more damaging witnesses file by to testify against him. One example will do.

At one point Rosaria folded her gilt-edged paper napkin into a little ship and with the bill, a smaller slip of paper, she made a second, smaller boat which she put on the table beside the first, explaining that they were mother and daughter. Edoardo laughed heartily as if he thought this a wonderful game and thus encouraged, the girl went on to pretend that the table was an ocean; pushing the little barks along with her plump fingers, she announced: "Ship is sailing! The biggest ship goes to my Francesco and the little one to Signor Cerentano." "And what are they carrying?" asked Edoardo. "The big one is carrying kisses." "And the little one?" "I'm not going to tell you," Rosaria exclaimed, hiding her face on Francesco's shoulder. "Why not? Francesco wants you to tell me, don't you Francesco?" "Yes, tell him." "Well, all right, if you like. Your ship carried littler kisses." "I don't want littler ones," Edoardo declared. "If you want them, there they are," she laughed, "and if you don't, throw them away." "I want the big ship," the young man said, with a stubborn smile. "That one, oh, no, that's Francesco's. Take it, Francesco." But Francesco, frowning and grim, did not take the boat and said not a word. "Take it, take it," Rosaria repeated in her drunken, laughing voice. "Keep quiet!" Francesco muttered. "Can't you see that everybody is staring at you?" "What do I care?" she retorted, her face afire and her hat askew. And she added: "Then the big ship is for Signor Cerentano. Take it!" and she threw the paper ship at Edoardo's chest. With a victorious glance he picked it up and placed it carefully in his breast pocket, as if it were a love letter.

Francesco thought this was all inevitable. How could any woman resist his friend's charm, his wealth and his courteous manner? His affection for Edoardo was too strong for him to feel resentment; rather, he was surprised to see someone like Edoardo who had known such noble, pure and splendid girls, now taken with Rosaria. It raised Rosaria's prestige in his eyes while at the same time he felt so awkward, so disfigured, that it seemed impossible he could ever have pleased her. His pitted face burned and stung and a dull nausea robbed him of any desire to drink. He felt like an ugly, inert puppet and imagined all the clients in the café were pointing at him with scornful pity; anger alternated with a sense of desperate abandon in which he seemed to drift away from his surroundings and his humiliation toward remote, silent, somnolent shores. It was a bitter, unforgettable evening which had a strange conclusion. As they left the café, Rosaria asked gaily where they were going and Francesco told her that he and Edoardo would accompany her home and leave her at the door, and that he would go home to bed since he had to be up early the next morning for a lecture. But Rosaria seemed put out at this news and paying no attention to Edoardo's presence, she clung to Francesco and begged him to go to her room with her. She was so drunk that she was oblivious of the social decencies Francesco had tried to train her in; she implored her lover with completely shameless frankness, telling him without modesty or reserve what she wanted to do once she reached her room with him. As she talked, she leaned close to Francesco and stroked his cheeks and throat; alluring and full of desire, her hat awry, her red hair disheveled and her throat uncovered and throbbing under her cat fur. In a strangled voice, Francesco kept saying to her: "Are you crazy? Aren't you ashamed?" and pushed her from him. "Don't you want me?" asked Rosaria in a languid, tearful voice (she had begun willfully and shamelessly to cry): "Doesn't my Don Francesco want his girl when she is dying for him? Doesn't he want to kiss these hands and this mouth . . ." And one by one she enumerated her charms, even the most secret. She seemed remorseful for her recent flirting with Edoardo and anxious to win her lover back with such promises. Meanwhile they had arrived at her house; with trembling hands Francesco took her key from her bag and opened the door. In the dim light of the entrance way, the crazy girl leaned against the wall, laughing and flushed, with great tears rolling down her cheeks. "Go on, go up to your room, go on," repeated Francesco, pale with agitation. But Edoardo, who had come in with them and who had been silent until then, suddenly laughed strangely and exclaimed: "I want to see who wins. I bet she wins."

"No," Rosaria stammered, laughing too but with a tearful grimace, "Francesco doesn't want me, Francesco doesn't love me any more," and almost as if to show what Francesco was losing by refusing her, with the excuse of adjusting her garter she raised her skirt and exposed a generously proportioned and attractive leg well above the knee. "Go on, go on upstairs!" repeated Francesco and forgetful of all the obligations of a gentleman, he was about to push the shameless girl toward the stairs. But at that moment, Edoardo, quite unexpectedly, went over to Rosaria, tore her hat from her head with a high, triumphant laugh, and threw it to the middle of the hallway. "Get along," he ordered. "March! Pick up your hat and get along!"

At this unexpected and fantastic gesture, Francesco turned pale and stared at his friend; in a voice he did not recognize (he felt as if he were moving through some mad comedy or dream) he exclaimed: "What have you done? Ask her pardon at once! Ask her pardon." "I beg your pardon, madam," said Edoardo ironically, with a little bow. "And now pick up her hat," added Francesco. "Ah, no," replied Edoardo, laughing, "that she has to pick up herself. That will be the affected young lady's punishment." Trembling, he stared defiantly back at Francesco.

"Pick it up," the other repeated, with hatred in his voice. "Oh Lord," said Rosaria like one shaking herself awake, "what's going on? You don't want to fight. I'll pick up my own hat," she added with a sob, "and then I'll go, yes, then I'll go, good night." As she spoke, she went over and picked up her hat with its dirty, bedraggled feathers and started up the stairs, not, however, without turning first to Francesco, to say to him: "Come tomorrow afternoon, Francesco mine. Forgive me." And with a rolling, drunken step she climbed the stairs out of sight.

When they were alone, Francesco did not look at Edoardo but stood with his head bowed, his face fixed and stormy, as if he were about to fall upon him. "You want to fight," said Edoardo with a little laugh. "All right, let's go out on the street. I'm not as strong as you and I was sick until yesterday, but I'll do my best, too." Francesco did not look at him nor did he move. He clenched his fists in his torn gloves and he hated Edoardo in that moment as he had never hated anyone before. But he hesitated to strike him, and his friend's last remark drove the thought of violence still further from his mind; before this pale convalescent he felt the same control that a man feels in the presence of a girl who has mortally offended him but whom he cannot strike because her frailty protects her. For his part Edoardo seemed to be inviting the encounter and was tugging nervously at the heavy door; suddenly he turned to Francesco and exclaimed: "Stupid!" and kissed him on the forehead. The other man raised his head and his frowning eyes grew softer. "Stupid," repeated Edoardo. "Blessed stupid fool! Do you really want us to fight over that . . ." and he used a word I do not repeat out of deference to my well-bred readers. "Don't say that!" the other exclaimed, in a choked voice. "You know that she is my mistress, that she will be my wife." "You really want to marry that creature?" Edoardo said. They had gone out and had by now given up the idea of fighting. In an angry, mocking voice, Edoardo began to list Rosaria's faults, declaring that she was ugly, ridiculous and silly. The defects which made her all the more desirable in his eyes (since she really had pleased him) Edoardo described to his friend in such malicious, scornful terms that the poor girl lost all her charms as he talked and was reduced to a dirty rag. He talked about the fuzz on her body, her crinkled hair, her red hands and her heavy calves, and he made fun of her clothes, as if she was the funniest spectacle he had seen in a long time. "That's enough, don't say anything more, that's enough!" exclaimed Francesco, unable to refrain from saying in a low voice that, if one were to judge from

Edoardo's behavior toward Rosaria instead of his words, one would have said that the girl was not unattractive to him. To this Edoardo rejoined that he had been playing a part so that Francesco might realize how his supposed convert was actually the lightest creature in the world, who would forget every honest intention at the slightest invitation. At this, Francesco was silent.

But as we have seen Edoardo was lying when he said he despised Rosaria. He had not failed to note her address and the next morning when Francesco was at his lecture, Rosaria received a basket of hothouse flowers and a little note which said: "Forgive me for having thrown your very beautiful hat on the ground. E.C." She took the card to her landlady to read, and also hid the flowers in the latter's room so that Francesco should not see them. It was the first time in her life that Rosaria had received such an offering and in her enthusiasm, she not only forgave the donor the insult to her hat but lingered over the memory of his seductive person, boasting about his elegance and nobility to the landlady. It goes without saying that in her conversations with Francesco, the incident was never mentioned.

Edoardo's comments had thrown Francesco's feelings for Rosaria into confusion. On the one hand, he despised her for her frivolity and was ashamed of her for her humble origins and her clothes; and he could not see her now without finding fault secretly with those defects which had once seemed to him so attractive but which, ridiculed by his friend, now stood out unnaturally. On the other hand he pitied her not only for the reasons he had had before — that she was poor, entirely alone and on her own, and a victim of society — but because his friend had insulted her by calling her ugly and corrupt and cheap, and no one had come to her defense. One moment he hated her because he had been deceived in his hopes of redeeming her, and then he would say to himself that his friend was wrong: she had flirted with him that night only out of her natural, innocent friendliness, and not because she was corrupt. His confused feelings did not prevent Francesco from finding pleasure and happiness with his dear, impassioned mistress but his pleasure was spoiled by the suspicion that he might be betrayed by her, since Edoardo had judged her a loose woman. He persecuted Rosaria with accusations, doubts and questions. If she appeared in an unusually gaudy dress, he did not hide his distaste and often he accused her brutally of being careless and dirty. Then he would repent his unkindness and would be more passionately devoted than ever. He decided one day to give her up and the next day to marry her without delay. Once, on account of his classes or some trip with Edoardo, he did not go to see her; and the next day, crazy with jealousy, he cross-examined her endlessly on how she had spent those hours of freedom. But Rosaria forgave him his humors; by nature she was gay, indulgent and complacent. When the young man advised her, with a hostile stare to throw that necklace or shawl in the fire, or to be careful never to go out with him in that frightful hat, she would laugh and kiss him, remarking that men never understood women's clothes. When Francesco suddenly interrupted a kiss to say: "Wash your ears," or "You have dirty nails," she would look at her nails ruefully or tug on her silver earring and say: "Oh, *Madonnina mia*, yes, you're right. I forgot to wash. But you like your dirty little Rosaria just the same, don't you. Francesco? Come, kiss me, Rosaria's own heart, kiss me," and she would extend her downy hand or her ear for a kiss. She denied proudly his accusations of infidelity and would call her landlady to witness that she had not stirred from her room all day. And she would add, "But you, why didn't you come yesterday? Why do you make poor Rosaria cry?" Here, alas, it must be said that such goodness and indulgence did not spring wholly from a generous nature but from the fact that she had a sin to expiate. For some days, in fact, Rosaria had been unfaithful.

Not twenty-four hours had passed after the arrival of the flowers when a young man wrapped in a heavy cloak, slim and proud in bearing, who cupped a graceful pipe in one hand and a little package in the other, had climbed the stairs to Rosaria's room. She was lounging half-dressed in bed when the landlady came in and in the greatest excitement whispered in her ear. Pink with amazement, the girl jumped out of bed and slipped hurriedly into a skirt and blouse; a moment later Edoardo stood before her.

Paying no attention to the disorder about him (the room had not been tidied and the bed was unmade) he asked permission to lay his pipe on the shelf of the washstand. Then he asked if Rosaria had forgiven him and when she nodded assent, he offered her the little package with a self-assured air: "Here, this is a present for you." Instinctively Rosaria took the package in her hand, very curious to know what was in it, but he covered her hand with his own and asked what above everything else she would like to find in it. Rosaria confessed that for a long time she had wanted a ring. Somewhat vexed, Edoardo told her that it did not contain a ring but something else. Hurriedly and not without regret, Rosaria said in a low voice that, whatever it was, she would have to refuse it, for that was Francesco's wish. At this Edoardo's face darkened; he dropped Rosaria's hand and his own ceremonious manner and in a haughty, even threatening tone, such as one might adopt toward some inferior being, he declared that *never* would Francesco see that gift and *never* would he know that he had come. Rosaria did not know how to answer. He added: "It's up to you to keep the secret. Otherwise you will regret it. I will have my revenge."

Rosaria's first impulse was to let go and tell him: "What's all this you're saying? And who asked you to come? You can take your gift back and get out." But she was too curious to open the package and besides she felt a sharp urge not to chase this arrogant young man away but to keep him awhile. So, swinging her hips and preening herself as usual, she glanced at him and said: "Why make such a fuss? It's better for me, too, I should think, for Francesco not to know anything." Edoardo was restored to good humor but Rosaria suddenly bethought herself: "Oh dear Lord, I am sinning again, I will be damned, I'll go to hell! Oh Francesco!"

The box contained a pair of earrings, each in the form of a little gold chain from which hung a tear-shaped amethyst. Edoardo explained that he had bought them because he had thought the deep violet would become her and he wanted to try them on her in place of the old silver ones. As his fingers gently touched her ears, Edoardo remarked that she had tiny ears like a little lamb's and in a tone of compassion, he observed how it must hurt little girls to have their ears pierced. Laughing and wishing to be witty, Rosaria said she no longer could remember; then he told her how, as a child, he had envied his mother and his sister the little holes in their ears and he wanted some too and how his mother, to satisfy him, would hang her earrings on his ears with silken threads. "You must have been pretty as a baby," Rosaria observed admiringly. Edoardo agreed that he had been, according to what everyone said, and he added: "And you must have been pretty too."

In short, how could Rosaria resist her chief temptations, gifts and caresses, both offered at once? From that day Edoardo came to her room frequently; if he happened not to find her in, he threatened to write Francesco an anonymous letter saying that in spite of his prohibition she was loitering in the streets. Francesco's daily schedule permitted Edoardo to visit Rosaria at hours when he was certain to find her alone; indeed, sometimes he would take his friend in his carriage to the University, drop him off at his lecture, and proceed in the carriage to Rosaria's. He took the greatest precautions not to blunder: in his conversations with Francesco he continued to simulate indifference or distaste for Rosaria. Once and for all, he told him, the sound of her name was enough to annoy him, much less did he want to see her again. If he would persist in loving her, Francesco was requested at least to stop talking to his friend about her and above all to spare him her company. Francesco did not find it hard to observe this second wish. Edoardo's aversion for Rosaria seemed so genuine that Francesco was dumfounded to remember he could ever have been jealous of him. Actually, Edoardo did not hate Rosaria; he hated Francesco's mistress; it was the idea of that bond which he detested. From this to the hatred of Rosaria herself was a short step, as we shall see; but for the moment he found Rosaria a desirable person and being unable to explain to Francesco the true object of his rancor, he inveighed against the girl herself.

Wishing to avoid Edoardo's sarcasm and by now ashamed of his relationship with Rosaria, Francesco invented excuses when he had to leave Edoardo to go to his mistress. But Edoardo would shrug and say in a tone of ironic, insulting compassion: "You're ashamed, aren't you? You think I don't know where you're going? I envy you for being so easily pleased, but if you want to be putty in that woman's hands, by all means go to her. What does it matter to me?" Nevertheless, Edoardo searched in his mind for new pleasures to distract his friend and make his meetings with Rosaria less frequent.

Edoardo was exceedingly fearful that Francesco would discover he had been betrayed and that in spite of all their subterfuges, some indiscretion of Rosaria's would uncover their intrigue. He terrified the girl with every kind of threat; she would regret it, he warned her, if one day when she was being called to account by Francesco, she so much as mentioned Edoardo's name. The Cerentano family was omnipotent in the city and he was the head of the family. The police were his to command and in a matter of hours they would expel Rosaria from the city in disgrace, like a leper, and send her back to her peasant family; or he would have her shut up in a house of correction or a convent. This mythical, strange world of power cowed and dazzled Rosaria and she shook with fear, until anger against Edoardo, who showed himself to be her enemy by such threats, overcame her fear. Her face would blaze with fury; she could scarcely control the impulse to strike him, to tear at his blond hair and scratch his delicate skin, as she did when she quarreled with her women friends, to insult and bite him. The young man's prestige, however, was too great and intimidated her still childish mind so that she felt instead a kind of awed respect. In spite of the pleasure they enjoyed together, she did not feel for him the sense of trust that entered into her relations with Francesco. Grand and noble as he was, Francesco was still like her; but this one who came and went like a ghost, who held, according to him, her person and her fate in his hands, who wore silk shirts, whose feet were slender and white as his hands, he seemed to come from another race which did not live on bread like other men. She feared him for his power, much as she had feared God or the devil when Francesco had talked to her about them in his effort to save her soul.

When he was not persecuting her with his threats, Edoardo was very agreeable. In the midst of their embraces, he made Rosaria forget he came from another world and his white, slim body was like that of any mortal, caressing and responsive. He loved games and often, like two kittens or goats or some other wild creatures, Rosaria and he would tumble and struggle playfully, laughing and shouting on the bed or floor of the room. He often brought her gifts which, by agreement with him, she kept hidden so that Francesco would not find them.

Of all Edoardo's gifts to Rosaria, the most precious was a ring which has already appeared and is destined to reappear in our story: a ring in the form of a gold circlet, set with a ruby and a diamond. It is time to explain how the famous ring came to Rosaria.

Sometimes, Edoardo and Francesco would have a musical evening, Edoardo accompanying his friend on the piano. On such occasions, Edoardo often taught Francesco songs of his own composition which he took great pleasure hearing the other sing. Thus it was that one evening, I do not know whether out of heartlessness or nostalgia, he was pleased to revive a song we already know, the one which he had composed for Anna just a year before and had sung to her under her window that first day; the one which went: "*O, turn on me alone the dark splendor of your eyes. . . .*" When Francesco, who had no idea what lay behind the song, had quickly learned the words and the music, Edoardo made a proposal. They were to go, the two of them, to the house of a beautiful cousin of his and brighten her dreams with a serenade. In those days and in that part of the country, serenades were a frequent, customary ritual; sought after because of his fine voice, Francesco had sung them often with friends or fellow-students for one girl or another in the city. Protected by the night and emboldened by the certainty that the sleeping beauty could not see his pitted face, he would pour his most intense romantic feelings into the serenades, even if he did not know the girl to whom he sang.

He accepted Edoardo's proposal most willingly and the two friends went to the narrow little street Edoardo had walked along so many times and stationed themselves under the windows he had stared at so often in anxiety, curiosity and jealousy.

It was a winter night, as it had been the year before, but this time the sky was cloudy and the air was warm. In the house where Anna lived all the windows were closed and dark; the street was lighted by a single lamp and by its dim glow, Edoardo pointed out Anna's windows to Francesco. In teaching the song to his friend, he had substituted another name but now, as the serenade was about to begin, he told Francesco that his cousin was called Anna and suggested that he use that name when he sang rather than the other. With that he bent his face over his guitar and after striking a few chords, he began to sing the melody. Warm and resonant, Francesco's baritone voice rose, repeating with every melodious refrain the name of the unknown girl. Lights appeared at a few windows and one curious person opened his shutter a crack. It was clear that the Massias had a bad reputation with their neighbors for when they heard the name of *Anna*, several made unkind remarks about her; but the Massias' windows remained closed. When the song ended, Edoardo suggested that they leave; as they walked away, he seemed by turns tense and bemused.

The following afternoon when he met Francesco, Edoardo suddenly proposed they should go together to call on his cousin. To Francesco's objection that the girl might think him impertinent since she did not know him, Edoardo replied that she would be very much pleased, for she led a very lonely life, being of good family but poor. So they went to Anna's house; when they had knocked, they waited a long time for an answer. Then they heard wooden heels clattering on the floor and a lazy, harmonious but almost irritated voice ask: "Who is it?" Edoardo replied: "It is you cousin, Edoardo." There was a silence of some seconds but the girl must have stayed by the door for they could not hear the sound of her heels. Finally the door opened and Anna appeared. She held out a small, damp hand to her cousin and said: "Good afternoon. How are you?"

It was dusk and in the uncertain light Anna's face was hard to distinguish but Francesco was sure he had seen her before; only after some time did he remember that she was the same girl he had seen in the Cerentanos' reception hall. That of course did not lead him to suspect any connection between the two cousins other than their family relationship, for it seemed quite natural that she should go to her aunt's home. Later, when Edoardo gave him to understand that the Massias had no resources other than what they received from their rich relatives, he imagined that the girl might have come to ask for help and been refused and that this explained her bitter, distracted behavior that day. Francesco also set down her strange manner toward Edoardo as the rebellious pride of a poor girl. In fact, because of his nature and the ideas which obsessed him, Francesco was in the habit of explaining people's feelings in terms of social motives when he found them mysterious.

The disorder of her hair indicated that until a moment ago it had been free and undone and that she had hastily put it up, just as her faded rose jacket was carelessly laced. A button was missing from one of her shoes, her heels were worn, and she dragged her foot a little as she walked. The poverty and disorder of her clothes were reflected in the room where she received the two young men, but the girl seemed to be scornful of that poverty and her manner was so out of keeping with the room and her dress that Francesco felt awkward and ill at ease as if he were in the presence of a great lady.

She was alone at home and the room was almost dark. Edoardo presented his companion with the words: "This is my dearest friend, Baron Francesco de Salvi," and Francesco, bowing in confusion, shook the hand she extended to him. He had a sensation of mixed surprise and awe as he had the girl's hand in his large farmer's paw; it was so small in comparison to her tall body, so terribly small, thin, damp and cold.

"How you've changed," Edoardo said to his cousin, looking at her in the uncertain light. "You have changed, too," she said. "I," replied Edoardo gently and with a kind of childish boastfulness, "have been very, very sick, as you know. Now I am well again but the doctors have ordered a clearer air for me. So I shall be going away soon and I have really come today to say good-bye to you."

At that moment Anna turned away in search of something; she was looking for matches to light the lamp but only after having looked here and there did she realize that they were on the table by which her guests stood. She reached toward the oil-lamp which hung from the ceiling but before she lighted it, she asked coldly: "When will you leave?" "In a few days," Edoardo replied. Francesco was painfully surprised; he had heard his friend talk about his departure but did not know that it was imminent. Edoardo had always said he would wait for good weather.

Timidly Francesco expressed his regret and the other explained that he had decided only a few days ago to leave at once, on the advice of his doctors, and he had said nothing to his friend to spare him the displeasure.

When she had lighted the lamp, Anna sat down and the others sat with her at the table, on which she leaned her tightly clasped hands. A beautiful ring glittered on the girl's engagement finger, a ring which we already know, a ruby and a diamond set in a gold circlet. Edoardo marveled to see it because during the time of their meetings, his cousin had never worn the ring so that no one else should ever see it. He glanced away quickly and made no comment. And he said nothing of the serenade. For a few moments they were all silent. Francesco, disturbed as he was by Anna, was filled with bitter regret at the thought of his friend's departure; Anna, whether from disdain or timidity, did not look at her guests and her flaring dark eyebrows stood out against her white skin. In her faded little flannel jacket her body looked pitifully thin; her neck seemed longer, so wasted had it become, but with all her frailty she carried her head with its great crown of hair erect and proud. But her face grew visibly paler; she looked as if she might collapse at any moment.

Taking up the conversation Edoardo explained that he had wanted to present his friend, Baron de Salvi, to his cousin, with the hope that he might visit her occasionally (since she led such a secluded life), and thus make up for his own absence. As he spoke his brown eyes glanced now at Anna, now at Francesco. The latter blushed and quickly murmured assent; Anna, without raising the eyelids which concealed her stormy eyes, smiled bitterly and the smile remained on her lips as if forgotten there. Perhaps it was the small scar at the corner of her mouth that made it seem so bitter. Suddenly Edoardo looked at the scar and pretending to know nothing about it, he asked Anna how she had come to hurt her face.

This time it was Anna who blushed and when her severe face was flooded with color, it suddenly seemed girlish, even like that of a pink-cheeked doll. She raised rebellious, shining eyes to Edoardo's and stammered that she had burned herself.

"Burned yourself? There? How could that have happened?" Edoardo demanded. Still stammering, like a person lost in confusion, she said: "With a curling iron."

"With a curling iron!" Edoardo exclaimed, shaking his head reprovingly. "That's what happens when one cares too much about one's looks."

This seemed too severe to Francesco who secretly disapproved of his friend at this moment but did not dare enter into the conversation. The girl's face had grown pale again and she shook as she struggled to regain her self-control. She frowned and murmured with a slight grimace: "That hardly applies to me."

"That's true," Edoardo said, laughing pleasantly. Then, glancing down at the ring as if he had just noticed it, he exclaimed; "An engagement ring! So you are engaged?"

Anna shook her head and shrugged. The flippant gesture contrasted with her reserved manner and betrayed the confusion of her heart: "No," she said. "Then what?" inquired Edoardo. "Why are you wearing an engagement ring on your left hand? That's what you do when you are engaged."

Anna's small, proud mouth trembled a little. Edoardo thought she would bury her face in her hands at any moment, and burst into tears, but she did not. As before, she smiled a tight, bitter smile and her body stiffened. Her lips were as pale as her cheeks.

Francesco could not forgive his friend for putting such indiscreet questions to the girl since they clearly offended her pride and modesty. In her presence he felt an emotion he had not experienced since childhood in the presence of his mother. Anna's beauty seemed to him the most sublime a human being could achieve. Her manner and the delicacy of her body revealed her noble birth. She seemed untouchable to him, like a saint breathing a holy atmosphere unknown to him, and at the same time defenseless and weak, as if she were a little girl.

At last Edoardo apparently decided to give up tormenting her and he inquired courteously after her mother. Recovering her calm, Anna replied simply that her mother was quite well but that she had aged greatly and was always of the same uncertain humor. Edoardo asked that she give his aunt greetings and Anna nodded slightly in thanks.

At that point Edoardo drew a little gold watch from his waistcoat and flipping back the engraved cover, said that it was late and he would have to go. Anna jumped to her feet and Francesco moved to go with his friend, but Edoardo urged him strongly to stay so that Anna would not be alone until her mother returned. Francesco did not know what to say and in his confusion, he looked at the girl who seemed not to have heard her cousin's proposal. Torn between the fear of offending her by refusing and of seeming indiscreet if he remained, the young man turned back to Edoardo questioningly. Edoardo renewed his suggestion. "I have another appointment and I must go," he explained, "but there is no reason why you should interrupt your call so soon. Is there, Anna?" The girl nodded coldly and absently; she picked up a lamp and accompanied her cousin toward the entrance hall, while Francesco remained alone in the room.

A long hallway separated the parlor from the door so that Francesco could not hear the conversation between the two cousins or even catch the sound of their low voices. When they reached the door Anna handed her cousin his coat and helped him submissively to put it on; she was violently thrilled at the touch of it. As he slipped it on, he bent his head slightly and Anna saw again the well-remembered parting-line in his curly hair. With all her strength she strained to fix clearly in her mind those handsome, adored features but the dim light of the lamp on the chest made them indistinct. Edoardo was on the threshold when she whispered to him hoarsely:

"I heard someone singing last night."

"It wasn't I who sang," Edoardo said, shaking his head.

"I know. But who was it, then?"

"Francesco." And her cousin motioned toward the young man they had left in the parlor. "He has a fine voice, hasn't he? I was playing the guitar for his accompaniment. But when I saw your window did not open, I supposed you were sleeping and did not hear."

"Yes, I heard. . . ."

"And if it had been my voice singing, would you have opened the window?"

As he put this question he looked curiously at Anna but without waiting for her answer he said quickly: "Good-bye." He went out and had already reached the landing when Anna's hand seized his shoulder with nervous strength. "Wait, wait a moment," she said precipitately. He turned and in the darkness that blurred its features, he looked at her fearful, longing face, which quivered now as if she had been struck.

"Go back in," he said to her then, with the almost motherly solicitude one sometimes finds in boys like him who have grown up in a family of doting women. "Go on in, you have nothing on and it's cold here on the stairs." But at the same time he shook off her hand with impatience and added: "What is it?"

"When . . . will you come back from your trip?" Anna asked him.

"When? Well, for you, never," he replied and as if this unkind answer had given him wings, he leapt down the dark stairs.

However, as he went down, it seemed to him that he could hear Anna breathing hard as she stood motionless on the landing. Then her voice rang out sharply: "Edoardo!" and she ran down to him. "Edoardo," she repeated weakly and seizing his hand, she began to kiss it. Again he slipped away from her and leaning against the balustrade in a position of defiant revolt, he asked: "Didn't you get my letter? The one I sent by the servant to the door?"

Anna was silent. "Did you get it? Did you?" he insisted. And he went on in an arrogant, vexed voice as if he had been wronged: "Then why do you insist? Why do you keep running after me? Haven't you any shame? Perhaps when you saw me coming here today, you imagined . . . Well, you were wrong. If I paid you one more farewell visit, it was first of all out of politeness, since you are my cousin, after all. And secondly, and above all, this is why. When I wrote you that last letter, I thought it would be enough to make you understand that you meant nothing to me any more. But then, afterwards, I had a presentiment and some dreams which made me understand that you were still stubbornly waiting for me, in spite of the letter, that you were living only in the hope that I would come. Now, since I've known this is true, I've been sorry for you day and night and I cannot bear being sorry for you because I no longer love you. To pity someone you love is a good feeling, a delicious feeling which I would gladly exchange for all other pleasures. Actually, the only way I can tell I love someone is when I am glad to be sorry for her and as you know, I deliberately make occasions for this pity in a thousand ways, to realize more and more how I love her. But pity for someone who doesn't belong to me, who isn't mine, someone I don't love, that is the most hateful, painful feeling, that is something for gloomy priests. Really, it is so selfish of you, you're taking such advantage when you force this pity on me! I have been very sick and this pity makes me even weaker. At night when I am alone, it begins, it begins . . . and I toss in bed . . . and I fret over it . . . and it gives me a fever. Why do you persecute me so, why are you so jealous and heartless, you witch? I want to be free of this pity, do you understand? I don't want you to wait for me any more! That is why I came to warn you that I was going away and that you will never see me again, so it's useless to wait for me. I tell you again, I wanted to take advantage of this visit to prove to myself for the last time that I don't love you at all. That was it. I wanted to pity you, to see if I enjoyed it and that is why I said the things I did, to hurt you, and I saw you suffer and I felt a terrible, terrible pity."

"And this pity . . . did you like it?" Anna murmured, scarcely realizing that she spoke.

"No! It bored me, it disgusted me! And just now, to listen to your little voice asking 'Did you like it?' makes me feel a crazy, an unbearable pity. And this pity bores me, it disgusts me! You, too, you bore me and disgust me! Go away! Please go away!'

And since the dim light from the open door above did not reach them, he lit a match and holding it so that it lighted the steps, he repeated: "Go away! Go away, go upstairs!"

In the light of the match he saw Anna hesitate, her eyes dilated and terrified, her chin trembling; she began to laugh and her twisting, uncertain lips drew back and bared her bloodless gums. Suddenly the laughter stopped and her face grew stubborn. The match flickered out and Edoardo could no longer distinguish his cousin's expression when she said in a strange, shrill voice: "I came after you to give you this back." Furiously she tore off the ring and thrust it into the surprised young man's open hand; then she turned and began to run up the stairs toward the lighted doorway.

She had almost forgotten the stranger who was waiting for her and as Francesco jumped to his feet when he saw her, she turned to him blindly, full of hate that this dark-skinned person should have sung the serenade instead of Edoardo and should now be standing in the room from which the other had vanished. Though she tried hard to control her agony, Anna was grim and distraught. In the short time they were together, Francesco felt he was in the presence of a legendary Chimera, at once beautiful and fierce. Their conversation was halting but when Francesco, after a few moments, prepared to take his leave, Anna suddenly asked him to come back to see her. "Come soon," she insisted, "come soon," and he did not know what to make of the strange intensity with which she said this, apparently at the same time in haste to dismiss him and fearful of losing him. As she said good-bye, Anna had in fact suddenly realized that he was her last link with her cousin; but this Francesco could not know or understand, and that afternoon the mysterious splendor of Anna possessed him forever. Those who, like me, do not know the glory and the pain which a great and arduous love brings as it first makes itself felt, at the time when, just issuing from adolescence, the heart still sees before it a vista of great adventures (when even the tedium of death can seem heroic), will have to forego, as I must, accompanying Francesco as he walked through the dimly lighted streets to his home, already bearing within him a sense of the profound myth of Anna.

The next day Edoardo was the first to speak of their visit, thus satisfying the secret desire of Francesco who could not conceal the admiration Anna aroused in him. How is one to explain the strange situation? Usually so jealous of his friend, Edoardo not only did not mind his admiration but sought artfully to intensify it. Was it perhaps because his distaste for the relationship between Francesco and Rosaria was so strong that it made him welcome eagerly any way of breaking up that hateful affair? Or were his feelings, first toward Anna and now toward his friend, such that he wished to join the sentiments into one, uniting two persons close to him in a single destiny? Perhaps he thought he was making Francesco's future blissful by giving him Anna? Or, on the contrary, that he was working his ruin? Perhaps he was merely taking pleasure in playing the role of fate whether for good or evil? I offer all these suggestions which have in common only the fact that they are very tentative and, now that I think of it, of a kind that might very well have occurred to my readers without my assistance. The one hypothesis, however, which only I can advance at this point since it derived from my knowledge of what was to happen later and from my incurable partiality for my character, Edoardo; the most generous, moving, even tenderly tragic hypothesis possible, I know and do not want to reveal. May my readers forgive me. To reveal it now would mean that I should have to give away with it all the rest of my story and that would not be to my liking.

5

A Catastrophe Brought About By An Anonymous Person. The Mysterious Monocle. A Beautiful Woman Driven Out Of The City.

EDOARDO'S PRAISES OF ANNA fed Francesco's growing love. With great pride (which Francesco attributed to their being related but which sprang from Edoardo's secret conviction *I have only to say I want this girl and she is mine*) Edoardo exclaimed that, yes, Francesco was right, Anna was a beauty, an angel. If, he added she could dress and get herself up like rich girls, she would outshine every woman in the city. Francesco could scarcely suppress the question that leapt up in him: "You are the one who could raise her to her rightful place, you could make her queen of the city, and yet you do nothing about it. Why?" Edoardo sensed his friend's unspoken question: "I can guess what you are thinking. You know, it's strange that someone like you who despises wealth and class, should think about such things. But can't you see that my cousin is much more beautiful as she is, because she is poor and badly dressed? Of course, she lives in obscurity and it will be given to very few to enjoy her beauty, perhaps only to one. Is beauty a prostitute to be shared by many, in your opinion? But I had forgotten that you like prostitutes for the pleasure of reforming them." Edoardo laughed and Francesco blushed, for it was true that from the day he had visited Anna, he could not help making comparisons between her and Rosaria, and the always triumphant Anna haunted his thoughts more and more.

"Her beauty will be for one man alone," repeated Edoardo, "and if I were that man, Anna would certainly be rich and a lady. But I don't love her and even if I wanted to heap gifts on her, she wouldn't take them from someone who does not love her. She is too proud for that." Francesco was silent at this but deep in his heart, he cried out: "How can you not love her?"

Such conversations about Anna took the place of the visits Francesco did not dare pay her even though he had been invited. He would have liked to ask his friend if it would be proper to call on her but dignity and shyness held him back. That feeding of passion which in the beginning of love comes from seeing and talking with the desired person, he obtained by talking about her with Edoardo. His friend had told him the story of Teodoro and the quarrels between his family and his uncle, never saying but allowing it to be understood that the Massias owed their modest means to the Cerentanos' bounty. But, her cousin added proudly, Anna was a true Massia in heart and in appearance; he praised her black curly hair, her tiny wrists, her wild, proud nature, capable of making a supreme sacrifice for love. Francesco listened and in imagination he saw her beautiful black hair falling richly over her graceful, queenly shoulders and her stormy gray eyes glittering with mysterious emotions. After talking with Edoardo, Francesco went back to his room full of excitement and fantasies. The one consolation he found in solitude where he had no one with whom he could talk of Anna was the play of memory which, although it did not satisfy him, gave him its own delicious pleasure; one by one he revived her words and gestures during that famous visit. One memory above all made him tremble with hope and that was her invitation at the last moment to return soon.

Edoardo said nothing more about traveling. He had lied to Anna in announcing his immediate departure; it was true that the doctors advised him to seek a change of climate but he who had so longed to travel, now found himself bound to his native city by various intricate and fascinating ties which he only obscurely understood, and he had no intention of going away before spring. Unwilling to admit to Francesco that he had lied, he satisfied his friend's questions by saying that on the day of his visit to his cousin he had really almost decided to go but had returned to his first idea of waiting for good weather. "However," he added, "don't tell my cousin this; let her think I am going soon. I don't want any more good-byes." At this Francesco's face flamed. "I don't think," he stammered, "that I will have any occasion to see your cousin again." "Why? Didn't she invite you?" Edoardo asked with an air of surprise. And again he encouraged Francesco to visit Anna who would certainly welcome an occasional interruption in her solitude.

But when the moment of decision came Francesco's courage failed him. He forced himself to go as far as Anna's house and after waiting a long time in a fine winter rain, he saw the girl turn into the little square and enter the house. Anna did not notice him; she was walking absently, she had no umbrella and her untidy dress was drenched with rain. Her face with the little scar appeared frowning and defiant. Her pallor, her thinness and her deeply circled eyes made Francesco all the more enamored but they also touched his heart. That evening, having broken an engagement with Rosaria to meet Edoardo, he accompanied his friend to a bar where they found a guitarist. The wine lifted their spirits; they decided on a second serenade and took the poor guitarist with them. As always when he was drinking, Francesco felt full of confidence and courage. He had already begun to sing Edoardo's song when his friend interrupted and asked him to sing something else. So he sang a serenade that was rather famous at the time and not without excitement, Edoardo was able to tell from his voice that he loved Anna. Had he himself not been the one to will it? He was like a necromancer who has fashioned a magic mirror and then trembles to see the deceits he can create. I do not know how long the mirror would have remained a favorite toy; destiny, as we shall see, had other plans for Edoardo. And if this were not so, where would my story be?

In the days that followed Francesco again drank in the evenings to give himself courage and went twice alone to sing under Anna's windows, but they never were opened. Cesira would have like to open them; she was delighted with the serenades. At the first notes of the guitar, she would shake Anna, saying: "Listen! Listen!" and since both the first and second times Anna's name rang out, her mother was immensely curious to know who the singer was. But Anna replied carelessly that she did not know. Cesira praised the voice of the unknown singer warmly. She was thrilled to recognize a phrase here and there from a song especially dear to her. She would get up and sit on the side of the bed, her sparse hair hanging about her shoulders, and sometimes she went as far as the window and tried to peer down into the street. But Anna ordered her quickly not to open the window and then turned on her pillow, her heart hammering at the thought that her cousin might be below. So he had not gone away? But why have someone else sing for him? And why these serenades after such a cruel leave-taking? This nightly enigma upset her but even if it was nothing more than a joke or still another insult, it brought her hope and freed her from the disconsolate lassitude in which Edoardo had left her.

Meanwhile, the girl felt a growing animosity for the man who sang in her lover's place. Like an awkward, black puppet his face now blurred into Edoardo's comely features in her disturbed mind. His dark skin, his heavy hands and scarred face filled her with revulsion. Although Anna knew that her cousin liked to associate with people socially beneath him, and knew also that the title of baron is rather common and rarely genuine in our region, some prestige did attach to his poor person by virtue of such a title and such a friendship. Anna hoped he would call for this seemed to her the only way of having news of her cousin. But, although invited, the young man never appeared until one day Anna met him by chance on the street in the quarter where she lived. He seemed lost in thought and was walking along with his coat collar turned up and his hands thrust in his pockets. Blushing violently at he own boldness, Anna went up to him and in a voice at once imperious and timid asked him why he had never come again. He snatched his hands from his pockets and whipped off his hat, standing before her with his jet-black curls uncovered, and he seemed so upset that she suspected he was hiding some mysterious news. Not daring to ask him any questions and too upset herself to talk then, she invited him to come to see her later that afternoon.

He appeared promptly at the hour they had fixed and their talk turned naturally to Edoardo; Anna learned that her cousin had not yet left and although the repeated serenades had made her hope as much, this definite news overjoyed her. Though Francesco hastened to add, it is true, that his friend's departure was expected any day, at the thought that Edoardo was still in the same city with her, Anna was transfigured. A lovely glow revived in her cheeks and, animated by hope, her manner became light and gracious. The serenades were not mentioned but Francesco talked of Edoardo with such enthusiasm that Anna almost forgave him for having sung in his place. Francesco praised his friend's warm and affectionate nature and his brilliant mind but deplored the fact that such gifts would be wasted in idleness.

Unfortunately, he added, in an allusion that fell like a sybilline utterance on Anna's ear, the time has not come, although many signs indicate it is not far distant, when idleness will no longer exist, nor social injustice, when neither wealth nor poverty will be able to break the spirit and the heart of man. To this Anna replied that the rich are not the only ones who live in idleness; for example, although she was not rich, she did nothing. She loved to be idle, she added with a blush, but now that she was grown up she would have to look for some kind of work, for her mother was old and tired and the little she earned from her lessons was not enough for them to live on. In spite of the valiant tone in which this was said, it was easy to see that Anna despaired of ever being able to earn her own living. Francesco looked at her small hands and heard the fear in her voice, and once more he had the sense that he was not talking to a contemporary (as she was, more or less) but to some creature still in its infancy, needing care and help. Looking about the room which was lighted this time by daylight, he could see better than on the occasion of his first visit the signs of poverty. A defiant, impetuous emotion flooded his heart. He who said he detested any show of wealth and who preached modesty and decency to Rosaria felt now the most frivolous desires. For days he had been pausing by every shop window he saw, and each display of vanity excited him with longing as if he were a woman. All those precious, fragile, gorgeous objects, were they not invented to make girls like Anna happy and adorn their beauty like trophies? And why should the most beautiful of all women be deprived of them? On the other hand, must he not bless the poverty which allowed him a proximity and friendship which would have been impossible if she were rich? Anna seemed to him quite unattainable and in youth's grand way, this was one more reason for him to love her. The ambitious utopias he had dreamed of as a boy became more human and more compelling now that he had learned to love. It was no longer for himself or for society that he longed to become great, but for her of whom he wished to be worthy and who, thanks to him, would know the ideal splendor for which she was born. Francesco had not broken with Rosaria but how she was overshadowed by Anna. Had he not planned at one time to make Rosaria his companion for life? And although he had never revealed this to her, did not the intention bind him to her like a promise? He did not dare think of abandoning Rosaria to whom, in spite of his new passion, he felt bound by pleasure, by duty and compassion. But now that he had seen Anna, he had to admit that he had been wrong in thinking he loved Rosaria and that Edoardo had been right in showing him how unworthy she was. In the grandiose scheme of his life, Rosaria had been an event but Anna, now, was the goal itself.

As he discovered, remembered, and even invented Anna's virtues one by one Francesco did not doubt that he had found in her his ideal companion, that the propitious stars had contrived her birth and their meeting, and that there was no one like her in the world. The woman that in his bookish dreams he projected for his perfect society, the strong spirit able to grasp the destiny of man and share it with him on the basis of equal rights, was this woman not the image of Anna? Her pale forehead promised him an intelligence to which he could teach the most secret and arduous truths. And if Anna no less than Rosaria was a victim of the social order, this very injustice which made Rosaria worthy of compassion made Anna more beautiful, enriched her, in Francesco's thoughts, with a more experienced and profound awareness. By uniting himself forever with Rosaria he meant to defy the world, but could not Anna help him to redeem it? If Rosaria was beneath him, Anna was above him, etc., etc.

We have seen before that Francesco was not insensible to the prestige of aristocratic birth; and this made Anna seem even more splendid in his eyes. In Rosaria he saw a kind of animal whom he was duty-bound to awaken to more human feelings but Anna seemed to him a kind of Madonna who would inspire him to true manhood. And Rosaria's free, flirtatious manners which he had found so seductive, while still agreeable, seemed nonetheless stupid and trivial to him now that he compared them with Anna's unaffected simplicity in which an almost womanly dignity was combined with girlish artlessness.

But, along with all this, we must confess that our Francesco did not always or only dream of Anna as man's ideal, free companion. Quite often he could not keep from dreaming of her and desiring her as a wife. Wife, that is, in the sense in which the word is still used in parts of our country where customs are almost oriental. He longed to be rich so that he could dress her like a favorite, he played with the thought of protecting her, of hiding her from the eyes of other men, of working so that she might never know fatigue or trouble. Now he was no longer proud of his studious nature which he had thought might make him worthy of Anna. He wished he were as handsome as she, and did not have that pock-marked face. He was horrified at the thought that she might be repelled by him or that she might find out about his farmer family and come to despise him. Then he would try to drive all thought of her from his mind and go back to Rosaria who forgave him everything. But often the memory of Anna assailed him so strongly that he would cut short his visits with Rosaria and go off alone to think of her, preferring the shadow of the one to the living kisses of the other.

Anna's expression, in the short time he had had to study it, was certainly not that of a happy girl. Passion and melancholy glowed in her eyes and, despite its reserve, her manner nevertheless betrayed a tempestuous spirit and thoughts far heavier than are usual in young girls. Still, as lovers will, Francesco often envied Anna her happiness to the point of longing to enter into her very being in order to share in it. What happiness: The happiness of being Anna. For the fire and the splendor with which we invest the beloved seems to us to be an innate virtue of theirs, never a deception we practice on ourselves. We cannot imagine those we love to be without an awareness of their own splendor and fire, and we dream that, like Narcissus, they take as much pleasure in themselves as we do. The bitterness of every success in love, even the most fortunate, lies in the insane desire to lose one's self entirely in another person; and, as we search for possession or repose in such a transformation, the ultimate limit of this desire is the mad pretense that we are no longer ourselves but the beloved. If this holds true for fortunate lovers, the unfortunate ones must know in addition the pain of self-hatred. Hatred for their own ugliness (since the beloved is beautiful), their dullness (since the beloved is brilliant), and their agony (since the beloved is calm and indifferent, like to the gods).

As Francesco longed to be Anna, so Anna in those days longed to be Edoardo — Edoardo sick, Edoardo away, but always Edoardo, Edoardo, and not an Anna without him. These days were filled with pain and difficulty for her. Although he had lied about his departure, Edoardo had not lied in saying that his visit was a farewell. That he had really meant. Perhaps he would have felt differently had he found Anna indifferent or hostile. But since he saw that he was still loved, he lost all interest in her. We know that after the visit to his cousin, he gave the famous ring to Rosaria. But this gift had no symbolic value for him; he merely happened to have a valuable piece of jewelry appropriate for a girl and he offered it to Rosaria (who had said she longed for a ring) without telling her, of course, where it came from. And Rosaria's pleasure was equal to those splendid jewels.

On Edoardo's advice, she looked for a more secure hiding place for the ring than the chest where her other jewels were hidden, which the landlady at least knew of. She discovered a little hole under a broken brick in her floor and there she hid the ring which was destined to lie buried and rarely to see the light.

Another consequence of his visit to Anna and his conversations with Francesco was that Edoardo inquired of his mother about the monthly allowance to the Massias. Now that his affair was over, the subject was no longer a delicate one between them. Concetta knew that Anna's star had set and her son's cold, imperious tone in discussing this matter of business assured her, once and for all, that he no longer loved his cousin. When he heard the amount the Massias received, Edoardo's face darkened and he declared that, for the honor of the family, it should be suitably increased. In a low voice, Concetta ventured that it was enough to live modestly and she was about to add other objections when she saw that her son's pale face was clouding ominously; she interrupted herself and asked what amount he thought of contributing to the Massias. The young man was quite ignorant of the needs of the poor and not knowing what to say, he replied heatedly: "Give twice, give three times as much!" Concetta thought that the joy of having won her son back from a hated rival was worth the sacrifice and she promised to give orders at once that her son's wishes be carried out. A few hours later she informed him that arrangements had already been made and that the Massias would enjoy their new beneficence starting that same month.

But the Massias were never to know that they had come so close to ease. The envelope left as usual with the Cerentano steward contained more than double the previous amount. But the clerk did not see the usual, thin, frivolously dressed little woman whose ceremonious manners contrasted so oddly with her hurried movements and her sickly, exhausted face. In her place there came a girl he had never seen before, a tall, black-haired, pale young woman who asked coldly for the envelope for Signora Massia. When the clerk objected that he could not give the envelope without a signed receipt from Signora Massia, the girl retorted that she did not intend to accept the envelope but to return it to its sender, who was her aunt. Since the clerk seemed in doubt, she repeated her request imperiously and the intimidated man handed her the envelope. She did not open it or even look at it but slipped it into a second envelope she had brought with her, addressed to Concetta Cerentano. When she had passed the flap over her delicate, fresh lips to seal it, she handed the envelope back to the clerk and walked haughtily out of the office. Thus the magnificent allowance returned to Concetta, accompanied by a note announcing in Anna's ungrammatical style and still childish hand that Anna and Cesira Massia thanked their Cerentano relatives for the generosity they had showed them until now, a generosity which they intended in the future no longer to accept, renouncing any and every advantage that might accrue to them by their family connection or by the magnanimity of the Cerentanos. It went on to say that Anna, the daughter of Teodoro Massia, would have refused to accept such charity from the beginning, had she previously not been prevented because of her youth from exercising sufficient authority and decisions. She and her mother extended their most sincere greetings to Signora Cerentano and her illustrious family. In tall, elaborate and childish script, there followed the signature: Anna Massia di Corullo.

The tone of this letter was so haughty that Concetta took it as an affront. Her cheeks reddened in annoyance and her first impulse was to run to Edoardo's room and punish him with a violent scene for having favored his insolent cousin. But before she reached her son's room, she realized the mistake she was about to make; what assurance could she have that Anna's presumption would not appear to Edoardo's irrational judgment as a virtue and would not revive in him the feelings which had so recently subsided? Later, calmly and without attaching undue importance to it, she could tell Edoardo about the matter, but only when it became necessary.

And so Concetta composed herself and went back to her room without speaking to him, she gave orders to her administrator to suspend the Massias' allowance.

Subsequently Concetta congratulated herself on her foresight. Having agreed with his mother about the aid to their poor relatives, Edoardo showed no further concern about them or their allowance and in his irresponsible way, never brought up the subject; either he supposed that everything was settled and further discussion useless, or other livelier interests occupied his mind. Thus Anna's sacrifice was not known to the one person on whose altar it had above all been offered. A few months later Edoardo did learn of it by chance but by then his once winged, all-conquering spirit was gripped in its own dark agony and the smoke of sacrifice meant nothing to him.

As Anna was reaching this heroic decision to renounce the allowance, Francesco had grown more courageous and had called on her twice. But both times Anna was not alone at home. Her mother was there and, although she did not take part in their conversation, she came in and out on one pretext or another, driven by her restless curiosity. She would sit down for a few moments and then vanish into some other room, only to reappear again like a feeble, flickering flame. She was cordial, she chatted in a lively, conventional way like someone who knows the proper style of the salons, and she called Francesco "Baron." In her eyes, Francesco had more than one attraction: first of all, she was impressed by the title (less subtle than Anna, she did not notice his evident rusticity), and we have already seen how she was attracted to youth and love. And, had he not referred to country estates and to great projects for the future? Was he not an eligible young man, probably rich, and with a promising future? Cesira's enthusiasm grew in proportion to Anna's diffidence and coldness. Anna detested even the suggestion that another man — and of all men, this one! — might take the place of her cousin. Cesira's occasional presence was enough to make her avoid any reference to Edoardo and that robbed Francesco's visits of any pleasure or consolation they might hold for her. Cesira had not been able to refrain from taunting her daughter savagely in their quarrels about her cousin, telling the girl *he was only playing with you* because, she added, Anna did not have it in her to attract men, no one could ever love her seriously, no one would ever want to marry her; what is more, she went on, Anna was now disgraced because of her loose contact with Edoardo who had only wanted to amuse himself at her expense; she was the talk of the neighborhood. To hear her, one would have said Cesira took some cruel pleasure in Anna's disappointment. Actually, we know that she had entertained the wildest hopes about Edoardo and his betrayal had embittered her not a little, especially on account of the satisfaction it had provided their neighbors. Mixed with this bitter disappointment was the vague, malign satisfaction of a woman who has missed emotional fulfillment in her own life and who witnesses the frustrations of another.

All of this made Anna behave with the most rigid reserve in her mother's presence and her desire to hide her feelings from her grew stronger than ever. Francesco was dismayed to see her so hostile and taciturn where once she had been so pleasant. She seemed, with difficulty and a kind of passionate anger, to be repressing some deep burning defiance. Sometimes, with a combination of hardness and ingenuous boastfulness, she alluded to her unvanquished spirit and to certain plans she had for the future (she imagined that he was in Edoardo's confidence). At other times, she sat silent. And if Francesco (heartened by the wine he drank to give himself courage as he girded himself to come to see her) began to talk to her about his pet theories and arguments, his much coveted pupil seemed as indifferent to his revelations as to his prophecies. When he described to her the future, holy, atheistic Republic where beauty, honesty and intelligence (her particular qualities, in other words) would reign supreme, Anna would glance at him absently and severely as if to say: "What do you mean? Am I not, by any chance, already queen and goddess?"

It was Cesira now who invited him to return, not Anna. He did not dare go often, fearing that he was not welcome to the girl. Unable to suppress his feelings, he went more and more often to sing under her window at night; only then, in the wintry, dark silence of the alley, could he give free course to the desires that tormented him during the day. The popular ballards and the snatches of opera seemed like poems to him, such was the fire he put in the banal words. Anyone would have guessed to hear him that it was something more than love of the music that lent eloquence to his voice. Anna still continued to persuade herself that it was all a lover's trick, that Edoardo was somehow behind those serenades, like a sovereign who commands his mimes to act out on the stage his own confession of love. The serenades which neither of them ever mentioned added a secret source of emotion to their conversations. Two unexpressed questions agitated them: Francesco's was: "Haven't you heard me singing? Haven't you understood why I come?" And Anna's: "Don't you bring any message from your friend, the guitarist?"

Intimidated by Anna's coldness, Francesco had suspended his visits for some days at the time when the grave decision about the allowance was reached. Undaunted and full of threats, Anna informed her mother of her intention not to accept aid from the Cerentanos in the future; they would live by their own means. Now these means, beyond Cesira's few lessons, were her mother's tiny savings which would scarcely have been enough to keep them for more than a few months. Cesira discovered that neither grief, nor fear, not recriminations could shake her daughter's decision; Anna declared that the Cerentanos' assistance had been meant for her alone and that, having reached the age of reason, she had decided after due reflection not to accept their charity any longer. For that matter, she did not intend to live at anyone's expense; she had been promised employment, she affirmed; this was a lie. Her earnings would be enough not only for herself but for her mother. And, she added, if her mother wished to avoid trouble, she would not try in any way, openly or secretly, to oppose this decision. With that, Anna wrote the famous letter and took it herself to the office of the Cerentano steward.

What was she thinking of doing in the future? Confused, tumultuous plans passed through her mind. It was not wounded pride alone which had made her take this step but also a superstitious impulse; she felt that her sacrifice must surely bring Edoardo back to her. Perhaps desperation had broken the spell which had bound her for so many months. She also thought of turning to Francesco to ask his help in finding employment. She knew the young man's address but the idea of going to him was repugnant to her and besides for some days he had not come to see her.

So Anna spent her days in her usual, indolent fashion, stretched out on the divan or bed, careless about her appearance, daydreaming or reading cheap novels. As for Cesira, fatigue had left her so spiritless that she could scarcely take pleasure in her vague satisfaction over Anna's revenge on the Cerentanos. Sometimes her fear of the future inspired her with vast plans for going to them, without Anna's knowledge, and begging for their help. But the absurdity of the idea struck her immediately and furthermore the thought of having to do it disgusted her. She preferred to submit to Anna and withdraw from the struggle; authority passed entirely to Anna almost as it she were the mature woman and the other had become a child again. Cesira did not, however, renounce the right to quarrel about the money, but Anna would tell her sharply not to worry, that soon everything would be settled, or, in exasperation, she would turn on her like a fury, or break into sobs.

And so the days passed when, according to her presentiment, Anna's fate was being decided, but it was a fate far different from what her hope had led her to think.

We know that Francesco had not broken off his meetings with Rosaria, and it could not be said, either, that his heart was not in them. During those disturbed days, a strange figure of a girl, a shifting, double shadow, dominated him waking and dreaming. Clasping Rosaria in the most passionate embrace, he would think of Anna; but when his battles with the ambiguous shadow of Anna left him exhausted, it was with the familiar, simple Rosaria that he found repose. He was torn continually between his need for affection, his scorn of Rosaria, his desire for Anna and his despair of ever having her.

If a sense of duty held him to Rosaria, a stronger sense of duty toward himself and his destiny moved him to love Anna. He thought of her, not the other, as his true fiancée. A longing for simple pleasures led him to Rosaria's room but a more violent desire in which innocent delight combined with ambition, hope and grand fantasies drove him toward Anna.

Rosaria noticed the change in Francesco; at first her bad conscience made her fear that he had some inkling of her meetings with Edoardo, but the trustful admiration he sometimes expressed for his friend made this unlikely. On the other hand, instead of watching her more closely, he had left her in unaccustomed freedom for some time; with the excuse of his studies and private lessons, he remained away from her for long periods of the day and night. This allowed her, it is true, more leisurely meetings with Edoardo but it also embittered her. She began to suspect that Francesco preferred some other girl; unable to contain herself, she spoke of her jealous doubts not only to Francesco but to Edoardo. The latter laughed and told her not to fear: Francesco was by nature faithful. But as he said it, he laughed in a certain malicious way that increased Rosaria's doubts: "You know something!" she said, frowning intently. At this Edoardo became annoyed and said it was not pleasant to talk to him about another man like that and show that she loved the other more than she did him. Besides, was she not betraying Francesco at this very moment? What had she to complain of? "It's true," Rosaria stammered but wringing her hands, she added that even if she betrayed Francesco, she could not bear to have him be unfaithful to her. "Oh, you selfish, loose creature!" Edoardo cried. "How can you try to deprive a man of his rights when you fall short in your duties?" This language was a little too difficult for Rosaria; in perplexity she looked at him with great, troubled eyes.

"It's you," she murmured finally, "who makes me fail in my duty." Edoardo burst out laughing. "As if you didn't share in the blame!" he said, shaking her with contemptuous affection. "Why don't you leave me, then?" In reply she glanced at him agitatedly, but in her eyes was that meekness which made her resemble at times a gentle calf. It is a fact that she sometimes thought of breaking with Edoardo in order to be worthy of Francesco once more. Especially since she knew Edoardo certainly did not love her and only wanted pleasure and amusement from her. Indeed he seemed less and less eager even for these since his visits were becoming regularly less frequent. But she could not decide to leave him; either because she did not dare deny herself to him or because it cost her too much to give up the prestige of his visits and the precious gifts he brought her. "Because you're greedy, that's why," Edoardo said now, reading her thoughts, "because you like the ring I gave you too much, even if you can't wear it, and the earrings and the gold pin. When, when did you ever, even in your wildest dreams, my poor little mountaineer, think you would have such jewels?" Resentment filled Rosaria and she would have liked to throw his gifts in his face and turn him out, but her love of those precious stones and her joy in that hidden wealth held her back. Torn between opposing impulses, she burst into tears: "Don't cry, don't cry," Edoardo told her. "What are you afraid of? I told you Francesco is faithful to you, he cannot not be faithful, he will be faithful unto eternity. And he loves you enough to marry you." "To marry me! Francesco!" she cried, flushing with sorrow and sudden hope. "Yes, he doesn't say anything about it but he means to marry you, he plans to make you a baroness. He hasn't told you yet because he wants to watch you and make sure you deserve it. But since you have betrayed him, you don't deserve it and he won't marry you." Rosaria tried to laugh and looked anxiously at Edoardo. "In any event, be careful," he added, in a threatening tone, "be careful never to mention my name or let slip that you have seen me again. You know what would happen to you if he suspected anything." "Don't worry," said Rosaria, full of fear and remorse, "he will never know anything from me." She tried to understand if Edoardo had been joking or not when he said Francesco wanted to marry her; and she could not get rid of her doubts about Francesco's fidelity. She planned to have him followed secretly by some friend, or to find out by some other stratagem.

I wonder, at this point, what scenes would have taken place among my four characters if a mysterious intervention had not hurried their involved relations toward an end. I can imagine with a narrator's pleasure a possible encounter between Anna and Rosaria, if Rosaria had discovered the existence of her rival. The two women did meet, in fact, but that was many years later and under vastly different circumstances. But what would their lives have been if an anonymous person had not prompted Francesco to the decisive break he himself would never have been able to make? Feeling that he was not loved by Anna and abandoned by Edoardo, might he perhaps have married Rosaria? And, in this case . . . But there is no point in wasting paper and ink on such conjectures. In actuality, events developed as follows: the day after the conversation between Edoardo and Rosaria which I recounted above, Francesco received an anonymous letter. From what the cabdriver's family said, the letter, which was carefully sealed, had been delivered by a little boy they had never seen before. When he had left it in their keeping, the messenger had gone his way whistling. The letter was written on fine paper in a hand Francesco did not recognize and it bore no signature or salutation. It simply said:

> You poor, deluded man, listen to what one who wishes you well must tell you. The woman you trust has not given up her true inclinations and she is betraying you with a man who has more money than you have. If you want proof of this, look for it in the little chest with the mirror top which is on the commode of Signorina Rosaria. The chest, please note, has a secret compartment. So, be warned. Your well-wisher sends you greetings.

This was the message; when he had read it, Francesco rushed to Rosaria's house. It was one o'clock. Late that afternoon Edoardo climbed in his turn up to Rosaria's room, after having sent a boy ahead to make sure she was alone. She was alone, indeed, but quite unlike the gay Rosaria who usually welcomed Edoardo. The room was topsy-turvy, the bed was undone, the little chest was smashed and lying on the floor, its mirror top in fragments; Rosaria's few possessions were tossed here and there on the floor or on the chairs. In the midst of this disorder Rosaria was half-lying on the bed, undressed, her face red and her eyes swollen with weeping. "What's happened here?" Edoardo asked, looking around him in amazement. Between sobs Rosaria told him that a few hours earlier Francesco had stormed into the room and without saying a word to her, had gone to the commode, raised the lid of the chest and pulled out pell-mell the ribbons, buttons and other trifles it contained. While she stared at him, stupefied, he ran his finger feverishly around the inside of the chest and demanded that she show him the secret catch. She felt as if she were the victim of witchcraft or sorcery and with a shriek she had thrown herself on Francesco to tear the chest from him. But he had pushed her away and in the struggle the chest had fallen. As if overcome by hatred for this malignant object, Francesco had kicked it furiously, crushing it and breaking the mirror, while she sat terror-stricken, thinking that to break a mirror brought bad luck. And then from the smashed chest had rolled the earrings, the pendant and the pin which she kept hidden there. "Who gave you this stuff?" he had demanded and while in her distraction she sought for some suitable lie, he raged about the room like a wild beast; and he found something in the folds of the coverlet at the foot of the bed. It was a monocle on a gold chain.

Rosaria was more than ever convinced that some evil spell was upon her; she knew that Edoardo never wore a monocle, yet who else (he had been in her room the night before) could have left it there? She swore to Edoardo that no other man ever set foot in her room. However that might be, the monocle seemed infallible proof to Francesco, if the jewels were not enough in themselves, that Rosaria had a lover. While she cursed herself secretly for the laziness which made her lie in bed late every morning instead of making her bed and straightening her room, Francesco dropped the monocle on the bed, as if the touch of it were unbearable. And in a choked, frozen voice which seemed not to be his, he told her that from that moment their paths divided forever, that he was leaving her to the ignoble fate for which she was born and from which in his stupid trustfulness, he had thought to rescue her. At these words Rosaria felt that hell yawned at her feet. She ran to Francesco who was already at the door and falling on her knees, she had clasped his legs but he seized her by the shoulders and forcibly threw her to the floor. When she had recovered from her stunned surprise, she rushed out to the landing in pursuit of him. But Francesco was already at the bottom of the stairs and, half-dressed as she was, she could not go into the street. The landlady had appeared at that point to caution Rosaria not to make scenes on her stairs and had pushed her back into her room, consoling her with the comment that for one man lost, she would find a new and better one. Smarting at this remark and having to loose her anger on someone, Rosaria thought for a moment that she saw through everything. Turning on her landlady, she screamed that she and she alone could have played the spy. Who else could have known the secret of the chest and the hiding place of jewels? Of course it was she, an old, finished creature whom nobody loved, who for jealously of Rosaria had wanted to drive away her lover. Naturally she did not like Francesco, he was too poor to satisfy her dirty greed, procuress that she was, and she had thought to get rid of him by telling him what she knew. The landlady swore that she had not breathed a word to a soul about any of Rosaria's secrets, feeling under obligation, as she did, particularly to Signorino Edoardo. And she added that if it were not for him, she would have repented her discretion since she saw now how it was appreciated. Having cleared herself on this score, she answered Rosaria's insults with new insults and a fine altercation developed which the landlady terminated by ordering Rosaria to leave her room that very day. In her anger she had wrenched open the drawers and pulled out the girl's linen, inviting her to pack her bags without delay. At that point a neighbor called and she had gone out, leaving Rosaria alone in the room and in the state in which Edoardo discovered her.

As Rosaria concluded her hysterical account, the landlady (who perhaps had been listening at the door) asked: "May I come in?" and without waiting for a reply, she slipped meekly into the room. Turning to the young man, she declared in a voice of passionate respect that she could not wait one moment longer to clear herself of the cruel accusations against her, adding that she could not have slept that night if the suspicion even crossed Signorino Edoardo's mind that she could ever betray the confidence he had placed in her. Everything she knew about her young tenant and about Signorino Edoardo would lie buried within her forever, as in a tomb. Elaborating these thoughts with the greatest eloquence and with gestures and facial expressions no less colorful than her words, the landlady finally broke into tears and, unable to contain her emotion a moment longer, she threw her arms forgivingly about Rosaria's neck. Rosaria in turn dissolved in a shower of tears and clung to the woman seeking comfort and sympathy. "Come, come, be brave, girl," the woman murmured to her, "how can anyone cry who is pretty and young like you, and has such a handsome young man for a friend? This one is a thousand times handsomer that the other one, isn't he?" But such words did not console Rosaria who, hiding her head on the landlady's shoulder, collapsed into still more terrible tears and sobs. "Be so kind as to leave," Edoardo said at this point to the landlady. "I have taken note of your obliging remarks and good intentions. I do not know who played the traitor but in any event, remember that if you let slip anything about me or my visits, you will regret it all your life. And as for your evicting the young lady, there is no need to take that back. That was an excellent idea and the young lady will give up the room today. Good afternoon." "What do you mean?" the landlady stammered, while Rosaria held back a sob and turned her tearful, contorted face to look at him. "Oh, Lord, I made myself quite clear," Edoardo answered, "now I must ask you to leave."

"Well, if she can be any better off than here . . ." grumbled the landlady and she went out, closing the door behind her.

Edoardo stood in silence, staring at the floor. Hesitant, but already somewhat consoled by a vague hope, the girl asked: "Why . . . did you say . . . I am giving up the room?" "Why?" Edoardo shrugged. Looking firmly at Rosaria, he continued: "Because that is not mine, that monocle." "It's not yours! Then how . . .?" "It is not mine, and it was not I who left it here." "It wasn't you!" Rosaria replied, turning pale, "but then . . . whose can it be?" "Oh, my own angel," Edoardo said, "that is precisely what I would ask you, if I were even a little interested. The fact is that that monocle is not mine, it is not Francesco's, and therefore it is some other man's. And that monocle was found in your bed." "What do you mean?" Rosaria asked. "I mean that you are a shameless, faithless little hussy," Edoardo replied, "and therefore I am withdrawing my support. Now, I do not believe the lady of the house will feel the same enthusiasm to have you keep this room when she knows I have taken away my protection. That is why I frankly warned her not to go back on her eviction." Rosaria was silent, unable to utter a word for indignation and amazement stifled her. "On the other hand," Edoardo continued, "I have my own reasons for wanting you to leave this room and, for that matter, the city not later than today. Your presence here and your caprices could compromise me and my friends. No one can tell what you will take it into your head to do. Don't be afraid, by the way, that I am sending you away without any consolation. It happens that I have just withdrawn some money for my mother from the bank and my mother generously allows me to dispose of our income as I like. This money is yours, as well as the jewelry I have given you; together they should make more than enough capital for you to open your little shop elsewhere . . ." As he spoke, Edoardo drew a package of bank notes from his jacket and put them on the chest of drawers. But Rosaria was so beside herself that she was not even moved by the sight of those bills which a few months before would have seemed to her a fortune. "So I am a faithless hussy!" she shouted, controlling her gasping anger by sheer force of will. "I am, am I?

And you, what are you, if not a traitor and a liar? You betrayed your own friend, coming here and making love to me, and you know you're lying now when you say that monocle isn't yours. Why don't you admit you're just looking for excuses to leave me? Maybe you yourself put that damned monocle in my bed! Yes, I see, you put it there last night while you were pretending to kiss me, you brought it and left it on the coverlet, half covered up, so you would have an excuse to get rid of me. I've known for a long time that you were getting tired of me. And do you think I care? No, thank God, I've never loved you! If Francesco could take my heart out of my body, he would know that even if I was unfaithful to him, he was always first in my heart. But you, you force me into betraying a man I love like a brother, like an angel, like my father and my mother! You should kiss his feet because compared with him you and I are like two worms. And after all this, you insult me and make fun of me! Oh, Francesco, Francesco mine, my brother, my saviour, why won't you forgive me? Why won't you come back to me?" and Rosaria, overcome, broke into fresh sobs.

"Crocodile tears," Edoardo observed with a sneer, "you'd do better not to bother and anyhow, what good will they do you? It is pleasant and even touching sometimes to see decent girls cry. But you women! When you were crying on the shoulder of that woman, the two of you sniffling away together, you made such a stupid, ridiculous picture that I didn't know whether to laugh or cry myself. Look at yourself in the mirror and see how ugly you are when you cry."

"Oh, so now I'm ugly!" cried Rosaria belligerently. "And what if I don't go, what if I tell Francesco that it was you who tempted me, that you betrayed him?"

"Try it," Edoardo replied. "I don't have to tell you for the thousandth time what the consequences would be."

"You take advantage of me," cried Rosaria, foaming slightly at the lips, "you take advantage because I'm a poor girl with no one to protect me or help me and you, with your fine friends, you can scare me. But I'm not afraid of you, so there!" and in violent rage, Rosaria struck Edoardo on the cheek.

Edoardo turned so pale that a moment later Rosaria regretted her impulsive gesture and was terrified. The young man glared at her with hatred and amazement. "What have you done?" he exclaimed. "Get down on your knees!" he added. "Get down on your knees as if you were in church!" She was afraid and obeyed at once. "Now ask my pardon," he continued, leaning against the chest of drawers, almost choked by his vengeful passion. "Oh God, what will become of me?" she said in a loud voice. "Forgive me, I didn't know what I was doing." "Now pack your bag and get out," he ordered her as if speaking to a servant. "My carriage will take you to the station." Rosaria thought that she would never see Francesco again and she moaned over and over: "Oh God, oh God!"

But he did not allow her even a few hours to say good-bye to her friends. Between sobs Rosaria stooped to collect her few scattered belongings and stuffed them in the same sack she had brought to the city from her mountain home, since she did not own a bag. She carried out these hasty preparations under the frowning, pitiless eyes of the outraged Edoardo; finally, she slipped the jewels and money he had given her inside her blouse. He asked it she was ready; she was moaning and dabbing at her eyes under her fantastic hat and did not reply. "Remember," Edoardo said threateningly, with his hand on the door, "remember that you have sworn never to mention my name. The best luck I can wish for you is that you never hear of me again."

Rosaria turned on him suddenly and with a wild laugh full of hatred and pain, she cried: "Don't be afraid, I won't ever mention your name. You never think of anything but yourself. I hate you, I've never loved you, you pale, sickly blond little chicken — you're as weak as a woman! Don't you see you've lost your looks, why, you've got Death in your face!" Rosaria noticed that as she spoke the triumphant expression on his face slowly faded only to vanish entirely at her last words and give way to a weak, questioning smile which seemed to ask her what it was she meant. But it was enough for her to know she had hurt him and about that there was no doubt; although he pretended indifference, Edoardo was so upset that his fingers trembled as he paid the landlady Rosaria's bill.

Very probably she had been eavesdropping all the while and during her fervid, ceremonious farewell, she looked at her tenant with mocking curiosity. The girl promptly composed herself, putting on an appearance of dignified complacence. When Edoardo handed the woman her money, she permitted herself to remind him gently about the broken chest and without a word he immediately gave her more money. The young man's attitude seemed entirely changed; from being insulting and aggressive, he had become silent and almost submissive. Every so often he would glance covertly at Rosaria and as he entered the carriage after her, he looked intently and doubtfully in the little mirror, questioning his own face as if it were that of a sphinx; but immediately fearing to give his enemy any satisfaction and to excuse his looking into the mirror, he smoothed his hair with his hands. During the entire drive to the station, the two did not speak to each other again. Edoardo bought Rosaria a first-class ticket on an express train to the capital and since the train was soon to leave, he helped her into her compartment. "Good-bye," he said, "and good luck." He stood waiting on the platform for the train to leave. "That damned pale-faced ninny, that devil straight from hell," Rosaria thought.

Fresh sobs came to her throat but finding herself for the first time in her life on the velvet of first-class seats, and watching her gentlemen traveling companions come in, she assumed a lady-like posture as if she were entirely accustomed to traveling in luxurious compartments. It was then perhaps that Edoardo remembered the blow, and forgetting the anxiety which had swept over him at her gloomy prophecy, he wanted to taste his triumph to the full. Not knowing how better to offend the traveler, he knocked on the window and with a gay and maddening laugh, cried to her: "Good-bye, Signora." She pretended not to hear that mocking greeting, but Edoardo repeated it: "Good-bye, Signora," so that the travelers in her compartment looked curiously from Rosaria to him. Rosaria did not bat an eyelash. She deigned to glance absently out the window only when the train was moving and the remote little figure of her enemy was fading into the blur of red lights in the train shed.

But it was not Rosaria's nature to surrender without a fight. Several days after this scene she returned for a few hours to the city from which Edoardo had exiled her. Bravely defying his threats, she arrived incognito and went directly to the house where Francesco lived. She wanted to see her lover again, to talk to him once more, before she returned to the capital again. At the tinkling of the bell, the cabdriver's little boy came to the door and was so struck by timid admiration at the sight of that rich, perfumed lady that he remained mute to all her questions. She stepped into the hall with beating heart but at that moment the cabdriver's wife appeared. From her Rosaria learned that Francesco had gone away a few days before but insist as she might, she could learn nothing further. The woman had the reputation of her family very much at heart and one glance at the appearance of the lady and her furs had made her suspicious. Judging in her timid heart that any conversation with her was dangerous and dishonorable, she cut Rosaria's questions short and having repeated that Signor Francesco had gone and that she knew nothing more, she accompanied her to the door.

Several months passed and the same lady appeared at the cabdriver's house again, fresh from the capital. This time she was in a summer costume so very decolleté that it almost exposed her breasts. Seductive, twirling a parasol as if it were a flag, she asked for Francesco but the lady of the house eyed her from head to foot with the greatest contempt and without even inviting her to come in, stood firmly in the doorway and announced that Francesco was no longer there, that he had married and was living elsewhere. "Married? When? Who?" the other stammered, turning red. But the woman replied brusquely "Good-day" and almost slammed the door in her face. The same evening the girl once more left that inhospitable city.

And now let us bid farewell to Rosaria whom we shall not see again for some time. And let us return to Francesco where we left him, at the moment when he had discovered Rosaria's betrayal and left her room forever.

As he rushed downstairs and out into the street, Francesco was in the grip of such incoherent, conflicting emotions that it would have been difficult to judge which of them was the most genuine or the most violent. He had been betrayed by a mistress he had trusted too much, but he had been betrayed just when he himself had stopped loving her. He had continued his relationship with Rosaria not only for the pleasure he still found in it, in spite of his dying love, but even more because of the responsibilities he had assumed toward her. The memory of his pleasures caused Francesco pain and jealousy now. And the sense of responsibility which had bound him to the girl gave rise to a sense of wounded pride; for, if it had not been for Edoardo's ironies, would he not even to this moment have believed in the reformation of the woman who was secretly deceiving him all the time? He should, he felt, be grateful for the discovery which had brought about a break he had already known was inevitable but still, a sense of offended honor tormented him, although he often proclaimed himself free of such social superstitions. He felt an overwhelming impulse to go back up and beat the unfaithful girl, to kill her, to discover his unknown rival, challenge him, and kill him, or be killed. But immediately he laughed at the idea, telling himself it would be absurd, ridiculous to avenge a betrayal by such a woman. Rosaria belonged to every man and it was no wonder that she gave herself to the richest; the fault was his for having believed in her, not hers, and not his unknown rival's. But what of the hopes he had placed in her, what of his plans for their life together, their honest, hard-working life? All that was over now.

Francesco mourned for the little room where he had felt he was loved and no longer alone, where he had given and received such warm embraces. Then, in the full flood of his regret a feeling of liberation and relief welled up within him; his loneliness no longer weighed on him for now he could give himself completely to his true passion, to Anna who held utter sway over him. "But will Anna be able to love me?" he asked and with a sense of humiliation and scorn he answered himself that no one could love him. Even that peasant, that streetwalker had played with him. How could he hope, with his face and his humble future, with nothing to offer but absurd promises, how could he hope to be loved by a princess like Anna? *Peasant, princess*! words that should have rung hollow in his ears, if he had been faithful to his much vaunted principles! But alas, the slave of a confused mind, Francesco was in frequent conflict with himself, and the most foolish passion could obscure principles which had once been radiant truths to him. One persistent feeling now dominated him: his lack of confidence in himself, his terror at being alone in a hostile world where no one would accept his offer of himself, where for him there was nothing but emptiness and contempt. From childhood he had found a kind of comfort in this feeling. Lost in this despairing sense of himself (which is for the weak, a most common and clumsy form of self-adulation), he wandered through the streets, pausing finally at the corner of a little square where market was held in the mornings but which was deserted at this hour. He sat down at the top of a flight of steps leading to a lower street and contemplated himself morosely: a black, ragged, wild creature seeking shelter from the autumn wind in a dirty corner of the city. It was a pathetic and menacing vision of his world he conjured up for the occasion.

"See," he said to himself, "in the world around me people come together, they fall in love, they make plans, they look toward the future — but never with me. The lights go on in their houses, families gather together, lovers linger in doorways, instruments tune up in ballrooms. The stores close down, the lights gleam in the windows of rich shops, the day's accounts are drawn up, people exchange thoughts, and plans. But I am never with them. And who is with me, then? Not Edoardo. He is the only one who allows me a kind of friendship but he keeps me out of his circle, away from his family, as if I belonged to some inferior race. Not my mother, poor illiterate peasant, who in her simplicity is nearer to her animals than to her own son. Rosaria is unfaithful. Nicola Monaco is dead. Let's look elsewhere: the family I live with, the cabdriver's family, don't they change their ways and their talk in my presence because I am a student, because I am of a different breed? And the people who would be glad to take me in, haven't I rejected them because for one reason or another they are not what I want? I am alone, that's the simple truth, I am as alone as when I was a boy and wandered over the fields to cry because I was lonely and unhappy."

This was the elegy our hero sang to himself during this sorrowful hour, in the melancholy period between light and dark. It requires no great penetration to understand, after carefully considering his soliloquy, that Francesco was in effect calling for a mother. There is nothing wrong in that: even Achilles called tearfully on his mother to rise from her chambers under the sea and comfort him on an occasion not unlike the one before us. And if Homer did not hesitate to show Achilles to us in such a moment, we need feel no compunction in doing the same with our hero, Francesco De Salvi.

Francesco, however, could not turn to his real mother because, for the various reasons we know, he was ashamed of Alessandra. In her place another mother came to his aid; this other mother often comes to console young men who are a little weak and immature — I mean, Imagination. As is her custom, she assumed the features most likely to lift Francesco from the depths of his gloom, in this case, the features of Anna. Not the true Anna, of course, but an absolutely imaginary Anna, as simple and gentle as the real Anna was obscure and unyielding. This unreal Anna began to sing in Francesco's ear an unreal bridal song (in the florid style, naturally, that appealed to Francesco) which went about like this:

"Oh, Francesco mine! Have you forgotten me? Or have you confused me with the others? Do you not understand how all that has happened has had one purpose, to bring us together? There is a time for work and a time for fear, there is a time for rest and a time for love. I am your time for love. I am your beauty, your justice, your faith. I am yours, Francesco mine. I will love you, I will love you so that I shall be able to show myself in all nakedness to you without shame, for I shall be your true wife. You will be able to tell me all that you hide from others, I will be your friend. Am I not also alone, like you, poor De Salvi, and am I not like you, but more beautiful? But you must not fear my beauty, for between man and wife all wealth is shared and if one is beautiful, the other is mirrored in him. When two people are as one, united even in their innermost secret selves, what does it matter how they look? They remain young for each other to the end, for their feelings are confounded with their features. Oh, Francesco mine, why do you doubt? I am the revelation, the confession and the absolution."

These, or others like them, were the fanciful arguments proffered by the consoling mother and our deluded friend was suddenly transported from despair to joy. Every motive for self-mortification seemed now a source of grace: the solitude in which he had been isolated since childhood now seemed to him the sign of his election to greatness; physical and social inferiority became a pretext to spur him on to the greatest accomplishments; his adventure with Rosaria had been an experience which made him more mature; her betrayal was his opportunity to be free again. And the brute jealousy which in spite of himself stung him at the thought of her infidelity, became a flame of desire for his true beloved.

Transformed thus from victim to victor, Francesco turned homeward for dusk had long since fallen. At home he found a telegram which had arrived a few moments after the anonymous accusation had sent him flying to Rosaria. In it his mother informed him that his father, Damiano, was gravely ill and that he was to come home at once.

There were no trains which stopped at that little station until noon of the next day. Meanwhile, as soon as he had read the telegram, Francesco went to the Cerentano house to inform his friend of his own immediate departure, but Edoardo was not there. The next morning Francesco went again to the Cerentano palace and again Edoardo had gone out; only a few hours later, when Francesco returned to his room for his bag, did he learn that Edoardo had been there looking for him and having heard from the landlord that his friend was leaving, had waited a long time for him. Since he had an appointment, he had finally left, much grieved at the thought of not being able to see Francesco before he went away.

And how had Francesco spent those morning hours while Edoardo looked and waited for him? Disappointed not to find Edoardo, he had preferred not to go home immediately after leaving the Cerentano palace; his little bag was packed and there was nothing for him to do. He sensed that the telegram meant Damiano was dying or dead and although his attachment to the old man was slight, the thought of that trip across the autumn fields, surrounded on all sides by the mournful spectacle of dying nature, and his arrival at a deathbed, depressed him deeply. He longed for the comfort of someone who would talk to him but his friend was out and Rosaria, the little room he knew so well, was now cut off from him forever. The thought of another visit occurred to him as necessary and wonderful, a kind of talisman for his journey; how could he leave town for what might be a long time without saying good-bye to Anna? If she gave him one single word of hope, it would be enough to transform the days ahead. But his exaltation of the evening before had died down and in the place of the imaginary Anna, the consoling mother, he now saw only the ambiguous, chill Anna of his last visits. So it was after much hesitation and battling against his cowardice that he dared climb the stairs to the Massias' apartment. As he climbed, the beating of his heart grew louder and his decision to speak to Anna grew more passionate. Like a frightened little boy, he had to assure himself before leaving of a prospect of happiness, no matter how distant. A trip under the sign of solitude seemed unbearable to him, and made him feel as if the train he soon would take would lead him to a kind of polar night, a region of ice and darkness where the final boundaries of his young life were already irrevocably marked, and where his heart would fail him.

In this mood of desperate decision he rang Anna's bell. A short silence, and then came the well-known clicking of her wooden heels on the floor. Anna was alone and to judge from her pallor, she had just got out of bed. She seemed to him to have grown thinner since his last visit and he thought he could see traces of tears in her deeply shadowed eyes. She looked at him dully and he explained hurriedly that he had come to see her because he was leaving. He saw her grow paler at this but he could not divine her thought which was: Edoardo is leaving, perhaps, and you go with him?

He took her sudden pallor as an enchanting confession and much moved he added at once that he hoped to return almost immediately, that his father was ill and he had to go to him. He noticed that Anna revived but not even then did he grasp the real cause of the change in her. She offered sympathy and polite wishes for his father's recovery. They stood silent, not knowing what further to say. Suddenly the blood rushed to Francesco's cheeks, and he stammered : "I haven't come to see you lately but you will have understood that I . . . you will have understood who it is that has been singing under your windows." Anna raised her head boldly and said, also flushing: "Yes, my cousin told me."

"Edoardo came with me the first two times," Francesco continued rapidly, "but then I came alone. I didn't tell anyone." Anna's face hardened and her eyes shone with shame and antagonism. Remembering the nights when she had stubbornly persisted in imagining Edoardo standing under her window, she said to herself: "Fool, fool that I've been!" and she sensed that she would not be able to control a flood of angry tears. "Leave me now, please," she murmured, and her mouth trembled. Seeing her color change once more and her breast shaking with rough sobs, Francesco, forgetting all restrain, exclaimed: "Anna, why are you crying?" His emotion drove out every trace of timidity, although he had not had the wine he usually drank to give himself courage. Tenderness and adoration made his hands tremble as he added: "Oh, if something is making you sad . . . do this for me at least, let me share your sorrow. It will do me great honor to bear every burden for you, to be able to comfort you. This is what I came to tell you — that I love you, that I am yours. Tell me if you want me, if there is any hope, and you will never have to take another step on this earth. I will carry you, light as a feather, and even if you have to pass through fire, you will not be touched by the flames, my dear one!"

As she listened to this speech, Anna stared with dry, pitiless eyes at Francesco. In the chaos of her crashing hopes, she was moved by animosity and a cruel desire for revenge on this interloper.

She remained wordless for a moment, furious at finding herself too confused to humiliate him as he deserved. Her silence, however, could not encourage the young man who saw the cold rejection in her eyes. A deep gloom came over him and he smiled bitterly, but at the thought of his coming trip and the depressing scene awaiting him at home, suddenly and unexpectedly he felt a heroic, almost a defiant impulse of pride: "This is how I feel," he exclaimed, "and I had to tell you before I left. I am going away now and I ask nothing of you, not even hope. I only want you to know that if for any reason you ever need someone, there is one person who would ask nothing in return, not even thanks, and would be happy to offer you all he has. What I have is yours, and the offer of my life is little to tell you how I feel."

These bold and ardent words aroused in Anna such a violent desire to strike him down for his audacity that she grew drunk with it. Her angry and uncertain smile lent her an unaccustomed vulgarity; suddenly she seemed not a girl but a grown woman: "How dare you," she exclaimed hotly, "how dare you talk to me so familiarly . . . as if I were one of your . . . one of your . . . What do I care about you? What do I care about your songs? You . . . I would rather give myself to the devil! What are you doing here? This is my house . . . my cursed house! Get out! Get out, I tell you! Go away!" She shook her head violently and an angry foam flecked her pale, swollen lips. Francesco obeyed without another word and found himself once more in the street feeling stunned and lost, like someone who had swallowed a poison or an overdose of sleeping pills, and imagining the walls were crumbling about him with an absurdly soft, almost gentle sound.

When Francesco got home it was well past noon and although he could not hope to catch the train he went directly to the station. He put down his bag and waited on a bench for the next train which was to leave at about three; it was an express which did not stop at his station, but at a larger and more important town some miles to the south. But he had decided to leave that day under any circumstances, to get off at the nearest stop and walk to his own village if necessary. Much as the idea of leaving frightened him, the idea of remaining in a city which had suddenly become foreign and hostile terrified him even more. He avoided even the thought of meeting Edoardo for their friendship was based on snobbery and illusion rather than on mutual trust. It would be unthinkable to confess to him the defeats of the last two days. For there was no doubt, Edoardo did not love the weak or the unhappy unless he could tyrannize over them, and true sympathy wearied him.

The three o'clock train stopped only for a few minutes at the station and choosing a third class carriage, Francesco was about to sit down when he heard from the platform an excited voice calling: "Francesco! Francesco!" He recognized Edoardo's voice and wished desperately he could hide, ashamed to be seen traveling third class. But from a distance Edoardo had seen him get on the train and had run along the cars, looking up to find his friend. Francesco leaned out hurriedly, for the doors were already slamming shut. "I've finally found you," Edoardo exclaimed, raising his flushed face, "this is the fourth train I've seen off, I came here at noon, and again later, and then I went to your house . . . But where were you? Oh Lord . . ." he went on, breathless from his chase, "how it upset me that you should be able to go away without saying good-bye. When will you come back?" "Soon, I hope, very soon," replied Francesco. "How I would like to come with you!" said Edoardo, drawing a deep breath. "But now, it just so happens there is something . . ." He laughed and his eyes sparkled. "Just the same," he went on, with a shiver at the sound of the train whistle, "I would love to come with you. But perhaps I would be in the way?" he asked hesitantly, looking beseechingly at his friend.

"It's better . . . it's better for me to go alone . . . it doesn't matter . . ." Francesco stammered hurriedly. "I'll be back soon and I will write you at once." "You will write me at once?" Edoardo repeated skeptically, "Will you really write me at once? You won't forget? Well, then, good-bye, the train is moving. Have a good trip!" As he said "good-bye, have a good trip" his expression was bitter and vexed, as if his friend were leaving him for some caprice or for a pleasure trip, to be away for years. He shook Francesco's hand through the window and pressing it hard, he added: "Now remember, write me really and don't deceive me. I love you more than all my other friends . . . more than my mother . . . more than my sister! More than my girl!" He ran along the train as he spoke until finally he pressed his friend's hand once more and shouted to him with a sweet smile: "Good-bye!"

Francesco saw to his distress that Edoardo's eyes were filled with tears.

As a handful of diamonds may console the fugitive in exile, so Edoardo's tears consoled our hero on his trip. The gloomy oppressiveness of the present and the immediate future could not dismay him. Impetuously he rushed on toward a future full of hope and delight in which he imagined himself successful, easy, graceful and wealthy like his incredible friend. Then Anna Massia would have no reason to scorn Francesco De Salvi and bending her proud head slightly she would say to him: "Yes, I want you." And perhaps one day Edoardo Cerentano di Paruta, as he rode by his side over a boundless estate, would say to him: "You remember, cousin, the autumn we met, when you were having an affair with that prostitute, that dreadful, red-haired woman . . . I used to ask myself, *what does he find in her?*" and Francesco would answer with a slighting laugh: "Her? Oh, yes . . . who knows what ever happened to her? Didn't I tell you? Well, I let her go . . . dropped her, just like that . . . she was upset, poor thing. But on the other hand, women should know better; never believe a student. She's dead, maybe, in some hospital . . ." And with that, the conversation would cease and cynical, wealthy Francesco would spur his horse onward.

Busy with such fantastic visions, it seemed to our traveler that the train was not taking him away from Anna but toward her. Then he fell asleep; when he awoke, the winter twilight had descended on the fields and a dark melancholy once more possessed him.

It was already night when he reached his destination, too late to start out for his village, and Francesco stayed at an inn near the station. The next morning he could have waited for a train which stopped near his home but he decided to get up at dawn and make the trip on foot. This would save him several hours and besides he looked forward to the solitary walk as a flight that would bring him respite and repose.

IGNAZIO SILONE

FROM *Bread and Wine*

Ignazio Silone.
Courtesy of Agenzia Giornalistica Italia.

PERHAPS HE'LL BE LATE," Don Benedetto said to his sister. "Perhaps he won't come till after dark."

"Don't you think that having him here might be dangerous?" Marta said.

The way her brother looked at her made her correct herself immediately. "What I meant was that it might be unwise for him."

"By now he must be pretty expert in these matters," Don Benedetto said. "He has been doing nothing but hiding and getting away for years. At all events, you had better leave us alone," he went on. "He might want to tell me things it's wiser to confide to one person only."

"I shan't disturb you," Marta said. "But what I've been wanting to say is that he can't remain an outlaw for the whole of his life. Don't you think we ought to tell his grandmother? She and his uncle are rich, they might be able to get him a lawyer and have him pardoned by the government."

"I don't think Pietro would want to be pardoned."

"But there's no disgrace in a pardon. Why should he refuse one?"

"The point is I don't think he feels guilty. Only those who repent are pardoned."

"But he won't be able to live in the woods for the rest of his life," Marta repeated. "He must still be young. How old is he?"

"The same age as Nunzio, thirty-four or thirty-five."

"But ruining your whole life just for a political opinion isn't right, it isn't decent. You were his teacher, you ought to tell him that."

"I don't think he does it just for politics," Don Benedetto said. "He has seemed to me to have been picked for a hard life ever since he was a boy."

"But if he's persecuted it's because of his political opinions."

"Do you remember when he came to see us here immediately after taking the school leaving exam? It was the summer after the earthquake."

"Yes, he was wearing mourning, his parents had been killed."

"Well, I remembered the occasion a short time ago," Don Benedetto said. "He told me something in confidence that must have been very important for his future development. His parents' death had affected him deeply, as was natural enough, but something else happened in those terrible days after the earthquake, when we were all wandering about among the rubble and taking shelter where best we could, something that actually shattered him. I don't think I've ever mentioned it before, because Pietro himself asked me not to tell anyone. But now a long time has passed. Well," Don Benedetto went on, "he had the misfortune to see, without being seen, a monstrous incident that filled him with horror. He was the only witness, and he kept the secret. He didn't tell me exactly what it was, but it was obvious from what he said that the person concerned was a relative of someone from his immediate environment."

"Crimes have always happened," said Marta.

"The person concerned enjoyed universal respect and after the crime he went on living as before, honestly, so to speak and enjoying general esteem. That was where the monstrosity of the thing lay."

"Can't you tell me what sort of crime it was?" said Marta.

"It was robbery with violence at the expense of an injured or dying man who was still half buried in the rubble," Don Benedetto said. "The criminal was not in need, the crime was committed at night and, as I said, Pietro witnessed it by chance. He was fifteen at the time. He fainted out of sheer horror. When he told me about it some months later he was still trembling. The killer was a neighbor and acted in the certainty of not being discovered. He was what is called a decent, respectable man. Thinking about it now, I feel that Pietro's fugue began at that time. At one time I used to think that he would end up in a monastery."

"Didn't you hear a noise?" Marta said. "Someone's knocking."

Marta hurriedly withdrew to her room. The expected guest was at the threshold. He was in lay clothing and without a hat, but a black garment he was carrying on his arm like a coat might have been the cassock he had taken off just previously. Pietro and Don Benedetto greeted each other and shook hands. Both were embarrassed by emotion.

"Did you come on foot?" Don Benedetto asked.

"I left the carriage down in the village," Pietro replied.

Don Benedetto pointed to a big armchair and sat beside him on a stool that was rather lower. As he was bent with age, this made him seem smaller than his former pupil. Pietro tried to react against the emotion of the scene and to appear perfectly at ease.

"Behold the lost lamb returning to the shepherd of its own accord," he said with a laugh.

Don Benedetto, who was looking with surprise at the young man's precociously aged face, failed to see the joke and shook his head. "It's not easy to tell which of us is the lost lamb," he said sadly.

"Many people talk about you in the villages round here," Pietro said. "What I've heard has been enough to convince me that you're the only person who keeps Christian honor alive in these parts."

"That is not at all my opinion," said Don Benedetto with bitterness in his voice. "and I assure you that that is not false modesty.

The truth of the matter is that I know I'm useless. I have lost my teaching job, and I have no cure of souls. It's true that I have the reputation that you mention, but if someone comes here to tell me about some wrong he has suffered I don't know what to say to him. That's the situation, I'm useless. Making certain discoveries at my time of life is sad, believe me."

Pietro had tears in his eyes. In his hours of discouragement in banishment or exile the mere thought of Don Benedetto had been sufficient to restore his calm and confidence, and now the poor old man was reduced to this state. What was he to say to him that would not seem to be inspired by compassion?

"For the rest," Don Benedetto went on, "it is not those who say mass and profess themselves to be ministers of the Lord who are closest to him in the intimacy of the spirit."

Hearing the old man talking of God as in the old days, Pietro suspected that there might be a grave misunderstanding in his mind that might falsify the whole meeting.

"I lost my faith many years ago," he said quietly but distinctly.

The old man smiled and shook his head. "In cases such as yours that is a mere misunderstanding," he said. "It would not be the first time that the Lord has been forced to hide Himself and make use of an assumed name. As you know, He has never attached much importance to the names men have given Him; on the contrary, one of the first of His commandments is not to take His name in vain. And sacred history is full of example of clandestine living. Have you ever considered the meaning of the flight into Egypt? And later, when He had grown up, did not Jesus several times have to hide himself to escape from the Pharisees?"

This religious apologia for the conspiratorial life brought back serenity to Pietro's face and gave it a childish cheerfulness.

"I have always felt the lack of that chapter in the *Imitation of Christ*," he said with a laugh.

Don Benedetto went on in the same sad tone with which he had begun. "I live here with my sister, between my garden and my books," he said. "For some time past my mail has obviously been tampered with, newspapers and books arrive late or get lost in transit. I pay no visits and receive few, and most of them are disagreeable. All the same, I'm well informed about many things, and they are demoralizing. In short, what should be given to God is given to Caesar and what should be left to Caesar is given to God. It was to such a brood that the Baptist spoke the words: 'O Generation of vipers, who have warned you to flee from the wrath to come?'"

Marta came in and said good evening to Pietro. She did so in a faint voice and with a frightened smile that seemed to have been prepared outside the door and then kept fixed with pins. She put a jug of wine and two glasses on the table and hurried back to her room.

The old man continued, "There is an old story that ought to be brought to mind whenever belief in God is doubted. Perhaps you will remember that it is written somewhere that in a moment of great distress Elijah asked the Lord to let him die, and the Lord summoned him to a mountain. Elijah went there, but would he recognize the Lord? And there arose a great and mighty wind that struck the mountain and split the rocks, but the Lord was not in the wind. And after the wind the earth was shaken by an earthquake, but the Lord was not in the earthquake. And after the earthquake there arose a great fire, but the Lord was not in the fire. But afterwards, in the silence, there was a still, small voice, like the whisper of branches moved by the evening breeze, and that still small voice, it is written, was the Lord."

Meanwhile a breeze had arisen in the garden, and the leaves began to rustle. The garden door that led into the sitting room creaked and swung open.

"What is it?" Marta called out from the next room. Pietro shuddered. The old man put his hand on his shoulder and said with a laugh, "Don't be afraid, you have nothing to fear."

He rose and shut the door that had been opened by the evening breeze. After a short pause he went on, "I too in the depth of my affliction have asked, where then is the Lord and why had He abandoned us? The loudspeakers and the bells that announced the beginning of new butchery to the whole county were certainly not the voice of the Lord. Nor are the shelling and bombing of

Abyssinian villages that are reported daily in the press. But if a poor man alone in a hostile village gets up at night and scrawls with a piece of charcoal or paints 'Down with war' on the walls the Lord is undoubtedly present. How is it possible not to see that behind that unarmed man in his contempt for danger, in his love of the so-called enemy, there is a direct reflection of the divine light? Thus, if simple workers are condemned by a special tribunal for similar reasons, there's no doubt about which side God is on."

Don Benedetto poured a little wine into a glass, raised it and held it against the light to make sure it was clear, since it came from a new barrel, and sipped it before filling the two glasses.

"I don't know if you can imagine what it is like to reach certain conclusions at my age, on the brink of the tomb," he went on. "At seventy-five it's still possible to change one's ideas, but not one's habits. A retired life is the only kind that fits in with my character. I lived in seclusion even when I was young. Revulsion from vulgarity always kept me away from public life. On the other hand, inaction irks me. I look around and don't see what I can do. With the parish priests there's nothing I can do. Those who know me personally now avoid me, are afraid of meeting me. The few priests who have left the Church in the past fifty years in the Marsica diocese have done so because of scandalous breaches of celibacy. That is sufficient to give you an idea of the spiritual state of our clergy. If news spread in the diocese that a priest had abandoned the priesthood, the first thing that would naturally occur to the minds of the faithful would be that another one had eloped with his housemaid."

"I had to call on Don Angelo Girasole this afternoon," Pietro said. "He gave me the impression of being a very decent man, a good clerk in an administrative office."

"You're quite right," Don Benedetto said, "but Christianity is not an administration."

"The others, those who believe they have historical vision, are worse," said Pietro. "They believe, or pretend they believe, in a Man of Providence."

"If they allow themselves to be deceived it is their own fault," Don Benedetto interrupted, livening up. "They were warned about two thousand years ago. They were told that many would come in the name of Providence and seduce the people, that there would be talk of wars and rumors of wars. They were told that all this would come to pass, but that the end was not yet. They were told that nation would rise up against nation and kingdom against kingdom; that there would be famines and pestilences and earthquakes in divers places; but that all these things would not be the end, but the beginning. Christians were warned. We were told that many would be horrified and many would betray, and that if someone, whoever it might be, should say here is a man of Providence, there is a man of Providence, we must not believe him. We have been warned. False prophets and false saviors shall arise and shall show great signs and wonders and deceive many. We could not have asked for plainer warning. If many have forgotten it, it will not change anything of what will come to pass. The destiny of the Man of Providence has already been written. *Intrabit ut vulpis, regnabit ut leo, morietur ut canis.*"*

"What a fine language Latin is," said Pietro. "And what a difference there is between that honest old church Latin and the modern sibylline Latin of the encyclicals."

"What is lacking in our country, as you know, is not the critical spirit," Don Benedetto said. "What is lacking is faith. The critics are grumblers, violent men, dissatisfied men, in certain circumstances they may sometimes even be heroes. But they are not believers. What is the use of teaching new ways of talking or gesticulating to a nation of skeptics? Perhaps the terrible sufferings that lie ahead will make Italians more serious. Meanwhile, when I feel most disheartened, I tell myself I'm useless, a failure, but there's Pietro, there are his friends, the unknown members of underground groups. I confess to you that that is my only consolation."

Pietro was taken aback by the despondency in his former master's voice. "My dear Don Benedetto," he said, "we have not met for fifteen years, and after this perhaps we shall not meet again. You are an old man, my health is uncertain, the times are hard. It would

*He will come in like a fox, reign like a lion, die like a dog.

be wrong to waste this short visit exchanging compliments. The trust you have in me terrifies me. I genuinely believe I'm no better than my former school fellows. My destiny had been more fortunate than theirs because I was helped by a whole series of misfortunes and cut the cord in good time. For the rest, you must forgive me for not sharing the optimism of that only consolation of yours."

"There's no salvation except putting one's life in jeopardy," Don Benedetto said. "But that is not for everyone. After his first meeting with you at Acquafredda Nunzio, that poor soul in torment, came here and told me everything. He told me again about his position, which I already knew. Under dictatorial régime how can one exercise a profession in which one depends on public offices and yet remain free? he asked me. What good fortune that at least Pietro is saved, he said."

"Saved?" said Pietro. "Is there a past participle of saving oneself? Alas, recently I have had plenty of occasions to consider what is undoubtedly the saddest aspect of the present degeneracy, because it concerns the future. My dear Don Benedetto, perhaps the future will resemble the present. We may be sowing contaminated seed."

Don Benedetto signaled to him to be silent. "There's someone at the door," he said in an undertone. "Come into the next room."

They rose and went into Marta's room. At that moment there was a knock at the door.

"Go and see who it is," Don Benedetto said to his sister. "Don't let anyone in. Never mind who it is, say you don't know whether I can see him. And please, before you open the door bring the wine and the two glasses in here."

There was another knock at the door, and Marta opened it. It was Don Piccirilli.

"Good evening," he said. "Am I disturbing you? I was told that Don Angelo Girasole was here with Don Benedetto, and I should like to see him too."

"You have been misinformed," Marta said. "Don Girasole is not here."

"Didn't a priest arrive here in a carriage from Fossa a short while ago?" Don Piccirilli said.

"No priest and no carriage have been seen here," Marta said. "You have been misinformed."

This conversation took place at the front door. Marta showed no inclination to let him in.

"I hope I'm not being troublesome," Don Piccirilli said, "but as I've come all this way I should like at least to say good evening to Don Benedetto."

"I don't know whether he can see you," Marta said. "He may be resting. I'll go and see."

In the next door room she found her brother alone. Pointing to the window that gave on to the gardens, he indicated that his first visitor had left. "Now we must try and keep Don Piccirilli here as long as possible," he said to his sister in an undertone. "Bring us some wine immediately."

He went to meet the newly arrived guest.

"What are you doing standing there in the doorway?" he said reproachfully. "Come in, come in, don't stand on ceremony. You must tell me what you think of the wine from a new barrel."

MATALENA WAS PREPARING flour for bread making on the ground floor of the inn, and Don Paolo was keeping her company. At Pietrasecca bread was baked once a fortnight in a communal oven. It was a ritual with strict rules. The woman's head was wrapped in a cloth rather like a nun's veil and she was passing the flour through a sieve over an open bin. Thus she separated the white flour from the chaff and the best from the ordinary flour. The chaff went to the chickens and the pig, the ordinary was used for bread and the best for pasta. The woman's face and hands were covered with dust from the flour that rose from the rhythmical movement of the sieve. Chiarina, the goatherd's wife, was having difficulty in lighting the green wood under the copper in which potatoes were being cooked that were to be added to the flour to make the bread heavier and more lasting.

The sieving stopped when a strange young man, looking halfway between a cafone and a workman, came into the bar and asked for Don Paolo. He had a letter in his hand. He seemed rather surprised and embarrassed at the sight of Don Paolo, and was on the point of apologizing and going away again.

"Don Benedetto told me he was sending me to someone in whom I could have full confidence. To tell the truth, I didn't expect to find a priest here," he said.

"Never mind," said the priest. "Don Benedetto will have had his reasons." The youth handed over the letter of introduction.

It consisted of these few words, written in Don Benedetto's fine, tremulous hand: '*Ecce homo*, my friend, here is a poor man who has need of you, and perhaps you also have need of him. Please listen to him to the end."

Don Paolo took the young man to his room and made him sit beside him.

"If you had come here as one goes to a priest," he said, "I should certainly have asked you to apply elsewhere. How long have you known Don Benedetto?"

"We belong to the same village," the young man said. "Every family at Rocca knows every other. Everyone knows everything, or nearly everything, about everyone else. When you see someone going out you know exactly where he's going, and when you see him coming back you know where he has been. My family has a vineyard near Don Benedetto's garden halfway up the hill above the village. We use water from his well to spray sulfur on the vines, and he borrows our stakes for his tomatoes, beans and peas. My mother always consulted him about my education. His advice may not always have been good, but his intentions always were. He has always liked me, ever since I was a boy." After a pause he added, "He told me to tell you everything."

As he spoke the young man's personality became better defined. At first sight, particularly because of his plain, patched clothing, the earthy marks on his face and hands, and his untidy, ruffled hair, he created the impression of being half-workman, half-cafone, but on closer inspection he turned out to have extraordinarily lively and intelligent eyes, and his manners were controlled and polite. Also instead of using dialect he spoke very correct Italian with complete ease. After some hesitation he started telling his story.

"I was a delicate and sickly boy, and also I was an only son," he said. "So my mother decided that I should not work on the land. 'Our family has always worked the land, and we're still where we always were,' she said. 'For generations we have hoed, dug, sowed and manured the land, and we're still poor. Let the boy study. He's not strong and he needs a less tough way of living.' My father didn't agree. 'Working the land is hard, but it's safe,' he said. 'Education is for the sons of gentlemen. We have no-one to back us.' Our backing was Don Benedetto. 'Since the boy wants to study, let him,' he said. He helped my mother with his advice. As long as I was at grammar school my family could still regard itself as being prosperous. Apart from the vineyard, my father had two fields on which he grew wheat and vegetables and a shed with four cows. While I was a student the money orders my mother sent me to pay for my keep never arrived regularly, but they arrived. But during my three years at high school the family situation went from bad to worse, because of two bad harvests and an illness of my father's. On top of this were my heavy expenses. The result was that one of the two fields had to be sold to pay off my father's debts. Two cows died in an epidemic; the two that were left were sold at the fair, and the shed was let. 'No matter,' my mother said. 'When our son has passed his exams he'll be able to help us.' I passed the state exam three years ago and the following October I went to Rome, where I registered in the faculty of arts. Actually my mother didn't know where to find the money to keep me in Rome until I got my degree."

"Why did you choose the faculty of arts?" Don Paolo asked. "It's not the best from the point of view of earning a living."

"Don Benedetto said that was what I was best at. In Rome I led a life of severe privations. I lived in a small room without electric light. My midday meal consisted of white coffee and bread, and for dinner I had soup. I was permanently hungry. I was comically dressed and had no friends. The first time I tried to approach other students they laughed at me and made stupid jokes because of my provincial appearance. Two incidents of that kind were enough to make me completely unsociable. I often wept with rage and mortification in my little room. I resigned myself to a life of solitude.

After the warm family atmosphere to which I was used I was ill at ease in the noisy, vulgar, cynical students' world. Most of the students were interested in sport and politics, both of which offer frequent opportunities for rowdiness. One day I saw a typical piece of rowdiness from the tram. About a dozen students belonging to my faculty beat a young workman till the blood flowed. I can still see the scene in my mind's eye. The workman lay on the pavement with his head on one of the tramlines while the students who had surrounded him went on kicking and hitting him with sticks. 'He didn't salute the flag,' they shouted. Some policemen arrived on the scene, congratulated the aggressors on their patriotic action and arrested the injured man. A crowd had gathered, but no-one protested. I was left alone on the stationary tram. What cowardice, I muttered to myself. Behind me I heard someone mutter, 'Yes, it's a real disgrace.' It was the conductor. We said goodbye to each other that day, but that was all. But as he was often on duty on the line that went down my street, we saw each other every so often and got into the habit of greeting each other like old acquaintances."

There was a long pause as if he had lost the thread. Then he went on, "I met him in the street one day when he was off duty. We shook hands and went into a tavern for a glass of wine. Each of us told the other about himself, and so we struck up a friendship. He asked me to his home, where I met other persons, nearly all of them young. There were five of them altogether and they constituted a cell, and those meetings were cell meetings. All this was strange and new to me. Thanks to the tramwayman's introduction, I was admitted to the cell, and I regularly attended the weekly meetings. Those were my first personal contacts with townspeople. The other members of the cell were workers or artisans, and they liked me for being a student, and I enjoyed those meetings too. The purely human pleasure they gave me meant that I did not at first realize the gravity and significance of the step I had taken. At the meetings badly printed little newspapers and pamphlets were read in which tyranny was denounced and the revolution was proclaimed as a certain, inevitable and not distant event that would establish fraternity and justice among men. It was a kind of secret and prohibited weekly dream in which we indulged, and it made us forget the wretchedness of our everyday lives. It was like a secret religious rite. There was no link between us apart from those meetings, and if by chance we met in the street we pretended not to know one another.

"When I went out one morning I was arrested by two policemen, taken to the central police station and shut up in a room full of other policemen. After some formalities they started slapping my face and spitting at me, and that went on for an hour. Perhaps I might have put up better with a more violent beating, but the slapping and spitting were intolerable. When the door opened and the official who was to interrogate me appeared, my face and chest were literally dripping with spittle. The official railed at, or pretended to rail at, his subordinates, made me wash and dry myself, took me to his office, and assured me that he had studied my case with benevolence and understanding. He knew I lived in a small room, he knew the milk bar where I had my midday bread and coffee and the inn where I went for my soup in the evening. He had detailed information about my family, and he knew about the difficulties that endangered the continuation of my studies. He could only guess the motives that had led me towards the revolutionary groups but, he said, that impulse could not in itself be regarded as reprehensible; on the contrary, in fact. He said youth was inherently magnanimous and idealistic, and it would be disastrous if it were otherwise. However, the police had the socially necessary but perhaps distasteful role of keeping a close watch on the magnanimous and idealistic impulses of the young."

"In short," Don Paolo interrupted, "he suggested that you should put yourself in the service of the police. And what did you reply?"

"I agreed."

Matalena appeared at the door and said, "Dinner's ready. Shall I lay for two?"

"I'm not hungry this evening," the priest replied. He rose from his seat because he was tired and lay on the bed.

In a soft voice the young man continued, "I was given 100 lire to pay the rent of my room, and in return I wrote a short report, like an academic essay, on 'How a cell works, what its members read and what they talk about'. The official read it and praised it. 'It's very well written,' he said. I was proud that he was pleased with me, and I undertook to remain in contact with him in return for an allowance of 500 lire a month. That enabled me to have soup at midday as well as in the evening and to go to the cinema on Saturday night. One day he also gave me a pack of cigarettes. Actually I had never smoked, but I learnt to out of politeness."

"And what did you write in your next reports?" Don Paolo asked.

"They went on being very general, and he began to be dissatisfied with them," the young man said. "I always sent him a copy of the printed matter that was distributed in the cell, but that was not enough for him, probably because he received the same material from other sources. Eventually he advised me to leave that cell and join a more interesting one, and I had no difficulty in doing so. I told my friends that I wanted a transfer to a cell in which there were other intellectuals, and it was arranged immediately. In the new cell I met and struck up a friendship with a girl, a dressmaker. She was the first woman I had ever met. Very soon we were inseparable, and it was then that I began to have the first twinges of conscience. With her I began to have glimpses of a pure, honest and decent way of living the possibility of which I had not previously imagined. At the same time an insuperable abyss opened up between my apparent and my secret life. Sometimes I managed to forget my secret. I worked for the cell with genuine enthusiasm, translated into Italian and typed out whole chapters of revolutionary novels that we received from abroad, stuck manifestos on the walls at night. But I was deceiving myself. When my new comrades admired my courage and my activity they reminded me that in reality I was betraying them. So I tried to get away from them. Also I told myself that I too had a right to live. No more money was being sent to me from home. When I was hungry and the rent was due I lost all restraint. I had no other resources. I regarded politics as absurd. What did all that stuff matter to me? I should certainly have preferred to live in peace, to have two or three meals a day, consigning both 'economic democracy' and 'the necessity of imperial expansion' to the devil. But that was impossible. I had no money to buy food or pay the rent. But that kind of cynicism collapsed when I was with my girl. We were very much in love. To me she did not represent a way of thinking, in fact she argued very little but kept silent and liked listening to others; to me she was a way of being, a way of living, a way of giving oneself in an unparalleled human and pure way. I could no longer think of life without her, because she was really more than a woman, she was a light and a flame, she was concrete proof of the possibility of living honestly, cleanly, unselfishly, seeking harmony with one's fellows with the whole of one's soul. It seemed to me that only after I met her had I become spiritually alive. But I did not blame my parents. They were good, honest people, but they were traditional. That girl did not follow the rules, but her heart. She seemed to me to invent her life as she lived it. But in the face of her ingenuous confidence in me how could I not remember that I was deceiving and betraying her? Thus our love was poisoned at the roots. Being with her, though I loved her so much, was an insupportable pretense, a torment . . ."

"Why, when your relations with the police became morally reprehensible to you, did you not break with them?" Don Paolo asked.

"I tried to get away from them and cover my tracks several times," the young man said. "Once I moved, but they had no difficulty in tracking me down to my new address. For a time I tried to quiet my conscience by writing harmless, phony reports that told them nothing. At that time I was beginning to receive a small monthly allowance from my mother again. I tried to deceive the police by telling them I had left the cell because my comrades no longer trusted me. But they had other informers who satisfied them of the opposite. Finally I became obsessed with the idea that my situation was irremediable. I felt condemned. There was nothing that I could do. It was my destiny."

The young man spoke with difficulty, almost struggling for breath. Don Paolo avoided looking him in the face.

"I don't want to make my behavior seem less ugly than it was," he went on. "I don't want to make my case more pitiful. This is a confession in which I want to show myself in all my repulsive nakedness. Well, then, the truth of the matter was this. Fear of being discovered was stronger in me than remorse. What was I to tell my girl if my deception were revealed? What would my friends say? That was the idea that haunted me. I feared for my threatened reputation, not for the wrong that I was doing. I saw the image of my fear all round me everywhere."

The young man paused. His throat was dry. There was a bottle of water and a glass on the table, but it did not occur to Don Paolo to ask him to help himself.

"I knew I was being trailed by the police who no longer trusted me," he went on. "I kept away from my friends to avoid having to denounce them. The police threatened me with arrest if I associated with suspects without informing them. I lived in terror of being arrested again. I tried to live in complete seclusion, with the result that every meeting with my girl was a torment. But in spite of that she was always patient, gentle and affectionate with me. On Christmas Day last year we went together to a little eating-place outside the walls . . ."

Don Paolo went on listening to a story every detail of which he already knew. The unusually cheerful lunch. The invitation to go home with the girl. The buying of flowers, fruit, sweets, and a bottle of Marshal. The arrival of the police and the escape on to the roof. The long wait on the roof. But the young man did not finish. He hid his face in his hands and burst into tears. After a while he resumed his story.

"I went home to Rocca dei Marsi. I told my parents that the doctors had insisted on my returning to my native climate. I spent the winter at home without seeing anyone. Sometimes I went to see Don Benedetto, who gave me books to read. In the spring I started working in the fields with my father, winnowing, pruning the vines, hoeing and reaping. I went on working as long as I could stand on my feet, to the point of physical exhaustion. Immediately after dinner I went to bed, and in the morning, at dawn, it was I who woke my father. He looked at me with admiration. He said, 'It's obvious that you come of a race of peasants; if you come from the land you cannot free yourself from it.' But if you come from the land and have lived in a town you're no longer a peasant and you're not a townsman either. Memory of the town, of my girl, of the cell, of the police, was a perpetually open wound, a wound that still bled and was beginning to putrefy and threatened to poison the rest of my life. My mother said town air had ruined me and put sadness in my blood. 'Let me work,' I said, 'perhaps work will make me better.' But in the fields my girl would often appear before me in my mind's eye. How could I forget her? Having glimpsed the possibility of another way of living, a clean, honest and courageous way of living, having seen the possibility of open and frank communication and dreamed of a better humanity, how could I resign myself to village life? On the other hand, how could I undo the irremediable? In my solitary brooding, that left me not a moment's peace, I passed from fear of punishment to fear of non-punishment. The idea that I was haunted by the wrong I had done only because of the continual risk of being found out began to frighten me. So I began to wonder whether, if better technique enabled one to betray one's friends with the certainty that one would never be found out, that would make it more supportable."

Don Paolo looked him in the face, in the eyes.

"I must confess," the young man went on, "that my religious faith has never been very strong. I have never believed very deeply. I was baptized, confirmed and received holy communion like everyone else, but my faith in the reality of God was very vague and fitful. That was why I put up no resistance in Rome to accepting the so-called scientific theories that were propagated in the cells. These theories began to strike me as too comfortable. The idea that everything was matter, that the idea of right was inseparable from that of utility (even if it were social utility) and was backed only by the idea of punishment, became intolerable to me. Punishment by whom? The state, the party and public opinion? But supposing the state, the party and public opinion were immoral? And then, if favorable circumstances or an appropriate technique made it possible to do evil with impunity, what was morality based on? So might technique be capable of destroying the distinction between right and wrong by eliminating the risk of punishment? The idea frightened me. I began to be seriously afraid of the absurd. I don't want to weary you with these digressions, which may seem abstract to you; nor do I want you to suppose that by moralizing I'm now trying to put myself in a more favorable light. No, those ideas became the very substance of my life. I no longer believed in God, but with all the strength of my mind I began to want Him to exist. I had an absolute need of Him to escape from the fear of chaos. A night came when I could no longer stand it, and I got up to go and knock at the door of a Capuchin monastery in our part of the world. On the way I met a monk whom I already knew, one Brother Gioacchino. I said to him, 'I want so much to believe in God and I can't manage it, won't you please explain to me how it's done?' 'One mustn't be proud,' he replied, 'one mustn't claim the right to understand everything, one mustn't try, one must resign oneself, shut one's eyes, pray. Faith is a grace.' But I could not let myself go. I wanted to understand. I couldn't not try to understand. My whole being was in a state of extreme and painful tension. I couldn't resign myself. I wanted God by force. I needed Him."

The young man fell silent, as if exhausted.

"You must be thirsty," Don Paolo said. "Drink some water."

"Eventually I went to see Don Benedetto," the young man went on. "I went to see him, not because he was a priest, but because to me he'd always been a symbol of the upright man. He has known me since childhood, as I said. When I went to see him I told him that actually he did not know me yet, because he had no suspicion of what was hidden inside me. My confession lasted for five hours. I made a tremendous effort and told him everything, and in the end I was lying almost unconscious on the ground. I seriously believed I was dying. On that first occasion the words came out of me as if I were bringing up blood. When I had finished only a vague gleam of consciousness remained. I felt like an empty sack. Don Benedetto sent his sister Marta to tell my mother that I would be sleeping at his house that night, and that for the next few days I would be helping him working in his garden. We worked together for the next few days, and every now and then he stopped and talked to me. He taught me that nothing is irreparable while life lasts, and that no condemnation is ever final. He explained to me that, though evil must not of course be loved, nevertheless good is often born of it, and that perhaps I should never have become a man but for the infamies and errors through which I had passed. When at last he had finished with me and said I could go home I had no more fear and I seemed to have been reborn. I was struck by the air coming from the mountain. Never before had I breathed such fresh air in my village. Having stopped being afraid, I stopped brooding and started rediscovering the world. I started seeing the trees again, the children in the streets, the poor people laboring in the fields, the donkeys carrying their loads, the cows pulling the plow. I went on seeing Don Benedetto from time to time. Yesterday he sent for me and said, 'I should like to spare you the repetition of a painful experience, but there's a man near here to whom I want you to repeat your confession. He's someone in whom you can have complete confidence.' He gave me the necessary information, added some advice, and here I am."

By now it was dark, and the young man's exhausted voice faded away in the shadows. After a pause the other man's voice emerged from it.

"If I were a leader of a party or of a political group," Don Paolo said, "I would have to judge you according to the party rules. Every party has a morality of its own, codified in rules. Those rules are often very close to those with which moral feeling inspires everyone, though sometimes they are the exact opposite. But I'm not (or am no longer) a political leader. Here and now I'm an ordinary man, and if I am to judge another man I can be guided only by my conscience, respecting the very narrow limits within which one man has the right to judge another."

"I did not come here to ask for pardon or absolution," the young man said.

"Luigi Murica," the other man said quietly, "I want to tell you something that will show you how much I now trust you. I'm not a priest. Don Paolo Spada is not my real name. My name is Pietro Spina."

Murica's eyes filled with tears.

Meanwhile Matalena of her own accord had laid the table for two, and she now insisted on their coming down for dinner. "Convalescents mustn't miss meals," she said. "And if they have visitors the least they can do is to invite them."

She had put a clean tablecloth and a bottle of wine on the table. The two men dined in silence. The wine was the previous year's and the bread was a fortnight old. They dipped the bread in the wine. When they had finished Murica wanted to go straight back to Rocca, and Don Paolo went up to his room to fetch a coat and go with him for some of the way. Matalena did not conceal a certain amount of jealousy at this sudden friendship between a stranger and her priest.

"You talked for such a long time," she said to Murica. "Do you still have things to say to each other?"

"I confessed," the young man said.

When the two men parted in the road leading down to the valley Murica said. "Now I'm ready for anything."

"Good, we'll meet again soon," Don Paolo said.

The priest delayed returning to the inn. He sat on the grassy edge of the road, oppressed by many thoughts. Voices could be heard in the distance, shepherds calling to their flocks, the barking of dogs, the low bleating of sheep. A slight odor of thyme and wild rosemary rose from the damp earth. It was the time of day when the cafoni put their donkeys back in their sheds and went to sleep. Mothers called their children from the windows. It was a time favorable to humility. Man returned to the animal, the animal to the plant, the plant to the earth. The stream at the bottom of the valley was full of stars. Pietrasecca was submerged in shadow; all that could be seen was the cow's head with its two big horns at the top of the inn.

NATALIA GINZBURG

Valentino

Natalia Ginzburg.
Courtesy Angelo Riverone Agrigento.

I LIVED WITH MY FATHER, mother and brother in a small rented apartment in the middle of town. Life was not easy and finding the rent money was always a problem. My father was a retired school-teacher and my mother gave piano lessons; we had to help my sister who was married to a commercial traveler and had three children and a pitifully inadequate income, and we also had to support my student brother who my father believed was destined to become a man of consequence. I attended a teacher-training college and in my spare time helped the caretaker's children with their homework. The caretaker had relatives who lived in the country and she paid in kind with a supply of chestnuts, apples and potatoes.

My brother was studying medicine and the expenses were never-ending: microscope, books, fees . . . My father believed that he was destined to become a man of consequence. There was little enough reason to believe this, but he believed it all the same and had done ever since Valentino was a small boy and perhaps found it difficult to break the habit. My father spent his days in the kitchen, dreaming and muttering to himself, fantasizing about the future when Valentino would be a famous doctor and attend medical congresses in the great capitals and discover new drugs and new diseases. Valentino himself seemed devoid of any ambition to become a man of consequence; in the house, he usually spent his time playing with a kitten or making toys for the caretaker's children out of scraps of old material stuffed with sawdust, fashioning cats and dogs and monsters too, with big heads and long, lumpy bodies. Or he would don his skiing outfit and admire himself in the mirror; not that he went skiing very often, for he was lazy and hated the cold, but he had persuaded my mother to make him an outfit all in black with a great white woolen balaclava; he thought himself no end of a fine fellow in these clothes and would strut about in front of the mirror first with a scarf thrown about his neck and then without and would go out on to the balcony so that the caretaker's children could see him.

Many times he had become engaged and then broken it off and my mother had had to clean the dining-room specially and dress for the occasion. It had happened so often already that when he announced that he was getting married within the month nobody believed him, and my mother cleaned the dining-room wearily and put on the gray silk dress reserved for her pupils' examinations at the Conservatory and for meeting Valentino's prospective brides.

We were expecting a girl like all the others he had promised to marry and then dropped after a couple of weeks, and by this time we thought we knew the type that appealed to him: teenagers wearing jaunty little berets and still studying at high-school. They were usually very shy and we never felt threatened by them, partly because we knew he would drop them and partly because they looked just like my mother's piano pupils.

So when he turned up with his new fiancée we were amazed to the point of speechlessness. She was quite unlike anything we had ever imagined. She was wearing a longish sable coat and flat rubber-soled shoes and was short and fat. From behind tortoiseshell glasses she regarded us with hard, round eyes. Her nose was shiny and she had a moustache. On her head she wore a black hat squashed down on one side and the hair not covered by the hat was black streaked with gray, crimped and untidy. She was at least ten years older than Valentino.

Valentino talked non-stop because we were incapable of speech. He talked about a hundred things all at once, about the cat and the caretaker's children and his microscope. He wanted to take his fiancée to his room at once to show her the microscope but my mother objected because the room had not been tidied. And his fiancée said that she had seen plenty of microscopes anyway. So Valentino went to find the cat and brought it to her. He had tied a ribbon with a bell around its neck to make it look pretty, but the cat was so frightened by the bell that it raced up the curtain and clung there, hissing and glaring at us, its fur all on end and its eyes gleaming ferociously and my mother began to moan with apprehension lest her curtain should be ruined.

Valentino's fiancée lit a cigarette and began to talk. The tone of her voice was that of a person used to giving orders and everything she said was like a command. She told us that she loved Valentino and had every confidence in him; she was confident that he would give up playing with the cat and making toys. And she said that she had a great deal of money so they could marry without having to wait for Valentino to start earning. She was alone and had no ties since both her parents were dead and she was answerable to no one.

All at once my mother started to cry. It was an awkward moment and nobody knew quite what to do. There was absolutely no emotion behind my mother's tears except grief and shock; I sensed this and felt sure that the others sensed it too. My father patted her knee and made little clicking noises with his tongue as if comforting a child. Valentino's fiancée suddenly became very red in the face and she went over to my mother; her eyes gleamed, alarmed and imperious at the same time, and I realized that she intended to marry Valentino come what may. "Oh dear, Mother's crying," said Valentino, "but Mother does tend to get emotional." — "Yes," said my mother, and she dried her eyes, patted her hair and drew herself up. "I'm not very strong at the moment and tears come easily. This news has taken me rather by surprise; but Valentino has always done whatever he wanted to do." My mother had had a genteel education; her behavior was always correct and she had great self-control.

Valentino's fiancée told us that she and Valentino were going to buy furniture for the sitting-room that very day. Nothing else needed to be bought as her house already contained all that they would need. And Valentino sketched a plan, for my mother's benefit, of the house in which his fiancée had lived since her childhood and in which they would now live together: it had three floors and a garden and was in a neighborhood where all the houses were detached and each had its own garden.

For a little while after they had gone we all sat silently looking at each other. Then my mother told me to go and fetch my sister, and I went.

My sister lived in a top-floor flat on the outskirts of town. All day long she typed addresses for a firm that paid her so much for each addressed envelope. She had constant toothache and kept a scarf wrapped around her face. I told her that our mother wanted to see her and she asked why but I wouldn't tell her. Intensely curious, she picked up the youngest child and came with me.

My sister had never believed that Valentino was destined to become a man of consequence. She couldn't stand him and pulled a face every time his name was mentioned, remembering all the money my father spent on his education while she was forced to type addresses. Because of this, my mother had never told her about the skiing outfit and whenever my sister came to our house one of us had to rush to his room and make sure that these clothes and any other new things that he had bought for himself were out of sight.

It was not easy to explain to my sister Clara the turn that events had taken. That a woman had appeared with lashings of money and a moustache who was willing to pay for the privilege of marrying Valentino and that he had agreed; that he had left all the teenagers in berets behind him and was now shopping in town for sitting-room furniture with a woman who wore a sable coat. His drawers were still full of photographs of the teenage girls and the letters they had written him. And after his marriage to the bespectacled and mustachioed woman he would still manage somehow to slip away from time to time to meet the teenagers in berets and would spend a little money on their amusements; only a little, because he was basically mean when it came to spending on others the money he regarded as his own.

Clara sat and listened to my father and mother and shrugged her shoulders. Her toothache was very bad and addresses were waiting to be typed; she also had the washing to do and her children's socks to mend. Why had we dragged her out and made her come all this way and forced her to waste a whole afternoon? She wasn't the slightest bit interested in Valentino, in what he did or whom he married; the woman was doubtless mad because only a mad woman could seriously want to marry Valentino; or she was a whore who had found her dupe and the fur coat was probably fake — Father and Mother had no idea about furs. My mother insisted that the fur was genuine, that the woman was certainly respectable and that her manners and bearing were those of a lady, and she was not mad; only ugly, as ugly as sin. And at the memory of that ugliness my mother covered her face with her hands and started to cry again. But my father said that that was not the main consideration; and he was about to launch into a long speech about what was the main consideration but my mother interrupted him. My mother always interrupted his speeches, leaving him choking on a half-finished sentence, puffing with frustration.

There was a sudden clamor in the hall: Valentino was back. He had found Clara's little boy there and was greeting him boisterously, swinging him high over his head and then down to the floor, then up and down again while the baby screamed with laughter. For a moment Clara seemed to enjoy the laughter of her child, but her face soon darkened with the emotions of spite and bitterness that the sight of Valentino invariably aroused in her.

Valentino started to describe the furniture they had bought for the sitting-room. It was Empire style. He told us how much it had cost, quoting sums that to us seemed enormous; he rubbed his hands together hard and tossed the figures gleefully around our little living-room. He took out a cigarette and lit it; he had a gold lighter — a present from Maddalena, his fiancée.

He was oblivious of the uneasy silence which gripped the rest of us. My mother avoided looking at him. My sister had picked up her little boy and was pulling on his gloves. Since the appearance of the gold cigarette lighter, her lips had been compressed into a grim smile which she now concealed behind her scarf as she left, carrying her child. As she passed through the door, the word "Pig!" filtered through the scarf.

The word had been uttered very softly, but Valentino heard it. He started after Clara, intending to follow her downstairs and ask her why she had called him a pig and my mother held him back with difficulty. "Why did she say that?" Valentino asked my mother. "Why did the wretched woman call me a pig? Because I'm getting married? Is that why I'm a pig? What's she thinking about, the old hag!"

My mother smoothed the pleats in her dress, sighed and said nothing; my father refilled his pipe with fingers that trembled. He struck a match against the sole of his shoe to light his pipe but Valentino, noticing this, went up to him holding out his cigarette lighter. My father glanced at Valentino's hand proffering the light, then he suddenly pushed the hand away, threw down his pipe and left the room. A moment later he appeared in the doorway, puffing and gesticulating as if about to launch into a speech; but then he thought better of it and turned away without a word, slamming the door behind him.

Valentino stood as if transfixed. "But why?" he asked my mother. "Why is he angry? What's the matter with them? What have I done wrong?"

"That woman is as ugly as sin," said my mother quietly. "She's grotesque, Valentino. And since she boasts about being so wealthy, everyone will assume that you are marrying her for her money. That's what we think too, Valentino, because we cannot believe that you are in love with her, you who always used to chase the pretty girls, none of whom was ever pretty enough for you. Nothing like this has ever happened in our family before; not one of us has ever done anything just for money."

Valentino said we hadn't understood anything at all. His fiancée wasn't ugly, at least he didn't find her ugly, and wasn't his opinion the only one that really mattered? She had lovely black eyes and the bearing of a lady, apart from which she was intelligent, extremely intelligent and very cultured. He was bored with all those pretty little girls with nothing to talk about, while with Maddalena he could talk about books and a hundred other things. He wasn't marrying her for her money; he was no pig. Deeply offended all of a sudden, he went and shut himself in his room.

In the days that followed he continued to sulk and to act the part of a man marrying in the teeth of family opposition. He was solemn, dignified, rather pale and spoke to none of us. He never showed us the presents that he received from his fiancée but every day he had something new: on his wrist he sported a gold watch with a second hand and a white leather strap, he carried a crocodile-skin wallet and had a new tie every day.

My father said he would go have a talk with Valentino's fiancée, but my mother was opposed to this, partly because my father had a weak heart and was supposed to avoid any excitement, partly because she thought his arguments would be completely ineffectual. My father never said anything sensible; perhaps what he meant to say was sensible enough, but he never managed to express what he meant, getting bogged down in empty words, digressions and childhood memories, stumbling and gesticulating. So at home he was never allowed to finish what he was saying because we were always too impatient, and he would hark back wistfully to his teaching days when he could talk as much as he wanted and nobody humiliated him.

My father had always been very diffident in his dealings with Valentino; he had never dared to reprove him even when he failed his examinations, and he had never ceased to believe that he would one day become a man of consequence. Now, however, this belief had apparently deserted him; he looked unhappy and seemed to have aged overnight. He no longer liked to stay alone in the kitchen, saying that it was airless and made him feel claustrophobic and he took to sitting outside the bar downstairs sipping vermouth; or sometimes he walked down to the river to watch the anglers, and returned puffing and muttering to himself.

So, seeing that it was the only thing that would set his mind at rest, my mother agreed to his going to see Valentino's fiancée. My father put on his best clothes and his best hat, too, and his gloves; and my mother and I stood on the balcony watching him go. And as we did so, a faint hope stirred within us that things would be sorted out for the best; we didn't know how this would come about nor even what we were hoping for precisely, and we certainly couldn't imagine what my father would find to say, but that afternoon was the most peaceful we had known for a long time. My father returned late looking very tired; he wanted to go straight to bed and my mother helped him to undress, questioning him while she did so; but this time it was he who was reluctant to talk. When he was in bed, with his eyes closed and his face ashen, he said: "She's a good woman. I feel sorry for her." And after a pause: "I saw the house. A beautiful house, extremely elegant. The kind of elegance that is simply beyond the experience of people like you and me." He was silent for a minute, then: "Anyway, I'll soon be dead and buried."

The wedding took place at the end of the month. My father wrote to one of his brothers asking for a loan, because we had to be well turned out so that we should not disgrace Valentino. For the first time in many years, my mother had a hat made for her: a tall, complicated creation with a bow and a little veiling. And she unearthed her old fox fur that had one eye missing; by arranging the tail carefully over the head she could hide this defect, and the hat had been so expensive that my mother was determined not to spend any more on this wedding. I had a new dress of pale blue wool trimmed with velvet, and around my neck I too had a little fox-fur, a tiny one that my aunt Giuseppina had given me for my ninth birthday. The most expensive item of all was the suit for

Valentino, navy blue with a chalk stripe. He and my mother had gone together to choose it, and he had stopped sulking and was happy and said he had dreamed all his life of possessing a navy blue suit with a chalk stripe.

Clara announced that she had no intention of coming to the wedding because she wanted nothing to do with Valentino's disgraceful goings-on and had no money to waste; and Valentino told me to tell her to stay at home by all means as he would be happier if she spared him the sight of her ugly face on his wedding day. And Clara retorted that the bride's face was uglier than hers; she had only seen it in photographs but that was enough. But Clara did turn up in church after all, with her husband and eldest daughter; and they had taken pains to dress nicely and my sister had had her hair curled.

During the whole of the ceremony my mother held my hand and clutched it ever more tightly. During the exchange of rings she bent towards me and whispered that she couldn't bear to watch. The bride was in black and had on the same fur coat that she always wore and our caretaker who had been keen to come was disappointed because she had expected a veil and orange-blossom. She told us later that the wedding wasn't nearly as splendid as she had hoped after hearing all the rumors about Valentino marrying such a rich woman. Apart from the caretaker and the woman from the paper-shop on the corner, there was no one there that we knew; the church was full of Maddalena's acquaintances, well-dressed women in furs and jewels.

Afterwards we went to the house and were served with refreshments. Without even the caretaker and the woman from the paper-shop there, we felt utterly lost, my parents and I and Clara and Clara's husband. We huddled in a group close to the wall and Valentino came over to us for a moment to tell us not to stick together in a group like that; but we still stuck together. The garden and the ground-floor rooms of the house were crowded with all the people who had been in church; and Valentino moved easily among these people, speaking and being spoken to; he was very happy with his navy blue suit with a chalk stripe and took the ladies by the arm and led them to the buffet. The house was extremely elegant, as my father had said, and it was difficult to imagine that this was now Valentino's home.

Then the guests left and Valentino and his wife drove off in the car; they were to spend a three-month honeymoon on the Riviera. We went home. Very excited by all the food she had eaten from the buffet and all the strange new things that she had seen, Clara's little girl jumped and skipped, chattering non-stop about how she had run round the garden and been frightened by a dog and how she had then gone into the kitchen and seen a tall cook all dressed in light blue, grinding coffee. But as soon as we were indoors our first thought was of the money that we owed to my father's brother. We were all tired and cross and my mother went to Valentino's room and sat on the unmade bed and had a little cry. But she soon started to tidy up the room and then put the mattress in mothballs, covered the furniture with dust-sheets and closed the shutters.

There seemed to be nothing to do now that Valentino had gone: no more clothes to brush or iron or spot with spirit. We seldom spoke about him for I was preparing for my exams and my mother spent much of her time with Clara, one of whose children was poorly. And my father took to wandering about the town because the solitary kitchen had become distasteful to him now; he sought out some of his old colleagues and attempted to indulge his taste for long speeches with them, but always ended up by saying that he might as well not bother as he would soon be dead anyway and he didn't mind dying since life had had precious little to offer. Occasionally the caretaker would come up to our flat bringing a little fruit in return for my help with her children's homework, and she invariably asked after Valentino and said how lucky we were that Valentino had married such a rich woman because she would set him up in a practice as soon as he qualified and we could sleep easy now that he was provided for; and if his wife was no beauty so much the better because at least one could be reasonably certain that she would never be unfaithful.

Summer drew to a close and Valentino wrote to say that they would not be back for a while yet; they were swimming and sailing and had planned a trip to the Dolomites. They were having a good holiday and wanted to enjoy it for as long as possible because once they returned to town they would have to work really hard. He had to prepare for his exams and his wife always has a heap of things to attend to: she had to see to the administrations of her farmland and then there was charity work and suchlike.

It was already late September when he walked in through the door one morning. We were happy to see him, so happy that it no longer seemed important whom he had married. Here he was, sitting in the kitchen once more with his curly head and white teeth and deeply-cleft chin and big hands. He stroked the cat and said that he would like to take it away with him: there were mice in the cellar of the house and the cat would learn to kill and eat them instead of being afraid of them as he was at present. He stayed a while and had to have some of my mother's home-made tomato sauce on bread because their cook couldn't make it like this. He took the cat with him in a basket but brought it back a few days later: they had put it in the cellar to kill the mice but the mice were so big and the cat was so frightened of them that he had meowed all night long and kept the cook awake.

The winter was a hard one for us: Clara's little boy was constantly unwell; he had, it seemed, something seriously wrong with his lungs and the doctor prescribed a substantial, nourishing diet. And we also had the continual worry of the debt towards my father's brother which we were trying to repay a little at a time. So, although we no longer had to support Valentino, it was still a struggle to make ends meet. Valentino knew nothing of our troubles; we rarely saw him as he was preparing for his exams; he visited us from time to time with his wife and my mother would receive them in the living-room; she would smooth her dress and there would be long silences; my mother would sit very erect in the armchair, her pretty, pale, fragile-looking face framed in white hair that was as smooth and soft as silk; and there, would be long silences broken from time to time by her kind, tired voice.

I did the shopping every morning at a market some distance away because this meant a little saving on the purchases. I thoroughly enjoyed my morning walk, particularly on the way there with the empty shopping-basket; the open air, cool and fresh, made me forget all the troubles at home and my thoughts would turn instead to the questions that normally occupy a young girl's mind, wondering if I should ever get married and when and to whom. I really had no idea whom I could marry because young men never came to our house; some had come from time to time when Valentino was still at home, but not now. And the idea that I might marry seemed never to have crossed my parents' minds; they always spoke as if they expected me to stay with them for ever and looked forward to the time when I should be selected for a teaching post and would be bringing in some money. There were times when I was amazed at my parents for their never considering the possibility that I might wish to get married, or even have a new dress or go out with the other girls on Sunday afternoons; but although their attitude amazed me, I did not resent it in the slightest, for my emotions at that time were neither profound nor melancholic and I was confident that sooner or later things would improve for me.

One day as I was returning from the market with my basket, I saw Valentino's wife; she was in a car and was driving herself. She stopped and offered me a lift. She told me that she got up at seven every morning, had a cold shower and went off to attend to her agricultural interests: she had a property some eighteen kilometers outside town. Valentino, meanwhile, stayed in bed and she asked me if he had always been as lazy as this. I told her about Clara's child who was sick and her expression became very serious and she said that she had known nothing about this: Valentino only mentioned it in passing as a matter of no great importance and my mother had said nothing at all about it. "You all treat me as a complete outsider," she said. "Your mother can't stand the sight of me — as I realized the first time I came to your house. It never even occurs to you that I could help when you have problems. And to think that people I don't even know come to me for help and I always do everything I can for them." She was very angry and I could think of nothing to say; we were outside our flat by now and I asked her, rather timidly, if she would like to come in but she said she preferred not to visit us because of my mother's dislike for her.

But that very day she went to see Clara; and she hauled Valentino — who hadn't been to see his sister for some time, ever since she had called him a pig — along with her. The first thing that Maddalena did on arriving was to open wide the windows, saying that the place smelt dreadful. And she said that Valentino's couldn't-care-less attitude towards his family was disgraceful, while she who had no family of her own found herself getting emotionally involved with the problems of perfect strangers and would willingly go miles out of her way to be of help. She sent Valentino off to fetch her own doctor and he said that the child should be in hospital and she said that she would pay all the expenses. Clara packed the child's suitcase in a state of alarm and bewilderment while Maddalena bullied and scolded her, making her more confused than ever.

But once the child was in hospital we all felt a great sense of relief. Clara wondered what she could do to repay Maddalena. She consulted my mother and together they bought a big box of chocolates which Clara took to Maddalena; but Maddalena told her that she was an idiot to spend money on chocolates when she had so much to worry about, and what foolishness was this about repayment. She said that none of us had any idea about money: there were my parents, struggling to make ends meet and sending me off to a market miles away in order to save a few lire when it would have been so much simpler had they asked her to help; and here was Valentino who didn't give a snap of his fingers but was always buying himself new clothes and prancing about in front of the mirror and making a fool of himself. She said that from now on she would make us a monthly allowance and would provide us with fresh vegetables every day so that I would no longer have to trail across town to the market, because her own farm yielded more vegetables than she could use and they simply rotted in the kitchen. And Clara came to beg us to accept the money; she said that after all the sacrifices we had made for Valentino it was only right that his wife should give us a bit of help. So once a month

Maddalena's steward arrived with the money in an envelope, and every two or three days a case of vegetables would be left for us at the caretaker's flat and I no longer had to get up so early to go to the market.

My father died at the end of the winter. My mother and I had gone to the hospital to visit Clara's little boy, so my father was all alone when he died. We found him already dead when we got home; he had lain down on the bed and had dissolved some of his tablets in a glass of milk, presumably because he had felt unwell, but hadn't drunk the mixture. In the drawer of his bedside table we found a letter addressed to Valentino which he must have written some days before, a long letter in which he apologized for having always believed that Valentino would become a man of consequence, it would be enough if he became a man at all, because at present he was merely a child. Valentino and Maddalena came and Valentino cried; and Maddalena, for the first time was sweet to my mother, showing great tact and kindness; she phoned her steward and asked him to see to all the funeral arrangements and stayed with my mother all night and throughout the following day. When she had left, I remarked on her kindness but my mother said that even when she was kind she couldn't bear her and shuddered every time she saw her beside Valentino; and she said that she was sure that this was the cause of my father's death, his grief at Valentino's having married for money.

Maddalena had a baby in the summer and I believed that this would soften my mother's heart and that she would become fond of the child; I fancied I could see a tiny dimple in the baby's chin and that he looked like Valentino. But my mother denied that there was even a shadow of a dimple; she was very sad and depressed and kept thinking about my father and regretting that she had not shown him more affection; she had never had the patience to let him finish what he was saying but always shut him up and humiliated him. Only now did she realize that my father was the best thing that had ever happened to her in her life; she had no complaints about Clara and me, but still we didn't keep her company as much as we should; and Valentino had married that woman just for her money. She gradually ceased to give piano lessons because she had arthritis and a great deal of pain in her hands; and anyway, the money in the envelope that the steward delivered each month was sufficient for the two of us. When the steward came I always received him alone in the dining-room; my mother stayed in the kitchen with the door shut and never allowed me to mention the envelope; yet this was the money that fed us every day.

Maddalena came to ask me if I would like to spend August with them near the sea. I should have loved to accept but felt I should not leave my mother alone, so I refused. Maddalena told me that I was a fool and a stay-at-home and could rest assured that I should never find a husband; but it was untrue, and August was a long, dreary month. Every evening I took my mother out for a breath of cool, fresh air and we would walk through the tree-lined roads or beside the river with her long, slender hand, now deformed by arthritis, resting on my arm and a yearning in my heart to be able to stride out alone and speak to someone who was not my mother. Then she began to keep to her bed all day because her back ached, too, and she complained ceaselessly about it. I begged Clara to come as often as possible but she always had stacks of addresses to type for the company that employed her. She had sent the children away to the countryside for a holiday, including the one who had been so ill but had now recovered; all week long she typed away furiously at her addresses and on Sunday she visited her children. So I was alone in the house when my mother died on the Sunday of the mid-August holiday. All through the night she had complained of the ache in her bones; she was delirious and thirsty and got cross with me for being slow to bring her glasses of water and to plump up her pillows. In the morning I fetched the doctor and he said that there was no hope. I sent off a telegram to Valentino and another Clara in the country but by the time they arrived my mother was already dead.

I had loved her very much. I would have given anything now to be able to repeat those evening walks that had bored me at the time, with her long, slender, deformed hand resting on my arm. And I felt guilty for not having shown her more affection. I remembered the times when I stood on the balcony eating cherries and heard her calling me but didn't turn round and let her call and call while I hung over the railing and pretended not to hear. I hated the courtyard now, and the balcony and the four empty rooms of the flat; and yet I wanted nothing and had no desire to leave the place.

But Maddalena came and asked me to go and live with them. She was very sweet to me, just as she had been to my mother when my father died: full of kindness and caresses and not at all authoritarian. She said I was free to do as I liked but it was hardly sensible to stay in the flat alone when there were so many rooms in her house where I could get on quietly with my studies and when I felt sad they would be there to cheer me up.

So I left the house in which I had grown up and which was so familiar to me that I could hardly conceive of living anywhere else. As I was tidying the rooms before I left, I discovered in a trunk all the letters and photographs sent to Valentino by the teenage girls he used to date, and Clara and I spent an afternoon reading the letters and laughing over them before we burnt them all on the gas stove. I left the cat with the caretaker, and when I saw him again a few months later he had learnt to kill mice and had grown into a big, strong, self-possessed animal, not in the least bit like the wild, timid kitten who had raced up the curtain in fright.

In Maddalena's house I had a room with a big, pale blue carpet. I loved the carpet, and every morning when I woke up the sight of it gladdened my eyes and when I walked on it with bare feet it felt warm and soft. I should have liked to stay in bed for a little while in the morning, but I remembered that Maddalena despised late risers and I could, indeed, hear her ringing the bell furiously and giving orders for the day in her imperious voice. Then she went out in her fur coat and hat squashed to one side, yelled again at the cook and the nursemaid, climbed into the car and slammed the door.

I went to fetch the baby and dandled him for a while in my arms. I had grown very fond of the child and hoped that he was growing fond of me too. Valentino came down to breakfast yawing and unshaven; when I asked him if he intended to sit for his exams he changed the subject. The steward Bugliari, the same man who used to bring the envelope to the flat when my mother was alive, soon arrived; and a cousin of Maddalena's whom they called Kit would come too. Valentino would play cards with them, but as soon as Maddalena's car was heard in the drive the cards would be hastily hidden because Maddalena didn't like Valentino to waste his time at cards. Maddalena always arrived tired and disheveled, her voice husky from shouting at the farm workers, and she would start to argue with the steward, pulling out files and ledgers and discussing business at some length. I was constantly amazed that she neither asked after her child nor went to see him: the baby hardly seemed to matter to her; when the nursemaid brought him to her she would cuddle him for a moment and while the moment lasted her face became young, gentle and maternal, but then she would sniff the baby's neck and complain that he didn't smell clean and hand him straight back to the nursemaid to be washed.

Kit was a man of forty, tall, thin and slightly balding. The sparse hairs at the back of his neck were long and damp and looked like those of a new-born baby. He had no definite work, and although he owned some land adjacent to Maddalena's he never went there and relied on Maddalena to keep an eye on it; she was always complaining about having quite enough work of her own without being saddled with the responsibility for Kit's land as well. Kit spent every day with us; he played with the baby, chatted to the nursemaid, played cards with Valentino and sprawled in an armchair, smoking. Then, towards evening, he and Valentino would go into town and sit outside a bar watching the elegantly-dressed women as they passed by

I was very worried about Valentino because he never seemed to study. He would go to the room where he kept his microscope, his books and a skull, but was incapable of sitting at his desk for a minute without ringing down for an egg-flip, and then he would put a lighted candle inside the skull, darken the room completely, call the maid and frighten her out of her wits. Since his marriage he had sat two of his exams and passed them both; he seldom failed an exam because he had a way with words and could bluff examiners into thinking that he knew much more than he really did. But there were still many more exams to go before he qualified and several of his friends who had begun their studies at the same time as he did had been qualified for quite a while. Whenever I mentioned the subject of exams he shied away from it and there was nothing I could do. When Maddalena got home she always asked him if he had been studying and he said yes and she believed him; or maybe she was just tired after spending the whole day working and talking business and preferred to avoid arguments at home. She would sit on the settee with her feet up and Valentino sitting near her on the floor. I found her abject manner towards Valentino embarrassing at these times; she would take his head between her hands and stroke it, and her face shone and her expression became gentle and maternal. "Has Valentino been studying?" she would ask Kit, and he would reply: "Indeed he has." And she would sit there quietly with her eyes closed, stroking Valentino's forehead with her fingertips.

Maddalena had another baby and we went to the coast for the summer. She bore her children with no difficulty at all and continued to go back and forth between the house and her farm throughout the pregnancy; then, once they were born, she found a wet-nurse and had little more to do with them; it was enough for her to know that they were there. She had a similar attitude towards Valentino: she was content to know that he was there but she spent her days apart from him; it was enough to find him at home when she returned, to caress his hair for a while and lie on the settee with his head in her lap. I recalled his telling my mother that with Maddalena he could talk about anything, yet I never noticed them talking at all. Meanwhile, there was always Kit; he was always the one who did the talking, relating endless boring anecdotes about his housekeeper who was simple-minded and nearly blind, or moaning about his bad health and his doctor. And if Kit were not there, Maddalena would ask one of us to telephone and tell him to come at once.

So we went to the seaside, and Kit and Bugliari and the maid and the wet-nurse came too. We stayed in a hotel, a very smart hotel, and I was ashamed of my scant wardrobe but was unwilling to ask Maddalena for money and it did not occur to her, apparently, to offer it; nor did she trouble to look elegant herself but always wore the same sun-dress with blue and white spots; and she said that she had no intention of spending money on clothes because Valentino already spent so much on his. Valentino certainly dressed well, sporting linen trousers and a constant succession of sweaters and tee shirts. Kit advised him in the matter of clothes even though he himself always wore the same slightly shabby trousers with the excuse that he was so unprepossessing that clothes gave him no pleasure. Valentino went off sailing with Kit while Maddalena, Bugliari and I waited on the beach; and Maddalena said that she was already bored with this way of life because she was incapable of sitting idly in the sun. In the evening Valentino and Kit went out dancing. Maddalena suggested that they might take me with them but Valentino retorted that one did not take one's sister to a dance.

We returned to town and I took my teaching diploma. I was appointed to a temporary post at a school and Maddalena drove me there every morning before going to the farm. I told her that I could live on my own and look after myself now, but she treated the suggestion as an affront and said there was no reason why I should have to fend for myself with such a big house at my disposal and plenty of food to eat; did I really want to rent some tiny room and cook soup over a gas ring? She could see no sense in the idea. And the babies were fond of me and I could keep an eye on them when she was away, and I could also keep an eye on Valentino and make sure that he got on with his studies.

At that point I took my courage in both hands and told her that I was worried about Valentino: he seemed to be spending less and less time on his studies and now Kit had persuaded him to learn to ride and they went to the riding-stables every morning. Valentino had acquired a riding outfit complete with boots, tight-fitting jacket and crop and would stand in front of the mirror at home brandishing the whip and doffing the hat. On hearing this, Maddalena called Kit and gave him a tongue-lashing; she told him that even if he was a failure and a layabout, Valentino was not to become a failure too and he was to leave him alone. Kit listened with his eyes half-closed, his mouth open and one hand gently massaging his jaw; Valentino, meanwhile, angrily retorted that riding was doing him good, that he had been much healthier since he started to ride. Maddalena then ran to fetch the breeches, boots, hat, jacket, and whip, parceled them up and said that she was going to throw them all into the river. She went out with the big bundle under her arm; she was pregnant again and her swollen belly protruded from her fur coat as she ran, limping slighty from the combined weight of her belly and the package. Valentino ran after her and Kit and I were left alone. "She's right," said Kit, heaving a deep sigh, he scratched his head with its few straggly hairs and pulled such a comic face that I had to laugh. "Maddalena is right," he repeated. "I'm nothing but a failure and a layabout. She's right. There's no hope for someone like me. But there's no hope for Valentino either: he's just like me, just the same type. Or rather, he's worse than me, because he cares about nothing. I do care a bit about some things; not a great deal, but I do care." — "And to think that my father always believed that Valentino would be a man of consequence," I said. "Oh really?" said Kit, suddenly bursting into laughter with his head thrown back and his mouth wide open. He rocked backwards and forwards in his chair, clasping his hands between his knees and guffawing. There was something unpleasant in his laughter and I left the room. When I returned he had gone. Valentino and Maddalena did not appear for the evening meal, and there was still no sign of them when darkness had fallen; after I had been in bed for some time I heard them come upstairs and the sound of whispers and laughter told me that they had made it up. The following day

Valentino went off to the stables in his riding outfit; Maddalena had not thrown it into the river and the only damage was to the jacket which had got slightly creased and had had to be ironed. Kit stayed away for a few days, but then reappeared, his pockets bulging with socks to be mended which he gave to the maid because he had no one at home to mend his socks, living alone as he did with the old housekeeper who was half blind and incapable of mending anything.

Maddalena's third child was born. It was another boy and she said she was glad that her children were all boys because had she had a girl she would have been scared that it might have grown up to look like her, and she was so ugly that she would not wish that on any woman. She had become reconciled to her ugliness because she had Valentino and the children, but as a girl it had been a source of grief and she had been afraid that she would never get married, afraid that she would grow old alone in the big house with only carpets and pictures for company. Perhaps the reason why she had so many children was in order to forget her previous fears by surrounding herself with toys and nappies and the sound of voices; but having given birth to her children, she had little to do with them.

Valentino and Kit went off on a trip together. Valentino had sat another examination and had passed and said he now needed a little rest. They visited Paris and London because Valentino had never been abroad and Kit said that to know nothing about the great capitals of the world was a disgrace. He criticized Valentino's provincial background saying that it had to be corrected and Valentino must visit dance-halls and famous art galleries. I taught every morning and in the afternoon I played with the children in the garden; and I tried my hand at making toys for them with rags and sawdust as Valentino used to do for the caretaker's children. When Maddalena was out the maid and the cook came to sit with me in the garden; they said that they were not in the least bit shy with me but were very fond of me; and they took off their shoes and put them on the grass beside them, and they made themselves paper hats and read Maddalena's newspapers and smoked her cigarettes. In their opinion I was too much alone and cut off from the rest of the world, and they thought that Maddalena should take me out and about a bit; but all she thought about was her farm. And they said that if things went on like this, I should never find myself a husband: no one ever came to the house apart from Kit and Bugliari; Bugliari was too old for me so they decided that I should marry Kit: he was a nice man but so disorganized, roaming about the city half the night instead of going to bed; and perhaps what he really needed was a woman to look after him and mend his socks and care for him generally. But they were both scared stiff of Maddalena and as soon as they heard her car approaching they put their shoes on and slipped back to the kitchen as quickly as possible.

I visited Clara from time to time but she always made me feel unwelcome and complained that I cared nothing about her or her children any more but only thought of Valentino's boys. All that Maddalena had done for her child when he was ill, arranging for him to go into hospital and paying all the expenses, had already faded from her memory; she no longer had a good word for Maddalena and said that Valentino's marriage to her had completely ruined him: everything was provided for him and we could wave goodbye to our cherished hopes of seeing him qualified. He would fritter away the whole of his wife's fortune eventually. While she spoke she continued to type out addresses; the work had given her corns on her fingers, she had continuous pain in her back and hardly slept at night for toothache. She needed treatment but it was very expensive and she couldn't afford it. I suggested that she ask Maddalena for a loan but this made her indignant and she said she refused to ask favors from people like that. So I got into the way of handing over my stipend to her every month; after all, I had food to eat and a bed to sleep in and wanted for nothing. I hoped that this would make her happier, that she would see a dentist and not tire herself out so much by typing addresses. In the event she continued to type addresses and did not go to see a dentist: she told me that her daughter needed a new coat and her husband a new pair of shoes and that I had no idea what her life was like but if I ever got married I would find out for myself what a bed of roses marriage really was. Because I , she was convinced, if I got married at all, was bound to land myself with a man without a penny to his name as she had done and after all as a family we already had Valentino who had married money and could hardly expect a second stroke of luck but in reality was the opposite, because for Valentino having money only meant that he could slouch around doing nothing and frittering it all away bit by bit.

Valentino and Kit returned and we all left for the coast; but Valentino was in a very bad mood and he and Maddalena quarreled continually. Valentino drove off alone every morning without saying where he was going; and Kit spent the day under the beach umbrella with us and was very unhappy. Half way through August Valentino announced that he was tired of the sea and wanted to go up into the Dolomites: so we went to the Dolomites, but the weather there was wet and the youngest child became feverish. Maddalena blamed the child's illness on Valentino because he had dragged us away on the spur of the moment from the coast where we had been perfectly content to a hotel that was uncomfortable and where you couldn't find a corner out of the draught. Valentino retorted that he could just as well have come alone: he hadn't asked us to come with him but he couldn't move a step without our dogging his heels and he was fed up with babies and nursemaids and the whole lot of us. Kit drove off in the dark to fetch a doctor, and when the child had recovered he went home.

All at once relations between Maddalena and Valentino seemed to have deteriorated and there was never a moment of peace when they were together. Maddalena was very tense and irritable and as soon as she got up in the morning she began to shout at the maid and the cook. She was irritable with me, too, and snapped at me every time I opened my mouth. And I heard her and Valentino quarreling loudly late into the night: she would tell him that he was a layabout and a failure just like Kit, but that whereas Kit was a decent person, he, Valentino was not: he was an egoist, he never thought of anyone but himself and he was throwing away money on clothes and on other things that she knew nothing about. And Valentino shouted back at her that it was she who had ruined him, that her shouting in the morning was driving him mad and that to see her sitting opposite him at table made him shudder. Sometimes they made it up, Valentino crying and asking her to forgive him and she asking his forgiveness too; and for a while everything was as peaceful as before: he would sit on the carpet and she would lie on the sofa stroking his hair, and they would send for Kit and listen to all his gossip about the town. But these interludes never lasted very long and became increasingly rare: there was many a long-drawn-out day of grim faces and silence succeeded by an outburst of raised voices late at night.

After one particular scene with Maddalena the maid gave in her notice, and Maddalena asked me if I would go to a certain village near her farm to see if I could engage a replacement from among a list of names that she had been given. She would ask Kit to drive me there. So one morning Kit and I drove off. Driving through the countryside, neither of us spoke for some time; every now and then I glanced at Kit's slightly comic profile with the balding head topped by a little beret and the rather pointed nose. I noticed that he was wearing Valentino's gloves. "Are those Valentino's gloves?" I asked to break the silence. He took his hands off the wheel for a moment and looked at them. "Yes, they're Valentino's. He didn't want to lend them to me: he likes to keep his possessions to himself." I leant my face against the window and looked at the countryside; and the thought of a whole day of freedom ahead, away from that house and its constant quarrels, filled me with a sense of relief and of peace; and it occurred to me that I had to get away from that place: I no longer enjoyed living there, it was too oppressive; I had even taken a dislike to the pale blue carpet in my room which I had liked so much at first. I said: "What a splendid morning!" And Kit said: "Isn't it just! And we shall find a splendid girl and we'll have lunch at a little place I know where the wine is excellent. It'll be a holiday, a little one-day holiday: life must be very trying for you with those two quarreling all the time and never a moment's peace." — "Yes," I said, "there are times when it become unbearable. I should like to get away for good." — "Where to?" asked Kit. "Oh, I don't know, just somewhere." — "We could go away together, you and I," he said. "Find some peaceful little place and leave those two to get on with it. I've had enough of them too. Many a time when I get up in the morning I tell myself that I shan't go to the house, but somehow I always do in the end. It's a habit; for years I've been used to dining with Maddalena, it's nice and warm there and they mend my socks. My own house is a hovel: there's a coal-burning stove that doesn't draw properly and one day I shall probably die of asphyxiation, and my housekeeper does nothing but gossip. I should put in central heating. Maddalena comes to my place every so often and tells me all the things I should do to improve it. I tell her that I can't afford the money but she says that I could if I would only manage my property sensibly, selling one plot and buying another; she knows all about it. But I don't want to have to make decisions. Maddalena also says that I should get married, but that's something I shall never do. I don't believe in marriage. When Maddalena and Valentino told me that they were getting married, I spent a whole day trying to dissuade them. I even told Valentino to his face that I could have no respect for him. If only they had listened! But now you see what a mess they're in: always squabbling, always making each other unhappy."

"Do you really have no respect for Valentino?" I asked.

"No. Do you?"

"I love him, because he's my brother."

"Loving is another matter. It could be that I, too, love him dearly." He scratched his head under the beret. "But I have no respect for him. I've no respect for myself, either; and he is just like me, just the same type. The type that will never do anything positive. The only difference between us is this, that he cares for nothing at all, not things nor people nor anything else. He only worships his own body, his sacred body that has to be cared for daily with good food, good clothes and must be allowed to lack for nothing. But I do care a bit, both about things and people, though there's no one who cares about me. Valentino is lucky: self-love never leads to disappointment; but I'm just a poor unfortunate for whom nobody on this earth gives a snap of the fingers."

We had now reached the village to which Maddalena had told us to go, and Kit drew up and parked the car. "Now to find this girl," he said.

We made some enquiries in the village and someone pointed to a house in the distance, high on a hillside, where they thought a girl lived who might be prepared to work in town. We climbed up a narrow pathway with vineyards on either side and Kit became breathless and fanned himself with his beret. "It's a bit much," he puffed, "to expect us to find their maid for them. Why can't they do their own dirty work?"

The girl was out working in the fields and we had to wait for her to return. We sat in a small, dark kitchen and the girl's mother gave us a glass of wine and some little wrinkled pears. Kit chatted away rapidly in dialect to the woman, praising the wine and asking a hundred and one detailed questions about the work on the farm. I sat sipping my wine in silence, my thoughts gradually becoming blurred: the wine was very strong and all at once I felt happy to be in that little kitchen with the open fields beyond the windows and the taste of wine on my tongue and Kit there with his long legs and his beret and his pointed nose; I found myself thinking, "I do like Kit, he's such a nice person."

Then we went out into the sunshine and sat on a stone bench in front of the house, eating the pears and enjoying the warmth of the sun. "How nice this is!" said Kit. He took my hand and, having removed the glove, examined it. "Your fingers are just like Valentino's," he said. He pushed my hand away suddenly. "Did your father seriously believe that Valentino would become a man of consequence?" — "Yes," I replied, "He did. We went without a great many things so that he could study; life was pretty hard and it was always a struggle to make ends meet. But Valentino always had everything he wanted and my father said that one day we would have our reward when Valentino was a famous doctor making important discoveries."

"Well, well," he said. For a moment I thought he was about to start guffawing as he had on the previous occasion when we were discussing the same subject in the sitting room. He rocked backwards and forwards on the bench with his hands clasped between his knees; but then he quickly glanced at my face and his expression became serious again.

"You know," he said, "fathers always have peculiar ideas. My father wanted me to be an Air Force officer. An Air Force officer! Me! I can't even go on a switch-back because when I look down I get giddy!"

The girl arrived: she had red hair and thick legs with black stockings rolled down to her ankles. Kit fired an interminable series of meticulous, probing questions at her in dialect; he seemed to have an excellent knowledge of all the skills required by a housemaid. The girl said that she would be happy to enter service; she would make her preparations and be ready to leave within two or three days.

We returned to the village for a meal and then went for a long walk through the streets and out into the fields. Kit was in no hurry to get home. Every courtyard that we passed, he pushed open the door, went through and nosed around; on one occasion an irate old woman chased us away and threw a shoe at us as we fled. We went for a long walk through the fields and vineyards. Kit's pockets were still stuffed with little pears and he gave some to me now and then. "How nice it is to be away from those two!" he exclaimed repeatedly. "See how happy and relaxed we are! We really should go away together to some peaceful spot."

It was dark by the time we got back into the car. "Will you marry me?" Kit said suddenly. He hadn't switched on the engine and was sitting with his hands on the wheel; the expression on his face was a comical mixture of fear and solemnity, his beret sat askew on his brow and his eyebrows were drawn together in a frown. "Will you marry me?" he repeated sharply; I laughed and said yes. Then he started the car and we drove off.

"I'm not in love," I said.

"I know; nor am I. And I don't believe in marriage. But who knows? It could be a good thing for both of us; you're such a calm, sweet girl that I see no reason why we shouldn't be happy. We wouldn't do anything extraordinary, we wouldn't travel all over the place, but we could go on little trips like this one occasionally and look at a village or two and nose around the courtyards."

"Do you remember the old woman who threw a shoe at us?"

"Oh yes," he said, "what a temper!"

"Perhaps I should think about it for a while," I said.

"Think about what?"

"Whether we should get married."

"Oh yes," he said, "we mustn't rush things. But, you know, this isn't the first time that it's occurred to me. Watching you, I've often thought how fond I am of you. I'm basically a decent sort of chap; I've got some bad faults, I'm lazy and I don't get round to doing things: in my house the chimneys don't draw properly and I don't have them seen to. But basically I'm a decent fellow. If we get married, I shall have something done about the chimneys and I'll take an interest in my business. Maddalena will approve."

When we got back to the house, he opened the car door for me and said good night. "I shan't come in," he said, "I'll just put the car away and then go home to bed. I'm tired." He pulled off the gloves and handed them to me, saying: "Give these back to Valentino."

I found Valentino in the sitting room reading *Mysteries of the Black Jungle*. Maddalena had already gone up to bed.

"Did you find a housemaid?" Valentino asked. "Where's Kit?"

"He's gone home to bed. Here are your gloves," I said and tossed them to him. "But aren't you a bit past *Mysteries of the Black Jungle*?"

"Stop talking like a schoolmistress," he replied.

"I am a schoolmistress," I said.

"I know; but you needn't talk like one to me."

My supper had been left on a side-table in the sitting-room and I sat down to eat. Valentino went on reading. When I had finished my meal I sat on the settee next to him. I put my hand on his head. He frowned and muttered something under his breath without raising his eyes from the book.

"Valentino," I said, "Kit has asked me to marry him. I may accept."

He let the book drop and stared at me. "Are you serious?" he asked.

"Quite, Valentino," I said. He smiled crookedly, as if embarrassed, and moved away from me.

"You're not serious, are you?"

"Indeed I am."

Neither of us spoke for a while. He continued to smile crookedly; I couldn't look at him because there was something unpleasant in that smile: I couldn't understand what was behind it; I sensed shame and embarrassment but didn't understand why he should be ashamed or embarrassed, nor could I understand what was going through his mind.

"I'm getting on, Valentino," I said, "I'm nearly twenty-six. And I'm no great beauty and I haven't any money. And I should like to get married; I don't want to grow old alone. Kit's a nice person; I'm not in love with him but my reason tells me that he's a decent person, unpretentious, sincere and good-hearted. If he wants to marry me, I shall be happy to accept; I would like to have children and a home of my own."

"Ah yes," he said, "I see. But don't go rushing into anything. I'm not the best person to be giving advice. But give it some more thought."

He got up, stretched his arms and yawned. "He's a dirty fellow," he said, "he never washes properly."

"But that's not a serious fault," I said.

"I tell you, he hardly ever washes. It is a serious fault. I don't like people who don't wash. Good night," he said, and patted my cheek. A caress of any kind from Valentino was rare, and I was grateful for it. "Good night, Valentino dear," I said.

All night long I lay thinking about whether I should marry Kit. I was too agitated to sleep. My mind went back over the day we had spent together and I recalled every detail: the wine, the little pears, the girl with red hair, the courtyards and the fields. It had been such a happy day, and it occurred to me that there had not been many happy days in my life, days of freedom to do as I liked.

The next morning Maddalena came to sit on my bed. "I hear that you and Kit are to be married," she said. "It might not be such a bad idea, actually. You would have been better off with a steadier sort of person: Kit's disorganized and lazy, as I keep telling him; and his health is not too good, either. But perhaps you will manage to change his life for the better. There's no reason why you shouldn't. Of course, you will have to be very firm with him: his house is in a dreadful state; he must put in central heating and have the walls painted. And he must keep an eye on his farmland every day like I do. It's good land and would yield well if he would only take some trouble over it; and you must help too. I expect you're thinking that I should be firmer with Valentino; I do my best to persuade him to study, but we always end up having a dreadful row and things are bad. They're so bad, in fact, that I sometimes think we shall have to separate; but there are the children to think of and I haven't the heart to do it. But let's not think about such miserable things for the moment; you're engaged to be married and this is a time for happiness. I've known Kit all his life, we grew up together like brother and sister; his heart's in the right place and I'm very fond of him and want him to be happy."

My engagement to Kit lasted for twenty days. For twenty days we toured the shops with Maddalena, looking at furniture; but Kit never decided on anything. These were not particularly happy days: I kept thinking about the day we went to find the housemaid, Kit and I, and expected a return of the happiness we had shared that day; but that happiness never returned. We went round the antique shops, always with Maddalena, and Maddalena quarreled with Kit because he never made up his mind about anything and she told him that he was missing out on some good bargains. The girl with red hair was now installed at the house; she wore a black dress and a little lace cap and I found it difficult to identify her with the muddy peasant girl we had met that day, yet every time I saw her red hair I recalled the little pears and the wine and the dark kitchen and the stone bench in front of the cottage and the wide expanse of the fields; and I wondered if Kit remembered too. It occurred to me that Kit and I should have been spending some time alone together, but he appeared not to want this and invariably asked Maddalena to accompany us when we went to look at furniture, and when we were in the house he continued to play cards with Valentino as he had always done.

Everyone in the house was happy for me. The cook and the nursemaid were delighted and reminded me that they had always said that Kit and I should get married. I had asked the school for a three months' leave of absence on grounds of health; I rested and played with the children in the garden whenever I was not looking at furniture with Kit and Maddalena. Maddalena had told me that she would provide my trousseau, and she insisted on going to tell my sister Clara about the engagement. Clara had met Kit two or three times and couldn't stand him; but she always found Maddalena very intimidating and dared say nothing to her; she was probably impressed, too, by the fact that I was to marry a landed proprietor and not the penniless nobody that she had always predicted for me.

One afternoon when I was in the garden winding some wool, the maid came to tell me that Kit was in the sitting-room and wanted to see me. I took the wool in with me intending to ask him to hold the skein for me. Maddalena was out and Valentino sleeping, so I thought we might be able to have an hour or two to ourselves.

I found him slumped in an armchair with his long legs stretched out in front of him. He was still wearing his coat and was crushing his beret between his hands; he looked pale and depressed.

"Are you unwell?" I asked.

"Yes; I'm not well at all. I feel shivery. I may be in for a bout of 'flu. I won't hold the wool," he said, glancing at the skein over my arm and wagging a long finger to emphasize his refusal. "Forgive me. I've come to tell you that we won't be getting married."

He got up and started pacing up and down the room. He continued to crush his beret in his hands, then suddenly flung it down and came to a stop in front of me. We stood facing each other and he put a hand on my shoulder. His face was that of a very old new-born baby, with the sparse hairs plastered damply to the elongated head.

"I'm deeply sorry that I ever proposed to you. I realize that I can never marry. You're a dear girl, so quiet, so sweet, and I had woven a whole world of fantasy for the two of us. It was a beautiful fantasy but all made up and with no basis in reality. I beg you to forgive me. I cannot marry. I'm terrified."

"That's all right," I said, "it doesn't matter, Kit." I wanted very much to cry. "I don't love you, as I told you before. If I'd fallen in love with you it would have been difficult for me; but as things are, it won't be too hard. There's no point in brooding; some things we just have to put behind us and soldier on."

I turned towards the wall, my eyes brimming with tears.

"I really cannot, Caterina," he said. "You mustn't cry over me, Caterina: I'm not worth it. I'm a wreck. I spent the whole night thinking how to break this to you; and throughout these past weeks my mind has been in a turmoil. I hate having to hurt someone as dear to me as you are. You would have regretted it bitterly after a while: you would have come to realize the sort of person that I am, a wreck not fit for civilized society."

I said nothing but stood fiddling with the wool. "Now I'll hold the skein for you," he said, "now I've got all that off my chest and I'm feeling calmer. On my way here, my head seemed to be spinning; and I didn't sleep a wink all night."

"No, I don't want to wind the wool now," I said, "but thank you."

"Forgive me," he said. "I wish there was something I could do to make you forgive me. Tell me, is there anything I can do that would persuade you to forgive me?"

"You don't have to do anything," I said, "really, Kit. Nothing has happened; we hadn't bought any furniture, nothing was really settled. We were only toying with the idea and were only half-serious about it."

"Yes, yes, only half-serious," he repeated. "Deep down, no one really believed us. But we can still have the odd day out together; that day we had was such fun. Do you remember the old woman with the shoe?"

"Yes."

"No one can stop us going out for the day together. We don't need to be married to do that. We'll do it again sometime, won't we?"

"Yes, we'll do it again."

I went slowly up to my room. I still had the wool to wind, but all at once the effort seemed too much; it was even an effort to drag myself up the stairs, undress, fold my clothes on the chair and get into bed. I wanted to call the maid and tell her that I had a headache and should not be down to supper; but I didn't want to see the maid, I didn't want to see her red hair and be reminded of that day. I decided that I had to leave the house as soon as possible, the very next day, and never see Kit again. And I thought how even the quality of beauty was lacking in my pain because I was not in love with Kit: I felt only shame, shame that he should have asked me to marry him and then changed his mind. And it seemed to me that attempts over the past weeks to push into the background those things about Kit which I disliked and highlight the things I liked, learning to reconcile myself to the thought of living with his old-baby face, had all been so much wasted effort, a silly, humiliating waste of effort! And how ridiculous Kit had been, panicking at the thought of actually having to marry me!

When Maddalena came into my room, I told her that Kit and I had come to a joint decision not to get married, and that I wanted to go away for a time. I spoke very quietly and kept my face turned to the wall; I had worked out exactly what I wanted to say and had rehearsed the words to myself; now I recited them by heart, very quietly and slowly and completely without expression, as if recounting events that had happened a long time ago; I had chosen to explain things in this way so that Maddalena wouldn't be angry with Kit and also to spare myself some embarrassment. But in the event Maddalena was entirely unconvinced about the decision having been made by both of us.

"You both changed your minds? No; only Kit changed his mind," she said, and appeared not in the least surprised.

"We both did," I repeated in a low voice. "Both of us."

"Only Kit," she said. "I know him too well. You're not the sort of person to change your mind. Anyway, it's no great misfortune; you'll find someone much better than Kit. He's so disorganized. He'll probably come round tomorrow and proposed to you again. I know him. Just forget him; you've seen how muddle-headed and indecisive he is; remember how he couldn't even make a decision about the furniture?"

"I want to go away for a while," I said.

"Where would you go?"

"I don't know. I want to be alone, I don't mind where."

"As you wish," she said, and left the room.

I left early the next morning, before Valentino had even got up. Maddalena helped me pack, insisted on giving me some money and drove me to the station. She kissed me goodbye.

"Please don't quarrel too much with Valentino," I said.

"I'll try not to," she said. "And you mustn't give way to tears and bitterness. That idiot Kit is really not worth it."

I went to stay with my aunt Giuseppina, my mother's sister. Aunt Giuseppina lived in the country, in the same village where she had spent her whole working life as a schoolteacher. She was retired now and spent her time knitting; the knitting brought in a little money and she lived on that and her pension. I hadn't seen her for many years and I was struck by her likeness to my mother; looking at her white hair gathered into a chignon and her delicate profile, I almost had the impression of being with my mother again. I had told her that I had been ill and needed to rest and she was full of concern for me, taking pains to see that I had everything I needed and preparing my favorite dishes. We went for a walk every evening before supper; she walked very slowly, resting her thin hand on my arm, and it was just like walking with my mother.

Every now and then a letter would arrive from Maddalena, short and concisely informative: she and Valentino were getting on so-so, the children were well, they were thinking of me and looking forward to my return. I told Aunt Giuseppina all about Valentino's children and Clara's children; I found myself repeating the same things over and over again and Aunt Giuseppina repeated the same questions over and over again. She was especially curious to hear about Valentino's wealthy wife and that house of hers with all those servants and carpets; and she was rather surprised that I should have left such a comfortable house and come to stay with her in the poor little village with its muddy streets and so out of the way.

After two months with Aunt Giuseppina, the time when I was due to return to my teaching was drawing near and I wrote to our old caretaker to ask if she knew of a room I could rent, for I had no wish to return to Maddalena's house. I prepared to leave and went with Aunt Giuseppina to say my farewells to all her friends and promise them postcards.

One morning I received a letter from Valentino. It was all blots and disjointed sentences. He wrote: "With Maddalena life has become impossible for us to stay together. I'm extremely unhappy. Come as soon as you possibly can." And at the bottom of the page he wrote: "I suppose you heard about Kit's death."

I had heard nothing. Kit, dead? I could almost see him lying there, dead, his long legs stiffened by rigor mortis. All this time I had tried not to think about him, because although I hadn't loved him his rejection had been a blow. And now he, Kit, was dead!

I wept. I recalled the death of my father and that of my mother; their faces were receding ever more completely from my mind and I would try in vain to recall the phrases they had used every day. And what of Kit's phrases, what had he said? "Do you remember the old woman with the shoe?" he had said. "There's nothing to stop us going out for the day together. I'm a wreck," he had said, "unfit for civilized society."

I said goodbye to Aunt Giuseppina. In the train I re-read Valentino's almost illegible scrawl. Another quarrel with Maddalena, then; but I was used to their rows and it was quite possible that they would have made it up before I arrived. But that phrase: "I'm extremely unhappy" struck a note which puzzled me: it didn't sound like Valentino at all. And how strange, too, that he, who had a horror of picking up a pen, should have written to me at all!

I had never read the papers during my stay with Aunt Giuseppina because in the first place she didn't buy them and in the second place they were always days out of date by the time they got to her little village. So I had known nothing about Kit's death. But why had Maddalena not written? Anxiety clutched at my heart, I was shivering and felt feverish; and the train was rattling at high speed through the countryside past the places we had seen from the car that day when Kit and I had gone to find the new housemaid and had been so happy; and I remembered the wine, the little pears and the old woman throwing a shoe at us.

I got to the house at four o'clock in the afternoon. The children ran across the garden to meet me and made a great fuss of me. The nursemaid was doing the washing in the scullery, the gardener was watering the flowerbeds; everything seemed perfectly normal. I went up to the sitting room.

Maddalena was sitting in an armchair, her glasses on the end of her nose and a pile of socks beside her to darn. It was unusual for her to be at home at that hour and unknown for her to darn socks. "Hello," she said, looking at me over the top of her spectacles. She seemed, all of a sudden, to have grown very old, to be a little old lady.

"Where's Valentino?" I asked.

"Not here any more. He doesn't live here now. We have separated. Sit down."

I sat down. "You're surprised to find me darning socks," she said, "but I find it soothes the nerves. Apart from which, I needed a change; from now on I intend to spend my time darning socks and looking after the children and sitting down a lot. I'm tired of managing farmland and shouting at people and wearing myself out. We've got enough money to live on, and now there's no Valentino to throw it away on clothes and all the other things. As for Valentino, I've told him that I shall make him a monthly allowance; I shall send him an envelope."

"Valentino will come to live with me," I said. "We can rent a couple of rooms. Just until there's a reconciliation."

She made no reply. She was darning very carefully, her lips compressed and her brow furrowed.

"You may make it up very soon," I said. "You've had quarrels before and then made it up. He said in his letter that he was extremely unhappy."

"Ah, so he wrote to you?" she said. "What did he tell you?"

"He said that he was extremely unhappy, that's all," I said. "That was why I came back at once. And he told me that Kit was dead."

"Ah, so he told you about it. Yes, Kit committed suicide." Her voice was cold and distant. Suddenly she put down the sock she was mending, the needle still stuck through it. She snatched off her glasses and stared at me with wide, unfriendly eyes.

"I'll tell you what happened," she said. "Kit killed himself. He sent his housekeeper away with some excuse or other, lit the stove in his bedroom, opened the top and shut the flue. He left a letter for Valentino. I read it."

Breathing heavily, she mopped her face, hands and neck with a handkerchief.

"I read it. And then I went through every drawer in the house. There were photographs of Valentino and letters from him. I never want to see Valentino again." She suddenly began to sob convulsively. "I never want to see him again," she said. "Never let me see him again. I couldn't bear it. I could have borne anything to do with another woman, no matter what had happened. But not this." She lifted her head and gave another hard look. "And the same goes for you: I never want to see you again. Go away."

"Where is Valentino?" I asked.

"I don't know. Bugliari knows where he is. We have started separation proceedings. Tell him not to worry, Bugliari will bring him his money every month."

"Goodbye, Maddalena," I said.

"Goodbye, Caterina," she replied. "Don't come here again. I would rather not see any member of your family ever again. I want to be left in peace." She had picked up her darning again. "I shall make sure that you can see the children as often as possible," she said, "but not here. I'll make arrangements with the lawyer. And I'll send the money every month."

"The money is not important," I said.

"It is," she said, "it is."

I was half-way down the stairs when she called me back. I returned. She embraced me, weeping; not angrily this time, but softly and piteously.

"It's not true that I never want to see you again," she said. "Come back to see me, Caterina, darling Caterina!" And I wept too and we stood with our arms around each other for a long time. Then I went out into the peace of the sunny afternoon and went to phone Bugliari to ask where I could find Valentino.

Valentino and I live together now. We share two small rooms, a kitchen and a little balcony that overlooks a courtyard very much like the courtyard of my parents' flat. Valentino sometimes wakes up in the morning with his head full of ideas for some commercial enterprise, and he comes and sits on my bed and juggles with figures and dreams about barrels of oil and ships; and then he complains about father and mother and their having insisted on his studying when his real métier was in commerce. I let him talk.

I teach in school every morning and give private lessons in the afternoon; and when I teach at home I ban Valentino from the kitchen because when he's at home he will insist on wearing a shabby old dressing-gown. I find Valentino reasonably docile and obedient and affectionate, too, and when I get home cold and tired after school he prepares a hot-water bottle for me. He has grown fatter because he no longer plays any sport, and the occasional tuft of white hairs is now visible among his dark curls.

He seldom goes out in the morning but wanders around the flat in his shabby dressing-gown, reading magazines or doing crossword puzzles. In the afternoon he shaves, dresses and goes out. I watch him until he turns the corner; but after that I do not know where he goes.

Once a week, on Thursdays, the children come to visit us. They come with their nanny; the nurse has gone now and been replaced by a nanny. And Valentino makes the same rag and sawdust toys for his own children that he used to make for the caretaker's children, dogs and cats and monsters with lumpy bodies.

We never mention Maddalena. Nor do we speak about Kit. Our conversation is strictly limited to daily trivia, to our food or the tenants of the flat opposite. I visit Maddalena from time to time. She has got very fat and her hair is completely gray; she is an old lady. She occupies herself with her children, taking them skating and organizing picnics in the garden. She seldom visits her farm; she is tired of it and says that she has more than enough money already. She spends whole afternoons at home and Bugliari keeps her company. She enjoys my visits but I have to avoid talking too much about Valentino. With her, as with Valentino, I am always careful to keep the conversation on topics which cannot cause pain. We talk about the children, Bugliari, the nanny. So there is no one to whom I can speak the words that most need to be spoken, about the events which most closely concern our family and what has happened to us; I have to keep them bottled up inside me and there are times when they threaten to choke me.

Sometimes I have a feeling of intense anger towards Valentino. I see him there, mooching about the flat in his tatty dressing-gown, smoking and doing crosswords, he who my father always believed was destined for greatness, he who has always taken from others with never a thought of giving anything in return, he who has never neglected for one day to pamper his curls in front of the mirror and smile at his reflection; he who most certainly did not omit that mirrored smile on the very day of Kit's death.

But I can never remain angry with Valentino for very long. He is the only person left in my life; and I am the only person left in his. So I have to repudiate my anger: I must be loyal to Valentino, I must stay at his side that he may find me there if he chances to look in that direction. I watch him walk down the road when he goes out and my eyes follow him until he has turned the corner; and I rejoice in his beauty, in his small curly head and broad shoulders. I rejoice in his step, still so joyful, triumphant and free; I rejoice in his step, wherever he may go.

ALBERTO MORAVIA

Agostino

Alberto Moravia, 1980.

1

During those days of early summer Agostino and his mother used to go out every morning on a bathing raft. The first few times his mother had taken a boatman, but Agostino so plainly showed his annoyance at the man's presence that from then on the oars were entrusted to him. It gave him intense pleasure to row on that calm, transparent, early morning sea; and his mother sat facing him, as gay and serene as the sea and sky, and talked to him in a soft voice, just as if he had been a man instead of a thirteen-year-old boy. Agostino's mother was a tall, beautiful woman, still in her prime, and Agostino felt a sense of pride each time he set out with her on one of those morning expeditions. It seemed to him that all the bathers on the beach were watching them, admiring his mother and envying him. In the conviction that all eyes were upon them his voice sounded to him stronger than usual, and he felt as if all his movements had something symbolic about them, as if they were part of a play; as if he and his mother, instead of being on the beach, were on a stage, under the eager eyes of hundreds of spectators. Sometimes his mother would appear in a new dress, and he could not resist remarking on it aloud, in the secret hope that others would hear. Now and again she would send him to fetch something or other from the beach cabin, while she stood waiting for him by the boat. He would obey with a secret joy, happy if he could prolong their departure even by a few minutes. At last they would get on the raft, and Agostino would take the oars and row out to sea. But for quite a long time he would remain under the disturbing influence of his filial vanity. When they were some way from the shore his mother would tell him to stop rowing, put on her rubber bathing cap, take off her sandals and slip into the water. Agostino would follow her. They swam round and round the empty raft with its floating oars, talking gaily together, their voices ringing clear in the silence of the calm, sunlit sea. Sometimes his mother would point to a piece of cork bobbing up and down a short distance from them and challenge him to race her to it. She gave him a few yards start, and they would swim as hard as they could toward the cork. Or they would have diving competitions from the platform of the raft, splashing up the pale, smooth water as they plunged in. Agostino would watch his mother's body sink down deeper and deeper through a froth of green bubbles; then suddenly he would dive in after her, eager to follow wherever she might go, even to the bottom of the sea. As he flung himself into the furrow his mother had made it seemed to him that even that cold, dense water must keep some trace of the passage of her beloved body. When their swim was over they would climb back onto the raft, and gazing all round her on the calm, luminous sea his mother would say: "How beautiful it is, isn't it?" Agostino made no reply, because he felt that his own enjoyment of the beauty of sea and sky was really due above all to his deep sense of union with his mother. Were it not for this intimacy, it sometimes entered his head to wonder what would remain of all that beauty. They would stay out a long time, drying themselves in the sun, which toward midday got hotter and hotter; then his mother, stretched out at full length on the platform between the two floats, with her long hair trailing in the water and her eyes closed, would fall into a doze, while Agostino would keep watch from his seat on the bench, his eyes fixed on his mother, and hardly breathing for fear of disturbing her slumber. Suddenly she would open her eyes and say what a delightful novelty it was to lie on one's back with one's eyes shut and to feel the water rocking beneath; or she would ask Agostino to pass her her cigarette case or, better still, to light one for her himself and give it to her. All of which he would do with fervent and tremulous care. While his mother smoked, Agostino would lean forward with his back to her, but with his head to one side so that he could watch the clouds of blue smoke which indicated the spot where his mother's head was resting, with her hair spread out round her on the water. Then, as she never could have enough of the sun, she would ask Agostino to row on and not turn around, while she would take off her brassière and let down her bathing suit so as to expose her whole body to the sunlight. Agostino would go on rowing, proud of her injunction not to look as if he were being allowed to take part in a ritual. And not only did he never dream of looking around, but he felt that her body, lying so close behind him, naked in the sun, was surrounded by a halo of mystery to which he owed the greatest reverence.

One morning his mother was sitting as usual under the great beach umbrella, with Agostino beside her on the sand, waiting for the moment of their daily row. Suddenly a tall shadow fell between him and the sun. He looked up and saw a dark, sunburnt young man shaking hands with his mother. He did not pay much attention to him, thinking it was one of his mother's casual acquaintances; he only drew back a little, waiting for the conversation to be over. But the young man did not accept the invitation to sit down, pointing to the white raft in which he had come, he invited the mother to go for a row. Agostino was sure his mother would refuse this invitation as she had many previous ones; so that his surprise was great when he saw her accept at once, and immediately begin to put her things together — her sandals, bathing cap and purse, and then get up from her chair. His mother had accepted the young man's invitation with exactly the same spontaneity and simple friendliness which she would have shown toward her son; and with a like simplicity she now turned to Agostino, who sat waiting with his head down, letting the sand trickle through his fingers, and told him to have a sun bath, for she was going out for a short turn in the boat and would be back soon. The young man, meanwhile, as if quite sure of himself, had gone off in the direction of the raft, while the woman walked submissively behind him with her usual calm, majestic gait. Her son, watching them, could not help saying to himself that the young man must now be feeling the same pride and vanity and excitement which he himself always felt when he set out in a boat with his mother. He watched her get onto the float: the young man leaned backward and pushed with his feet against the sandy bottom; then, with a few vigorous strokes, lifted the raft out of the shallow water near the shore. The young man was rowing now, and his mother sat facing him, holding onto the seat with both hands and apparently chatting with him. Gradually the raft grew smaller and smaller, till it entered the region of dazzling light which the sun shed on the surface of the water, and slowly became absorbed into it.

Left alone, Agostino stretched himself out in his mother's deck chair and with one arm behind his head lay gazing up at the sky, seemingly lost in reflection and indifferent to his surroundings. He felt that all the people on the beach must have noticed him going off every day with his mother, and therefore it could not have escaped them that today his mother had left him behind and gone off with the young man in the bathing raft. So he was determined to give no sign at all of the disappointment and disillusion which filled him with such bitterness. But however much he tried to adopt an air of calm composure, he felt at the same time that everyone must be noticing how forced and artificial his attitude was. What hurt him still more was not so much that his mother had preferred the young man's company to his as the alacrity with which she had accepted the invitation — almost as if she had anticipated it. It was as if she had decided beforehand not to lose any opportunity, and when one offered itself to accept it without hesitation. Apparently she had been bored all those times she had been alone with him on the raft, and had only gone with him for lack of something better to do. A memory came back to his mind that increased his discomfiture. It had happened at a dance to which he had been taken by his mother. A girl cousin was with them who, in despair at not being asked by anyone else, had consented to dance once or twice with him, though he was only a boy in short trousers. She had danced reluctantly and looked very cross and out of temper, and Agostino, though preoccupied with his own steps, was aware of her contemptuous and unflattering sentiments toward himself. He had, however, asked her for a third dance, and had been quite surprised to see her suddenly smile and leap from her chair, shaking out the folds of her dress with both hands. But instead of rushing into his arms she had turned her back on him and joined a young man who had motioned to her over Agostino's shoulder. The whole scene lasted only five seconds, and no one noticed anything except Agostino himself. But he felt utterly humiliated and was sure everyone had seen how he had been snubbed.

And now, after his mother had gone off with the young man, he compared the two happenings and found them identical. Like his cousin, his mother had only waited for an opportunity to abandon him. Like his cousin, and with the same exaggerated readiness, she had accepted the first offer that presented itself. And in each case it had been his fate to come tumbling down from an illusory height and to lie bruised and wounded at the bottom.

That day his mother stayed out for about two hours. From under his big umbrella he saw her step on to the shore, shake hands with the young man and move slowly off toward the beach cabin, stooping a little under the heat of the midday sun. The beach was deserted by now, and this was a relief to Agostino, who was always convinced that all eyes were fixed on them. "What have you been doing?" his mother asked casually. "I have had great fun," began Agostino, and he made up a story of how *he* had been bathing too with the boys from the next beach cabin. But his mother was not listening; she had hurried off to dress. Agostino decided that as soon as he saw the raft appear the next day he would make some excuse to leave so as not to suffer the indignity of being left behind again. But when the next day came he had just started away when he heard his mother calling him back. "Come along," she said, as she got up and collected her belongings, "we're going out to swim." Agostino followed her, thinking that she meant to dismiss the young man and go out alone with him. The young man was standing on the raft waiting for her. She greeted him and said simply: "I'm bringing my son, too." So Agostino, much as he disliked it, found himself sitting beside his mother facing the young man, who was rowing.

Agostino had always seen his mother in a certain light — calm, dignified and reserved. During this outing he was shocked to see the change which had taken place, not only in her manner of talking but, as it seemed, even in herself. One could scarcely believe she was the same person. They had hardly put out to sea before she made some stinging personal remark, quite lost on Agostino, which started a curious, private conversation. As far as he could make out it concerned a lady friend of the young man who had rejected his advances in favor of a rival. But this only led up to the real matter of their conversation, which seemed to be alternately insinuating, exacting, contemptuous and teasing. His mother appeared to be the more aggressive and the more susceptible of the two, for the young man contented himself with replying in a calm, ironical tone, as if he were quite sure of himself. At times his mother seemed displeased, even positively angry with the young man, and then Agostino was glad. But immediately after she would disappoint him by some flattering phrase which destroyed the illusion. Or in an offended voice she would address to the young man a string of mysterious reproaches. But instead of being offended, Agostino would see his face light up with an expression of fatuous vanity, and concluded that those reproaches were only a cover for some affectionate meaning which he was unable to fathom. As for himself, both his mother and the young man seemed to be unaware of his existence; he might as well not have been there, and his mother carried this obliviousness so far as to remind the young man that if she had gone out alone with him the day before, this was a mistake on her part which she did not intend to repeat. In the future she would bring her son with her. Agostino felt this to be decidedly insulting, as if he was something with no will of his own, merely an object to be disposed of as her caprice or convenience might see fit.

Only once did his mother seem aware of his presence, and that was when the young man, letting go the oars for a moment, leaned forward with an intensely malicious expression on his face and murmured something in an undertone which Agostino could not understand. His mother started, pretending to be terribly shocked, and cried out, pointing to Agostino sitting by her, "Let us at least spare this innocent!" Agostino trembled with rage at hearing himself called innocent, as if a dirty rag had been thrown at him which he could not avoid.

When they were some way out from shore, the young man suggested a swim to his companion. Agostino, who had often admired the ease and simplicity with which his mother slipped into the water, was painfully struck by all the unfamiliar movements she now put into that familiar action. The young man had time to dive in and come up again to the surface, while she still stood hesitating and dipping one toe after another into the water, apparently pretending to be timid or shy. She made a great fuss about going in, laughing and protesting and holding on to the seat with both hands, till at last she dropped in an almost indecent attitude over the side and let herself fall clumsily into the arms of her companion. They dived together and came up together to the surface. Agostino, huddled on the seat, saw his mother's smiling face quite close to the young man's grave, brown one, and it seemed to him that their cheeks touched. He could see their two bodies disporting themselves in the limpid water, their hips and legs touching, and looking as if they longed to interlace with each other. Agostino looked first at them and then at the distant shore, with a shameful sense of being in the way. Catching sight of his frowning face, his mother, who was having her second dip, called up to him: "Why are you so serious? Don't you see how lovely it is in here? Goodness! what a serious son I've got"; a remark which filled Agostino with a sense of shame and humiliation. He made no reply, and contented himself with looking elsewhere. The swim was a long one. His mother and her companion disported themselves in the water like two dolphins, and seemed to have forgotten him entirely. At last they got back onto the raft. The young man sprang on at one bound, and then leaned over the edge to assist his companion, who was calling him to help her get out of the water. Agostino saw how in raising her the young man gripped her brown flesh with his fingers, just where the arm is the softest and biggest, between the shoulder and the armpit. Then she sat down beside Agostino, panting and laughing, and with her pointed nails held her wet suit away from her, so that it should not cling to her breasts. Agostino remembered that when they were alone his mother was strong enough to climb into the boat without anyone's aid, and attributed her appeal for help and her bodily postures, which seemed to draw attention to her feminine disabilities, to the new spirit which had already produced such unpleasant changes in her. Indeed, he could not help thinking that his mother, who was naturally a tall, dignified woman, resented her size as a positive drawback from which she would have liked to rid herself; and her dignity as a tiresome habit which she was trying to replace by a sort of tomboy gaucherie.

When they were both back on the raft, the return journey began. This time the oars were entrusted to Agostino, while the other two sat down on the platform which joined the two floats. He rowed gently in the burning sun, wondering constantly about the meaning of the sounds and laughter and movements of which he was conscious behind his back. From time to time his mother, as if suddenly aware of his presence, would reach up with one arm and try to stroke the back of his neck, or she would tickle him under the arm and ask if he were tired. "No, I am not tired," he replied. He heard the young man say laughingly: "Rowing's good for him," which made him plunge in the oar savagely. His mother was sitting with her head resting against his seat and her long legs stretched out; that he knew, but it seemed to him that she did not stay in that position; once, for instance, a short skirmish seemed to be going on; his mother made a stifled sound as if she were being suffocated and the raft lurched to one side. For a moment Agostino's cheek came into contact with his mother's body, which seemed vast to him — like the sky — and pulsing with a life over which she had no control. She stood with her legs apart, holding on to her son's shoulders, and said: "I will only sit down again if you promise to be good." "I promise," rejoined the young man with mock solemnity. She let herself down again awkwardly on to the platform, and it was then her body brushed her son's cheek. The moisture of her body confined in its wet bathing suit remained on his skin, but its heat seemed to overpower its dampness and though he felt a tormenting sense of uneasiness, even of repugnance, he persisted in not drying away the traces.

As they approached the shore the young man sprang lightly to the rower's seat and seized the oars, pushing Agostino away and forcing him to take the place left empty beside his mother. She put her arm round his waist and asked how he felt, and if he was happy. She herself seemed in the highest spirits, and began singing, another most unusual thing with her. She had a sweet voice, and put in some pathetic trills which made Agostino shiver. While she sang she continued to hold him close to her, wetting him with the water from her damp bathing suit, which seemed to exude a violent animal heat. And so they came in to the shore, the young man rowing, the woman singing and caressing her son, who submitted with a feeling of utter boredom; making up a picture which Agostino felt to be false, and contrived for appearance sake.

Next day the young man appeared again. Agostino's mother insisted on her son coming and the scenes of the day before repeated themselves. Then after a few days' interval they went out again. And at last, with their apparently growing intimacy, he came to fetch her daily, and each time Agostino was obliged to go too, to listen to their conversation and to watch them bathing. He hated these expeditions, and invented a thousand reasons for not going. He would disappear and not show himself till his mother, having called him repeatedly and hunted for him everywhere, succeeded at last in unearthing him; but then he came less in response to her appeals than because her disappointment and vexation aroused his pity. He kept completely silent on the float, hoping they would understand and leave him alone, but in the end he proved weaker and more susceptible to pity than his mother or the young man. It was enough for them just to have him there; as for his feelings, he came to see that they counted for less than nothing. So, in spite of all his attempts to escape, the expeditions continued.

2

ONE DAY AGOSTINO WAS SITTING on the sand behind his mother's deck chair, waiting for the white raft to appear on the sea and for his mother to wave her hand in greeting and call to the young man by name. But the usual hour for his appearance passed, and his mother's disappointed and cross expression clearly showed that she had given up all hope of his coming. Agostino had often wondered what he should feel in such a case, and had supposed that his joy would have been at least as great as his mother's disappointment. But he was surprised to feel instead a vague disappointment, and he realized that the humiliations and resentments of those daily outings had become almost a necessity of life to him. Therefore, with a confused and unconscious desire to inflict pain on his mother, he asked her more than once if they were not going out for their usual row. She replied each time that she didn't know, but that probably they wouldn't be going today. She lay in the deck chair with a book open in her lap, but she wasn't reading and her eyes continually wandered out to sea, as if seeking some particular object among the many boats and bathers with which the water was already swarming. After sitting a long time behind his mother's chair, drawing patterns in the sand, Agostino came round to her and said in a tone of voice which he felt to be teasing and even mocking: "Mamma, do you mean to say that we're not going out on the raft today?" His mother may have felt the mockery in his voice and the desire to make her suffer, or his few rash words may have sufficed to release her long pent-up irritation. She raised her hand with an involuntary gesture and gave him a sharp slap on the cheek, which did not really hurt, probably because she regretted it almost before the blow fell. Agostino said nothing, but leaping up off the sand in one bound, he went away with his head hanging down, in the direction of the beach cabin. "Agostino! . . . Agostino! . . ." he heard his name called several times. Then the calling stopped, and looking back he fancied he saw among the throng of boats the young man's white raft. But he no longer worried about that, he was like someone who has found a treasure and hastens to hide it away so that he may examine it alone. For it was with just such a sense of discovery that he ran away to nurse his injury; something so novel to him as to seem almost incredible.

His cheek burned, his eyes were full of tears which he could not keep back; and fearing lest his sobs should break out before he got into shelter, he ran doubled up. The accumulated bitterness of all those days when he had been compelled to accompany the young man and his mother came surging back on him, and he felt that if only he could have a good cry it would release something in him and help him to understand the meaning of all these strange happenings. The simplest thing seemed to be to shut himself up in the beach cabin. His mother was probably already out in the boat and no one would disturb him. Agostino climbed the steps hurriedly, opened the door and, leaving it ajar, sat down on a stool in the corner.

He huddled up with his knees tucked into his chest and his head against the wall, and holding his face between his hands, started weeping conscientiously. The slap he had received kept rising up before him, and he wondered why, when it seemed so hard, his mother's hand had been so soft and irresolute. With the bitter sense of humiliation aroused in him by the blow were mixed a thousand other sensations, even more disagreeable, which had wounded his feelings during these last days. There was one above all which kept returning to his mind: the image of his mother's body in its damp tricot pressed against his cheek, quivering with a sort of imperious vitality. And just as great clouds of dust fly out from old clothes when they are beaten, so, as the result of that blow to his suffering and bewildered consciousness, there arose in him again the sensation of his mother's body pressed against his cheek. Indeed, that sensation seemed at times to take the place of the slap; at others, the two became so mixed that he felt both the throbbing of her body and the burning blow. But while it seemed to him natural that the slap on his cheek should keep flaring up like a fire which is gradually going out, he could not understand why the earlier sensation so persistently recurred. Why, among so many others, was it just the one which haunted him? He could not have explained it, but he thought that as long as he lived he would only have to carry his memory back to that moment in his life in order to have fresh against his cheek the pulse of her body and the rough texture of the damp tricot.

He went on crying softly to himself so as not to interrupt the painful workings of his memory, at the same time rubbing away from his wet skin with the tips of his fingers the tears which continued to fall slowly but uninterruptedly from his eyes. It was dark and stuffy in the cabin. Suddenly he had a feeling of someone opening the door, and he almost hoped that his mother, repenting of what she had done, would lay her hand affectionately on his shoulder and turn his face toward her. And his lips had already begun to shape the word "Mamma" when he heard a step in the cabin and the door pulled to, without any hand touching his shoulder or stroking his head.

He raised his head and looked up. Close to the half-open door he saw a boy of about his own age standing in an attitude of someone on the lookout. He had on a pair of short trousers rolled up at the bottom, and an open sailor blouse with a great hole in the back. A thin ray of sunshine falling through a gap in the roof of the cabin lit up the thick growth of auburn curls round his neck. His feet were bare; holding the door ajar with his hands, he was gazing intently at something on the beach and did not seem to be aware of Agostino's presence. Agostino dried his eyes with the back of his hand and said: "Hello, what do you want?" The boy turned around, making a sign not to speak. He had an ugly, freckled face, the most remarkable feature of which was the rapid movement of his hard blue eyes. Agostino thought he recognized him. Probably he was the son of a fisherman or beach attendant, and he had doubtless seen him pushing out the boats or doing something about the beach.

"We're playing cops and robbers," said the boy, after a moment, turning to Agostino. "They mustn't see me."

"Which are you?" asked Agostino, hastily drying his eyes.

"A robber, of course," replied the other without looking around.

Agostino went on watching the boy. He couldn't make up his mind whether he liked him, but his voice had a rough touch of dialect which piqued him and aroused his curiosity. Besides, he felt instinctively that this boy's hiding in the cabin just at that moment was an opportunity — he could not have explained of what sort — but certainly an opportunity he must not miss.

"Will you let me play too?" he asked. The boy turned round and stared at him rudely. "How do you get into it?" he said quickly. "We're all pals playing together."

"Well," said Agostino, with shameless persistence, "let me play too."

The boy shrugged his shoulders. "It's too late now. We've almost finished the game."

"Well, in the next game?"

"There won't be any more," said the boy, looking him over doubtfully, but as if struck by his persistence. "Afterwards we're going to the pine woods."

"I'll go with you, if you'll let me."

The boy seemed amused and began to laugh rather contemptuously. "You're a fine one, you are. But we don't want you."

Agostino had never been in such a position before. But the same instinct which prompted him to ask the boy if he might join their game suggested to him now a means by which he might make himself acceptable.

"Look here," he said hesitatingly, "if you . . . if you'll let me join your gang, I . . . I'll give you something."

The other turned round at once with greedy eyes.

"What'll you give me?"

"Whatever you like."

Agostino pointed to a big model of a sailboat, with all its sails attached, which was lying on the floor of the cabin among a lot of other toys.

"I'll give you that."

"What use is that to me?" replied the boy, shrugging his shoulders.

"You could sell it," Agostino suggested.

"They'd never take it," said the boy, with the air of one who knows. "They'd say it was stolen goods."

Agostino looked all round him despairingly. His mother's clothes were hanging on pegs, her shoes were on the floor, on the table was a handkerchief and a scarf or two. There was absolutely nothing in the cabin which seemed a suitable offering.

"Say," said the boy, seeing his bewilderment, "got any cigarettes?"

Agostino remembered that that very morning his mother had put two boxes of a very good brand in the big bag which was hanging from a peg; and he hastened to reply, triumphantly, "Yes, I have. Would you like some?"

"I *don't* think!" said the other, with scornful irony. "Are you stupid! Give them here, quick."

Agostino took down the bag, felt about in it and pulled out the two boxes. He held them out to the boy, as if he were not quite sure how many he wanted.

"I'll take both," he said lightly, seizing the boxes. He looked at the label and clicked his tongue approvingly and said: "You must be rich, eh?"

Agostino didn't know what to answer. The boy went on: "I'm Berto. What's your name?"

Agostino told him. But the other had ceased to pay any attention. His impatient fingers had already torn open one of the boxes, breaking the seals on its paper wrapping. He took out a cigarette and put it between his lips. Then he took a match from his pocket and struck it against the wall of the cabin; and after inhaling a mouthful of smoke and puffing it out through his nose, he resumed his watching position at the crack of the door.

"Come on, let's go," he said, after a moment, making Agostino a sign to follow him. They left the cabin one behind the other. When they got to the beach Berto made straight for the road behind the row of beach cabins.

As they walked along the burning sand between the low bushes of broom and thistles, he said: "Now we're going to the Cave . . . they've gone on past . . . they're looking for me lower down."

"Where is the Cave?" asked Agostino.

"At the Vespucci Baths," replied the boy. He held his cigarette ostentatiously between two fingers, as if to display it, and voluptuously inhaled great mouthfuls of smoke. "Don't you smoke?" he said.

"I don't care about it," said Agostino, ashamed to confess that he had never even dreamed of smoking. But Berto laughed. "Why don't you say straight out that your mother won't let you? Speak the truth." His way of saying this was contemptuous rather than friendly. He offered Agostino a cigarette, saying: "Go ahead, you smoke too."

They had reached the sea-front and were walking barefoot on the sharp flints between dried-up flower beds. Agostino put the cigarette to his lips and took a few puffs, inhaling a little smoke which he at once let out again instead of swallowing it.

"You call that smoking!" he exclaimed. "That's not the way to do it. Look." He took the cigarette and inhaled deeply, rolling his sulky eyes all the while; then he opened his mouth wide and put it quite close to Agostino's eyes. There was nothing to be seen in his mouth, except his tongue curled up at the back.

"Now watch," said Berto, shutting his mouth again. And he puffed a cloud of smoke straight into Agostino's face. Agostino coughed and laughed nervously at the same time. "It's your turn now," said Berto.

A trolley passed them, whistling, its window curtains flapping in the breeze. Agostino inhaled a fresh mouthful and with a great effort swallowed the smoke. But it went the wrong way and he had a dreadful fit of coughing. Berto took the cigarette and gave him a great slap on the back, saying: "Bravo! There's no doubt about your being a smoker."

After this experiment they walked on in silence past a whole series of bath establishments, with their rows of cabins painted in bright colors, great striped umbrellas slanting in all directions, and absurd triumphal arches. The beach between the cabins was packed with noisy holiday-makers and the sparkling sea swarmed with bathers.

"Where is Vespucci?" asked Agostino, who had to walk very fast to keep up with his new friend.

"It's the last one of all."

Agostino began to wonder whether he ought not to turn back. If his mother hadn't gone out on the raft after all, she would certainly be looking for him. But the memory of that slap put his scruples to rest. In going with Berto he almost felt as if he were pursuing a mysterious and justified vendetta.

Suddenly Berto stopped and said: "How about letting the smoke out through your nose? Can you do that?" Agostino shook his head, and his companion, holding the stump of his cigarette between his lips, inhaled the smoke and expelled it through his nostrils. "Now," he went on, "I'm going to let it out through my eyes. But you must put your hand on my chest and look me straight in the face." Agostino went up to him quite innocently and put his hand on Berto's chest and fixed his eyes on Berto's, expecting to see smoke come out of them.

But Berto treacherously pressed the lighted cigarette down hard on the back of his hand and threw the butt away, jumping for joy and shouting: "Oh! you silly idiot! You just don't know anything." Agostino was almost blind with pain, and his first impulse was to fling himself on Berto and strike him. But Berto, as if he saw what was coming, stood still and clenched his fists, and with two sharp blows in the stomach almost knocked the breath out of Agostino's body.

"I'm not one for words," he said savagely. "If you ask for it you'll get it." Agostino, infuriated, rushed at him again, but he felt terribly weak and certain of being defeated. This time Berto seized him by the head, and taking it under his arm almost strangled him. Agostino did not even attempt to resist, but in a stifled voice implored him to let go. Berto released him and sprang back, planting his feet firmly on the ground in a fighting stance. But Agostino had heard the vertebrae of his neck crack, and was stupefied by the boy's extraordinary brutality. It seemed incredible that he, Agostino, who had always been kind to everyone, should suddenly be treated with such savage and deliberate cruelty. His chief feeling was one of amazement at such barbarousness. It overwhelmed him, but at the same time fascinated him because of its very novelty and because it was so monstrous.

"I haven't done you any harm," he panted, "I gave you those cigarettes . . . and you . . ." He couldn't finish. His eyes filled with tears.

"Uh, you crybaby," retorted Berto. "Want your cigarettes back? I don't want them. Take them back to Mamma."

"It doesn't matter," said Agostino, shaking his head disconsolately. "I only just said it for something to say. Please keep them."

"Well, let's get on," said Berto. "We're almost there."

The burn on Agostino's hand was hurting him badly. Raising it to his lips he looked about him. On that part of the beach there were very few cabins, five or six in all, scattered about at some distance from each other. They were miserable huts of rough wood. The sand between them was deserted and the sea was equally empty. There were a few women in the shade of a boat pulled up out of reach of the tide, some standing, some lying stretched out on the sand, all dressed in antiquated bathing suits, with long drawers edged with white braid, all busy drying themselves and exposing their white limbs to the sun. A signboard painted blue bore the inscription: "Amerigo Vespucci Baths." A low green shack half-buried in the sand evidently belonged to the bath man. Beyond this the shore stretched away as far as the eye could see, without either cabins or houses, a solitude of windswept sand between the sparkling blue sea and the dusty green of the pine trees.

One entire side of the man's hut was hidden from the road by sand dunes, which were higher at this point. Then, when you had climbed to the top of the dunes, you saw a patched, faded awning of rusty red, which seemed to have been cut out of an old sail. This awning was attached at one end to two poles driven into the sand, and at the other to the hut.

"That's our cave," said Berto.

Under the awning a man seated at a rickety table was in the act of lighting a cigarette. Two or three boys were stretched on the sand around him. Berto took a flying leap and landed at the man's feet, crying. "Cave!" Agostino approached rather timidly. "This is Pisa," said Berto, pointing to him. He was surprised to hear himself called by this nickname so soon. It was only five minutes ago that he had told Berto he was born at Pisa. Agostino lay down on the ground beside the others. The sand was not so clean as it was on the beach; bits of coconut shell and wooden splinters, fragments of earthenware and all sorts of rubbish were mixed up in it. Here and there it was caked and hard from the pails of dirty water which had been thrown out of the hut. Agostino noticed that the boys, four in all, were poorly dressed. Like Berto they were evidently the sons of sailors or bath men. "He was at the Speranza," burst out Berto, without drawing breath. "He says he wants to play at cops and robbers too, but the game's over, isn't it? I told you the game would be over."

At that moment there was a cry of "It's not fair! It's not fair!" Agostino, looking up, saw another gang of boys running from the direction of the sea, probably the cops. First came a thickset, stumpy youth of about seventeen in a bathing costume; next, to his great surprise, a Negro; the third was fair, and by his carriage and physical beauty struck Agostino as being better bred than the others. But as he got nearer, his ragged bathing suit, full of holes, and a certain coarseness in his handsome face with beautiful blue eyes, showed that he too belonged to the people. After these three boys came four more, all about the same age, between thirteen and fourteen. The big, thickset boy was so much older than the others that at first it seemed odd that he should mix with such children. But his pasty face, the color of half-baked bread; the thick, expressionless features, and an almost brutish stupidity were sufficient explanation of the company he kept. He had hardly any neck, and his smooth, hairless torso was as wide at the waist and hips as at the shoulders. "You hid in a cabin," he shouted at Berto. "I dare you to deny it! Cabins are out of bounds by the rules of the game."

"It's a lie!" retorted Berto, with equal violence. "Isn't it, Pisa?" he added, suddenly turning to Agostino. "I didn't hide in a cabin, did I? We were both standing by the hut of the Speranza, and we saw you go by, didn't we, Pisa?"

"You did hide in my cabin, you know," said Agostino, who was incapable of telling a lie. "There, you see!" shouted the other, brandishing his fist under Berto's nose. "I'll bash your head in, you liar!"

"Spy!" yelled Berto in Agostino's face. "I told you to stay where you were. Go back to Mamma, that's the place for you." He was filled with uncontrollable rage, a bestial fury which amazed and mystified Agostino. But in springing to punish him one of the cigarette boxes tumbled out of his pocket. He stooped to pick it up, but the big boy was quicker still, and darting down he pounced on the box and waved it in the air, crying triumphantly: "Cigarettes! Cigarettes!"

"Give them back," shouted Berto, hurling himself upon the big boy. "They're mine. Pisa gave them to *me*. You just give them back."

The other took a step back and waited till Berto was within range. Then he held the box of cigarettes in his mouth and began to pummel Berto's stomach methodically with his two fists. Finally he kicked Berto's feet from under and brought him down with a crash. "Give me them back!" Berto went on shouting, while he rolled in the sand, But the big boy, with a stupid laugh, called out: "He's got some more . . . at him, boys." And with a unanimity which surprised Agostino all the boys flung themselves upon Berto. For a moment there was nothing to be seen but a writhing mass of bodies tangled together in a cloud of sand at the feet of the man, who went on smoking calmly at the table. At last, the fair boy, who seemed to be the most agile, disentangled himself from the heap and got up, triumphantly waving the second box of cigarettes. Then the others got up, one by one; and last of all Berto. His ugly, freckled little face was convulsed with fury. "Swine! Thieves!" he bellowed, shaking his fist and sobbing.

It was a strange and novel impression for Agostino to see his tormentor in his turn, and treated as pitilessly as he himself had just been. "Swine! Swine!" Berto screamed again. The big boy went up to him and gave him a resounding box on the ear, which made his companions dance for joy. "Do you want any more?" Berto rushed like a mad one to the corner of the hut and, bending down, grabbed hold of a large rock with both hands and flung it at his enemy, who with a derisive whistle sprang aside to avoid it. "You swine!" yelled Berto again, still sobbing with rage, but withdrawing himself prudently behind a corner of the hut. His sobs were loud and furious, as if giving vent to some frightful bitterness, but his companions had ceased to take any interest in him. They were all stretched out again on the sand. The big boy opened one box of cigarettes, and the fair boy another. Suddenly the man, who had remained seated at the little table without moving during the fight, said: "Hand over those cigarettes."

Agostino looked at him. He was a tall, fat man of about fifty. He had a cold and deceptively good-natured face. He was bald, with a curious saddle-shaped forehead and twinkling eyes; a red, aquiline nose with wide nostrils full of little scarlet veins horrible to look at. He had a drooping mustache, which hid a rather crooked mouth, and a cigar between his lips. He was wearing a faded shirt and a pair of blue cotton trousers with one leg down to his ankle and the other rolled up below his knee. A black sash was wound round his stomach. One detail in particular added to Agostino's first feeling of revulsion, the fact that Saro — for this was his name — had six fingers instead of five on both hands. This made them look enormous, and his fingers like abbreviated tentacles. Agostino could not take his eyes off those hands; he could not make up his mind whether Saro had two first or two middle or two third fingers. They all seemed of equal length, except the little finger, which stuck out from his hand like a small branch at the base of a knotty tree trunk. Saro took the cigar out of his mouth and repeated simply: "What about those cigarettes?"

The fair boy got up and put his box on the table. "Good for you, Sandro," said Saro.

"And supposing I won't give you them?" shouted the elder boy defiantly.

"Give them up, Tortima; you'd better," called out several voices at once. Tortima looked all round and then at Saro, who with the six fingers of his right hand on the box of cigarettes, kept his half-closed little eyes fixed on him. Then, with the remark: "All right, but it isn't fair," he came over and put his box down on the table too.

"And now I'll divide them," said Saro, in a soft, affable voice. Without removing his cigar, he screwed up his eyes, opened one of the boxes, took out a cigarette with his stumpy, multiple fingers, which looked incapable of gripping it, and threw it to the Negro, with a "Catch, Homs!" Then he took another and threw it to one of the others; a third he threw into the joined palms of Sandro; a fourth straight at Tortima's stolid face — and so with all the rest. "Do you want one?" he asked Berto, who, swallowing back his sobs, had come silently back to join the others. He nodded sulkily, and was thrown one. When each of the boys had received his cigarette, Saro was about to shut the box, which was still half-full, when he stopped and said to Agostino: "What about you Pisa? Agostino would have liked to refuse, but Berto gave him a dig in the ribs and whispered: "Ask for one, idiot, we'll smoke it together afterward." So Agostino said he would like one, and he too had his cigarette. Then Saro shut the box.

"What about the rest? What about the rest?" shouted all the boys at once.

"You shall have the rest another day," replied Saro calmly. "Pisa, take these cigarettes and go and put them in the hut." There was complete silence. Agostino nervously took both boxes and, stepping over the boys' prostrate bodies, crossed to the shed. It appeared to consist of one room only, and he liked its smallness, which made it seem like a house in a fairy tale. It had a low ceiling with whitewashed beams, and the walls were of unplaned planks. Two tiny windows, complete with window sill, little square panes of glass, latches, curtains, even a vase or two of flowers, diffused a mild light. One corner was occupied by the bed, neatly made up, with a clean pillowcase and red counterpane; in another stood a round table and three stools. On the marble top of a big chest stood two of those bottles which have sailboats or steamships imprisoned inside them. Sails were hung on hooks all round the walls, and there were pairs of oars and other sea tackle. Agostino thought how he should love to own a cottage as cozy and convenient as this. He went up to the table, on which lay a big, cracked china bowl of half-smoked cigarettes, put down his two boxes and went out again into the sunlight.

All the boys were lying face downward on the sand around Saro, smoking with great demonstrations of enjoyment. And meanwhile they were discussing something about which they did not seem to agree. Sandro was just saying: "I tell you it *is* him."

"His mother's a real beauty," said an admiring voice. "She's the best looker on the beach. Homs and me got under the cabin one day to see her undress, but her chemise fell just above the crack we were looking through and we couldn't see anything at all. Her legs, gee, and her breasts. . . "

"You never see the husband anywhere about," said a third voice.

"You needn't worry, she satisfies herself. . . . D'you know who with? That young guy from Villa Sorriso . . . the dark one. He takes her out every day on his raft."

"He's not the only one either. She'd take anyone on," said someone maliciously.

"But I know it's not him," insisted another.

"Say, Pisa," said Sandro suddenly. "Isn't that your mother, that lady at the Speranza? She's tall and dark, with long legs, and wears a striped two-piece bathing suit . . . and she's got a mole on the left side of her mouth."

"Yes, why?" asked Agostino, nervously.

"It *is* her, it *is* her," cried Berto triumphantly. And then, in a burst of jealous spite: "You're just their blind, aren't you? You all go out together, her and you, and her gigolo. You're their blind, aren't you?" At these words everyone roared with laughter. Even Saro smiled under his mustache. "I don't know what you mean," said Agostino, blushing and only half-understanding. He wanted to protest, but their coarse jokes aroused in him a curious and unexpected sense of sadistic satisfaction. As if by their words the boys had, all unawares, avenged the humiliations which his mother had inflicted on him all these days past. At the same time he was struck dumb with horror at their knowing so much about his private affairs.

"Innocent little lamb," said the same malicious voice. "I'd like to know what they're up to; they always go a long way out," said Tortima with mock gravity. "Come on, tell us what they do. He kisses her, eh?" He put the back of his hand to his lips and gave it a smacking kiss.

"It's quite true," said Agostino, flushing with shame; "we do go a long way out to swim."

"Oh yes, to swim!" came sarcastically from several voices at once.

"My mother does swim, and so does Renzo."

"Ah, yes, Renzo, that's his name," affirmed the boy, as if recovering a lost thread in his memory. "Renzo, that tall dark fellow."

"And what do Renzo and Mamma do together?" suddenly asked Berto, quite restored. "Is it this they do?" and he made an expressive gesture with his hand, "And you just look on, eh?"

"I?" questioned Agostino, turning around with a look of terror.

They all burst out laughing and smothered their merriment in the sane. But Saro continued to observe him attentively, without moving. Agostino looked around despairingly, as if to implore aid.

Saro seemed to be struck by his look. He took his cigar out of his mouth, and said: "Can't you see he knows absolutely nothing?"

The din was immediately silenced. "How do you mean, he doesn't know?" asked Tortima, who hadn't understood.

"He just doesn't know," repeated Saro, simply. And turning to

Agostino, he said in a softer voice: "Speak up, Pisa. A man and a woman, what is it they do together? Don't you know?"

They all listened breathlessly. Agostino stared at Saro, who continued to smoke and watch him through half-closed eyelids. He looked round at the boys, who were evidently bursting with stifled laughter, and repeated mechanically, through the cloud which seemed to cover his sight: "A man and a woman?"

"Yes, your mother and Renzo," explained Berto brutally.

Agostino wanted to say "Don't talk about my mother," but the question awoke in him a whole swarm of sensations and memories, and he was too upset to say anything at all. "He doesn't know," said Saro abruptly, shifting his cigar from one corner of his mouth to the other. "Which of you boys is going to tell him?" Agostino looked around bewildered. It was like being at school, but what a strange schoolmaster! What odd schoolfellows! "Me, me, me! . . ." all the boys shouted at once. Saro's glance rested dubiously on all those faces burning with eagerness to be the first to speak. Then he said: "You don't really know either, any of you. You've only got it from hearsay. . . . Let someone tell him who really knows." Agostino saw them all eyeing each other in silence. Then someone said: "Tortima." An expression of vanity lit up the youth's face. He was just going to get up when Berto said, with hatred in his voice: "He made it all up, himself. . . . It's a pack of lies. . . ."

"What d'you mean, a pack of lies?" shouted Tortima, flinging himself upon Berto. "It's you who tells lies, you bastard!" But this time Berto was too quick for him, and from behind the corner of the hut he began making faces and putting out his tongue at Tortima, his red, freckled face distorted by hatred. Tortima contented himself with threatening him with his fist and shouting: "You dare come back!" But somehow Berto's intervention had wrecked his chances, and the boys with one accord voted for Sandro. His arms crossed over his broad brown chest on which shone a few golden hairs, Sandro, handsome and elegant, advanced into the circle of boys stretched out on the sand. Agostino noticed that his strong, bronzed legs looked as if they were dusted over with gold. A few hairs also showed through the gaps in his bathing trunks. "It's quite simple," he said in a strong, clear voice. And speaking slowly with the aid of gestures which were significant without being coarse, he explained to Agostino what he now felt he had always known but had somehow forgotten, as in a deep sleep. Sandro's explanation was followed by other less sober ones. Some of the boys made vulgar gestures with their hands, others dinned into Agostino's ears coarse words which he had never heard before; two of them said: "We'll show you what they do," and gave a demonstration on the hot sand, jerking and writhing in each other's arms. Sandro, satisfied with his success, went off alone to finish his cigar. "Do you understand now?" asked Saro, as soon as the din had died down. Agostino nodded. In reality he hadn't so much understood as absorbed the notion, rather as one absorbs a medicine or poison, the effect of which is not immediately felt but will be sure to manifest itself later on. The idea was not in his empty, bewildered and anguished mind, but in some other part of his being; in his embittered heart, or deep in his breast, which received it with amazement. It was like some bright, dazzling object, which one cannot look at for the radiance it emits, so that one can only guess its real shape. He felt it was something he had always possessed but only now experienced in his blood.

"Renzo and Pisa's mother," he heard someone say close beside him. "I'll be Renzo and you be Pisa's mother. Let's try." He turned suddenly and saw Berto, who with an awkward, ceremonious gesture was making a bow to another boy. "Madam, may I have the honor of your company on my raft? I'm going for a swim. Pisa will accompany us." Then suddenly blind rage took possession of him and flinging himself upon Berto he yelled: "I forbid you to talk about my mother." But before he knew what had happened he was lying on his back on the sand, with Berto's knee holding him down and Berto's fists raining blows on his face. He wanted to cry, but realizing that his tears would only be an opening for more jeers, he controlled them with great effort. Then, covering his face with his arm, he lay as still as death. Berto left him alone after a bit, and feeling very ill-treated he went and sat down at Saro's feet. The boys were already busy talking about something else. One of them suddenly asked Agostino: "Are you rich, you people?"

Agostino was so intimidated that he hardly knew what to say. But he replied: "I think so."

"How much? . . . A million? Two millions? . . . Three millions?"

"I don't know," said Agostino, feeling bothered.

"Got a big house?"

"Yes," said Agostino; and somewhat reassured by the more courteous turn of the conversation, pride of possession prompted him to add: "We have twenty rooms."

"Bum . . ." came incredulously from someone.

"We've got two reception rooms and then there's my father's study . . ."

"Aha!" said a scornful voice.

"Or it *used* to be my father's," Agostino hastened to add, half-hoping that this detail might make them feel a little more sympathetic towards him. "My father is dead."

There was a moment's silence. "So your mother's a widow?" said Tortima.

"Well, of course," came from several mocking voices.

"That's not saying anything," protested Tortima. "She might have married again."

"No, she hasn't married again," said Agostino.

"And have you got a car?"

"Yes."

"And a chauffeur?"

"Yes."

"Tell your mother I'm ready to be her chauffeur," shouted someone.

"And what do you do in those reception rooms?" asked Tortima, on whom Agostino's account seemed to make more impression than on anyone else. "Do you give dances?"

"Yes, my mother has receptions," replied Agostino.

"Lots of pretty women, you bet," said Tortima, as if speaking to himself. "How many people come?"

"I don't really know."

"How many?"

"Twenty or thirty," said Agostino, who by now felt quite at his ease and was rather gratified by his success.

"Twenty or thirty . . . What do they do?"

"What do you expect them to do?" asked Berto ironically. "I suppose they dance and amuse themselves. They're rich . . . not like us. They make love, I suppose."

"No, they don't make love," said Agostino conscientiously, for the sake of showing that he knew perfectly well what they meant.

Tortima seemed to be struggling with an idea which he was unable to formulate. At last he said: "But supposing I was to appear at one of those receptions, and say: 'I've come too.' What would you do?" As he spoke he got up and marched forward impudently, with his hands on his hips and his chest stuck out. The boys burst out laughing. "I should ask you to go away," said Agostino simply, emboldened by the laughter of the boys.

"And supposing I refused to go away?"

"I should make our men turn you out."

"Have you got menservants?"

"No, but my mother hires waiters when she has a reception."

"Bah, just like your father." One of the boys was evidently the son of a waiter.

"And supposing I resisted, and broke that waiter's nose for him, and then marched into the middle of the room and shouted, 'You're a lot of rogues and bitches, the whole lot of you.' What would you say?" insisted Tortima, advancing threateningly upon Agostino, and turning his fist round and round, as if to let him smell it. But this time they all turned against Tortima, not so much from a wish to protect Agostino as from the desire to hear more details of his fabulous wealth.

"Leave him alone . . . they'd kick you out, and a good thing too," was heard on all sides. Berto said sneeringly: "What have you got to do with it? Your father's a boatman and you'll be a boatman too; and if you did turn up at Pisa's house you certainly wouldn't shout anything. I can see you," he added, getting up and mimicking Tortima's supposed humility in Agostino's house . . . "'Excuse me, is Mr. Pisa at home? Excuse me . . . I just came . . . Oh, he can't? . . . Never mind, please excuse me . . . I'm so sorry . . . I'll come another time.' Oh, I can see you. Why, you'd bow down to the ground."

All the boys burst out laughing. Tortima, who was as stupid as he was brutal, didn't dare stand up to their taunts. But in order to get even he said to Agostino: "Can you make an iron arm?"

"He don't know what an iron arm is," said several voices, derisively. Sandro came over and took hold of Agostino's arm and doubled it up, and told him to stay with his hand in the air and his elbow in the sand. Meanwhile Tortima lay face downward on the sand and placed his arm in a similar position. "You push from one side," said Sandro, "and Tortima will push from the other."

Agostino took Tortima's hand. The latter at one stroke brought down his arm and got up triumphantly.

"Let me try," said Berto. He brought down Agostino's arm just as easily and got up in his turn. "Me too, me too!" cried all the others. One after another they all beat Agostino. At last it was the Negro's turn, and someone said: "If you let Homs beat you, well, your arm must be made of putty." Agostino made up his mind not to let the Negro beat him.

The Negro's arms were thin, the color of roasted coffee. He thought his own looked stronger. "Come on, Pisa," said Homs, with sham bravado, as he lay down facing him. He had a weak voice, like a woman's, and when he brought his face to within an inch of Agostino's, he saw that his nose, instead of being flat, as you might have expected, was almost aquiline, and curved in on itself like a black, shiny curl of flesh, with a pale, almost yellow mole above one nostril. Nor were his lips broad and thick like a Negro's, but thin and violet-colored. He had round eyes with large whites, on which his protuberant forehead with its great mop of sooty wool seemed to press. "Come on, Pisa, I won't hurt you," he said, putting his delicate hand with its thin, rose-nailed fingers in Agostino's. Agostino saw that by raising himself slightly on his shoulder he could easily have brought his whole weight to bear on his hand, and this simple fact allowed him at first to keep Homs under his control. For quite a while they competed without either of them getting the upper hand, surrounded by a circle of admiring boys. Agostino's face wore a look of great concentration; he was putting his whole strength into the effort; whereas the Negro made fearful grimaces, grinding his white teeth and screwing up his eyes. Suddenly a surprised voice proclaimed: "Pisa's winning!" But at that very moment Agostino felt an excruciating pain running from his shoulder right down his arm; he could bear no more, and gave in, saying: "No, he's stronger than me." "You'll beat me next time," said the Negro in an unpleasantly honeyed voice, as he rose from the ground. "Fancy Homs beating you too, you're good for nothing," sneered Tortima. But the other boys seemed tired of ragging Agostino. "How about a swim?" said someone. "Yes, yes, a swim!" they all cried, and they set off by leaps and bounds over the hot sand to the sea. Agostino, trailing behind, saw them turning somersaults like fish into the shallow water, with shouts and screams of joy. As he reached the water's edge Tortima emerged, bottom first, like a huge sea-animal, and called out: "Dive in, Pisa. What are you doing?"

"But I'm dressed," said Agostino.

"Get undressed then," returned Tortima crossly. Agostino tried to escape, but it was too late. Tortima caught hold of him and dragged him along, struggling and puling his tormentor over with him. He only let him go when he had almost suffocated him by holding his head under water. Then with a "Good-bye, Pisa," he swam off. Some way out Agostino could see Sandro standing in an elegant posture on a raft, in the middle of a swarm of boys, all trying to climb on to the floats. Wet and panting he returned to the beach and stood a few moments watching the raft going further and further out to sea, all alone under the blinding sunshine. Then hurrying along the burnished sand at the water's edge, he made his way back to the Speranza.

3

IT WAS NOT SO LATE AS HE feared. When he reached the bathing place he found that his mother had not yet returned. The beach was emptying; only a few isolated bathers still loitered in the dazzling water. The majority were trailing languidly off in single file under the midday sun up the tiled path which led from the beach. Agostino sat down under the big umbrella and waited. He thought his mother was staying out an unusually long time. He forgot that the young man had arrived much later than usual with his raft and that it was not his mother who had wanted to go out alone, but he who had disappeared; and said to himself that those two had certainly profited by his absence to do what Saro and the boys had suggested. He no longer felt any jealousy about this, but experienced a new and strange quiver of curiosity and secret approval, as if he were himself an accomplice. It was quite natural for his mother to behave like that with the young man, to go out with him every day on the float, and at a safe distance from prying eyes to fling herself into his arms. It was natural, and he was now perfectly well able to accept the fact. These thoughts passed through his mind as he sat scanning the sea for the return of the lovers. At length the raft appeared, a bright speck on the sea, and as it drew rapidly nearer he could see his mother sitting on the bench and the young man rowing. Every stroke of the oars as they rose and fell left a glittering track in the water. He got up and went down to the water's edge. He wanted to see his mother land, and to discover some traces of the intimacy at which he had assisted so long without understanding, and which, in the light of the revelations that Saro and the boys had made, must surely be brazenly advertised in their behavior. As the raft came near the shore his mother waved to him, then sprang gaily into the water and was soon at his side. "Are you hungry? We'll go and have something to eat at once . . . Good-bye, good-bye till tomorrow. . . ." she added in a caressing voice, turning to wave to the young man. Agostino thought she seemed happier than usual, and as he followed her across the beach he could not help thinking there had been a note of joyous intoxication in her farewell to the young man; as if what her son's presence had hitherto prevented had actually taken place that day. But his observations and suspicious went no further than this; for apart from her naive joy, which was something quite different from her customary dignity, he could not really picture what might have happened while they were out together, nor imagine what their relations actually were. Though he scrutinized her face, her neck, her hands, her body with a new and cruel awareness, they did not seem to bear any trace of the kisses and caresses they had received. The more Agostino watched his mother the more dissatisfied he felt. "You were alone today . . . without me . . ." he began, as they approached the cabin; almost hoping she would say: "Yes, and at last we were able to make love." But his mother only seemed to treat this remark as an allusion to the slap she had given him, and to his running away. "Don't let's say any more about that," she said, stopping and putting her arm around his shoulders, and looking at him with her laughing, excited eyes. "I know you love me; give me a kiss and we won't say any more about it, eh?" Agostino suddenly felt his lips against her neck —

that neck whose chaste perfume and warmth had been so sweet to him. But now he fancied he felt beneath his lips, however faintly, a stirring of something new, as it were a sharp quiver of reaction to the young man's kisses. Then she ran up the steps to the cabin, and he lay down in the sand, his face burning with a shame he could not comprehend.

Later, as they were walking back together, he stirred up these new mysterious feelings in his troubled mind. Before, when he had been ignorant of good and evil, his mother's relations with the young man had seemed to him mysteriously tinged with guilt, but now that Saro and his disciples had opened his eyes, he was, strange to say, full of doubt and unsatisfied curiosity. It was indeed the frank jealousy of his childish love for his mother which had first aroused his sensibilities; whereas now, in the clear, cruel light of day, this love, though as great as ever, was replaced by a bitter, disillusioned curiosity compared with which those early, faint evidences seemed insipid and insufficient. Formerly, every word and gesture which he felt unbecoming had offended without enlightening him, and he wished he had not seen them. Now that he came to look back, those small, tasteless gestures which used to scandalize him seemed mere trifles, and he almost wished he could surprise his mother in some of the shameless attitudes into which Saro and the boys had so recently initiated him.

He would never have hit so soon on the idea of spying on his mother with the direct intention of destroying the halo of dignity and respect which had hitherto enveloped her, had he not that very day been driven by chance to take a step in that direction. When they reached home mother and son ate their luncheon in silence. His mother seemed distrait, and Agostino, full of new and, to him, incredible thoughts, was unusually silent. But after lunch he suddenly felt an irresistible desire to go out and join the gang of boys again. They had told him they met at the Vespucci bathing place early in the afternoon, to play the day's adventures, and when he had got over his first fear and repugnance the company of those young hooligans began to exercise a mysterious attraction over him. He was lying on his bed with the shutters closed; it was warm and dark. He was playing as usual with the wooden switch of the electric light. Few sounds came to him from outside; the wheels of a solitary carriage, the clatter of plates and glasses through the open windows of the *pension* opposite. In contrast with the silence of the summer afternoon the sounds inside the house seemed to stand out more clearly, as if cut off from the rest. He heard his mother go into the next room and her heels tapping on the tiled floor. She went to and fro, opening and shutting drawers, moving chairs about, touching this and that. "She's gone to lie down," he thought suddenly, shaking off the torpor which was gradually invading his senses; "and then I shan't be able to tell her I want to go to the beach." He sprang up in alarm at the thought, and went out on the landing. His room looked over the balcony facing the stairs, and his mother's room was next to his. He went to her door, but finding it ajar, instead of knocking as he generally did, he gently pushed the door half open, moved perhaps by an unconscious desire to spy upon his mother's intimacy. His mother's room was much bigger than his, and the bed was by the door; directly facing the door was a chest of drawers, with a large mirror above it. The first thing he saw was his mother standing in front of the chest of drawers. She was not naked, as he had pictured and almost hoped when he went in so quietly; but she was partly undressed and was just taking off her necklace and earrings in front of the glass. She had on a flimsy chiffon chemise which only came half-way down her loins. As she stood leaning languidly to one side, one hip was higher and more prominent than the other, and below her solid but graceful thighs her slender, well-shaped legs tapered to delicate ankles. Her arms were raised to unfasten the clasp of her necklace and, through the transparent chiffon, this movement was perceptible all down her back, curiously odifying the contours of her body. With her hands raised thus, her armpits looked like the jaws of two snakes and the long, soft hair darted out of them like thin black tongues, as if glad to escape from the pressure of her heavy limbs. All her splendid, massive body seemed to Agostino's fascinated eyes to lose its solidity and sway and palpitate in the twilight of the room, as if nudity acted on it as a leaven and endowed it with a strange faculty of expansion; so that at one moment it seemed to billow outward in innumerable curves, at another to taper upwards to a giant height, and to fill the space between floor and ceiling.

Agostino's first impulse was to hurry away again, but suddenly that new thought, "It is a woman," rooted him to the spot, with wide-open eyes, holding fast to the door handle. He felt his filial soul rebel at this immobility and try to drag him back; but the new mind which was already strong in him, though still a little timid, forced his reluctant eyes to stare pitilessly at what yesterday he would not have dared to look upon. And during this conflict between repulsion and attraction, surprise and pleasure, all the details of the picture he was contemplating stood out more distinctly and forcibly: the movements of her legs, the indolent curve of her back, the profile of her armpits. And they seemed to correspond exactly to his new conception, which was awaiting these confirmations in order to take complete sway over his imagination. Precipitated in one moment from respect and reverence to their exact opposite, he would almost have liked to see the improprieties of her unconscious nudity develop before his eyes into conscious wantonness. The astonishment in his eyes changed to curiosity, the attention which riveted them and which he fancied to be scientific in reality owed its false objectivity to the cruelty of the sentiment controlling him. And while his blood surged up to his brain he kept saying to himself: "She is a woman, nothing but a woman," and he somehow felt these words to be lashes of insult and contempt on her back and legs.

When his mother had taken off her necklace and put it down on the marble top of the chest of drawers, she began with a graceful movement of both hands to remove her earrings. In order to do so she held her head slightly to one side, turning a little away from the glass. Agostino was afraid she might catch sight of him in the big standing mirror which was nearby in the bay window; for he could see himself in it, standing furtively there, just inside the folding door. He raised his hand with an effort, knocked at the doorpost and said: "May I come in?"

"One moment, darling," said his mother calmly. Agostino saw her disappear from sight and, after rummaging about for a while, reappear in a long blue silk dressing gown.

"Mamma," said Agostino, without lifting his eyes from the ground, "I am going down to the beach."

"Now?" said his mother, abstractedly "But it's so hot. Hadn't you better sleep a little first?" She put out one hand and stroked his cheek, while with the other she rearranged a stray lock of her smooth black hair.

Agostino suddenly became a child again, said nothing but remained standing, as he always did when any request of his had been refused, obstinately dumb, and looking down, his chin glued to his chest. His mother knew that gesture so well that she interpreted it in the usual way. "Well, if you really want to very much," she said, "go to the kitchen first and get them to give you something to take with you. But don't eat it now . . . put it in the cabin . . . and mind you don't bathe before five o'clock. Besides, I shall be out by then and we'll swim together." They were the same instructions she always gave him.

Agostino made no reply, and ran barefooted down the stone stairs. He heard his mother's door close gently behind him. He put on his sandals in the hall and went out on to the road. The white blaze of the midday sun enveloped him in its silent furnace. At the end of the road the motionless sea sparkled in the remote, quivering atmosphere. In the opposite direction the red trunks of the pine trees bent under the weight of their heavy green cones.

He debated with himself whether to go to the Vespucci Baths by the beach or by the forest; but chose the former, for though he would be much more exposed to the sun he would be in no danger of passing the baths without seeing them. He followed the road as long as it ran by the sea, then hurried along as fast as he could, keeping close to the walls. Without his realizing it, what attracted him to the Vespucci, apart from the novel companionship of the boys, were their coarse comments on his mother and her supposed amours. He was conscious that his former disposition was changing into quite a different feeling, crueller and more objective, and he thought that their clumsy ironies, by the very fact that they hastened this change, ought to be sought out and cultivated. Why he so much wanted to stop loving his mother, why he even hated himself for loving her, he would have been unable to say. Perhaps because he felt he had been deceived and had thought her to be different from what she really was, or perhaps because, not being able to go on loving her simply and innocently as he had done before, he preferred to stop loving her altogether and to look on her merely as an ordinary woman. He was instinctively trying to free himself once and for all from the encumbrance of his old, innocent love which he felt to have been shamefully betrayed; for now it seemed to him mere foolishness and ignorance. And so the same cruel attraction which a few minutes ago had kept his eyes fixed on his mother's back now drove him to seek out the humiliating and coarse companionship of those boys. Might not their scoffing remarks, like her half-revealed nakedness, help to destroy the old filial relationship which was now so hateful to him? When he came within sight of the baths he slowed down, and though his heart was beating violently so that he could hardly breathe, he assumed an air of indifference.

Saro was sitting as before at his rickety table, on which were a half-empty bottle of wine, a glass, and a bowl containing the remains of fish soup. But there seemed to be no one else about, though as he got nearer the curtain opened and he saw the black body of the Negro boy Homs lying on the white sand.

Saro took no notice at all of the Negro, but went on smoking meditatively, a dilapidated old straw hat rammed down over one eye. "Aren't they here?" asked Agostino in a tone of disappointment. Saro looked up and observed him for a moment, then said: "They've gone to Rio." Rio was a deserted part of the shore, a few kilometers further on, where a stream ran into the sea between sandbanks and reeds.

"Oh dear," said Agostino regretfully, "they've gone to Rio . . . what for?"

It was the Negro who replied. "They've gone to have a picnic there," and he put his hand to his mouth with an expressive gesture.

But Saro shook his head and said: "You boys won't be happy till someone's put a bullet through you." It was clear that their picnic was only a pretext for stealing fruit in the orchards; at least, so it seemed to Agostino.

"I didn't go with them," put in the Negro obsequiously, as if to ingratiate himself with Saro.

"You didn't go because you didn't want to," said Saro calmly.

The Negro rolled in the sand, protesting: "I didn't go because I wanted to stay with you."

He spoke in a honeyed, singsong voice. Saro said contemptuously: "Who gave you permission to be so familiar, you little nigger? We're not brothers as far as I know."

"No, we're not brothers," said the other in an unruffled, even triumphant tone, as if the observation gave him profound satisfaction.

"You keep your place then," said Saro. Then, turning to Agostino: "They've gone to steal some corn. That's what their picnic'll be."

"Are they coming back?" asked Agostino anxiously. Saro said nothing but kept looking at Agostino and seemed to be turning something over in his mind. "They won't be back very soon," he replied slowly; "not till late. But if you like we'll go after them."

"But how?"

"In the boat," said Saro.

"Oh yes, let's go in the boat," said the Negro. He sprang up, all eagerness, and approached Saro, but the latter did not give him a glance.

"I have a sailboat . . . in about half an hour we shall be at Rio, if the wind's favorable."

"Yes, let's go," said Agostino happily. "But it they're in the fields how shall we find them?"

"Never you fear," said Saro, getting up and giving a twist to the black sash round his stomach. "We shall find them all right." Then he turned to the Negro, who was watching him anxiously, and added: "Come on, nigger, help me carry down the sail and mast."

"I'm coming, Saro, I'm coming," reiterated the jubilant Negro, and he followed Saro down to the boat.

Left by himself Agostino stood up and looked round him. A light wind had sprung up from the northwest, and the sea, covered now with tiny wavelets, had changed to an almost violet blue. The shore was enveloped in a haze of sun and sand, as far as the eye could see. Agostino, who did not know where Rio was, followed with a nostalgic eye the capricious indentations of the lonely coast line. Where was Rio? Somewhere out there, he supposed, where earth, sky and sea were mingled in one confused blackness under the pitiless sun. He looked forward intensely to the expedition, and would not have missed it for worlds.

He was startled from these reflections by the voices of the two coming out of the hut. Saro was carrying on one arm a pile of ropes and sails, while in the other he hugged a bottle. Behind him walked the Negro, brandishing like a spear a tall mast partly painted green. "Well, let's be off," said Saro, starting down the beach without glancing at Agostino. His manner seemed to Agostino curiously hurried, quite different from his usual one. He also noticed that those repulsive red nostrils looked redder and more inflamed than usual, as if all their network of little branching veins had suddenly become swollen with an inrush of blood. "*Si va . . . si va . . .*" intoned the Negro behind Saro, improvising a sort of dance on the sand, with the mast under his arm. But Saro had nearly reached the huts and the Negro slackened his pace to wait for Agostino. When he was near, the Negro signaled him to stop. Agostino did so.

"Listen," said the Negro, with an air of familiarity. "I've got to talk something over with Saro . . . please oblige . . . please . . . by not coming. Go away, please!"

"Why?" asked Agostino, much surprised.

"I told you I've got to talk something over with him . . . just the two of us," said the other impatiently, stamping his foot on the ground.

"I *must* go to Rio," replied Agostino

"You can go another time."

"No — I can't."

The Negro looked at him, and his eyes and trembling nostrils betrayed a passionate eagerness which revolted Agostino. "Listen,

Pisa," he said, "if you'll stay behind I'll give you something you've never seen before." He dropped the mast and felt in his pocket and brought out a slingshot made of a fork of pinewood and two elastics bound together. "It's lovely, isn't it," and the Negro held it up.

But Agostino wanted to go to Rio. Besides, the Negro's insistence aroused his suspicions. "No, I can't," he said.

"Take it," the other said again, feeling for Agostino's hand and trying to force the slingshot into his palm. "Take it and go away."

"No," repeated Agostino, "I can't."

"I'll give you the slingshot and these cards, too," said the Negro, feeling in his pocket again; and he drew out a small pack of cards with pink backs and gilt edges. "Take them all and go away. You can kill birds with the slingshot . . . the cards are quite new."

"I told you I won't," said Agostino.

The Negro turned on him an eye of passionate entreaty. Great drops of sweat shone on his forehead, his whole face was contorted in an expression of utter misery. "But why won't you?" he whined.

"I don't want to," said Agostino, and he suddenly ran towards the bath man, who was now standing by the boat. As he reached Saro he heard the Negro call after him: "You'll be sorry for this." The boat was resting on two rollers of unplaned fir a short way up the beach. Saro had thrown the sails into the boat and seemed to be waiting impatiently. "What's he up to?" he asked Agostino, pointing to the Negro.

"He's just coming," said Agostino.

And in fact the Negro came running over the sand with great leaps, holding the mast under his arm. Saro took hold of the mast with the six fingers of his right hand, and with the six fingers of his left reared it up and planted it in a hole in the middle seat. Then he got into the boat, fastened the sail and loosened the sheet. Saro turned to the Negro and said: "Now let's shove off from underneath."

Saro stood beside the boat, grasping the edges of the prow, while the Negro made ready to push from behind. Agostino, not knowing what to do, looked on. The boat was of medium size, part white and part green. On the prow, in black lettering, was written *Amelia*. "*Ah . . . issa*," commanded Saro. The boat slid forward on its rollers over the sand. As soon as the keel passed over the hindmost roller the Negro bent down and took it in his arms, pressing it to his breast like a baby; then leaping over the sand as in a novel kind of ballet, he ran and placed it under the prow. "*Ah . . . issa,*" repeated Saro.

The boat slid forward again quite a distance, and again the Negro gamboled and caracoled from stern to prow, with the roller in his arms; one last shove, and the prow of the boat dipped into the water and it was afloat. Saro got in and placed the oars in the rowlocks; then, grasping one in each hand, he motioned to Agostino to jump in, excluding the Negro as if by prearrangement. Agostino entered the water up to his knees and tried to climb in. He would never have succeeded had not the six fingers of Saro's right hand seized him firmly by one arm and pulled him up like a cat. He looked up. Saro was lifting him with one arm, without looking in the direction, for he was busy adjusting the left-hand oar. Agostino, in disgust at being grasped by those fingers, went off and sat in the stern. "Good," said Saro, "you stay there; now we are going to take her out."

"Wait for me, I'm coming too!" shouted the Negro from the shore. Exhausted by his efforts he sprang into the water and seized the edge of the boat. But Saro said: "No, you're not coming."

"What am I to do?" cried the boy, in an agony of disappointment. "What am I to do?"

"You can take the trolley," answered Saro, standing up in the boat and pulling hard. "You'll get there before us, see if you don't."

"But why, Saro?" wailed the Negro, thrashing along in the water beside the boat. "Why, Saro? I want to go too."

Without a word Saro dropped his oars, bent over and covered the Negro's face with his enormous hand. "I've told you you're not coming," he said quietly, and with one push sent the Negro over backward in the water. "Why, Saro?" he went on wailing. "Why, Saro?" and his melancholy voice, mingled with the splashing of the oars, made an unpleasant impression on Agostino and aroused in him an uneasy sense of pity. He looked at Saro, who smiled and said: "He's such a nuisance. What do we want with him?"

The boat was already some way from the shore. Agostino looked round and saw the Negro get out of the water and, as he thought, shake his fist threateningly at him.

Saro silently took out the oars and laid them down in the bottom of the boat. Then he went to the prow, undid the sail and fastened it to the mast. The sail fluttered uncertainly for a moment, as if the wind were blowing on both sides of it at once; then suddenly, with a violent shock swelled in the wind and leaned over to the left. The boat obediently settled down on its left side too, and began to skim over the waves, driven by the light breeze. "Good," said Saro, "now we can lie down and rest a bit." He settled down in the bottom of the boat and invited Agostino to lie beside him. "If we sit in the bottom," he explained, "the boat goes faster." Agostino obeyed, and lay down beside Saro.

The boat made swift progress in spite of its heavy build, rising and falling with the little waves and occasionally rearing up like a foal which feels the bit for the first time. Saro lay with his head resting against the seat, and one arm behind Agostino's neck, controlling the rudder. For a while he said nothing; then: "Do you go to school?" he asked at last.

Agostino looked up. Saro was half-lying and seemed to be exposing his wide, inflamed nostrils to the sea air, as if to refresh them. His mouth was open under his mustache, his eyes half-shut. His unbuttoned shirt revealed the dirty, grey, ruffled hair on his chest. "Yes," said Agostino, suddenly trembling with fear.

"What class are you in?"

"The third."

"Give me your hand," said Saro; and before Agostino could refuse he seized hold of it. To Agostino his grasp felt like a vice. The six short, stumpy fingers encircled his whole hand and met below it. "What do they teach you?" Saro went on, stretching himself out more comfortably and sinking into a kind of ecstasy.

"Latin . . . Italian . . . geography . . . history . . ." stammered Agostino.

"Do they teach you poetry . . . lovely poetry?" asked Saro, in a low voice.

"Yes," said Agostino, "poetry as well."

"Recite some to me."

The boat plunged, and Saro shifted the rudder without changing his beatific attitude. "I don't know what . . ." began Agostino, feeling more and more embarrassed and frightened. "I learn a lot of poetry . . . Carducci . . ."

"Ah yes, Carducci," repeated Saro mechanically. "Say a poem by Carducci."

"*Le fonti del Clitunno*," suggested Agostino, terrified by that hand which would not let him go, and trying little by little to escape from it.

"Yes, *Le fonti del Clitunno*," said Saro in a dreamy voice.

Ancor dal monte che di foschi ondeggia
frassini al vento mormoranti e lunge

began Agostino in a shaky voice.

The boat sped on, and Saro, still stretched at full length with closed eyes and his nose to the wind, began to move his head up and down as if scanning the lines. Agostino clung to poetry as the only means of escape from a conversation which he intuitively felt to be dangerous and compromising, and went on reciting slowly and clearly. Meanwhile, he kept trying to release his hand from those six imprisoning fingers; but they held him more tightly than ever. With terror he saw the end of the poem drawing near, and not knowing what to do he joined the first line of *Davanti a San Guido* on to the last line of *Fonti del Clitunno*. Here would be proof, if any were needed, that Saro didn't care a bit about the poetry but had something quite different in view; *what*, Agostino could not understand. The experiment succeeded. "*I cipressi che a Bolgheri alti e schietti*" suddenly began without Saro giving the faintest sign of noticing the change. Then Agostino broke off and said in an exasperated voice: "Let go, please," and tried at the same time to pull his hand quite away.

Saro started, and without letting go of him, opened his eyes and turned to look at him. He must have read such violent antipathy and such obvious terror on Agostino's face that he suddenly realized that his plan, for he certainly had a plan, was a complete failure. He slowly withdrew one finger after another from Agostino's aching hand and said in a low voice, as if speaking to himself: "What are you afraid of? We're going ashore now."

He dragged himself to his feet and pulled round the rudder. The boat turned its prow towards the shore.

Still rubbing his cramped fingers, Agostino got up from the bottom of the boat without a word and went to sit in the prow. By now the boat was not far from the shore. He could see the whole beach, the white stretch of sunbleached sand which at that point was very wide, and beyond the beach the dense, brooding green of the pines. Rio was at a gap cut in the high dunes, overhung by a greenish-blue mass of reeds. But before they got to Rio, Agostino saw a group of people on the beach, and from the center of this group there rose a long thread of black smoke. He turned to Saro, who was sitting in the stern controlling the rudder with one hand. "Is this where we get out?"

"Yes, this is Rio," replied Saro indifferently.

As the boat drew nearer and nearer to the shore Agostino saw the group gathered round the fire suddenly break up and start running down to the water's edge, and he at once saw that it was the boys. He could see them waving and probably calling out, but the wind carried their voices away. "Is it them?" he asked nervously.

"Yes, it's them," said Saro.

The boat drew nearer still and Agostino could clearly distinguish the boys. They were all there: Tortima, Berto, Sandro, and the others. And there was the Negro Homs, leaping along the shore and shouting with the others, a discovery which for some reason gave him a very uncomfortable feeling.

The boat made straight for the shore where with a rapid turn of the rudder, Saro brought it crosswise, and throwing himself upon the sail clasped it in both arms and lowered it to the deck. The boat swung motionless in the shallow water. Saro took a small anchor from the bottom and threw it into the water. "Let's go ashore," he said. He climbed over the edge of the boat and waded through the water to meet the boys who were waiting on the beach.

Agostino saw the boys crowding around him and apparently offering him congratulations, which Saro received with a shake of his head. Still louder applause greeted his own arrival, and for a moment he was deceived into thinking they were welcoming him cordially. But he soon realized he was mistaken. Their laughter was mocking and sarcastic. Berto called out: "Good old Pisa, he enjoys going out for a sail," while Tortima, putting his fingers into his mouth, gave a rude whistle. The others imitated him. Even Sandro, usually so reserved, looked at him with contempt. As for the Negro, he did nothing but jump about around Saro, who went on ahead towards the fire the boys had lit on the beach. Surprised and vaguely alarmed, Agostino went and sat down among the others around the fire.

The boys had made a sort of rough oven out of damp compressed sand. Inside was a fire of dried pine cones, pine needles and twigs. Heaped up in the mouth of the oven were about a dozen ears of corn, slowly roasting. Spread out on a newspaper near the fire were masses of fruit and a watermelon. "He's a fine one, is our Pisa," said Berto, when they had sat down. "You and Homs are buddies now, you ought to be sitting together . . . you're brothers, you two; he's black, you're white . . . that's all there is to it . . . and you both like going for a sail."

The Negro chuckled appreciatively. Saro was bending down to give the corncobs another turn in front of the fire. The others laughed derisively. Berto went so far as to give Agostino a push which sent him against Homs, so that for a moment their backs were touching; one chuckling with depraved self-satisfaction, the other bewildered and disgusted. "But I don't know what you mean," said Agostino suddenly. "I went out in the boat; what harm is there in that?"

"Aha, what harm is there in that? He went out in the boat. What harm is there in that?" repeated many scoffing voices. Some were holding their sides with laughter.

"Yes, indeed, what harm?" repeated Berto, turning to him again. "No harm at all! Why Homs thinks it's grand, don't you Homs?"

The Negro assented ecstatically. And now the truth began dimly to dawn on Agostino, for he couldn't help seeing some connection between their taunts and Saro's odd behavior in the boat. "I don't know what you mean," he declared. "I didn't do anything wrong in that boat. Saro made me recite some poems, that's all."

"Ah, ah, those poems," was heard on all sides.

"Isn't it true what I say, Saro?" cried Agostino, red in the face.

Saro didn't say yes or no; he contented himself with smiling, watching him all the while with a certain curiosity. The boys interpreted his air of pretended indifference, which was really a cloak for his treachery and vanity, as giving the lie to Agostino. "Oh, of course," they all struck up together: "He asks the host if the wine is good, eh, Saro? That's a good one! Oh, Pisa, Pisa!" The Negro was having his revenge, and enjoying himself particularly. Agostino suddenly turned on him, trembling with rage, and said: "What is there to laugh at?"

"I'm not laughing," he replied, edging away.

"Now, don't you two quarrel," said Berto. "Saro will have to see about making you friends again." But the boys lost all interest when the issue seemed to be settling itself peacefully, and were already talking of other things. They were telling how they had crept into a field and stolen the corn and fruit; how they had seen the enraged farmer coming towards them with a gun; how they had run away, and the farmer had fired salt at them without hitting anyone. Meanwhile, the ears were ready, beautifully toasted on the embers. Saro took them out of the oven and with his usual fatherly air parceled out one to each. Agostino took advantage of a moment when they were busy eating, and sprang across to Sandro, who was sitting a little apart, eating his corn grain by grain.

"I don't understand," he began. The other gave him a knowing look and Agostino felt he need say no more. "The Moor came by trolley," said Sandro slowly, "and he said you and Saro had gone sailing."

"But what harm is there in that?"

"It's no business of mine," replied Sandro, casting down his eyes. "It's up to you . . . you and the Moor. But as for Saro," he stopped and looked at Agostino.

"Well?"

"Well, I wouldn't have gone out alone with Saro."

"But why?"

Sandro looked carefully round him, then in a low voice gave the explanation which Agostino somehow expected, without being able to say why. "Ah," he said . . . but he could say no more and went back to the others. Squatting in the middle of the boys, with his imperturbable, good-natured head on one side, Saro had the air of a kind paterfamilias surrounded by his sons. But Agostino felt a deep loathing when he looked at him, greater in fact than he felt for the Negro. What made Agostino hate him more was his silence when appealed to, as if he wanted the boys to believe that what they had accused him of had really taken place. Besides, he could not help noticing that their scorn and derision had set a wide gulf between him and his companions — the same gulf which he now realized separated them from the Negro; only the Negro, instead of being humiliated and offended, as he himself was, seemed somehow to relish it. He tried more than once to turn the conversation on to the subject which so tormented him, but was met with laughter and an insulting indifference. Moreover, in spite of Sandro's only too clear explanation, he still could not quite grasp what had really happened. Everything seemed dark around him and within him, as if instead of beach, sea and sky, there were only shadows and vague, menacing forms.

Meanwhile, the boys had finished eating their roasted corn and tossed the bare cobs away in the sand. "Let's go swim at Rio," suggested someone, and the proposal was immediately accepted. Saro went with them, for it was agreed that he should take them all back to Vespucci in the boat.

As they walked along the sand Sandro left the others and came over to Agostino. "If you're offended with the Moor," he said, "why don't you put the fear of God into him?"

"How?" asked Agostino, in a discouraged tone.

"Give him a good hiding."

"But he's stronger than me," said Agostino, remembering the duel of the iron arm. "Unless you will help me."

"Why should I help you? It's your concern . . . yours and his." Sandro pronounced these words in such a way as to make it quite clear that he took the same view as the others as to the reason for Agostino's hatred of the Negro. A sense of terrible bitterness pierced Agostino to the heart. So Sandro, the only one who had shown him any kindness, believed that calumny too. After giving him this advice Sandro went off to rejoin the others, as if he were afraid of being seen with Agostino. From the beach they had passed through a forest of young pines; then they crossed sandy path and entered the reed beds. The reeds grew thick and tall, and many had a white, plumy crest; the boys appeared and disappeared between their long green spears, slipping about on the damp earth and pushing the stiff, fibrous leaves aside with a dry, rustling sound. At last they came to a place where the reed bed widened around a low, muddy bank, at sight of them big frogs leaped from all sides into the opaque, glassy water; and here they began to undress, all together, under the eyes of Saro, who sat fully clothed on a rock overlooking the reeds, and appeared to be absorbed in his cigar, but was really watching them all the time through his half-closed eyelids. Agostino was ashamed to join them, but he was so afraid of being laughed at that he too began to unbutton his trousers, taking as long as he could about it and keeping an eye on the others. The rest seemed to be overjoyed at getting rid of their clothes, and bumped into each other shouting with glee. They looked very white against the background of green reeds, with an unpleasant, squalid whiteness from groin to belly, and this pallor only emphasized a sort of graceless and excessive muscularity which is especially to be found in manual workers. The graceful, well-proportioned Sandro, whose pubic hair was as fair as that of his head, was the only one who hardly seemed to be naked, perhaps because his skin was equally bronzed over his whole body; in any case his nakedness was quite different from that repulsive nakedness displayed in the public baths.

Before diving in the boys played all sorts of obscene pranks; opening their legs wide, poking and touching each other with a loose promiscuity which astounded Agostino, to whom this sort of thing was quite new. He was naked too, and his feet were black from the cold, filthy mud, but he would have liked to have hidden himself in the reeds, if only to escape the looks which Saro, who sat hunched up motionless like one of those huge frogs native to the reed bed, darted at him through half-closed eyes. But as usual his repugnance was less strong than the mysterious attraction which bound him to the gang; the two were so indissolubly mixed up together that it was impossible for him to distinguish between his horror and the pleasure which underlay it. The boys displayed themselves each in turn, boasting of their virility and bodily prowess. Tortima, the vainest of all, and in spite of his disproportionate strength the most squalid and plebeian looking, was so elated as to call out to Agostino: "Suppose I was to appear before your mother, one fine morning, naked like this, what would she say? Would she go along with me?"

"No," said Agostino.

"And I tell you that she'd come along at once," said Tortima. "She'd just give me one good look over, to see what I was good for, and then she'd say: 'Come along, Tortima, let's be off'" The gross absurdity of his suggestion made them all laugh, and at his cry: 'Come, Tortima let's be off!' they flung themselves one after another into the water, diving in head over heels, just like the frogs whom their coming had disturbed.

The shore was so entirely surrounded by reeds that only a short stretch of the river was visible. But when they got into the middle of the stream they could see the whole river which, with an imperceptible motion of its dark, dense waters, flowed toward the mouth further down among the sandbanks. Up-stream the river continued between two lines of large silvery bushes which cast delightful reflections in the water; till one came to a little iron bridge, beyond which the reeds, pines and poplars were so dense as to prevent further passage. A red house, half-hidden among the trees, seemed to keep guard over this bridge.

For a moment Agostino felt happy, as he swam in that cold, powerful water which seemed to be trying to bear his legs away with it; he forgot for a moment all his wrongs and crosses. The boys swam about in all directions, their heads and arms emerging from the smooth green surface. Their voices resounded in the limpid, windless air; seen through the transparency of the water their bodies might have been the white shoots of plants blossoming out of the depths and moving hither and yon as the current drew them. Agostino swam up to Berto, who was not far off, and asked: "Are there many fish in this river?"

Berto looked at him and said: "What are you doing here? Why don't you keep Saro company?"

"I like swimming," replied Agostino, feeling miserable again; and he turned and swam away.

But he was not so strong or experienced a swimmer as the others; he soon got tired, and let the current carry him towards the mouth of the river. He had soon left the boys and their clamor behind him; the reeds grew thinner; through the clear, colorless water he could see the sandy bottom over which grey eddies flowed continually. At last he came to a deeper green pool, the stream's transparent eye as it were; and when he had passed this his feet touched the sand, and after struggling a moment against the force of the water he climbed out on to the bank. Where the stream flowed into the sea it curled round itself and formed a knot of water. The stream then lost its compactness and spread out fanwise, growing thinner and thinner till it was no more than a liquid veil thrown over the smooth sands. The tide flowed up into the river with tiny foam-flecked wavelets. Here and there in the watery sand, pools forgotten by the stream reflected the bright sky. Agostino walked about for a little, naked on the soft, mirroring sand, and enjoyed stamping on it with his feet and seeing the water suddenly rise to the surface and flood his footprints. There arose in him a vague and desperate desire to ford the river and walk on and on down the coast, leaving far behind him the boys, Saro, his mother and all the old life. Who knows whether, if he were to go straight ahead and never turn back, walking, walking on that soft white sand, he might not at last come to a country where none of these horrible things existed; a country where he would be welcomed as he longed to be, and where it would be possible for him to forget all he had learned and then learn it again without all that shame and horror, gently and naturally as he dimly felt that it might be possible. He gazed at the dark, remote horizon which enclosed the utmost boundaries of sea and shore and forest and felt drawn to the immensity as to something which might set him free from his bondage. The shouts of the boys racing across the shore to the boat roused him from his melancholy imaginings. One of them was waving his clothes in the air, and Berto was calling: "Pisa, we're off!" He shook himself and walked along at the edge of the sea to join the gang.

The boys were thronging together in the shallow water. Saro was warning them in fatherly tones that the boat was too small to hold them all, but he was clearly only teasing them. Screaming, the boys flung themselves like mad upon the boat; twenty hands at once clutched the sides, and in a twinkling the boat was filled with their gesticulating bodies. Some lay down on the bottom, others sat in a heap in the stern around the rudder, some in the prow, others on the seats; others again sat on the edge and let their feet dangle in the water. The boat really was too small for so many, and the water came almost to the top.

"We're all here then, are we?" said Saro in great good humor. He stood up, let out the sail, and the boat sped out to sea. The boys cheered its departure loudly.

But Agostino did not share their happy mood. He was looking out for a favorable opportunity to prove his innocence and remove the unjust stigma which oppressed him. He took advantage of a moment when the other boys were deep in some discussion, to scramble up to the Negro who was sitting alone in the bow and resembled in his blackness a new kind of figurehead. Squeezing one arm hard, Agostino demanded: "What did you go and say about me just now?"

It was a bad moment to choose, but it was Agostino's first opportunity of getting near the Negro who had taken good care to keep at a distance while they were on shore. "I spoke the truth," said Homs, without looking at him.

"What is the truth?"

The Negro's reply terrified Agostino. "It's no good your squeezing my arm like that. I only spoke the truth. But if you go on setting Saro against me I shall tell your mother everything. So look out, Pisa."

"What!" cried Agostino, seeing an abyss open beneath his feet. "What do you mean? Are you crazy? I . . . I . . ." He stammered, unable to follow up in words the frightful vision his imagination suddenly summoned up. But he had no time to continue. Shouts of derision broke out all over the boat.

"Look at them both side by side," laughed Berto. "Look at them! What a shame we haven't got a camera to take them both together." Agostino turned round, his face burning, and saw them all laughing. Even Saro was smiling under his mustache, as with half-closed eyes he puffed at his cigar. Agostino drew back from the Negro, as from the touch of a reptile, and with his arms around his knees sat watching the sea, his eyes full of tears.

On the horizon the sun was setting in clouds of fire above a violet sea, shot with pointed, glassy rays. The wind had risen and the boat made slow progress, listing heavily to one side under its load of boys. The prow of the boat was turned out to sea and seemed to be directed towards the dark profiles of far-off islands which rose among the red smoke of sunset like mountains at the end of a distant plateau. Saro, holding firmly between his knees the boys' stolen watermelon, split it open with his seaman's knife and cut off large slices which he distributed to them paternally. They passed the slices and bit into them greedily, spitting out the seeds and tearing off pieces of the flesh. Then one after another the sections of red, close-gnawed rind flew overboard into the sea. After the melon it was the turn of the white flask, which Saro solemnly produced from under the stern. The bottle made the round of the boat, and even Agostino was obliged to swallow a mouthful. It was warm and strong and at once went to his head. When the empty bottle had returned to its place Tortima sang an indecent song, and they all joined in the refrain. Between verses they pressed Agostino to sing too, for they had noticed his black mood; but no one spoke to him except to tease him and incite him to sing. Agostino felt within him a heavy weight of pent-up grief which the windy sea and magnificent fires of sunset on the violet waters only made more bitter and unbearable. It seemed to him horribly unjust that it was on such a sea and under such a sky that a boat like theirs should be sailing, so crowded with malice, cruelty, falsehood and corruption. That boat, overflowing with boys gesticulating like obscene monkeys, with the fat and blissful Saro at the helm, was to him an incredible and melancholy sight in the midst of all that beauty. At moments he wished it would sink; he would have liked to die himself, he thought, and no longer be infected and stained by all that impurity. How far away seemed the morning when he had for the first time looked upon the red awning of the Vespucci Baths; far away and belonging to an age already dead. Each time the boat rose on an unusually high wave they gave a yell which made him shudder; each time the Negro addressed him with his revolting and hypocritically slavish humility, he tried not to listen and drew back still further into the prow. He was dimly conscious of having on that fatal day entered upon an age of difficulties and miseries from which he could see no way of escape. The boat made a long trip, going as far as the port and then turning back again. When they at last touched land Agostino ran off without saying good-bye to anyone. But he had not gone far before he slackened his pace and looking back saw the boys helping Saro to pull the boat up on the beach. It was already getting dark.

4

THAT DAY WAS THE BEGINNING of a dark and troubled time for Agostino. On that day his eyes had been opened for him by force, but what he had learned was too much for him, a burden greater than he could bear. It was not so much their novelty as the quality of the things he had learned which oppressed and poisoned him; they were too appalling and too portentous for him to assimilate. He thought, for example, that after that day's disclosures about his mother his relations with her would have become clarified; that the uneasiness, distaste and even disgust which, after Saro's revelations, her caresses awoke in him would somehow, as if by enchantment, be resolved and reconciled in a new and serene consciousness. But it was not so; the uneasiness, distaste and disgust remained, rising in the first instance from the shock and bewilderment to his filial love occasioned by his obscure realization of his mother's femininity, and after that morning in Saro's tent rising from a bitter sense of guilty curiosity which his traditional and abiding respect for his mother rendered intolerable to him. At first he had unconsciously tried to break loose from that affection by an unjustified dislike, but now it seemed to him a duty to separate his newly won reasoned knowledge from his sense of blood relationship with someone whom he wanted to consider only as a woman. He felt that if only he could see in his mother what Saro and the boys did — just a beautiful woman — then all his unhappiness would disappear; and he tried with all his might to seek out occasions which would confirm him in this belief. But the only result was that his former reverence and affection gave place to cruelty and sensuality.

At home his mother did not hide herself from him any more than she had before, and was unaware of any change in his attitude towards her. As his mother, she had no sense of shame; but to Agostino it seemed that she was wantonly provocative. He would hear her calling him, and would go to her room to find her at her toilet, in her negligee and with her breasts half-uncovered. Or he would wake to find her bending over him to give him his morning kiss, with her dressing gown open so that he could clearly see the shape of her body through her fragile, crumpled nightgown. She would go to and fro in front of him as if he were not there; putting on or taking off her stockings, putting on her clothes, applying perfume or make-up; and all those acts which Agostino had once thought so natural now seemed to him the outward and visible signs of a much more embracing and more dangerous reality, so that his mind was torn between curiosity and pain. He kept saying to himself: "She's only a woman," with the objective indifference of a connoisseur. But a moment later, unable to endure either her maternal unselfconsciousness or his own watchfulness, he would have liked to shout: "Cover yourself up, go away, don't let me see you any more, I'm not the same as I used to be." But his hope of judging his mother as a woman and nothing more almost immediately suffered shipwreck. He soon saw that even if she had become a woman she remained in his eyes all the more his mother; and he realized that the cruel sense of shame which he had at first attributed to the novelty of his feelings would now never leave him. He saw in a flash that she would always remain for him the person he had loved with such a free and pure love; she would always mix with her most feminine gestures those purely affectionate ones which for so long had been the only ones he knew; never would he be able to separate his new conception of her from his now wounded memory of her former dignity. He did not for a moment doubt that the facts of her relationship with the young man really were as reported by the boys in Saro's tent. And he wondered secretly at the change which had taken place in him. At first he had only felt jealously of his mother and antipathy towards the young man; both feelings being rather veiled and indefinite. But now, in his effort to remain objective and calm, he would have wished to feel sympathy for the young man and indifference towards his mother. But this sympathy seemed somehow to make him an accomplice, and his indifference to make him indiscreet. He very seldom went out with them now on the raft, for he generally contrived to avoid being invited. But whenever he went he was conscious of studying the young man's gestures and words almost as if he wanted him to overstep the limits of permitted social gallantry, and of studying his mother almost in the hope of having his suspicions confirmed. At the same time these sentiments were intolerable to him because they were the exact opposite of what he wanted to feel, and he would almost have liked to feel again the pity which his mother's foolish behavior had once aroused in him; it was more human and affectionate than his present mercilous dissection.

Those days of inner conflict left him with a confused sense of impurity. He felt that he had exchanged his former state of innocence, not for the manly calm he had hoped for, but a dark, indeterminate state in which he found no compensating advantages, but only fresh perplexities in addition to the old. What was the good of seeing clearly, if this clarity only brought with it deeper shades of darkness? Sometimes he wondered how older boys than himself managed to go on loving their mother when they knew what he knew; and he concluded that such knowledge must at once destroy their filial affection, whereas in his own case the one did not banish the other, but they existed side by side in a dreary tangle.

As sometimes happens, the place which was the scene of these discoveries and conflicts — his home — became almost intolerable to him. The sea, the sun, the crowd of bathers, the presence of many other women at least distracted him and deadened his sensibilities. But here, between the four walls of his home, alone with his mother, he felt exposed to every kind of temptation, beset by every kind of contradiction. On the beach his mother was one among many other sun bathers; here she seemed overpowering and unique. Just as on a small stage the actors seem larger than life, so here every gesture and word of hers stood out with extraordinary definition. Agostino had a very lively and adventurous sensibility in regard to the familiar things of his home. When he was a child every passage, every nook and corner, every room had had for him a mysterious and incalculable character; they were places in which you might make the strangest discoveries and live through the most fantastic adventures. But now, after his meeting with those boys in the red tent, these adventures and discoveries were of a quite different kind, so that he did not know whether to be more attracted or frightened by them. Formerly he used to imagine ambushes, shadows, spirits, voices in the furniture and in the walls; but now his fancy, even more actively than in his exuberant childhood, attached itself to the new realities with which the walls, the furniture, the very air of the house seemed to him to be impregnated. And in place of his old innocent excitement which his mother's good night kiss and dreamless sleep could always calm, he was tormented by a burning and shameful curiosity which at night grew to giant proportions and seemed to find in darkness more food for its impure fire.

Everywhere in the house he seemed to spy out traces of a woman's presence, the only woman whom he had ever known intimately; and that woman was his mother. When he was with her he felt as if he were somehow mounting guard over her; when he approached her door he felt he was spying on her; if he touched her clothes he felt as if it was herself he was touching, for she had worn these clothes, they had held her body. At night he dreamed with his eyes open, and had agonizing nightmares. He would sometimes imagine himself to be a child again, afraid of every sound, of every shadow, and would spring up to run and take refuge in his mother's bed; but as soon as his feet touched the ground he realized, sleepy and bewildered though he was, that his fear was only a cunning mask for curiosity and that directly he was in his mother's arms his nocturnal vision would reveal its true purpose. Or he would wake suddenly and wonder whether by chance the young man of the raft were there at that very moment in his mother's room on the other side of the wall. Certain sounds seemed to confirm his suspicion, others to contradict it; he would toss restlessly in bed for a while, and at last, without the smallest idea how he had got there, would find himself in the passage in his nightshirt, listening and spying outside his mother's room. Once he could not resist the temptation of going in without knocking, and he stood motionless in the middle of the room in the diffused moonlight which entered through the open window, his eyes fixed on the bed where he could distinguish his mother's black hair spread out over the pillow, and her long, softly rounded limbs. "Is that you, Agostino?" she asked, waking up. Without saying a word he turned and hurried back to his room.

His reluctance to remain alone with his mother drove him more and more to Vespucci. But here other torments awaited him, and made the place as odious to him as his home. The boys' attitude towards him after he had been out alone in the boat with Saro had not changed at all; it had in fact assumed a definite and final form, as if founded on an unshakable conviction. For he was the one who had accepted that signal and sinister favor from Saro; it was impossible to get that idea out of their minds. So that, in addition to the jealousy and contempt they had felt for him from the first on account of his being rich, was now added another source of contempt . . . his supposed depravity. And in the minds of those young savages the one seemed to justify the other, the one to grow out of the other. They seemed by their humiliating and cruel treatment of him to imply that he was rich and therefore naturally depraved. Agostino was quick to perceive the subtle relation between these two charges, and he dimly felt that they were making him pay for being different from them and superior to them. His social difference and superiority were expressed in his clothes and his talk about the luxury of his home, in his tastes and manner of speech; his moral difference and superiority impelled him to refute the charge of having had any such relations with Saro, and kept showing itself in open disgust at the boys' manners and habits. So at last, prompted by the humiliating position in which he found himself rather than exercising any definite choice of his own, he decided to be what they seemed to want him to be . . . that is, just like themselves. He began wearing his oldest and dirtiest clothes, to the great surprise of his mother, who noticed that he no longer took any pride in his appearance; he made a point of never mentioning his luxurious home, and he took an ostentatious pleasure in ways and habits which up to that time had disgusted him. But worst of all, and it needed a great effort to nerve himself to it, one day when they were making their usual jokes about his going out alone with Saro, he said that he was tired of denying it, and that what they accused him of had really happened, and that he didn't care whether they knew it or not. Saro was startled by these assertions, but perhaps from fear of exposing himself did not deny them. The boys were also very much surprised to hear him admitting the truth of gossip which had seemed to torment him so much before. He was so timid and shy that they would never have given him credit for so much courage, but they very soon began raining down questions on him as to what had really happened; and then he lost heart, got red in the face and refused to say another word. Naturally the boys interpreted his silence in their own way, as being due to shame and not, as it really was, to his ignorance and incapacity to invent. And the usual load of taunts and low jokes became heavier than ever.

But in spite of this breakdown he really had changed. Without being conscious of it himself, without really trying to, he had, by dint of spending so much time with the boys every day, ended by becoming very like them, and had lost his old tastes without really acquiring any new ones. More than once, in a mood of revolt against Vespucci, he had joined in the more innocent games at Speranza, seeking out his playmates of earlier in the summer. But how colorless and dull those nicely brought-up boys now seemed to him, how boring their regulation walks under the eye of parents or tutors, how insipid their school gossip, their stamp collections, books of adventure and such-like. The fact is that the company of the gang, their talk about women, their thieving expeditions in the orchards, even the acts of oppression and violence of which he had himself been a victim, had transformed him and made him intolerant of his former friendships. It was during this time that something happened which brought this home to him more strongly. One morning when he arrived late at Vespucci he found no one there. Saro was off on some business of his own, and there were no boys to be seen. He wandered gloomily to the water's edge and seated himself on a float. Suddenly, as he was watching the beach in the hope of seeing at least Saro come in sight, a man and a boy about two years younger than himself appeared. He was a small man, with short, fat legs under a protruding stomach, a round face and pointed nose confined by pince-nez. He looked like a civil servant or professor. The boy was thin and pale, in a suit too big for him, and was hugging a large and evidently new leather ball to his chest. Holding his son by the hand, the man came up to Agostino and looked at him doubtfully for some time. At last he asked if it was possible to go for a row.

"Of course," replied Agostino, without hesitation.

The man considered him rather suspiciously over the top of his glasses, then asked how much it would cost to go out for an hour on a bathing raft. Agostino knew the prices and told him. Then he realized that the man had mistaken him for the bath man's son or for one of his boys, and that somehow flattered him. "Very well," said the man, "we will go."

Agostino didn't need telling twice. He at once took the rough pine log which served as roller, and placed it under the prow of the boat. Then, grasping the ends of the two floats in both hands, his strength redoubled by this singular spur to his pride, he pushed the raft into the water. He helped the boy and his father to get on, sprang after them and seized the oars.

For a while Agostino rowed without speaking. At that early hour the sea was quite empty. The boy hugged his ball to his chest and kept his pale eyes fixed on Agostino. The man sat awkwardly, with knees apart to make room for his paunch. He kept turning his fat neck to look about him, and seemed to be enjoying the outing. At last he asked Agostino who he was, the bath man's son, or employed by him. Agostino replied that he was employed by him. "And how old are you?" asked the man.

"Thirteen," replied Agostino.

"There," said the man, turning to his son, "this boy is almost the same age as you, and he's already at work." Then to Agostino: "And do you go to school?"

"I should like to, but how can I, sir?" he answered, assuming the hypocritical tone which he had heard the boys put on when asked a question like that. "We've got to live, sir."

"There, you see," said the father to his son. "This boy can't go to school because he has to work, and you have the face to make a fuss about your lessons."

"There's a lot of us in the family," said Agostino, rowing vigorously, "and we all work."

"And how much can you earn a day?" asked the man.

"It depends," replied Agostino. "If many people come, about twenty or thirty lire."

"Which of course you give to your father," interposed the man.

"Of course," replied Agostino, without a moment's hesitation, "except what I make in tips."

This time the man didn't think it necessary to point him out as an example to his son, but he nodded his head approvingly. His son said nothing, but hugged his ball still closer and kept his pale, watery eyes fixed on Agostino. "Would you like to have a leather ball like that, boy?" the man suddenly asked Agostino. Now Agostino had two identical balls, which had been lying about for a long time in his room with his other toys. But he said: "Of course I should, but how am I to get one? We have to buy necessities first." The man turned to his son and said to him, probably half in fun: "There now, Peter, give your ball to this boy who hasn't got one." The boy looked first at his father and then at Agostino, and greedily hugged his ball tighter; but still he didn't say a word. "Don't you want to?" asked his father gently. "Don't you want to?"

"It's my ball," said the boy.

"Yes, it's yours, but if you like you may give it away," persisted the father. "This poor boy has never had one in all his life; now, don't you want to give it up to him?"

"No," said his son emphatically.

"Never mind," interposed Agostino at this point, with a sanctimonious smile, "I don't really want it. I shouldn't have time to play with it . . . it's different for him."

The father smiled at these words, please at having found such a useful object lesson for his son. "He's a better boy than you," he went on, stroking his son's head. "He's poor, but he doesn't want to take away your ball, he leaves it to you; but whenever you want to grumble and make a fuss, I hope you'll remember that there are lots of boys like this in the world, who have to work, and who have never had balls or any toys of their own."

"It's my ball," repeated the boy obstinately.

"Yes, it's yours," sighed the father, absent-mindedly. He looked at his watch and said in a tone of command: "It's time we went back; take us in, boy." Without a word Agostino turned the prow towards the beach.

As they approached the shore he saw Saro standing in the water watching his maneuvers attentively, and he was afraid the bath man would give him away. But Saro didn't say a word; perhaps he understood, perhaps he didn't care; he gravely helped Agostino pull the boat up to the beach. "This is for you," said the man, giving Agostino the sum agreed on and something over. Agostino took the money and gave it to Saro. "But I'm going to keep the tip," he added, with an air of self-satisfied bravado. Saro said nothing; scarcely even smiling, he put the money inside the sash bound around his stomach and walked off slowly across the beach to his hut.

This little incident gave Agostino a definite feeling of not belonging any more to the world in which boys of that sort existed, and by now he had got so used to living with the poor that the hypocrisy of any other kind of life bored him. At the same time he felt regretfully that he wasn't really like the boys of the gang. He was still much too sensitive. If he had really been one of them, he thought sometimes, he would not have suffered so much from their coarse and clumsy jokes. So it seemed that he had lost his first estate without having succeeded in winning another.

5

ONE DAY, TOWARDS THE END of the summer, Agostino went with the boys to the pine woods to chase birds and look for mushrooms. This was what he enjoyed most of all their exploits. They entered the forest and walked for miles upon its soft soil along natural aisles, between the red pillars of the tree trunks, looking up in the sky to see if somewhere between those tall trunks there was anything moving among the pine needles. Then Berto or Tortima or Sandro, who was the most skillful of all, would stretch the elastic of his slingshot and aim a sharp stone in the direction they thought they had seen a movement. Sometimes a sparrow with a broken wing would come hurtling down, and go fluttering lamely along with pitiful little chirps till one of the boys seized it and twisted its neck between his fingers. But more often the chase was fruitless, and the boys would go wandering on deeper and deeper into the forest, their heads thrown back and their eyes fixed on some point far above them; going ever farther and farther till at last the undergrowth began and a tangle of thorny bushes took the place of bare, soft soil covered with dry husks. And with the undergrowth began their hunt for fungi. It had been raining for a day or two and the leaves of the undergrowth were still glistening with wet, and the ground was damp and covered with fresh green shoots. In the thick of the bushes . . . there were the yellow fungi, glittering with moisture; sometimes magnificent single ones, sometimes families of little ones. The boys put their fingers through the brambles and picked them delicately, to bring the stalk away too, with earth and moss still clinging to it. Then they threaded them on long, pointed sprigs of broom. Wandering thus from patch to patch of undergrowth, they would collect several kilos for Tortima's dinner, for he, being the strongest, confiscated their finds. That day their harvest had been a rich one, for after wandering about a good deal they had found some virgin undergrowth where the fungi were growing closely packed together in their bed of moss. It was getting late before they had even half-explored this undergrowth; so they began to tramp slowly homeward, with several long spits laden with fungi and two or three birds.

They generally followed a path which led straight down to the shore; but this evening they were led farther and farther in pursuit of a teasing sparrow which kept fluttering along among the low boughs and continually gave the illusion of being just within reach, so that they ended by walking the whole length of the forest, which to the east came to an end just behind the town. It was dark as they emerged from the last pine trees on to the piazza of a remote suburb, with rubbish heaps and thistles and broom scattered about and a few ill-defined paths winding over it. Stunted oleanders grew at intervals around the edge; there were no pavements, and the dusty gardens of the few little villas which bordered it alternated with waste ground enclosed by bits of fencing. These little villas were placed at intervals all round the piazza and the wide expanse of sky over the great square added to the impression of loneliness and squalor.

The boys cut diagonally across the piazza, walking two and two like a religious order. At the end of the procession came Tortima and Agostino. Agostino was carrying two long spits of fungi and Tortima held a couple of sparrows in his great hands, their bloody heads dangling.

When they had reached the far end of the piazza Tortima nudged Agostino with his elbow and, pointing to one of the little villas, said cheerfully: "Do you see that? Do you know what that is?"

Agostino looked. The villa was very like all the others; a little bigger perhaps, with three stories and a sloping slate roof. Its façade was gloomy and smoke-grimed, with white shutters tightly closed; while the dense trees in the garden almost hid it from view. The garden did not look very big; the wall around it was covered with ivy, and through the gate one could see a short path with bushes on either side, and a double-paneled door under an old-fashioned porch. "There's no one there," said Agostino, stopping.

"No one, eh?" laughed the other; and he explained to Agostino in a few words who it was lived there. Agostino had several times heard the boys talking about houses where women lived alone, and how they shut themselves in all day, and at night were ready to welcome anyone who came, in return for money; but he had never seen one of these houses before. Tortima's words roused in him to the full the sense of strangeness and bewilderment which he had felt when first he heard them discussing it. And now as then he could hardly believe that there really existed a community so singular in its generosity as to dispense impartially to all that love which seemed to him so far away and so hard to come by; so he now looked with incredulous eyes on the little villa, as if he hoped to read on its walls some trace of the incredible life that went on inside it.

Compared with his imaginary picture of rooms in each of which a naked woman shed her radiance, the house looked singularly old and grimy. "Oh yes," he said, with pretended indifference, but his heart had already begun to beat faster.

"Yes," said Tortima, "it's the most expensive in the town." And he added a number of details about the place and the number of women, the people who went there and the time you were allowed to stay. This information was almost displeasing to

Agostino, substituting as it did sordid details for the confused, barbaric image he had formed when he first heard tell of these forbidden places. But assuming a tone of idle curiosity he put a great many questions to his companion. For, after the first moment of surprise and disappointment, an idea had suddenly sprung up in his mind and soon laid fast hold of him. Tortima, who seemed to be well informed, gave him all the information he needed. Deep in conversation they crossed the piazza and joined the others on the esplanade. It was now almost dark and the party broke up. Agostino gave his fungi to Tortima and started home.

The idea which had come to him was clear and simple enough, however complicated and obscure its origin. He had made up his mind to go to that villa this very night and sleep with one of the women. This was not just a vague desire, it was an absolutely firm, almost desperate resolution. He felt that this was the only way he could escape from the obsession that had caused him such intense suffering all that summer. If he could only possess one of those women, he said to himself, it would forever prove the boys' calumny to have been ridiculous, and at the same time sever the thin thread of perverted and troubled sensuality which still bound him to his mother. Though he did not confess it to himself, his most urgent aim was to feel himself forever independent of his mother's love. A simple but significant fact had convinced him of this necessity, only that very day.

Up to now he and his mother had slept in separate rooms; but that night a friend of his mother's was arriving to spend a week with them. As the house was small it had been arranged that their guest should have Agostino's room, while a cot was to be made up for him in his mother's room. That very morning he had been disgusted to see the cot set up beside his mother's, which was still unmade and covered with bedclothes. His clothing and books and washing things had been carried in with the cot.

The fact of sleeping together only made Agostino hate still more that promiscuity with his mother which was already so hateful to him. He thought this new and still closer intimacy must suddenly reveal to him, without hope of escape, all that up to now he had only dimly suspected. Quickly, quickly he must find an antidote, and set up between his mother and himself the image of another woman to whom he could turn his thoughts if not his eyes. And the image which was to screen him from his mother's nakedness, and which would restore her dignity by removing her femininity . . . one of those women in the villa on the piazza was to supply that image.

How he was to get himself received in that house and how he would choose the woman and go off with her were matters to which Agostino did not give a thought — indeed, even if he had wanted to, he would never have been able to picture it. In spite of Tortima's information, the house and its inmates and everything belonging to it were surrounded by a dense atmosphere of improbability, as if one were not dealing with reality but with the most daring hypothesis which might at the last moment prove fallacious. The success of his undertaking depended on a logical calculation; if there was a house, then there were women too, and if there were women there was the possibility of meeting one of them. But it was not clear to him that the house and the women really were there; and this was not so much because he doubted Tortima's word as because he was totally lacking in terms of comparison. Nothing he had ever done or seen bore the faintest resemblance to what he was about to undertake. Like a poor savage who has heard about the palaces of Europe, and can only picture them as a slightly larger version of his own thatched hut, so he, in trying to picture those women and their caresses, could only think, with slight variations, of his mother; the love making could only be conjecture and vague desire.

But, as so often happens, his very inexperience led him to busy himself with practical aspects of the question, as if once these were settled he could also solve its complex unreality. He was particularly worried by the question of money. Tortima had explained to him in great detail exactly how much he would have to pay and to whom; and yet he could not quite grasp it. What was the relation between the money, which is generally used for acquiring quite definite objects with recognizable qualities, and a woman's caresses, a woman's naked flesh? Was there really a price, and was that price really fixed, and not different in each particular case? The idea of giving money in exchange for that shameful and forbidden pleasure seemed to him cruel and strange, an insult which the giver might find pleasant but which must be painful for the one who received it. Was it really true that he would have to pay the money directly to the woman, and in her very presence? He somehow felt he ought to hide it and leave her with the illusion of a disinterested relationship. And then, wasn't the sum Tortima had mentioned too small? No money would be enough, he thought, to pay for such an experience . . . the end of one period of his life and the beginning of another.

Faced with these doubts he decided to keep strictly to what Tortima had told him even if it turned out to be false, for he had nothing else on which to base his plan of action. He had found out from his friend how much it cost to visit the villa, and the figure did not seem higher than the amount he had been saving for a long time in his terra-cotta money box. With the small coins and paper money it contained he must surely be able to get the amount together, and it might even prove to be more. His plan was to take the money out of the money box, then wait till his mother had gone to the station to meet her friend, when he would go out in his turn, fetch Tortima and set off with him to the villa. He must have enough money for Tortima too, for he knew him to be poor and certainly not in the least disposed to do him a favor unless he was going to get something out of it himself.

This was his plan, and though it still seemed to him desperately remote and improbable he resolved to prepare for it with the same care and certainty as if it had only been an outing in a boat or some expedition into the pine woods.

6

EAGER AND EXCITED, freed for the first time from the poison of remorse and impotence, he almost ran all the way home from the distant piazza. The front door was locked, but the french windows of the drawing room stood open, and through them came the sound of music. His mother was at the piano. He went in; the two subdued lights over the piano lit up her face while the rest of the room was in darkness. His mother was sitting on the piano stool, and beside her, on another, sat the young man of the raft. It was the first time that Agostino had seen him in their house, and a sudden presentiment took his breath away. His mother seemed to divine his presence, for she turned her head with a calm gesture of unconscious coquetry, a coquetry of which Agostino felt the young man to be the object rather than himself. She at once stopped playing when she saw him, and called him to her, "Agostino, what do you mean by coming in at this hour? Come here."

He went slowly up to the piano, full of revolt and embarrassment. His mother drew him to her and put her arm around him.

He noticed that his mother's eyes were extraordinarily bright and young and sparkling. Laughter seemed to be on the brink of bubbling up through her lips, making her teeth glitter. She quite frightened him by the impetuosity, almost violence, with which she drew him to her, as if she were trembling with joy. He was sure that these manifestations had nothing to do with him personally. And they reminded him strangely of his own excitement of a few minutes before, as he ran through the streets in his eagerness to fetch his savings and go with Tortima to the villa and possess a woman.

"Where have you been?" his mother went on, in a voice which was at once tender, cruel and gay. "Where have you been all this time, you naughty boy?" Agostino made no reply; he did not feel his mother really expected one. That was just how she sometimes spoke to the cat. The young man was leaning forward, clasping his knees with both hands, his cigarette between two fingers, and gazing at his mother with eyes as sparkling and smiling as her own. "Where have you been?" repeated his mother. "How naughty of you to play truant like that." She rumpled up his hair on his forehead and then smoothed it again with her warm, slender hand, with a tender but irresistible violent caress. "Isn't he a handsome boy?" she said proudly, turning to the young man.

"As handsome as his mother," the young man replied. She smiled pathetically at this simple compliment. Full of shame and irritation, Agostino made an effort to free himself from her embrace. "Go and wash yourself," said his mother, "and make haste, because we are soon going in to supper." Agostino bowed slightly to the young man and left the room. Behind him, he immediately heard the music taken up again at the very point where he had interrupted it.

But once in the passage he stood still and listened to the sounds his mother's fingers were drawing from the keys. The passage was dark, and at the end of it he could see through the open door into the brightly lit kitchen, where the cook, dressed in white, was bustling about between the table and the kitchen range. His mother went on playing, and the music sounded to Agostino gay, tumultuous, sparkling, exactly like the expression in her eyes while she held him to her side. Perhaps that really was the character of the music, or perhaps his mother read into it some of her own fire and sparkle and vivacity. The whole house resounded to the music, and Agostino found himself thinking that out in the road lots of people must be stopping to listen, wondering at the scandalous wantonness which seemed to pour from every note.

Then, all at once, in the middle of a chord, the sounds stopped, and Agostino was convinced — he could not have told how — that the passion which had found expression in the music had suddenly found another outlet. He took two steps forward, and stood still on the threshold of the drawing room. What he saw did not much surprise him. The young man was standing up, and kissing his mother on the lips. She was bending backward over the low stool, which was too small to hold her body; one hand was still on the keyboard and the other was round the young man's neck. Even in the dim light he could see how her body was arched as it fell backward, with her chest thrust forward, one leg folded behind her, and the other stretched out toward the pedal. In contrast to her attitude of passionate surrender, the young man preserved his usual easy and graceful carriage. As he stood, he held on arm round the woman's neck, but apparently more from fear lest she might fall over than from any deep emotion. His other arm hung at his side and he still had a cigarette between his fingers. His white-trousered legs, planted far apart, expressed deliberation and complete mastery of the situation.

The kiss lasted a long time and it seemed to Agostino that whenever the young man wanted to interrupt it his mother clung to his lips more insatiably than ever. He really could not help feeling that she was hungry . . . famished for that kiss, like someone who has been starved too long. Then, at a casual movement of her hand two or three solemn, sweet notes sounded in the room. Suddenly they sprang apart. Agostino took a step forward and said: "Mamma." The young man wheeled about, and standing with his legs apart and his hands in his pockets, pretended to look out the window.

"Agostino!" said his mother.

Agostino went to her. She was breathing so violently that he could distinctly see her breasts rising and falling through her silk dress. Her eyes were brighter than ever, her mouth was half-open, her hair in disorder; and one soft, pointed lock, like a live snake, hung against her cheek.

"What is it, Agostino?" she repeated, in a low, broken voice, doing her best to arrange her hair. Agostino felt a sudden oppression of pity mingled with distaste. He would have like to cry out to her: "Calm yourself, don't pant like that . . . don't speak to me in that voice." But instead, he put on a childish voice and said, with exaggerated eagerness: "Mamma, can I break open my money box? I want to buy a book."

"Yes, dear," she answered, putting out a hand to stroke his brow. At the touch of her hand Agostino could not help starting back. His movement was so slight as to be almost imperceptible, but to him it seemed so violent that he felt every one must notice it. "Very well then, I'll break it," he said. And he left the room quickly, without waiting for a reply. The sand on the stairs made a gritty sound as he ran up to his room. The idea of the money box had really only been a pretext; the fact was he didn't know what to say when he saw his mother looking like that. It was dark in his room; the money box was on a table at the far end. Through the open window a street lamp lit up its pink belly and great black smiling mouth. He turned on the light, picked up the money box and flung it on the ground with an almost hysterical violence. It broke at once and from the wide opening poured a quantity of money of every description. There were several notes mixed with the coins, He went down on hands and knees and frantically counted the money. His fingers were trembling and, while he counted, the image of those two down in the drawing room kept getting mixed up with the money that was lying scattered over the floor — his mother, hanging backwards over the piano stool, and the young man bending over her. But when he had finished counting he discovered that the money did not amount to the sum he needed.

What was he to do? It flashed through his mind that he might take it from his mother, for he knew where she kept it, and nothing would have been easier; but this idea revolted him and he decided simply to ask her for it. But what excuse could he make? He suddenly thought of one, but at that moment he heard the gong sounding for supper. He hastily hid his treasure in a drawer and went downstairs.

His mother was already at table. The window was wide open and great velvety moths flew in from the courtyard and beat their wings agains the white lampshade. The young man had gone and his mother had again assumed her usual dignified serenity. Agostino, as he looked at her, wondered why her mouth bore no traces of the kisses which had been pressed on it a few minutes before, just as he had wondered that first time, when she went out on the raft with the young man. He could not have defined what feelings this thought awoke in him. A sense of pity for his mother, to whom that kiss seemed to be so disturbing and so precious; and at the same time a strong feeling of repulsion, not so much for what he had seen as for the memory which remained with him. He would have liked to expel that memory, to forget it altogether. How was it possible that such troublous and changing impressions could enter through one's eyes? He foresaw that the sight would be forever stamped on his memory.

When they had finished, his mother rose from the table and went upstairs. Agostino thought he would never find such an opportune moment to ask for the money. He followed her up and went into her room with her. His mother sat down at the dressing table and silently studied her face in the glass.

"Mamma," said Agostino.

"What is it?" she asked absentmindedly.

"I want twenty lire."

"What for?"

"To buy a book."

"But didn't you say you were going to break open your money box?" asked his mother, gently passing the powder puff over her face.

Agostino purposely made a childish excuse.

"Yes, but if I break it I shan't have any money left. I want to buy a book without opening my money box."

His mother laughed fondly. "What a baby you are." She studied herself a moment more in the glass, then she said: "You'll find my purse in the bag on my bed. Take out twenty lire, and put the purse back again." Agostino went to the bed, opened the bag, took out the purse and took twenty lire from it. Then clutching the two notes in his hand he flung himself on the cot beside his mother's. She had finished her make-up and came over to him. "What are you going to do now?" "I'm going to read this book," he said, taking a book of adventures at random from the bed table, and opening it at an illustration.

"Very well, but remember before you go to sleep to put out the light." His mother was still moving about the room, doing one thing and another. Agostino lay watching her, with his head pillowed on his arm. He obscurely felt that she had never been so beautiful as on that evening. Her dress of glossy white silk showed off brilliantly her brown coloring and the rich rose of her complexion. By an unconscious reflowering of her former character she seemed to have recovered all the sweet, majestic serenity of bearing she used to have; but with an indefinable breath of happiness. She was tall, but Agostino had never seen her look so imposing before. Her presence seemed to fill the room. White in the shadow of the room, she moved majestically about, with head erect on her beautiful neck, her black eyes calm and concentrated under her smooth brow. Then she put out all the lights except above the bed table, and bent down to kiss her son. Agostino drank in again the perfume he knew so well, and as he touched her neck with his lips he could not help wondering if those women . . . out there in the villa . . . would be as beautiful and smell as sweet.

Left alone, Agostino waited about ten minutes to give his mother time to have gone. Then he got up from the cot, put out the light, and tiptoed into the next room. He felt about in the dark for the table by the window, opened the drawer and filled his pockets with coins and notes. He felt with his hand in very corner of the drawer to see if it was really empty, and left the room.

When he was on the road he began to run. Tortima lived at the other end of town, in the caulkers' and sailors' quarter, and though the town was small he had a long way to go. He chose the dark alleys bordering on the pine woods, and walking fast and occasionally running, he went straight ahead until he saw, appearing between the houses, the masts of the sailboats in the dry dock. Tortima's house was just above the dock, beyond the movable iron bridge which spanned the canal leading to the harbor. By day this was a forgotten, dilapidated spot with tumble-down warehouses and shops bordering its wide, deserted, sun-baked quays, pervaded by the smell of fish and tar, with green, oily water, motionless cranes and barges laden with shingle. But now the night made it like every other part of the town, and only a ship whose bulging sides and masts overhung the footpath, revealed the presence of the harbor water lying deep in between the houses. Agostino crossed the bridge and headed toward a row of houses on the opposite side of the canal. Here and there a street lamp irregularly lit the walls of these little houses. Agostino stopped in front of an open lighted window, from which came the sounds of voices and clatter of plates, as if they were having a meal. Putting his fingers to his mouth he gave one loud and two soft whistles, which was the signal agreed upon between the boys of the gang. Almost at once someone appeared at the window. "It's me, it's Pisa," said Agostino, in a low, timid voice. "I'm coming," answered Tortima. He came down, still eating his last mouthful, red in the face from the wine he had been drinking. "I've come to go to that villa," said Agostino. "I've got the money here . . . enough for both of us." Tortima swallowed hard and looked at him. "That villa the other side of the piazza," Agostino repeated. "Where the women are."

"Ah," said Tortima, understanding at last. "You've been thinking it over. Bravo, Pisa. I'll be with you in a moment." He ran off and Agostino walked up and down, waiting for him, his eyes fixed on Tortima's window. He was kept waiting a long time, but at last Tortima reappeared. Agostino scarcely recognized him. He had always seen him as a big boy with trousers tucked up, or half-naked on the beach and in the sea. Now he saw before him a young working man in dark holiday clothes; long trousers, waistcoat, collar and tie. He looked older too, because of the brilliantine with which he had plastered down his usually unruly hair; and his spruce, ordinary clothes brought out for the first time something ridiculous and vulgar in his appearance.

"Shall we go now?" said Tortima as he joined him.

"But is it time yet?" asked Agostino, hurrying along beside him as they crossed the bridge.

"It's always time there," said Tortima with a laugh.

They took a different road than the one Agostino had come by. The piazza was not far away, only about two turnings further on. "But have you been there before?" asked Agostino again.

"Not to that one."

Tortima did not seem to be in any hurry and kept his usual pace. "They'll hardly have finished supper and there'll be no one there," he explained. "It's a good moment."

"Why?" asked Agostino.

"Why, don't you see, we can choose the one we like best."

"But how many are there?"

"Oh, about four or five."

Agostino longed to ask if they were pretty, but refrained. "What do we have to do?" he asked. Tortima had already told him, but the sense of unreality was so strong in him that he felt the need of hearing it reaffirmed.

"What does one do?" said Tortima. "Nothing simpler. You go in . . . they come and show themselves . . . you say: 'Good evening, ladies,' you pretend to talk for a bit, so as to give yourself the time to look them well over . . . then you choose one. It's your first time, eh?"

"Well," began Agostino rather shamefacedly. "Go along!" said Tortima brutally. "You're not going to tell me it isn't the first time. Tell that to the others, if you like, but not to me. But don't be afraid. She does it all for you. Leave it to her."

Agostino said nothing. The image evoked by Tortima of the woman initiating him into love pleased him . . . it had something maternal about it. But in spite of these facts he still remained incredulous. "But — but do you think they'll want me?" he asked, standing still suddenly and looking down at his bare legs.

The question seemed to embarrass Tortima for a moment. "Let's go on," he said, with feigned self-assurance. "Once there, we'll manage to get you in."

They came through a narrow lane to the piazza. The whole of it was in darkness, except for one corner where a street lamp shone peacefully down on a stretch of uneven sandy earth. In the sky above the piazza the crescent moon hung red and smoky, cut in two by a thin filament of mist. Where the darkness was thickest Agostino recognized the villa by its white shutters. They were closed, and no ray of light showed through them. Tortima, without hesitation, crossed over to the villa. But in the middle of the piazza, under the crescent moon, he said to Agostino: "Give me the money, I'd better keep it."

"But I . . ." began Agostino, who did not quite trust Tortima. "Are you going to give it to me or not?" persisted Tortima harshly. Agostino was ashamed of all that small change, but he obeyed and emptied his pockets into Tortima's hands. "Now keep your mouth shut, and come along with me," said his companion.

As they came near to the villa, the darkness grew less dense, and they could see the two gateposts, the garden path and the front door under the porch. The gate was not locked, and Tortima pushed it open and entered the garden. The front door was ajar. Tortima climbed the steps and went in, motioning to Agostino not to make a sound. Agostino, looking curiously about him, saw a quite empty hall, at the end of which was a double door, with brightly lit panes of red and blue glass. Their entrance was the signal for a ringing of bells, and almost immediately the massive shadow of someone seated behind the glass door rose against the glass, and a woman appeared in the doorway. She was a kind of servant, middle-aged and very stout, with a capacious bosom, dressed in black with a white apron tied round her waist. She came forward, sticking out her stomach, and with her arms hanging down. She had a swollen face and sulky eyes which looked out suspiciously from under a mass of hair.

The woman scrutinized them hostilely for a moment; then she made a sign, as if inviting Tortima to pass inside. Tortima smiled with renewed assurance, and hastened toward the glass door. Agostino made as if to follow him. "Not you," said the woman, putting her hand on his shoulder.

"What!" cried Agostino, at once losing all his fear. "Why him and not me?"

"You've really neither of you any business to be here," said the woman firmly; "but he will just pass, you won't."

"You're too little, Pisa," said Tortima mockingly. And he pushed the door open and disappeared. His stunted shadow stood out for a moment against the panes of glass; then it vanished in the brilliant light.

"But what about me?" insisted Agostino, exasperated by Tortima's treachery.

"You get off, boy, go away home," said the woman. She went to the front door, opened it wide, and found herself face to face with two men who were just coming in. "Good evening . . . good evening," said the first, who had a red, jolly face. "We're agreed, eh?" he added, turning to his companion, a pale, thin young man. "If Pina's free, I'm to have her . . . and no nonsense about it."

"Agreed," said the other.

"What's this little fellow doing here?" the jovial man asked the woman, pointing to Agostino.

"He wanted to come in," said the woman. A flattering smile framed itself on her lips.

"So you wanted to go in, did you?" cried the man, turning to Agostino. "At your age, home's the place at this hour. Home with you," he cried again, waving his arms.

"That's what I told him," the woman said.

"Suppose we let him come in?" remarked the young man. "At his age I was making love to the maid."

"Well, I'm blest! Get away home . . . home . . .*home*," shouted the other, scandalized. Followed by the fair man he entered the folding door, which banged-to behind him. Agostino, hardly knowing how he got there, found himself outside in the garden.

How badly it had all turned out; he had been betrayed by Tortima, who had taken his money, and he himself had been thrown out. Not knowing what to do, he went up the garden path, looking back all the time at the half-open door, the porch, the façade with its white shutters closed. He felt a burning sense of disappointment, especially on account of those two men who had treated him like a child. The laughter of the jovial man, the cold, experimental benevolence of his companion, seemed to him no less humiliating than the dull hostility of the woman. Still walking backward, and looking round at the trees and shrubs in the garden, he made his way to the gate. Then he noticed that the left side of the villa was illuminated by a strong light coming from an open window on the ground floor. It occurred to him that he might at least have a glimpse of the inside of the villa through that window; and making as little noise as possible he went towards the light.

It was a window open wide on the ground floor. The windowsill was not high; very quietly, and keeping to the corner where there was less chance of his being seen, he went up to the window and looked in.

The room was small and brilliantly lighted. The walls were papered with a handsome design of large green and black flowers. Facing the window a red curtain, hanging on wooden rings from a brass rod, seemed to conceal a door. There was no furniture visible, but someone was sitting in a corner by the window for he could see crossed legs with yellow shoes stretched out into the room. Agostino thought they must belong to someone lying in an armchair. Disappointed at not seeing more, he was going to leave his post when the curtain was raised and a woman appeared.

She had on a full gown of pale blue chiffon which reminded Agostino of his mother's nightgown. It was transparent and reached to her feet; looking at her long, pale limbs through that veil was almost like seeing them float indolently in clear sea water. By a vagary of design the neck of her gown was cut in an oval reaching almost to her waist; and from it her firm, full breasts seemed to be struggling to escape, so closely were they pressed together by the dress, which was gathered round them into the neck with many fine pleats. Her wavy brown hair hung loosely on her shoulders; she had a large flat, pale face, at once childish and vicious, and there was a whimsical expression in her tired eyes and mouth, with its full, painted lips. She came through the curtain with her hands behind her back and her bosom thrust forward, saying nothing and standing quietly, in an expectant attitude. She looked at the corner where the man with the crossed legs was lounging; then, silently as she had come, she turned and disappeared, leaving the curtain wide open. At the same time the man's legs vanished from the sight of Agostino. He heard someone get up and withdrew from the window in alarm.

He returned to the path, pushed the garden gate open, and came out on the piazza. He felt a keen sense of disappointment at the failure of his attempt, and at the same time a feeling almost of terror at what awaited him in days to come. Nothing had happened, he had not possessed any woman, Tortima had gone off with all his money, and tomorrow the same old jokes would begin again and the torment of his relations with his mother. Years and years of emptiness and frustration lay between him and that act of liberation. Meanwhile he had to go on living just as before, and his whole soul rebelled at the bitter thought that what he had hoped for had become a definite impossibility. When he got home, he went in without making any noise; he saw the visitor's luggage in the hall and heard voices in the sitting room. He went upstairs and flung himself on the cot in his mother's room. He tore off his clothes in the dark, and throwing them on the floor got into bed naked between the sheets. . . .

After a little he became drowsy and at last fell asleep. Suddenly he woke with a start. The lamp was lit and shone on his mother's back. She was in her nightgown and with one knee on the bed was just going to get in. "Mama," he said suddenly, in a loud, almost violent voice.

His mother came over to him. "What is it?" she asked. "What is it, darling?" Her nightgown was transparent, like the woman's at the villa; the lines and vague shadows of her body were visible, like those of that other body. "I want to go away tomorrow," said Agostino, in the same loud, exasperated voice, trying to look not at his mother's body but at her face.

His mother sat down on the bed and looked at him in surprise. "But why? . . . What is the matter? Aren't you happy here?"

"I want to go away tomorrow," he repeated.

"Let us see," said his mother, passing her hand gently over his forehead, as if she were afraid he was feverish. "What is it? Aren't you well? Why do you want to go away?"

His mother's nightgown reminded him so much of the dress of that woman at the villa: the same transparency, the same pale, indolent, acquiescent flesh; only the nightgown was creased, which made this picture even more intimate and secret. And so, thought Agostino, not only did the image of that woman not interpose itself as a screen between him and his mother, as he had hoped, but it actually seemed to confirm the latter's femininity. "Why do you want to go away?" she asked again. "Don't you like being with me?"

"You always treat me like a child," said Agostino abruptly, without knowing why.

His mother laughed and stroked his cheek. "Very well, from now on I'll treat you like a man . . . Will that be all right? But you must go to sleep now, it's very late." She stooped and kissed him. Then she put out the light and Agostino heard her get into bed.

"Like a man," he couldn't help thinking before he fell asleep. But he wasn't a man. What a long, unhappy time would have to pass before he could become one.

CARLO EMILIO GADDA

FROM *That Awful Mess on Via Merulana*

Carlo Emilio Gadda and Alberto Moravia in Rome, 1960.

THE SUN STILL HADN'T THE slightest intention of appearing on the horizon when Corporal Pestalozzi had already left (on his motorcycle) the barracks of the are-are-see see[1] at Marino to hurl himself on the tavern-workshop where he wasn't for one moment expected, at least not in his capacity as functioning corporal. The girls, and before them, the sorceress herself had sniffed in the air, yes, a certain, indefinable interest, then perceived a certain circumscribed buzzing of carabinieri (like the ugly horseflies when, of a sudden, a new miracle is scented, in the country), of the sergeant and the corporal, in particular, all around the sweet fragrance of the knitting shop, and finally to the very door of the tavern and even inside, at the counter: an attraction which wasn't the usual, for from the 17th to the 18th, from Thursday to Friday, in the space of twenty-four hours, it had become objectified in a scarf of green wool: yes: probably, if not surely, pinched: whence the urgency, for the beneficiary of the change of ownership, to take it to Zamira to be dyed. The new and, perhaps, even a bit intensified buzzing of the huge men in olive drab or black-and-red wasn't ascribable to private urges, that is to say to the exuberance of the eternal lymph from within the straits of discipline. No, no! The alert and ever closer circling of the workshop, or better of the little hovel that housed the same, had become, in the last couple of days, a royal, cabinierial buzz, obviously to be imputed to a determined case in point of the pinching variety: in short, a police-style buzzing. So that they, the girls, were? Silent! Lips sealed. And knitting, cutting, plying their needle: zum zum zum at the sewing machine. The two bechevroned men, sergeant and corporal, one after the other, and almost in mutual rivalry, had tossed out with effective nonchalance, as if it were a matter of mere passing curiosity, a couple of unforeseen questions, then foreseen and expected, concerning the scarf: and what was it like, and what color was it, was it made of cloth, or knitted, by hand or machine-made? An old lady had lost it, according to what they said . . . as she got off a tram. Zamira blew little bubbles of saliva from her hole and beaded her lips, at the corners: it was her way of palpitating, of participating. She had, one might say an invitation in her eyelids, the most melting, the most edulcorating invitation of *micarême*. But that other girl, that quasi-bride, the one who to the paternal heart of the sergeant was the opened, purplish rose in the bouquet of the white and still-closed buds, had shot into his eyes "her" eyes. A rapid, luminous adept's glance: and that arrow shot, so dewy with intelligence, had been more than sufficient for the sergeant. To concert with immediate parapathia an encounter, vespertine and casual, oh very casual indeed, halfway along the little road to Santa Margherita in Abitacolo: at an hour when no living soul was to be seen. Then and there the scarf was brought back to him (ideally): so green: and in the welling-up of whispers also there came to the surface the buggy, March, the horizontal rain and the new moon and all the strong March winds, and the offering of hot wine, poor horse! in a watering bucket: and, what was more important, the Ciurlani Dyers in Marino. And finally the first name, last name, alias, fixed abode of the denominated male or "boyfriend": with some further information, some hints about his appearance, his character, type, manners, figure, shoelaces. His overall, for that matter, not to mention the cap, were missing from the portrait: a precise question of the sergeant remained unanswered. In the workshop-tavern at I Due Santi, all the girls, every time, and Zamira also, on the other hand, had become lost in a dreamy innocence, had remained silent, or had answered in questions, with their eyes, their questioners: or else they had shrugged and had contracted their lips in a *moue* of ignorance.

Towards Monday, then, that rather rascally zeal of the carabinieri had become completely stilled. A private or two, true enough, had dropped in, descending from his bike; to order an orangeade. The swaying of the handle of the door with glass panes (colored ones) had given the swaying forewarning of a customer: and he had appeared: a carabiniere passing by. The orangeade having been ingested, when its respective gas, as usual, had erupted back again in the kind of nasal crypto-belch which follows a beverage of that kind, then the soldier had unbuttoned his tunic, had opened it slightly, for greater comfort and the drawing of breath: and had drawn out a kind of hamburger swollen with papers more than a generous salami sandwich: a rotten wallet: an organ indispensable, to the sweating, to the wretched, to effect the laborious payment of a "soft" drink. His fingering his buttonholes, restoring to a freer splendor the noble buttons of his uniform, had granted the girls — not to say to the mistress-seamstress — occasion to eye, in a furtive glimpse, but surely a connoisseur's glance, the vivid outlines of his chest, to appreciate the mood of the quenched man: peace, vigor, relaxation, inhibition, pride, and, to record it, this mood, on the positive side of the ledger of humanity's general heritage: excluded, in practice, any dutiful assignment any "casual motive" or rationale of service.

March the 23rd, in the carabinieri's barracks, at Marino. Having risen in the night, come down at daybreak, a private was waiting in the courtyard. Pestalozzi appeared, a dark person, from the shadows, from beneath the archway: he walked to his machine: his bandoleer stood out, white, to underline the dispatch of his actions in an elegant apparatus of authority. A few words to the subaltern, a brief inspection of the beast, splashed with mud up to its muzzle. Once he was in the saddle, with one foot on the ground, the left, he gave the kick to the motor: with his right. The sentry had opened the doors, as if for the exit of a great coach, of some Roman Apostolic Prince and Duke of Marino. Pestalozzi seemed lost in thought. Wednesday the 23rd, he thought. In fact. He raised his eyes to the tower, which a spout of almost-yellow light, from a screened bulb, tinged at its top, in a stripe, a little below the surviving roughness of the cordon at the pinnacle. Six twenty-five by the clock in the tower: the same as his own, exactly. To accompany him he had summoned this private, who was already weighing down the rear part of the seat with his behind and was about to draw his feet into the boat, too, clasping his superior by the waist, with both hands, and awaiting the motor's first explosion. Pestalozzi with his right foot, pressed down: he reiterated the starter. The cylinder began at last to gurgle, the whole machine to tremble, to beat its wings. The sentry saluted, at attention: the threshold was passed. The turn did not occasion falls. But they weighed, the two of them, on the tires. The cobbles were slippery, a steep slope: a little skin of mire, in some places, made it even more dangerous. The mare with the two riders on her withers rolled down, under restraint, grumbling, it bore to the right, then to the left towards the gate of the town, between black peperino walls and shadows, beneath little square windows, armed with rusty iron bars to incarcerate the darkness. An occasional civic lamp swayed its greeting to the fleeting men, in that dark and stony poverty of the village: a bracket coming from the lichened walls, which sloped back, like the curtains of a fort: electric flower of the willing budgets, ultimate sob from the bowels of the vice-mayor for the antelucan solitude of a street from which the north wind precipitates, whistling, at night: or the sirocco slows there and dies, three nights later. They descended to the gate of the town.

Once past the arch, the road started spreading out towards the Appian: it went among olive groves barely silvered by the dawn and the prone skeletons of vines in the vineyards. Then it was thrown back, like a stole, over the damp shoulders of the hill. At the first curve the view also turned back. Pestalozzi raised his head for a moment, cut the motor, put on the brake, stopped their course, with a certain caution: he paused for a couple of minutes, to cast the morning's horoscope.

It was dawn, even later. The peaks of the Algido, the Carseolani and the Velini unexpectedly present, gray. Soratte, sudden magic, like a fortress of lead, of ash. Beyond the passes of Sabina, through small openings, portholes that interrupted the line of the mountain's crest, the sky's revival manifested itself in the distance by thin stripes of purple and more remote and fiery dots and splendors of sulfur yellow, of vermilion: strange lacquers: a noble glow, as if from a crucible of the depths. The north wind of the day before had died away, and here, to alternate the auguries, the hot slavering on skin and face, the gratuitous and now subsiding breath of a sirocco's lashing. Further on, from behind Tivoli and Carsoli, flotillas of horizontal clouds, all curled with cirrus, with false ribbons of saffron, hurled themselves, one after the other, into battle, filed joyously towards their shredding: whither? where? who knows? but surely where their admiral ordered them, to get it in the neck, as ours orders us, all their little sails within the range of the winds. Labile, changing galleys, tacked at a high, unreal height, in that kind of overturned dream which is our perception, after waking at dawn, tacked along the ashen cliffs of the mountains of the Equi, the whitened nakedness of the Velino, the forewall of the Marsica. Their journey resumed, the driver obeyed the road, the machine addressed the curves, bending with the two men. The opposite half of the weather there, above the shore of Fiumicino and Ladispoli, was a brown-colored flock, shading into certain leaden bruises: gravied sheep pressed, compact, meshed in the ass by their dog, the wind, the one that turns the sky rainy. A roll of thunder, rummm, son-of-a-gun! had the nerve to raise its voice, too: on March the 23rd!

The sergeant pressed down with his foot, accelerating towards the fountain. From the right, where the plain was dense with dwellings and went down to the river, Rome appeared, lying as if on a map or a scale model: it smoked slightly, at Porta San Paolo: a clear proximity of infinite thoughts and palaces, which the north wind had cleansed, which the tepid succession of sirocco had, after a few hours, with its habitual knavishness, resolved in easy images and had gently washed. The cupola of mother-of-pearl: other domes, towers: dark clumps of pines. Here ashen: there all pink and white, confirmation veils: sugar in a *haute pâté*, a morning painting by Scioloja. It looked like a huge clock flattened on to the ground, which the chain of the Claudian aqueduct bound . . . joined . . . to the mysterious springs of the dream. There, stood the general H.Q. of the force: there, there, for many moons, his dreamed-of application lay waiting, waiting. Like pears, medlars, even an application's ripening is marked by that capacity for perfectible maceration which the capital of the ex-kingdom confers on all paper, is commensurate with an unrevolving time, but internal to the paper and its relative stamps, a period of incubation and of Roman softening. Bedecked, with silent dust, are all the red tapes, the dossiers of the files: with heavy cobwebs, all the great boxes of time: of the incubating time, *Roma doma*; Rome tames. Rome broods. On the haystack of her decrees. A day comes, at last, when the egg of the longed-for promulgation drops at last from her viscera, from the sewer of the decretal labyrinth: and the respective rescript, which licenses the gaunt petitioner to scramble that egg for the rest of his natural life, is whipped off to the addressee. In more cases than one, it arrives along with the Extreme Unction. It licenses the applicant, now sunk into coma — *verba volant, scripta manent* — to practice that sleeping art, that crippled trade that he had surreptitiously practiced until then, till the moment of the Holy Oil: and which from then on, *de jure decreto*, he will make an effort to practice, a little at a time, in hell with all the leisure granted him by eternity.

The sergeant sped downhill towards I Due Santi. It was a sultry day, the mugginess seemed to have drunk the swamps. But the wind of their speeding and an occasional rare drop, like a musket ball in the face, presaged the alacrity of their investigation, and the fecund interviews in the useful hours of the morning. Sounding the horn at a gander, which lingered to duck its ass in the road, he ripped a half-curse from his teeth: it was at that moment that there came to his mind, in a flash, haunted by his wakening at this early hour, the endless dream of the night before.

He had seen in his sleep, or had dreamed . . . what the hell had he managed to dream of? . . . a strange being, a topass: a topase. He had dreamed of a topaz: what is, after all, a topaz? a faceted glass, a kind of yellow stop light, which grew, and was enlarged from one moment to the next until it promptly became a sunflower, a malign disk that escaped him, rolling forward, almost beneath the wheel of the bike, in mute magic. The Marchesa wanted it, the topaz; she was drunk, yelling and threatening, stamping her feet, her face estranged in a pallor as she uttered obscenities in Venetian, or in some Spanish dialect, more likely. She had raised hell with General Rebaudengo because his carabinieri weren't bright enough to overtake it on any road, or path, the awful topaz, that yellow glass. So at the railroad crossing of Casal Bruciato, the glass sunflower . . . by the right flank, march! It had fled along the rails, changing its form into a yellow rat and snickering top-as-ass-ass: and the Rome-Naples express raced on and on, full speed after the sunset and almost already into the night, into the Circean darkness, diademed with flashes and spectral sparks on the pantograph, luminous stag saturated with electricity. Until, realizing that the mad rolling along the fleeting parallels was not enough to save him, the topaz-ass-rat had turned from the track and had sped into the countryside in the night towards the mouthless ponds of Campo Morto and the underbrush and the thickets of the Pometian shore: the women signal-keepers yelled, shouted that he was mad: they were to stop him, handcuff him: the locomotive chased him through the swamp, with two yellow eyes searching everything, cane brake and the darkness, to that point where place names become sparse, at the foot of the mountain of Contessa Circea, where Japanese lanterns and garlands swayed above the terraces on the shore, in the evening breeze from the sea. Nereids, there, freshly emergent from the waves and immediately denuded of their garments of seaweed and foam, amid the bustle of waiters in white jackets and of damp siphons and fistulas, were wont to make merry the enchanting night of Villa Porca. The Contessa, amid languid dirges, asked for a phial for sleep, for oblivion: for the vain arabesques, the bewilderments of dreams. Of the dream of not being. At Villa Porcina, under festoons of yellow ten-watt pears and drunken balloons, sweetly obese in the breathing and dying of every melody, the sorceress of the (perpetually) open snuffbox elicited at her scent the imminent swine, those who, at that philter, and that perfume, were to turn into snouted pigs, after having become eared-asses at the school: of the machiavellian club's hard knocks. Already the female pupils writhed, stark white except for the thicket triangle, from every austere veto of fathers, they wriggled in silent offering: which, from slow, restrained moorish saraband gradually was exalted to the trochaic rhythm of an *estampida*, where the resolute beating of the foot bestowed a fierce arsis on the floor: while the prompt erection and the shaking both of neck and head gave their hair back to the abyss, signifying the untamed pride both of the cervix and of the spirit, reiterated by the ta-ta-ta-tum of the castanets. Then as the aggression of the naked (but not for that hebefied) males broke into the chorus, the *estampida* was exacerbated to a sicinnis, to a dance simultaneously exozcizational: a swarm of frightened and bosomy nymphs pretended to abhor a herd of satyrs, to shield themselves and take shelter both with their hands and in flight towards their rubescent and fumigant thyrsi, already half-dazed, to tell the truth, by their excessive officiating: with their noses. Falling at that point among their legs, like the black thunderbolt of every prompt and every black happening, the crazed topaz had suddenly frightened the beauties. Shards of an exploded heart had flown off in every direction, to every corner, stopping — at the very sight of that possessed sewer rat, their hippy and mammary ritual. And there were shouts and shrills not to be told as the mustachioed one darted here and there like an arrow's notch, black, sharpened meatball. Many of the priestesses, forgetting their nakedness, had made a gesture as if to draw skirts down to their knees, protecting a defenseless delicacy: but the skirts were only a dream. And so was their delicacy.

Thus, in this delirium, they had sought safety in flight, in the ponds of the swamp, in the shadows of the canes, in the night, the silvery thicket of ilexes and pines on the shore, in the free wash of the beach, lorded over by a seething swell: others, poetesses and sea-creatures diving from the lunar rocks of the circeum, had plunged into the foam of the breakers. But the Contessa Circea, drunken, threw her head back, tossing her soaked hair (as yellow balloons laughed and swayed in Chinese) in the torpid benignity of the night: soaked in a shampoo of White Label: the cleft of her mouth, like an earthenware piggy-bank, arched, open and vulgar, till it could touch her ears, splitting the face like a watermelon after the first incision, in two slippers, in two soles of slogs: and from her rolling eyes, where you could see the white below the iris like that of a Teresa repossessed by the devil,[2] down her face dripped ethylic tears, bluish gouts: opalescent pearls of a contraband Pernod. She invoked the flask of *ratafia*, called for the subventions of Papa, Pappy, the great Aleppo, the invisible Omnipresent, who was, on the contrary, the Omnivisible pig, hailed savior of Italy, omnipresent in his tickling, in every kind of tickling: impotent as he was to achieve anything whatsoever, and even less his verbose braggings. There dripped azure pearls, tears of aloe, of terebene and vodka: the head thrown back, the hair lost in the night, with the two fingers, thumb and index, each with a yellow topaz, raising her skirt, in front, revealing to one and all that she was wearing underwear. She was wearing it, the sainted woman: yes, yes, she was. The wild rape had taken that path, which was the path of duty, for him and for his scenting scariness, climbing up her thighs now like ivy, fat and trembling in his terror, making her laugh and laugh in silly cascades, raving at his tickling: there: they were made of cardboard and plaster, her underpants, that time. Because once, in life, they had put a plaster cast on the trap.

The sergeant sped on, with a dry crackling, in the direction of I Due Santi, with the private grabbing his waist, blinking his eyelids at the oncoming wind, bothered by the dust. Disappointment wakened him abruptly. The time in which we would say that dreams extend has, instead, the diaphragming rapidity of a Leica's click, is measured in lightning segments of time, by fractions of the fourth degree on the orbital time of the earth, commonly known as solar time, the time of Caesar and of Gregory. And lo, now, beyond the flotilla of clouds that was skirting the rocks of the east, the opal became rose, the rose thickened and was stratified in carmine: the lividness everywhere, to the north, of broken day: then, at last, from the ridge, the splendid eyelash: a dot of fire, in a peak of the ridge of the Ernici or the Simbruni the unbearable pupil: the straight, arrowing gaze of the handsome Apollo, the spotlight. The gray latitudes of Latium were clarified, made plastic, emerging, purple-clad, almost like crumbling milestones of time, fragments of towers without names.

When the bam-bam-bam died out at I Due Santi, in a brief skid of the wheels, which the brakes quickly hindered, then blocked, the private found himself on the ground standing, as if he had fallen there: a mountain bear: stretching, from right to left, the lower edge of the olive-drab tunic, which was revealed to be an extremely short garment, over the rotund opulences of his anthropological type. To the right of the Appia, for those who went on in the direction of Albano, the door of opaque or colored panes to a little store, whose threshold of gray and worn peperino, on the outside, was at the level of the still damp asphalt. Opposite the door, to the left of the road that ascended straight and calm, between the mouths of the two connecting roads, one of which had brought them here from the barracks and the town, the low wall of a garden or a vineyard or something of the sort: above which there protruded, somewhat disheveled in the muggy dripping of the morning, the tops of some dried reeds. The wall was broken by a tall shrine, with two eaves and curlicues of pale stucco on the front. Two tumblers, and in them some primulas and periwinkles, consecrated to devotional use, flowered and colored the stone of that kind of window's sill: from which the Divinity, a bit stunned in the head, leaned out as if from a pulvinar over the bustle of the Appia. Framed by the jambs and the slightly cockeyed arch, the old painting, its color quite faded and chalky, demanded all one's attention: the Fara Filiorum Petri[3] gazed at it, though stupefied by sleep and dazed by the novelty of this excursion. Two figures, surely saints — he argued from the data: that is, dressed in clothes that weren't the pants-and-jacket of ordinary men, and their pates behaloed: of which the one, without beard, smaller, was dark and bald: the other, hard and boney, with a white blob on his chin, like a spoonful of lime, and thick hair halfway down his forehead, white, or once white, inside the halo's yellow circle. Those two little short cloaks, bunched like a bandoleer on the left shoulder of the two partners, did not cover the calves and still further, below the calves, the repainted malleoli: and that had allowed the first painter, their "creator," to bring on to the scene four unsuspected feet. The two right ones, enormous, had come to him in a flash: and they were generously tentacled in toes, stretched forward in their stride, to puncture the foreground, the ideal plane (vertical and transparent), to which every visual occasion is referred. With particular expressive vigor, in a remarkable adaptation to the mastery of the centuries, the big toes were depicted. In each of the two extended digits, the cross strap of otherwise unperceived footwear segregated and singled out the knuckled-toe in that august pre-eminence which is his, which belongs to the big toe, and to that toe alone, separating it from the flock of the toes of lower rank, less suitable for the day of glory, but still, in the osteologues' atlases and in the masterpieces of Italian painting, toes. The two haughty digits, enhanced by genius, were projected, hurled forward: they traveled on their own: they almost, paired off as they were, stuck in your eye: indeed, into both your eyes: they were sublimated to the central pathetic motif of the fresco, or alfresco, seeing as how it was plenty fresh. A bolt from heaven, a light of excruciated hours blanched them; however, when you came right down to it, the light seemed to rise from underground, since it struck them from below. The distant bray of a donkey, as the wind rose again, with the tinkle of bells. The glorious history of our painting, in a part of its glory pays tribute to the big toe. Light and toes[4] are prime ingredients, ineffable, in every painting that aspires to live, that wants to have its say, to narrate, persuade, educate: to subjugate our senses, win hearts from the Malign One: insist for eight hundred years on the favorite images. Not even the saints, then, so laden with so many gifts of the Lord — not even they could avoid the indispensable gift of feet: and still less these two, who walked the Appian Way together to Babylon,[5] towards decollation or upside-down crucifixion. They had, indeed, in their feet, the physical instrument of their itinerant apostolate: the trod on the feet of Ahenobarbus. Who, however, remained less than persuaded. No, the saints must not lack their full complement of toes: as soldiers must receive their full issue of tins: and even less when an Italian painter of the sixteenth or seventeenth century or, of the eighteenth, or worse, kneels before them and prepares to depict them, from below, with the soul of a pedicurist. Light, in Italy, is the mother of toes: and if one is an Italian painter, it's nothing to joke about, as Manneroni didn't joke at I Due Santi, neither with the light nor with the toes. The metatarsus of Saint Joseph has been peduncled with an inimitable big toe in the Palatine *tondo* by Michelangelo (the Holy Family): which huge digit, for a minimal portion, to tell the truth, has its pictorial tegument from the little toe of the Bride: a livid and almost surreal, or perhaps eschatological light, proposes the Toe-Idea, loftily incarnating — or in ossifying — it, in the foreground of the contingent: and salvages it promptly for the metaphysical bruises of eternity. The same metartarsus protuberates, the foot's thumb, rival of the Michelangelan-Palantine (to signify the miracle, or rather the audicle, of male chastity) in the Urbino master's Sposalizio, today at the Brera. The divarication of the solitary, bony toe from the remaining herd of other toes is rendered prominent by the perspectively charming joints of the cleansed pavement, where there is no husk or skin, neither orange's nor chestnut's, nor has any leaf or paper settled there, nor has man urinated there, nor dog. And the master toe, thought disjoined from the others, at its root is spurred and gnarled: and then it converges inwards, as if forced by gout or by the habitual constriction of a shoe momentarily removed, or I'd say *domum relapsa* as if too fetid for the hour of the wedding. And it responds, made august by its divarication, it responds to the tall, erect ecstasy of the slender stalk or staff which, overnight, miraculously flowered with three lilies, instead of the customary white carnation: and it picks up, from the rather rare juncture of carpenerial innocence with carpenterial poverty, the testimonial value of an artisan connotation: more than a toe of more than a barefoot carpenter, in that fashion.

As to the iconography of the two saints, and of the holy apostles in general, ah, didn't Manneroni dedicate to them the unspent energies of a velvet-bearded forty years of his own life? assisted on his scaffoldings not only by his believer's fervor, but by the tragic qualities of his genius and an iron constitution: by an athlete's physique, a prophet's appetite: and by a handful of cash, from time to time, given him, however, reluctantly, by the commissioner of those miracles. In the shrine of I Due Santi, adorned and curlicued with cheese-pale stuccos, he was finally enabled to collect and employ all of his talents: the talents which had been swelling his brush, in twenty years of initiation and pictorial apprenticeship, and of obstinate discipline through twenty more years of bearded mastery. Ejaculated impetuously and with free hand on the mortar, still fresh — that is alfresco — the two big toes, the Pietrine and the Pauline, display all the vigor and the urgency of their creation . . . inderogatable, of the enunciation . . . by coerced squeezing, as if splattered there by some source or spring . . . *"ch'alta vena preme."*[6] The "creator" couldn't bear another moment's delay, before creating. *"Fiat lux!"* And there were toes. Plip, plop.

Also of the painter Zeuxis, for that matter, it is rumored that he made a mountain, of lovely foam, at the mouth of a horse, splattering we don't know what sponge on his muzzle, at a whim, but catching it a little too low. And it worked out well. While Pestalozzi had taken to fiddling with his machine, bent over and absorbed, the short-tunicked young man, having crossed the road, moved under the shrine as if for a prayer or a vow: hinting, with his thumb alone, at the Sign of the Cross, he looked up, open-mouthed, and noticed that, with one hand, they held the edge of their garments, the two walkers, inasmuch as, if they didn't, their clothes would have been muddied along the way. It was muddy, in fact, towards the mire of the plain, even the road or row that they still had to travel: that same one, perhaps, that the Farafiliopetri now saw descending towards Le Frattocchie. A light must have spread from above, at one time, but the years, the decades or the centuries, had equated it to the squalor of the general wash: overcome by the light from underground. The bald saint, a little gnome with black hair at his temples, looked like somebody who knew a thing or two: able to read and write as smart as a lawyer, maybe even better: but he seemed to be slowing his pace, now, not even reluctantly, to allow his colleague to go ahead. A kind of right of primogeniture haloed the cervix of the latter, kindled and sharpened his pupils, it circumflowed, like rough beard, the mug that was greedily thrust forward to discern, a fisherman peering at his line: his nose was hardened to the task: granted the title of a Princedom which made his gray hair seem of stone, woolly as it was, to the forehead minimized of the harder. Beneath the figures of the two men, in the two waving scrolls one upon the other in exergue, the tubby Farafiliopetri managed to read, in silent parting and closing of the lips, barely forming the words without uttering them: "*Crescite ve-ro in gratia et in co . . . co . . . coccione Domini Preti Sec Ep.*"[7] The sergeant, in the meanwhile, had taken it into his head — despite all prearranged plans — to medicate his machine on the spot, bent over her greasy viscera. He persisted in titillating obstinately it wasn't clear what hot nipple or what teat, withdrawing his fingers immediately, every time, with a "damn" or a "Jesus Christ!" in a whisper, and snapping them each time in the air, as if to shake off the burning. "*Saepe,*" the Farafilio read on, "*proposui venire ad vos et pro-hi-bitus*" (still mentally) "*sum usque ad kuk Paul ad Rom*"[8] Whereupon he was certain that he had truly deserved his diploma: from grade school. He had received it the year before, as a Baptist received Baptism after his twentieth year, and immediately added it to the already presented and certified papers: hair, brown: eyes, gray: nose, straight: height: 1.74 meters: chest: 91, circumference of the behind . . . not required. And now, at last, after the diuturnal assistance of the goddess of learning (and penmanship), spreading even to within the range of Pallas the Speller, now, behind, the "certificate of studies": diploma, yessir, yes, elementary.

La Zamira, for it was truly she, so disheveled and ungirt, pushing a broom, preceded by a conspicuous cluster of domestic fluffs and straws and indefinable rubbish, received the two men with the salivary lubricity of her professional smile and the peasant falsity of her gaze. The resultant grimace, made livid by the window and the uncertain whiteness of the weather, then kindled by a sudden dart of the sun was meant to disguise as extremely welcome this most unwelcome visit.

"Come in, come in." Was she expecting it, this visit? Or did she guess its reason, if not its immediate purpose, then and there? The hard corporal wanted to bring his motorcycle inside, too well known to be left out in the road. When he had persuaded it to descend the step with both wheels, like an uneasy horse, he set it, with some difficulty, near the knitting machine. He looked at the *femme fatale*, at the sorceress. She hadn't yet combed her hair. Her bangs were a tangle: a gray clump of stubble and roots. Beneath the bumps of the forehead and the rain pipe of the two orbital arches, the pointed flashing of the irises, black, or almost: authentic fear, suspicion, reticence, derision, deception. Flanked by the four surviving canines, the barrel vault, obscene: her lips, at the corners, drooled revolting little bubbles, amid the irradiation of a thousand wrinkles, not yet smoothed or dispelled by cream. It seemed, that vault, the evil door whence like a snake, the head had to come blackened forth, followed then by the whole neck of an unforeseen stratagem, a cavil of the whoring peasant woman. The two dopes perceived, in alarm, the spell that misted towards them with her breath, like that of a gecko or a dragon whose experience in duel is not known. Pestalozzi had — and wanted — to make an effort in self-control: with one hand he seemed to dry his eyes, that is to say his eyelids, under the vizor, to clear his soul and his sensory faculties, which were commanded to pursue the investigation. "Goddamn whore!" he argued mentally. With this ejaculation he felt himself sergeant once again: "The below-named Farcioni Clelia, from Pozzofondo, and Mattonari Camilla, resident at Pavona, work here. Where are they?" The Farafiliorum, meanwhile, was scratching his behind with sweet leisure: or lifting from it, perhaps, the too-sheathing underpants. With both hands, and with two parallel and symmetrical gestures, he proceeded to press his tunic along his hips. It was still like a too-short undershirt: he was ashamed: that insufficience was embittering his whole day.

"Come right in, Corporal. They'll be along any minute. Who wants them?" Zamira counter-asked, insinuating, insolent. The handle of that filthy old broom, all burs, was now clasped in her two hands as if she leaned on it, in repose, and to listen. Pestalozzi, now master of his soul, gave the vile woman a thunderous look: "lousy old whore" was its meaning, mute, his lips closed, straight, "you can see for yourself who." She seemed to dissolve into attentions, pushing aside as best she could the filth to the flank of the sideboard, and allocating the broom there too, as if to guard what it had collected. "I'll go call them, if you'll mind the store for me: I can trust *you*!" she smiled, turning: after taking a shawl from the rag pile: and she started to go out, wagging her tail, for their joy as desiring but abstinent youths. He clenched his anger in his teeth, Pestalozzi did: and held her back promptly by one arm. A wink! and she whirled around suddenly, like a garter snake when you step on its tail.

"If they'll be along any minute, then we'll wait for them here. Don't move. Sit down," he fastened her to a chair, pressing her into it: "There. But if they don't come . . . we'll take *you* in, this time." The good dyeress paled: the harshness was rather, in him, descended from the hills, despite the noncommissioned officers' school. Santa Maria Novella had not shed on him the grace, oh no, of excessive refinement. The respectful glands were gadgets of the future, then, for a noncom; hopes, in the heart of evildoers, of a brighter morrow: the brighter morrow of those days. Harshness, at that time, was borne as a duty: the "courses in human relations" had not yet been set up. The chevrons of sergeanthood, a long promise waved under his nose like a shredded meal beneath a cat's, demanded wisdom, firmness: harshness, when required. Then, once sergeant, he could play the kindly man, the gruff bear with a heart of gold . . . full of understanding. So harshness it was: in that moment made even heavier by his annoyance. That breath, those mocking eyes of the sorceress, those lascivious *double-entendres* — their witchcraft had to be dispelled, the coils of her hypnosis had to be broken. "You, move away from that window," he ordered Cocullo, "hide over there." The motorcycle was now under cover, sheltered from the curious and from the rain. But along the provincial road, after the descent from Torraccio, its crackling had been heard more or less by everyone, and by some, he thought, seen, from the little window of the privy: at the hours of rising, when they yawn, in their trousers, wandering about the house with a train of suspenders at their shins, towards the sink, scratching the head in the prickly luxuriance of black hair, a ninth jawbreaking yawn, a rub of the eyelids with the most diligent knuckles and phalanges: whence sleep, so sweet in the morning, is dissipated and vaporizes away slowly, almost despite itself. Consciousness then identifies with itself, resumes its own skin, its lousy cloak. It begins to count again its chickens, the foolish events of the daylight hours. A motorbike on the road. The corporal seemed to reflect: "Have they come to work regularly, these last few days? Or have they had justified absences?"

"Worked . . ." the sly bag hesitated, "absence? justified?" she stammered, to gain time. No, with such legal language she couldn't, in all conscience, and therefore dared not pretend to be familiar. She was the sincere type, all heart, a woman of few words: deeds, rather, actions . . . to the succor of souls, of needful hearts: who had recourse to her . . . for disinterested advice. And hearts, as we all know, by their own nature . . . tend to fraternize.

In pairs. Nor could the corporal, from her, insist on law-court style. He had no reason and still less any right to demand it, with all the subtleties and circumlocutions and cavils that becloud it, on the lawyer's tongue. Oh! lawyers! they were so nice! And such good customers! She dreamed for a moment. But woe that she should be a customer of theirs, she pondered.

"Justified absence of who . . ."

"Don't play dumb. Don't pretend you don't understand; you know very well what I mean. The two girls I told you. Who?! Farcioni and Mattonati . . . Mattonari, that is. I have a feeling that last Tuesday, the fifteenth that is, I suspect . . . they didn't turn up. They said they were sick." He invented that "said" out of the whole cloth. He had never met them nor sought them: he also dropped that Tuesday instead of Saturday, to provoke a denial, and the consequent correction. Zamira seemed to be racking her memory.

"Come on, answer. You've got to answer right off, dear Madam, not think about it a year. If you have to think so long, it's surely to make up some lie. Have they come to work regularly? This is what I'm asking you. Or did they stay home some morning? I want to hear this from you, from your own lips. We know it already ourselves, never fear: the carabinieri know everything!"

"Why, what do you know? Why are you asking me, then, if you already know?"

"I told you. Because I want to hear it from you, from you in person, what you think about it and what you have to say. Yes, you, Signora Pàcori, Zamira, with your diploma in fortunetelling": and he sought it, on the wall, with his gaze: hanging like an engineering degree in a surveyor's office. But it must have been downstairs, with the Death's Head, in the consulting room, near the padlocked cupboard where the cheese was also stored.

She tried her smile again, her most lascivious one: she recalled her dribble, sucking in from the corners, despite the vault in the midst. She dried her lips, moving her little tongue in a rapid, scything motion, which then rested, for a moment, at the margin if impudence, of sluttidence, as Belli[9] might have said. It was, in general, a slimy and dark red tongue, as if it had also been painted:

and at that moment it crouched down among the canines, nice and docile, in a posture of waiting and perhaps of relaunching, since the fence of incisors had rotted away in the wayward years.

"Well, Sergeant dear, what can I tell you? You let me know . . ." and she swayed her head, here and there, looking like a silk moth, very coy: and she was careful, at the same time, to wriggle, with the larger part of her profferings, poorly concealed in this early hour, on the edge of the chair: to which she felt nailed. "You let me know, because I imagine, you know too, he he he, that we women, he he he, since we *are* women, he he he, have our little troubles . . . every so often . . . a punishment of the Lord, he he he, to try out patience, poor us! It isn't our fault if we're not like you men, he he he, who are always able to stand up!"

This time, revolted, it was he, the corporal, who played dumb.

"What troubles? Leave troubles out of it!"

She went one, haughtily:

"Well, Sergeant, just think a minute — with that kind heart of yours! You can't deny that it's so. My poor little girls, poor things!" Then, imploring: "You mean you don't have a wife?" shameless! "Or a couple of sisters? Not even one? . . . everybody had a sister, you might say. Where's the man these days, with all the men around, who doesn't have a couple of sisters to marry off? Even that big poet, the patriotic one, had one: the poet who made everybody cry, at Christmas, in Libya, at Ain Zara, with the Sixth Bersaglieri . . . what was his name? he's dead now, poor thing! What was his name? Giovanni . . . you know . . . those places where there's grass," and with her hand she drew the name from her forehead, "Giovanni . . . Giovanni Prati! No, no . . . not Giovanni Prati, wait a minute," and she continued, with her hand, "How can I have forgotten? It's all the trials I've been through . . . they've ruined my memory. Giovanni Pascoli![10] There, now I remember. I knew he had a name like the places where they make hay."

"Skip the grass and the hay, and the meadows and the pastures. And forget about the dead. Just answer me."

"But, Sergeant dear, let me get a word in. How can I answer you, otherwise? I was saying, how everybody nowadays has a sister, no? And if you have one, then I'm sure . . . that day comes around for your sister, too, poor lamb; maybe she has a little headache. We women, he he he, have our headaches here." And she touched her belly, almost caressing it. Her eyes flashed satanic, intoxicated. The black oven between the incisors' gap. The tongue drawn back, now, like a parrot's when he gurgles in this throat, in spite. Her hair seemed to be summoned aloft, by electricity, as if it were about to burst into flame and crackle like brambles, when a spark, on the baked earth, kindles them.

"Yes, I understand, you women here get a headache from all the knitting you have to do. But don't start nagging me with headaches now. Cut it short. Enough of this chatter. You have to tell me when it was that they stayed home, these two girls: Mattonari and Farcioni. I already know, but I want to check with you, to see if you're telling the truth, or if you're lying. If you're lying, if you're lying to put the investigation off the track, here, here are the handcuffs, all ready for them and for you." And he took from his pocket and dangled before her nose an example of the ill-famed hardware. Seated, the witch didn't bat an eye: those armillae, in any case, didn't concern her. "Well?"

"Well, let's see . . . it must have been last month, the one before this. Now that I think of it, we're just at the new moon." Obstinate, she harped on this theme: "How can I remember the monthlies of all the girls? I think that's asking too much . . ."

"Too much? Moons? Now look here, Zamira Pàcori! Have you lost your mind? Who do you think you're talking to?"

"But last month . . ."

"Last month my ass! Watch what you're saying. Last month! I'm asking you if they were absent on Tuesday the fifteenth, or Friday: one of the two." (he didn't dare bring his Saturday into play.) "This is what I'm asking you. And this is all I want you to answer, because you know very well."

At that point, as if summoned from the darkness, from the slightly opened door of the little stairway which led into the store (of which the young boys daydreamed, others mythicized, and more than one, because of the palm-reading, knew from experience), there peered in, then hopped onto the chill tile floor, here and there, with certain cluck-clucks of hers, among two piles of sweaters, a surly and half-featherless hen, lacking one eye, with her right leg bound by a string, all knots and splices, which wouldn't stop coming out, coming up: such, as from the ocean, the endless line of the sounding where the windlass of the poop summons it back aboard and yet a fringe of beard decks it out, from time to time: a mucid, green seaweed from the depths. After having hazarded, this way and that, more than one lifting of the foot, with the air, each time, of knowing quite well where she meant to go, but of being hindered by the contradictory prohibitions of fate, the pattering one-eyed fowl then changed her mind completely. She unstuck her wings from her body (and she seemed to expose the ribs for a more generous intake of air), while a badly restrained anger already gurgled in the gullet: a catarrhous commination. Her windpipe envenomed, she began a cadenza in falsetto: she pecked wildly at the top of that mountain of rags, whence she sprayed the phenomena of the universe with the supreme cockledoodledoo, as if she had laid an egg up there. But she fluttered down without any waste of time, landing on the tiles with renewed paroxysms of high notes, a glide of the most successful sort, a record: still dragging the string after her. Parallel to the string and its chain of knots and gnarls, a thread of gray wool had caught on one leg: and the thread this time seemed to be unwoven from a rhubarb-colored scarf, beneath the dyed rags. Once on the ground, and after yet another cluck-cluck expressing either a wrath beyond cure or restored peace and friendship, she planted herself on steady legs before the shoes of the horrified corporal, turning to him the highly unbersagliere-like plume[11] of her tail: she lifted the root of the same, revealed the Pope's nose in all its beauty: diaphragmed to the minimum, the full extent of the aperture, the pink rose-window of her sphincter, and, plop, promptly took a shit: not out of contempt, no, probably indeed to honor, following hennish etiquette, the brave noncom, and with all the nonchalance in the world: a green chocolate drop twisted *à la Borromini* like the lumps of colloid sulfur in the Abule water: and on the very tip-top a little spit of calcium, also in the colloidal state, a very white cream, the pallor of pasteurized milk, which was already on the market in those days.

All these aerodynamics, naturally, and the consequent release of chocolate, or mocha, as may be, were exploited by Zamira to avoid answering: while some surly little feathers, snowy and delicate as those of a baby duckling, lingered above, in midair, softly swaying, till they seemed the dissolving rings of smoke from a cigarette. In this new wonder Pestalozzi's imperative faded away. She got up quickly from the chair with all her bluish behind, and started kicking her slipper and waving her skirt after the sulky beast, since she had no apron, and screeching at it: "Get out! Out! dirty, filthy thing! The idea! Of anything so nasty! To the sergeant here! Filthy animal!"

So that the filthy thing in question, still trilling a thousand cluck-etyclucks, and spewing them, all together, towards the ceiling in a great cackling résumé, doubly anchored though she was by string and yarn, took flight up to the top of the sideboard: where, pissed off, and resuming her full dignity, she deposited, on the pewter tray, another neat little turd, but smaller than the first: plink! With which she seemed to have evacuated to the full extent of her possibilities. Fear (of the carabinieri) brings out the worst in all of us.

And there, at the glass door, the brass handle began also to show signs of restlessness. The door opened. A young girl, from the March outside, burst into the large room like a gust of wind. A dark shawl around her neck: umbrella in hand, already closed before her entry. A wave of handsome chestnut hair from the forehead back, almost in a cascade over the shawl: March had invaded it, with lunatic arabesques. At the sight of the olive drab, as soon as she had come down the step, she stopped, lips parted, dumfounded. The two soldiers and Zamira, all three, sensed an unexpected emotion which had flamed up from her uterus through the lymphatic glands and the vaginal tracts into the fullness of her boobs: in a faint gasping, but certainly a vivid palpitation. Her face paled, or so it seemed: it was, at this point, the slightly hysterical white of a desirable girl. She remained with her lips parted, then said: "Good morning, Corporal": and hurled a larboard glance at the other one, whom she had already discerned oncoming and descending the step, but whom she saw for the first time, cornered in his corner as if in a modest penumbra: over whom prevailed, in any case, the chevroned dazzle, that is to say the hierarchical precedence of Pestalozzi. After the glance at the other simpleton, she made as if to look around for a place to set her umbrella: but the lynx-like gaze (lynx was the word he used to describe himself) of the above-named sergeant . . . no, the lynx-like gaze did not miss a movement of her left hand (which held in the ring and little finger that scarecrow of an umbrella), to the charge or benefit of the other hand: a kind of scratching or massage inflicted or practiced with the thumb, from below, and externally with the index and middle finger, on the long, central fingers of the right hand: as if to warm them up, foreseeing the work to come. In the apparent casualness of the gesture there was an insistent, a premeditated quality: it was the gesture, not casual, of one who wishes to remove a ring, with some effort, and who proposes, at the same time, to conceal the not-easy operation from others present. The corporal glared at the girl, approached her by two paces, bang, bang, gently but firmly took her right hand by the fingertips: an invitation to the dance which admitted no refusal. He seemed to be pressing and squeezing them, one by one, those fingers, one after the other, as if to feel if there was a pimple, or a callus, as he went on looking into her eyes, fixed and perplexed, with the manner of a magician on the stage in a demonstration of hypnotism. Finally he turned it over, that hand, and stood there looking into its palm, to read her fate, one would have said. A handsome yellow stone, a topaz?, glowed like the headlight of a train, a hundred facets, on the inner part of the finger, the ring finger, after her surreptitious half-twist. It gave forth, from itself, the bumptious and slightly silly gaiety, at moments, of colored glass, under the sudden appearance and alternate fading, among the March clouds, of the sun, also seized with a uterine languor: for in that first month, when he has barely caught a whiff of the rain in the skies, he too is seized with the vapors and palpitations: like that Apollo that he is.

"You . . . who are you?" Pestalozzi, radiant, asked her, recognizing in his own desire the stimulating identity of the face, the eyes, the genteel figure of the girl, though not yet her name, in the filing cabinet of his mind. "Are you Clelia? Clelia Farcione? or Camilla Mattonari?"

"Why, Corporal, what's all this about? Yes, my name's Mattonari, all right: but I'm not Camilla. My name is . . . she hesitated, "Mattonari Lavinia."

"Then where is Camilla? And who is she? Your sister?"

"Sister?" she pursed her lips in disgust, "I don't have any sisters," disdaining the hypothesis of such a kinship.

"But you know her. She works here: you said her name, Camilla's. So you're friends." And in the meanwhile he was still holding her hand. She had set down, at last, the umbrella: she frowned: "Did I say that? Camilla? I just repeated the name you said, corporal." Pestalozzi thought he had caught a use of the article, in Tuscan or Lombard fashion,[12] which hadn't been spoken at all.

"Friends? I don't have any friends." The violence of this denial, a second time: no more than the corporal was expecting: "Well, if you don't have any friends, so much the better: you can speak out then: and no foolishness, because I don't have time to waste. Who's Camilla?" he continued to hold her hand, by the fingertips.

"She's . . . yes, a girl who . . . she's learning to be a seamstress, too . . . she works . . ."

"She works here?"

"Well yes," she admitted, hanging her head.

"She's her cousin: a distant cousin . . ." Zamira said calmly, in the tone with which the *Almanach de Gotha* asseverates, and all believe, that Charlotte Elisabeth of Coburg is the fourth cousin of Amalia of Mecklenburg.

"And where is she? Why isn't she here? Isn't she coming to work today?"

"How should I know?" the girl shrugged. "She'll be coming."

"You can see for yourself, Sergeant," Zamira insisted, haughtily. "We're out in the country. We work when there's something to do . . . to make or to mend: when there's need, I mean. Every other day, more or less. But in the winter, with the weather like this," and she took advantage of a fading of the sun, through the panes, and nodded towards the outside, "with these storms, you can't tell from one day to the next . . . whether it's spring or whether it's still January, with this weather maybe we work one day out of five. You know better than me, Sergeant, since you must have studied all about the weather and the signs of the moon, the way I did, when I got my fortunetelling diploma," she recited in a sententious tone:

Candlemas, Candlemas!
Winter's end has come at last.
But should rain fall or north wind blow
Winter then has weeks to go.

and three weeks ago, if you remember, just like today, the weather was something terrible; the water came right down into the shop, and that lousy hen," she sought the hen with her eyes behind the machine, "even stopped laying. Today maybe we have nothing to do, and tomorrow there may be a whole heap of stuff."

"It looks to me like you have a fine heap of lies, enough to last a month," and he indicated with his chin the little mound of things, piled as if in two peaks, like the back of a camel. Still holding the young girl by the hand, he abandoned the clucking hen to her doubts and the double train of yarn and string and the relative knots.

"Now . . . tell me something: who gave you this?" he raised his hand of the palpitating Lavinia, now clasping her by the wrist, and looking at the topaz which, from the inner part of the hand, she had turned again on her finger.

"Who gave it to me?" she made an effort to blush, as if at a tender secret.

"Signorina, hurry up. Take off the ring. I have to confiscate it. And tell me who gave it to you. If you tell me, all right. And if you don't tell me . . ." and he took from his pocket the familiar plaything: presenting it to her.

Lavinia blanched: "Corporal . . ."

"Skip the corporal. Take that ring off right now, and hand it over, make it snappy, because if you don't know, I'll tell you: it's stolen goods. It's in the list of jewels and gold objects stolen from the countess in Via Merulana, from Countess Menegazzi: it's here, in the list of jewels." And, to motivate his demand which, in spite of everything, he knew smacked a bit of bullying, he replaced the handcuffs and removed, from another pocket, Ingravallo's paper. The procedural timidity of that which in the *Barber* is marked in F sharp, the "force," had not yet sunk then, in 1927, into the present Oceanic depths: but it already knew certain aspects of today's taste. Even the most harsh official, alone in the countryside in the midst of the populace, deferred to it, as they defer to it today. Having therefore extracted the list, squaring off the two sheets as if he were reading a warrant, Pestalozzi pretended also to look there . . . for the legitimate authorization to proceed. "Mmm . . ." he went down the first lines, muttering, and stumbled at once at what he was seeking: "gold ring with topaz!" and his was the voice of victory. He waved the letterheaded paper, put it under her eyes, the girl's. She, Lavinia, didn't even know how to read it.

"Police Headquarters, Rome!" he chanted in her face, in a tone of importance, and of ironic detachment towards the rival organization, which, just because they could type a couple of sheets of paper, gave themselves such airs: "Police Headquarters, Rome!" He took the ring held out to him by the girl, her face pale with spite, livid, with the air of submitting, helpless, she, poor country girl, to this abuse of power. Zamira, silent, looked on: and listened. "Aha! this is the very one!" Pestalozzi ventured, examining the ring with a connoisseur's eye, turning it over and looking at it closely, as a fence would have done in Via del Gobbo, tending to sequester it at once: meanwhile he clasped the two sheets of paper in the other hand, between little finger and palm: "this is the topaz I've been hunting for two days: this is it!" as if his professional wisdom, operating in his cranium *ab aeterno*, had allowed him to recognize it instantly. In reality he was seeing it then for the first time, and he had been hunting it for two hours, if, after all, it really was a topaz, and not a piece of bottle, perhaps: "Who gave it to you? Tell the truth. He did, Retalli. You don't have the money to buy it: a ring like this! Enea Retalli gave it to you: he already confessed it yesterday to the sergeant." (Retalli was still a fugitive from justice.) "He's your lover, we know that: and he gave you this topaz"; which was rather a naïve remark. "Nobody's my lover: and Enea Retalli is out working somewhere: I don't know where; and it's not true that you caught him last night, or that he confessed anything."

"So much the worse for you then. Come on. Let's go," and he motioned to Farafiliopetri: and grabbed her by the arm.

"Corporal, you've got to believe me," the girl protested, freeing herself, " a girl friend of mine gave it to me; she's promised to buy it off a woman; she lent it to me for a couple of days, because today . . . today's my birthday. She gave it to me just for two days."

"Ah, and how old are you?"

"Well . . . I'm nineteen."

"Are you sure?"

"Yes, I was nineteen last night."

"So you were born at night then. And who lent you the ring, for your birthday? Speak up."

"Corporal, how could I know . . . that it belonged to the contessa that they murdered in Rome, or whose it was? The peddlers that go along the road on horseback, from town to town, you know? You think they know who owns or who made the stuff they sell?"

"That's enough fibs!" and he squeezed her arm, which he had taken again and was holding.

"Ouch!" she said: "You're bullying me."

"Who gave it to you? Come on. You can tell it to sergeant. He'll make you spill it, all right." He drew her towards the door. Fara also started to move, in compliance, he uprooted himself from where he was, left his corner. The hen had settled down, God knows where.

"I got it, Corporal, from a girl . . . A girl who works here gave it to me. We've been talking for ages about corals to wear around the neck, or earrings . . . And I was always saying that I didn't have anything to put on for my birthday."

"Then say who she is. You know her," Zamira prompted, pale.

"It's Camilla," she answered Zamira.

"Ah! Camilla Mattonari then? All this fuss to give us the name of Mattonari Camilla, your cousin, whose lover is a thief, or even a murderer, maybe. Come on: take me to her."

"What about the motorcycle?" Zamira stammered; to her the very thought of that machine in the shop without its master annoyed her unspeakably. She had got up from the chair. She wrung her hands before her belly, a little ball that made her look three months pregnant, considerably stained below her belt, where there were certain rivulets of dishwater or coffee; she had no apron. Her lips pursed, forgetting now every invitation and all her winks, with the foresighted and deducing gaze of one who guesses from a single movement the motives and intentions of the mover, with intent and glistening eyes, she followed the motions of the two men in their somewhat embarrassed footsteps between sideboard and bike, machine and table, counter and chair, between the heap of sweaters and the door: the door to the road. The light in her eyes changed, became evil, malevolent and almost sinister, at times. She seemed to see oscillating, like the oscillation of a charge, a tension in the spirit, as if it meant to break the sequence of acts and unacceptable deeds, the procedural validity of the carabinieresque miracle. Which she saw, at a given point, in its true light: in its certain meaning, compelling recognition: a gray and scarlet devilment of the Prince of Demons: he of the sergeant's stripes: he, in any case, whom she had been able to recognize on many occasions as the sworn enemy of I Due Santi: who took shelter in the fortress, at night, in Marino, when the mountain wind howled, to meditate before the bluish circle of the lampwick his malefactions for the day, ubiquitous then in the great hours of the sun like the view of the falcon, who peers and sees over all the land, in farmyard and meadow, on mountain or plain. A red-and-black, chevroned malefaction, filled like the September night with a thousand sophists' persistences, which from day to day press ever closer around the person of one who, perhaps, works honestly, who tries to get along as best he (or she) can, with the first expedient that comes to mind, to fight off the many tribulations of life. A duty though vain and maleficent, suited to justify, as well as to determine, one's corpulence, one's rubicund health, one's pension: an arbitrary and therefore illicit intervention into the private operations of magic, or of simple palm-reading, such as to spoil the outcome of everything: disputable then, on good grounds, with augural looks on the order of her own, zamirian gaze, as well as by a summons for help to the great king with the straight horns, Astarath: the very one that she, Zamira, had to call. So that she busied herself now, with her fingers, making on the sack of her paunch like the pharmacist on his marble counter, certain movements, certain twirls, certain jokes not comprehended by common ratiocination, as if she were shelling invisible peas or crumbling or snapping some invisible pill in the direction of the unaware Pestalozzi who had his back to her, still unsure what was to be done. Her lips began, little by little, to bubble up again, to twitch, and her cheeks to vibrate, to boil *motu proprio* in a grim contempt, which was being sharpened into the fideistic peroration of certain witch docto-priests of Tanganyika or African Kafirs or snub-nosed, kinky Niam-niams, their heads all curly, dusted with coal, gold rings hanging from their noses, their behinds like terraces, when they implore or imprecate from or to their animal gods in their monosyllabic-agglutinate language and in homologous and rather nasal chanting: "Nyam, nyam chep, chep, i-ti, i-ti, give that lousy missionary a humpback and get him off our balls." Mennonite missionary, of course. And meanwhile they give him a drink, their spit whipped up with coconut milk in a coconut shell, a sign of subtropical honor, or Tanganyika reverence.

"You, Signora, keep still with those fingers!" the Filiorum commanded her indignantly. His cheeks had become red, the red of tomato sauce, whitened to cheese color in the lower portion of his jaws. The objective clarity of ratiocination, in him, got the upper hand of the unreason of the powers of darkness: as if his elementary diploma had been countersigned by Filangieri himself with his own hand, Don Gaetano Filangieri, Prince of Arianello, Minister of the Realm.[13] He wouldn't admit, couldn't tolerate that the "superstition" of past centuries should rise again in magic, in the art of fashioning hunchbacks for one's neighbor, carabiniere as in this case, by that fingering of the witch. There is a uterus in us, always, a reasonable one, which is disturbed by a wink, a hint, a kneading of fingertips with which, despite every new enlightening of the Realm and every diploma on outsized paper, the most enlightened certainties are poisoned.

"Let's go," repeated Corporal Pestalozzi, making up his mind. "I'll leave the machine here," and he turned, "watch out for it: put a chair in front of it, and don't let anybody touch it."

Signora Pàcori smiled at him, a little automatic smile, though black in the center: a dry little smile, silly, the kind she was used to dispensing from the counter in gray moments, a habit of her art, of a saleswoman who knows how to look at smokers: she revealed, as usual, the hole: she could do nothing else. Her eyelids closed a moment, as if in foretasted voluptuousness: foretasted out of duty, out of professional obligation. Her little eyes signified, with a moment's flashing, the usual permission: to whom? to what? The malevolence meanwhile, on her forehead, had waxed and polished the two bumps, two strongholds still held by the devil.

"Where is Retalli?" the corporal was saying to the girl.

"Corporal, I don't know," she said: her face distraught.

"And your cousin? Where is your cousin? Take me to her. Come on." He seemed seized, really, by the mania to catch somebody, not to go back, empty-handed, to the barracks. A ring — and what a ring! — he had. All right. But now a suspect was needed, an accomplice, male or female, if not the guilty party in person.

"But I . . ." the girl whimpered again, forgetting the umbrella where she had placed it.

"Come on, that's enough. Show me where she is": and he opened the door, inviting her, with the other hand, to make use of both the step and the exit. Lavinia went outside first.

"At the railroad crossing," Zamira then hissed into his ear. But the private also heard her. Still, under her malevolent forehead, the pernicious light of her gaze was not spent. "She's the niece of the signal-keeper: at the crossing. That's where she lives."

"Which crossing?"

"The road to Castel de Leva, to the bridge; then to the left, the crossing at Casal Bruciato": she seemed a deaf-mute, explaining herself with her fingers, with the aphonous movement of her lips. She didn't want Lavinia to hear her, from the road. Farafilio stumbled over the step: "Careful!" she said, maternally: and repeated: "On the road to Divino Amore. Almost to the bridge. Then to the left."

And with that little thrust, with that viaticum, she succeeded in getting off the two comrades, with their four great boots. They would have plenty of dust to swallow! Old Nick had heard the boiling of her prayers, had graciously listened to her reiterated invocations and her pleas.

"Take care of the machine!" the corporal shouted to her again, from outside: as her gaze sharpened in meanness: "at the bridge of Divino Amore!" she shouted, as if to strike again at the rear guard of the vanquished. What fireworks exploded in their wake, what ejaculations, while the glass door was still open behind the departing men, history, past-mistress of life, has not troubled to record.

---

1. R.R.C.C., the Royal Carabinieri.
2. A reference to the Bernini St. Teresa in Ecstasy, in the church of the Santa Maria della Vittoria in Rome.
3. Fara Filiorum Petri is the peculiar name of a small town in the Abruzzo from which, apparently, this carabiniere private comes. Gadda refers to him at times by the name of the town, at times by combined forms of it ("Farafilio"), and at times by his surname, Cocullo.
4. This whole passage is underlined by an untranslatable play on the similarity of two words, *la luce* (light) and *l'alluce* (big toe).
5. Babylon, in this case, means Rome.
6. "At prompting of the Eternal Spirit's breath," Dante, *Paradiso*, XII, 99

7. "*Crescite vero in gratia et in cognitione Domini, Petri Secunda Epistula: (III-18).*" (Author's note). ". . . grow in grace, and in the knowledge of our Lord . . ."
8. "*Saepe proposui venire ad vos et prohibitus sum usque adhuc. Pauli ad Romanos: (I-13).*" (Author's note). ". . . oftentimes I purposed to come unto you, but I was let hitherto . . ."
9. Gioacchini Belli (1791-1863), Roman dialect poet.
10. A pun on the words *prati* (meadows) and *pascoli* (pastures), surnames of two Italian nineteenth-century poets. Pascoli, a bachelor, lived with his sister.
11. The soldiers of the *bersaglieri* (sharpshooters) regiments wear hats with special plumes of cock tailfeathers.
12. In Northern Italy proper names, in indirect reference, are often preceded by the definite article. Pestalozzi thought he heard her say *la* Camilla.
13. Gaetano Filangieri (1752-88), enlightened political thinker and author.

GIORGIO BASSANI

FROM *The Garden of the Finzi-Continis*

Giorgio Bassani, Rome 1947.

I

THE TOMB WAS BIG, MASSIVE, really imposing: a kind of half-ancient, half-Oriental temple of the sort seen in the sets of *Aïda* and *Nabucco* in vogue in our opera houses until a few years ago. In any other cemetery, the neighboring Municipal Cemetery included, a tomb of such pretensions would not have been the least amazing; indeed, confused in the general array, it would have gone unremarked. But in ours, it was unique; and so, though it rose quite far from the entrance gate, at the end of an abandoned field where no one had been buried for more than half a century, it stood out, it was immediately noticeable.

It seemed that the construction had been entrusted to a distinguished professor of architecture, responsible for many other contemporary outrages in the city, by Moisè Finzi-Contini, the paternal great-grandfather of Alberto and Micòl, who had died in 1863, shortly after the territories of the Papal States had been annexed to the Kingdom of Italy, with the consequent, definitive abolition, also in Ferrara, of the ghetto for the Jews. A great landowner, "reformer of Ferrarese agriculture" — as we could read on the plaque the community had placed along the stairs in the temple on Via Mazzini, at the top of the third landing, to immortalize his merits as "Italian and Jew" — but a man, obviously, of rather uncultivated artistic taste, once he had made the decision to set up a tomb *sibi et suis*, he had given the designer a free hand. The times seemed beautiful, flourishing: everything encouraged hope, daring. Overcome by the euphoria of the newly won civil equality, the same that, at the time of the Cisalpine Republic, had allowed him as a young man to make his first thousand hectares of reclaimed land, the stern patriarch had understandably been led, on that solemn occasion, not to pinch pennies. Very probably the distinguished professor of architecture had been given carte blanche. And with such quantities of fine marble available, snow-white Carrara, flesh-pink Verona, gray speckled with black, yellow marble, blue marble, green marble, he had, in turn, definitely lost all self-control.

The result was an incredible pastiche, in which architectonic echoes of Theodoric's mausoleum in Ravenna mingled with those of the Egyptian temples at Luxor, with Roman baroque, and even, as the squat columns of the peristyle indicated, the archaic Greek of Knossos. But so it went. Little by little, year after year, time, which, in its way, always adjusts everything, had succeeded in harmonizing that unlikely mixture of heterogeneous styles. Moisè Finzi-Contini, here called "austere and tireless worker," had died in 1863; his wife, Allegrina Camaioli, "angel of the household," in '75; in '77, still young, the only son, Menotti, doctor of engineering; followed twenty years later, in '98, by his wife, Josette, daughter of Baron Artom of the Treviso branch of that family. After that, the maintenance of the chapel, which, in 1914, had received only one more member of the family, Guido, a boy of six, had passed clearly into hands gradually less prompt in cleaning, tidying, repairing damage when necessary, and above all, fighting off the relentless siege of the surrounding vegetation. The clumps of grass, a dark, almost black grass, metallic in its toughness, and ferns, weeds, thistles, poppies, had been allowed to advance and invade with ever-greater license. So that in '24, or '25, sixty years after its inauguration, when I, as a little boy, was to see it for the first time, the funeral chapel of the Finzi-Continis ("A real horror," my mother, whose hand I was holding, never failed to call it) already looked more or less as it does now, when for a long time there has been no one left directly involved in taking care of it. Half-buried in the rampant vegetation, the surfaces of its polychrome marbles, originally smooth and brilliant, made opaque by gray accumulations of dust, the roof and the outer steps damaged by the baking sun and by frosts: even then it seemed transformed into that rich and wondrous thing into which any long-submerged object is transformed.

Who knows how, and why, a vocation for solitude is born? The fact is that the same isolation, the same separation with which the Finzi-Continis had surrounded their deceased, surrounded also the *other* house they possessed, the one at the end of Corso Ercole I d'Este. Immortalized by Giosuè Carducci and by Gabriele D'Annunzio, this Ferrara street is so well known to lovers of art and poetry throughout the world that any description of it would be superfluous. We are, as everyone knows, in the very heart of that northern section of the city added to the cramped medieval town during the Renaissance, and called for this reason the Addizione Erculea. Broad, straight as a sword from the Castle to the Mura degli Angeli, its entire length flanked by the dark forms of patrician dwellings, with that distant, sublime backdrop of brick-red, vegetal green, and sky, which seems to lead you, truly, to the infinite: Corso Ercole I d'Este is so beautiful, its tourist attraction is so great, that the Socialist-Communist coalition, responsible for the city government of Ferrara for more than fifteen years, has realized the necessity of leaving it untouched, defending it with all severity against any building or commercial speculation, preserving, in other words, its original aristocratic character.

The street is famous: moreover, substantially intact.

And yet, as far as the Finzi-Contini house in particular is concerned, though even today you enter it from Corso Ercole I — but to reach the house itself, you must cover more than a quarter-mile, through an immense open space, scantily cultivated or not at all — though it incorporates still those historic ruins of a sixteenth-century building, once an Este residence or "folly," bought by the same Moisè in 1850, and later transformed by his heirs, through successive remodelings and restorations, into a kind of neo-Gothic manor, English-style: despite such surviving points of interest, who knows anything about it, I wonder, who remembers it any more? The *Touring Club Guide* doesn't mention it, and so excuses the passing tourists. But in Ferrara itself, not even the few remaining Jews in the languishing Jewish community seem to recall it.

The *Touring Club Guide* doesn't mention it, and that, no doubt, is too bad. Still, we must be fair: the garden, or, to be more precise, the vast park that surrounded the Finzi-Contini house before the war, and spread over almost twenty-five acres to the foot of the Mura degli Angeli on one side, and as far as the Barrier of Porta San Benedetto on the other, representing in itself something rare, exceptional (The Touring Club guides of the early twentieth century never failed to speak of it, in a curious tone, half-lyrical, half-snobbish), today no longer exists, literally. All the big trees, the lindens, elms, beeches, poplars, planes, horse chestnuts, pines, firs, larches, cedars of Lebanon, cypresses, oaks, ilexes, and even palms and eucalyptuses, planted by the hundreds at the orders of Josette Artom, were cut down during the last two years of war for firewood, and the terrain for some time has returned to what it was once, when Moisè Finzi-Contini bought it from the Marchese Avogli's family: one of the many big vegetable gardens enclosed within the city walls.

There would still be the house proper. But the big, singular building, severely damaged by bombs in '44, is now occupied by about fifty refugee families, belonging to that same wretched urban subproletariat, not unlike the plebs of the Roman slums, that continues to huddle especially in the entrances of the Palazzone on Via Mortara: hard, wild people, intolerant (a few months ago, I was told, they received the city health inspector with a hail of stones, when he went there on his bicycle for an inspection);

and to discourage any eviction plan of the Fine Arts Commission of Emilia and Romagna, they have apparently had the fine idea of scraping from the walls anything that was left of the ancient paintings.

Now, why put poor tourists in jeopardy? — I imagine the compilers of the latest edition of the *Touring Club Guide* asked themselves. And, to see what, after all?

2

IF THE TOMB OF THE Finzi-Contini family could be called a "horror," and smiled at, their house, isolated down there among the mosquitoes and frogs of the Panfilio Canal and the outlets of the sewers, and nicknamed enviously the *magna domus*, at that, no, not even after fifty years could anyone manage to smile. Oh, it still took very little to feel offended by it! It was enough, say, to pass along the endless outside wall of the garden along Corso Ercole I d'Este, a wall interrupted, at about the halfway point, by a solemn door of dark oak, without any kind of knob; or else, in the other direction, from the top of the Mura degli Angeli, overlooking the park, to peer through the forestlike tangle of trunks, boughs, and foliage below, until you could glimpse the strange, sharp outline of the lordly dwelling, and behind it, much farther on, at the edge of a clearing, the tan patch of the tennis court: and the ancient offense of rejection and separation would smart once more, burning almost as it had at the beginning.

What a typical nouveau riche idea, what an outlandish idea! — my father used to repeat, with a kind of impassioned bitterness, every time he happened to mention the subject.

True, true — he admitted — the former owners of the place, the Marchese Avogli family, had "the bluest" blood in their veins; vegetable garden and ruins *ab antiquo* had boasted the highly decorative name of Barchetto del Duca: all excellent things, yes, indeed! and the more so since Moisè Finzi-Contini, who had to be granted the undoubted merit of having "seen" a good deal, in concluding that same deal must not have spent more than the proverbial pittance. But what of that? — he would add immediately. Was it really necessary, for this reason, that Moisè's son, Menotti, called, not without reason, *al matt mugnàga*, the apricot madman, after the color of his eccentric, marten-lined overcoat, to decide to move his wife, Josette, and himself into such an out-of-the-way part of the city, unhealthy even today, so imagine then! and moreover deserted, melancholy, and, especially, unsuitable?

You could even excuse the parents, who belonged to a different age, and after all could afford the luxury of investing all the money they liked in some old stones. You could especially excuse her, Josette Artom, descendant of the Artom barons of the Treviso branch (a magnificent woman in her day: blond, ample bosom, blue eyes, and in fact her mother had come from Berlin, an Olschky); besides being mad about the House of Savoy, to such a degree that in May of '98, shortly before her death, she had taken the initiative of sending a congratulatory telegram to General Bava Beccaris, who had turned his cannon on those poor devils, the Socialists and anarchists of Milan, she was also a fanatical admirer of Bismarck's studded-helmeted Germany, and had never troubled, since her husband, Menotti, eternally at her feet, had settled her in her Valhalla, to dissimulate her own aversion towards Ferrara's Jewish circles, too narrow for her — as she said — not to mention, in effect, though it was a fairly grotesque matter, *her own basic anti-Semitism*. Professor Ermanno and Signora Olga, nevertheless (he a scholar, she a Herrera from Venice: and therefore born of a western Sephardic family, *very* good, beyond a doubt, but somewhat badly off, however devout): what sort of people did they think they had become, the two of them as well? Real nobility? Oh, yes, it was comprehensible, yes: the loss of their son Guido, their first-born, who died in 1914 at the age of only six, after an attack of infantile paralysis, the American kind, galloping, against which even Dr. Corcos had been helpless, must have been a very hard blow for them: especially for her, for Signora Olga, who after that had never put off her mourning. But apart from this, wasn't it possible that, as time passed, living apart, they had got swelled heads, falling into the same absurd notions of Menotti Finzi-Contini and his worthy spouse? Aristocracy, indeed! Instead of giving themselves so many airs, they would have done much better, they at least, to remember who they were, where they came from, for it's a fact that Jews — Sephardic and Ashkenazic, western and Levantine, Tunisian, Berber, Yemenite, and even Ethiopian — in whatever part of the earth, under whatever sky History scattered them, are and always will be Jews, that is to say, close relatives. Old Moisè didn't give himself airs, not him! He didn't have any aristocratic fancies in his brain! When he was living in the ghetto, at number 24 Via Vignatagliata, in the house where, resisting the pressure of his haughty Treviso daughter-in-law, impatient as she was to move as quickly as possible to the Barchetto del Duca, he was determined at all costs to die, he would go out himself every morning to do the shopping in Piazza delle Erbe with his faithful shopping bag over his arm: he, who for this same reason, was nicknamed *al gatt*, the cat, had brought them up from nothing, his family. Yes, while there was no doubt that "la Josette" had come down to Ferrara, accompanied by a large dowry, consisting of a villa in the Treviso region frescoed by Tiepolo, a large check, and jewels obviously, many jewels, which at the opening nights of the Teatro Comunale, against the red-velvet background of their private box, attracted the eyes of the whole theatre to her, to her splendid décolletage, there was also no doubt that it had been *al gatt*, and he alone, who had put together, in the Ferrara plain, between Codigoro, Massa Fiscaglia, and Jolanda di Savoia, the thousands of acres on which the bulk of the family patrimony was still based today. The monumental tomb in the cemetery: that was the only mistake, the only sin (against taste, especially) of which Moisè Finzi-Contini could be accused. But apart from that, nothing.

So said my father: at Passover, especially, during the long suppers that continued to be held in our house even after the death of Grandfather Raffaello, at which about twenty friends and relations were present; but also at Kippur, when the same friends and relatives came back to our house to end the fast.

I remember, however, one Passover supper in the course of which, to the usual criticisms — bitter, generic, always the same, and expressed chiefly for the pleasure of summoning up the old tales of the community — my father added some new and surprising ones.

It was in 1933, the year of the notorious *infornata del Decennale*, Fascism's tenth-anniversary membership campaign. Thanks to the "clemency" of the Duce, who all of a sudden, as if inspired, had decided to open his arms to every "agnostic or adversary of yesterday," in the circle of our community the number of party members had also risen abruptly to 90 percent. And my father, sitting down there in his usual place at the head of the table, in the same place from which Grandfather Raffaello had pontificated for long decades with quite different authority and severity, had not failed to express his satisfaction at the event. The rabbi, Dr. Levi, had been quite right — he said — to mention it in the speech he had recently made at the Italian synagogue when, in the presence of the leading authorities of the city — prefect, provincial party secretary, mayor, the brigadier general in command of the garrison — he had commemorated the Fascist Statute!

And yet he was not wholly pleased, Papà. In his boyish blue eyes, filled with patriotic ardor, I could read a shadow of chagrin. He must have discerned a stumbling block, a little obstacle, unforeseen and unpleasant.

And in fact, having begun at a certain point to count on his fingers how many of us, us Ferrarese *judìm*, had still remained "outside," when he came at last to Ermanno Finzi-Contini, who had never taken out a party card, true, and after all, considering also the substantial agricultural holdings of which he was proprietor, it had never been quite clear why, suddenly, as if irked at himself and his own discretion, my father decided to reveal two curious events: perhaps unrelated — he premised — but no less significant for that.

First: that the lawyer Geremia Tabet, when in his position as a *Sansepolcrista*, a Fascist of the first days, and intimate friend of the party secretary, had gone to the Barchetto del Duca expressly to offer the Professor a card, already made out in his name, he had not only seen it handed back to him, but also a little later, very politely of course, but equally firmly, had been shown the door.

"And on what pretext?" someone asked, in a faint voice. "Ermanno Finzi-Contini has never been considered a lion."

"On what pretext did he refuse?" My father laughed violently. "Oh, one of the usual things: that he's a scholar (I'd like to know what subject!), that he's too old, that in his whole life he has never concerned himself with politics, et cetera, et cetera. For that matter he was sly, our friend. He must have noticed Tabet's grim expression, so then, *wham*! he slipped five thousand-lire bills into his pocket!"

"Five thousand lire!"

"That's right! To be contributed to the Seaside and Mountain Summer Camps of the Young Fascists. A nice thought, wasn't it? But now listen to the latest."

And he went on to inform the company that a few days ago, with a letter sent to the council of the community through the lawyer Renzo Galassi-Tarabini (could he have chosen a more stiff-necked, more obsequious, more "*halto*" lawyer than that?), the Professor had asked permission to restore, at his own expense, "for the use of his family and of anyone interested," the ancient, little Spanish synagogue on Via Mazzini, which had not been used for religious functions for at least three centuries and had long served as a storeroom.

3

In 1914, when little Guido died, Professor Ermanno was forty-nine, Signora Olga twenty-four. The child felt ill, was put to bed with a very high temperature, and sank at once into a deep drowsiness.

Dr. Corcos was urgently summoned. After a silent, endless examination, performed with a frown, Corcos abruptly raised his head, and stared, gravely, first at the father, then the mother. The doctor's gaze was long, severe, oddly scornful; meanwhile, beneath his thick, Umberto-style mustache, already completely gray, his lips curled in the bitter, almost vituperative grimace of desperate cases.

"Nothing can be done," Dr. Corcos meant, with that gaze and that grimace. But perhaps also something further. That he, too, ten years earlier (and who knows if he spoke of it that day, before taking his leave, or else, as certainly happened, only five days later, addressing Grandfather Raffaello, while they both slowly followed the impressive funeral?), he, too, had lost a child, his Ruben.

"I too have known this suffering, I also know well what it means to see a five-year-old son die," Elia Corcos had said abruptly.

Head bowed, his hands resting on the handlebar of his bicycle, Grandfather Raffaello was walking beside him. He seemed to be counting, one by one, the cobblestones of Corso Ercole I d'Este. At those words, truly unusual on the lips of his skeptical friend, he turned, amazed, to look at him.

And, in fact, what did Elia Corcos himself know? He had examined at length the child's inert body, decreed to himself the grim prognosis, and then, having raised his eyes, fixed them on the petrified eyes of the two parents: the father, an old man; the mother, still a girl. By what paths could he have descended, to read those two hearts? And who else could, ever, in the future? The epigraph dedicated to the dead child, on the monumental tomb of the Jewish cemetery (seven lines lightly carved and inked in a humble rectangle of white marble), was to say only:

Mourn
Guido Finzi-Contini
(1908-1914)
of exceptional form and spirit
your parents thought
to love you always more
not to mourn you

Always more. A subdued sob, and that was all. A weight upon the heart to be shared with no other person in the world.

Alberto was born in '15, Micòl in '16: more or less the same age as me. They were sent neither to the Jewish elementary school on Via Vignatagliata, where Guido had attended, without finishing, the first grade, nor, later, to the public Liceo-Ginnasio G. B. Guarini, the early crucible of the city's finer society, Jewish and non-Jewish, and therefore at least as sacramental. They studied together privately, both Alberto and Micòl, as Professor Ermanno interrupted from time to time his solitary studies of agronomy, physics, and history of the Jewish communities of Italy, to supervise closely their progress.

These were the mad but, in their own way, generous years of early Fascism in Emilia. All action, all behavior was judged — even by those who, like my father, happily quoted Horace and his *aurea mediocritas* — by the crude yardstick of patriotism or defeatism. To send one's children to the public schools was considered, in general, patriotic. Not to send them, defeatist: and therefore, towards all those who did send their children there, somehow offensive.

All the same, even in their segregation, Alberto and Micòl Finzi-Contini always maintained a fragile relationship with the outside world, with the young people, like us, who went to the public schools.

There were two professors of the Guarini whom we had in common, who acted as links.

Professor Meldolesi, for example, in the fourth year of *ginnasio* taught us Italian, Latin, Greek, History, and Geography; and every other afternoon he took his bicycle, and from the neighborhood of little villas, built in those years outside Porta San Benedetto, where he lived alone in a house he rented furnished, whose view and exposure he was accustomed to extol, he ventured all the way to the Barchetto del Duca, remaining there at times for three full hours. Signora Fabiani, our mathematics teacher, did the same.

From la Fabiani, to tell the truth, nothing had ever leaked. Bolognese by birth, a childless widow in her fifties, very devout, she would become preoccupied during question period, as she muttered to herself, constantly widening her sky-blue Flemish eyes, as if about to go into a trance. She was praying. For us, poor things, surely without any talent in algebra, almost all of us; but also, perhaps, to hasten the conversion to Catholicism of the Jewish family to whose house — and what a house theirs was! — she went twice a week. The conversion of Professor Ermanno, of Signora Olga, and especially of the two children, Alberto, so intelligent, and Micòl, so lively and pretty, must have seemed to her too important, too urgent a matter for her to risk compromising its probabilities of success through banal scholastic gossip.

Professor Meldolesi, on the contrary, did not remain silent at all. Born in Comacchio of a peasant family, educated in a seminary through the *liceo* years (and he much resembled a priest, a little, clever, almost feminine country priest), he had then moved on to study literature in Bologna, in time to attend the last lectures of Giosuè Carducci, whose "humble pupil" he boasted of being. The afternoons spent at the Barchetto del Duca, in an atmosphere steeped in Renaissance memories, with five o'clock tea taken in the company of the whole family — and Signora Olga often came in from the park at that hour, her arms filled with flowers — and then later, perhaps, up in the library, relishing until dark Professor Ermanno's learned conversation: those extraordinary afternoons obviously represented, for him, something too precious not to be made the subject, even with us, of constant discussion and digression.

And ever since one evening when Professor Ermanno had revealed to him how Carducci, in 1875, had been his parents' guest for about ten consecutive days, showing him then the room the poet had occupied, and letting him touch the bed where he had slept, and finally allowing him to take home, to examine at his convenience, a little "sheaf" of autograph letters sent his mother by the poet, Professor Meldolesi's agitation, his enthusiasm had known no limit. He had gone so far as to convince himself, and he tried to convince us as well, that the famous verse in the *Canzone di Legnano*:

> *O blond, O beautiful empress, O trusted one*

which clearly heralded the even more famous verses:

> *Whence did you come? What centuries handed you down,*
> *So mild and beautiful, to us . . . .*

and, at the same time, the sensational conversion of the great son of Maremma to the "eternal royal feminine" of Savoy, had been in fact inspired by the paternal grandmother of his private pupils, Alberto and Micòl Finzi-Contini. Oh, what a magnificent subject this would have been — Professor Meldolesi, once, in class, had sighed — for an article to send to that same *Nuova An-*

tologia where Alfredo Grilli, his friend and colleague Grilli, has been publishing for some time his acute notes on Serra! One of these days, naturally, with all the delicacy demanded by the situation, he would take care to mention this to the letters' owner. And heaven grant that, considering how many years had passed, and given the importance and, obviously, the perfect propriety of a correspondence in which Carducci addressed the lady only in such terms as "charming Baroness" or "most kind hostess" or the like, heaven grant that the owner would not say no! In the happy hypothesis of a yes, he, Giulio Meldolesi, would immediately take care — provided, also in this instance, that he was given explicit consent by the person who had every right to give it or deny it — to copy out the letters one by one, complementing later those sacred shards, those venerated sparks from the great forge, with a minimum commentary. What, in fact, did the text of the correspondence demand? No more than an introduction of a general nature, integrated perhaps, with a few sober, historical-philological footnotes . . .

But besides the teachers we had in common, there were also the examinations reserved for private students — examinations held in June, at the same time as the other examinations, national and local — which at least once a year brought us in direct contact with Alberto and Micòl.

For us regular students, especially if we were promoted, there were perhaps no days more beautiful. As if, all of a sudden, we regretted the just-ended hours of lessons and assignments, we could usually find no better place to meet than the entrance hall of the school. We would linger in the vast passage, cool and dark as a crypt, clustering in front of the big white sheets announcing the final grades, fascinated by our names and our companions', which, read there, written in handsome calligraphy and exposed behind glass, beyond a fine wire grille, never ceased to amaze us. It was beautiful to have nothing more to fear from school, beautiful to be able to go outside a moment later into the clear, blue light of ten o'clock in the morning, beckoning, there, through the postern of the front door, beautiful to have before us long hours of idleness and freedom, to spend as we liked best. Everything beautiful, everything stupendous, in those first days of vacation. And what happiness at the ever-current thought of our imminent departure for the sea or the mountains, when studying, which still burdened and tormented so many others, would be for us almost forgotten!

And there, among these *others* (rough boys from the country, for the most part, sons of peasants, prepared for their examinations by the village priest, who, before crossing the threshold of the Guarini, looked around bewildered, like calves led to the slaughterhouse), there were Alberto and Micòl Finzi-Contini, in fact: not at all bewildered, not they, accustomed as they were for years, to present themselves and triumph. Slightly ironic perhaps, especially towards me, when, crossing the hall, they glimpsed me among my companions and greeted me from the distance with a nod or a smile. But always polite, even too polite, and well behaved: like guests.

They never came on foot, or, still less, on bicycles. In a carriage: a dark-blue brougham with large rubber wheels, red shafts, all glistening in fresh paint, crystal, nickel.

The carriage would wait there, outside the door of the Guarini, for hours and hours, never moving, not even to seek shade. And it must be said that examining the equipage more closely, in all its details, from the great, heavy horse, with his bobbed tail and his cropped mane, calmly stamping a hoof from time to time, to the tiny, aristocratic crown that stood out, in silver, against the blue background of the doors, even obtaining, sometimes, from the indulgent coachman in summer uniform, permission to climb on one of the side steps, so that we could contemplate at our leisure, noses pressed against the crystal, the interior, all gray, padded, and in semidarkness (it seemed a drawing room: in one corner there were even some flowers in a slender oblong vase, like a chalice): all this could be another delight, indeed it certainly was, one of the many adventurous delights with which, then, for us, those marvelous adolescent mornings of late spring were prodigal.

4

As far as I personally am concerned, there had always been something more intimate, in any case, about my relations with Alberto and Micòl. The knowing looks, the confidential nods that brother and sister addressed to me, every time we met around the Guarini, alluded only to this, I well knew; something regarding us and only us.

Something more intimate. But what, exactly?

It's obvious: in the first place we were Jews, and this, in itself, would have been more than enough. Let me explain: between us there might have been nothing in common, not even the scant communion derived from having occasionally exchanged a few words. The fact, however, that we were what we were, that twice a year at least, at Passover and Kippur, we appeared with our respective parents and close relations at the same doorway on Via Mazzini — and it often happened that, having passed the door all together, the narrow hall that followed, half-dark, forced the grownups to hat-doffings, hand-clasps, obsequious bows, such as they would have no other occasion to exchange for the rest of the year — this would have been enough to ensure that when we young people met elsewhere, and especially in the presence of outsiders, there would immediately appear in our eyes the shadow or the smile of a certain special complicity and connivance.

That we were Jews, nevertheless, and inscribed in the ledgers of the same Jewish community, still counted fairly little in our case. For what on earth did the word "Jew" mean, basically? What meaning could there be for us, in terms like "community" or "Hebrew university," for they were totally distinct from the existence of that further intimacy — secret, its value calculable only by those who shared it — derived from the fact that our two families, not through choice, but thanks to a tradition older than any possible memory, belonged to the same religious rite, or rather to the same "school"? When we met on the threshold of the entrance to the temple, as a rule at dusk, after the embarrassed formalities exchanged by our parents in the gloom of the porch, in the end we almost always climbed, still a group, the steep stairs that led to the third floor, where, crowded with a mixed throng, wide, echoing with sounds of organ and singing like a church — and so high, among the rooftops, that on some May evenings, with the big side windows flung open towards the setting sun, at a certain point we found ourselves bathed in a kind of golden mist — that was the Italian synagogue. So only we, Jews, to be sure, but also brought up in the observance of a same rite, could realize actually what it meant to have the same family bench in the Italian synagogue, up there on the third floor, instead of on the second, in the German one, so different in its severe, almost Lutheran assemblage of wealthy, bourgeois bowler hats. And this was not all: because, even taking for granted, outside the strictly Jewish world, an Italian synagogue's being different from a German one, with everything in particular that such distinction involved on the social and the psychological planes, who, besides us, would have been able to provide specific information about "the Via Vittoria people," just to give one example? This expression regularly referred to members of the four or five families who had the right to attend the separate little Levantine synagogue, also known as the Fano synagogue, situated on the fourth floor of an old house on Via Vittoria: the Da Fano family of Via Scienze, in fact, the Cohens of Via Gioco del Pallone, the Levis of Piazza Ariostea, the Levi-Minzis of Viale Cavour, and I forget what other isolate family groups: all slightly odd people in any case, characters always a bit ambiguous and elusive, for whom religion in the Italian school had taken on too popular, theatrical a form, almost Catholic, with evident effect also on the character of the people, open and optimistic, for the most part, very "Po Valley," whereas religion for those others had remained essentially worship to be performed in a small group, in semiclandestine chapels to which it was best to go at night, slipping along the darkest and most infamous alleyways of the ghetto. No, no: only we, born and brought up *intra muros*, so to speak, could know, could really understand these things: very subtle, practically unimportant, but nonetheless real. It was futile to think that others, all the others, without excluding from the roster even school companions, childhood friends, playmates incomparably more beloved (at least by me), could be informed of such a private subject. Poor souls! In this respect, they were to be considered, all of them, only simple crude beings, sentenced for life, basically, to irreparable gaps of ignorance, or — as even my father would call them, with a benign grin — *goyishe blacks*.

And so, on occasion, we climbed the stairs together, and together we made our entrance into the synagogue.

And since our benches were neighboring, down front near the semicircular enclosure, marked all round by a marble railing, at the center of which stood the *tevá*, or reader's lectern, and both in excellent view of the black carved wooden cupboard that contained the scrolls of the Law, the so-called *sefarím*, we crossed together also the great hall's resounding pavement of white and pink rhombohedrons. Mothers, wives, aunts, and sisters had separated from us men in the vestibule. Vanishing in single file through a little door in the wall, which led into a closet, from there, by a circular stair, they had climbed even higher, into the women's section, and in a little while we would see them again, peering from above, from their coop set just below the ceiling, through the holes in the grille. But even in this way, reduced to males only — namely, me, my brother, Ernesto, Professor Ermanno, Alberto, as well as, now and then, Signora Olga's two bachelor brothers, the engineer and Dr. Herrera, who would come especially from Venice — even in this way we formed a fairly numerous group. Significant and important, at least: for, at whatever moment of the function we might appear, we were never able to reach our seats without arousing the liveliest curiosity around us.

As I said, our benches were neighboring, one behind the other. My family occupied the bench in front, in the first row, and the Finzi-Continis the one behind, in the second. And so, even if we had wanted to, it would have been difficult to ignore one another.

For my part, attracted by their diversity to the same degree my father was repelled by it, I was always very alert to any movement or murmur from the bench behind ours. I was never still a moment. Whether I chattered in whispers with Alberto, who was two years older than I, true, but still had to "enter the *mignàn*," and nevertheless, hastened, as soon as he arrived, to enfold himself in the large *talèd* of white wool with black stripes that had once belonged to "Grandpa Moisè," or whether Professor Ermanno, smiling at me kindly through his thick glasses, invited me with a gesture to observe the copper engravings that illustrated an ancient Bible, which he had taken especially for me from the drawer; or whether, fascinated, I listened, open-mouthed, to Signora Olga's brothers, the railway engineer and the physiologist, chatting among themselves half in Venetian dialect and half in Spanish ("What is it? *Cossa stas meldando?* Come, Giulio, *alevantate, ajde*! And see that *el chico* also stands up") only to stop then, suddenly, and join very loudly, in Hebrew, in the rabbi's chants; for one reason or another my head was almost always turned. In a row, on their bench, the two Finzi-Continis and the two Herreras were there, just a few feet away, and yet very remote, unattainable: as if they were protected all around by a wall of crystal. They did not resemble one another. Tall, thin, bald, with long pale faces shadowed by a growth of beard, dressed always in blue or black, and accustomed, moreover, to inject into their devotion an intensity, a fanatical ardor of which their brother-in-law and nephew — you only had to look at them — would never have been capable, the Venetian relations seemed to belong to a civilization completely alien to Alberto's sweaters and tobacco-colored long stockings, to Professor Ermanno's English woolens and tan cottons, a scholar's, a country gentleman's. And yet, different as they were, I felt a deep solidarity among them. What was there in common — all four seemed to say to themselves — between them and the distracted, whispering floor below, so *Italian*, which even in the temple, before the opened Ark of the Lord, continued to concern itself with all the pettiness of common life, business, politics, even sport, but never the soul and God? I was a boy then: between ten and twelve years old. An intuition, confused, yes, but substantially correct, was mingled with irritation and humiliation in me, equally confused, but searing, the intuition that I was part of the downstairs, the vulgar throng to be avoided. And my father? At the glass wall beyond which the Finzi-Continis and the Herreras, polite always, but distant, continued basically to ignore him, he behaved in a manner the opposite of mine. Instead of attempting approaches, as I did, I saw him react — he, with his doctorate in medicine, a freethinker, a war volunteer, a Fascist with a 1919 party card, an impassioned sports fan, he, a modern Jew, in other words — by exaggerating his own healthy intolerance of any excessively servile, shameless exhibition of devotion.

When there passed along the benches the happy procession of *sefarìm* (wrapped in rich short mantles of embroidered silk, with silver crowns askew and tinkling little bells, they seemed, the sacred scrolls of the Torah, an array of royal infants displayed to the populace to shore up a tottering monarchy), the doctor and the engineer Herrera were prompt to lean forward impetuously beyond the bench, kissing as many mantle hems as they could, with an almost indecent eagerness, greed. What did it matter that Professor Ermanno, imitated by his son, simply covered his eyes with a corner of the *talèd* and murmured a prayer with his lips?

"What a fuss, what *haltud*!" my father would comment later, at table: not that this prevented him, perhaps immediately afterwards, from returning once more to the hereditary pride of the Finzi-Continis, the absurd isolation in which they lived, as aristocrats, or even to their subterranean, persistent anti-Semitism. But for the moment, having no one else at hand, it was I that he took it out on.

As usual, I had turned to look.

"Would you do me the great favor of sitting properly!" he hissed at me, his teeth clenched, as his irate blue eyes glared at me in exasperation. "You don't know how to behave even in temple. Look at your brother here: four years younger than you, but he could teach you manners!"

I didn't hear. A little later, there I was again, turning my back to Dr. Levi's chanting, heedless of every prohibition.

Now, to have me again for some moments in his control — physical, mind you, only physical — my father could only wait for the solemn blessing, when all the sons would be gathered under the paternal *taletòd*, like so many tents. And there, finally (the sexton Carpanetti had already gone round with his pole, lighting one by one the synagogue's thirty candelabra of silver and ormolu: the hall blazed with light) there, awesomely awaited, Dr. Levi's voice, usually so colorless, suddenly assumed the prophetic tone suited to the supreme, and final, moment of the *berahà*.

"*Jevarehehà Adonài veishmerèha* . . ." the rabbi began solemnly, bent, almost prostrate, over the *tevà*, after having covered his towering white cap with the *talèd*.

"Now, boys," my father said then, happy and brisk, snapping his fingers, "come under here!"

In reality, even in that situation, escape was always possible. It was all very well for Papà to press his hard, athletic hands on our collars, on mine in particular. Though vast as a tablecloth, Grandfather Raffaello's *talèd*, which Papà used, was too worn and full of holes to guarantee the hermetic cloistering he dreamed of. And in fact, through the holes and rips produced by the years in the very fragile cloth, which smelled of age and must, it was not hard, for me at least, to observe Professor Ermanno as, there beside me, his hands placed on Alberto's dark hair and on the fine, light, blond hair of Micòl, who had rushed down from the women's section, he also said, one after the other, following Dr. Levi, the words of the *berahà*. Over our heads, my father, who knew no more than twenty words of Hebrew, the usual ones of family conversation — and moreover he would never have bent — kept silent. I imagined the suddenly embarrassed expression of his face, his eyes, at once sardonic and shy, raised towards the modest stucco decorations of the ceiling or towards the women's section. But meanwhile, from where I was, I looked up, with always renewed amazement and envy, at Professor Ermanno's wrinkled, keen face, as if transfigured at that moment, I looked at his eyes, which, behind his glasses, I would have said were filled with tears. His voice was faint and chanting, with perfect pitch: his Hebrew pronunciation, frequently doubling the consonants, and with the *z*, the *s*, and the *h* much more Tuscan than Ferrarese, could be heard, filtered through the double distinction of culture and rank . . .

I looked at him. Below him, for the entire duration of the blessing, Alberto and Micòl never stopped exploring, they too, the gaps in their tent. And they smiled at me and winked at me, both curiously inviting: especially Micòl.

5

ONE TIME, HOWEVER, in June of '29, the day when the final *ginnasio* examination results were posted in the entrance of the Guarini, something unusual happened.

During the orals I hadn't shone, and I knew it.

Though Professor Meldolesi had done his best to favor me, even managing, against all regulations, to have himself chosen to question me, nevertheless at the famous *pons asinorum* I had not by any means been at the high level of the numerous sevens and eights that dotted my report card. Even in the literary examinations I should have done much better. Questioned, in Latin, on the *consecutio temporum*, I had stumbled in a hypothetical sentence of the third type, namely the "contrary to fact." I also had trouble responding in Greek, on a passage of the *Anabasis*. It is true that later I regained some ground with Italian, history, and geography. In Italian, for example, I had done very well, both on *I promessi sposi* and on *Le ricordanze*. I had then recited from memory the first three octaves of *Orlando furioso*, without missing a word; and Meldolesi promptly rewarded me with a "bravo!" so ringing that it brought smiles not only from the rest of the examining board but also from me. In general, however, I repeat, my performance, even in the field of literature, had not been up to the reputation I enjoyed.

Even the year before, in the fourth year of *ginnasio*, algebra had refused to enter my head. Moreover, with Signora Fabiani, the teacher, my behavior had always been fairly despicable. I would study the minimum necessary to get a six out of her; and often, not even that minimum, as I was relying on the unfailing support I would receive, in the finals, from Professor Meldolesi. What importance could mathematics have anyway for someone, like me, who had declared more than once that, at the university, he was going to study literature? — I kept saying to myself, even that morning, as I rode on my bicycle up Corso Giovecca, towards the Guarini. In algebra and also in geometry, I had hardly opened my mouth, unfortunately. But what of it? Poor Signora Fabiani, who had never dared, during the past two years, give me less than a six in the council of professors, would never do so now. And as I avoided uttering even mentally the word "flunked," the very idea of flunking, with its consequent wake of the tiresome and depressing private lessons I would be subjected to in Riccione through the whole summer, seemed absurd, in my case. I, yes I, who had never suffered the humiliation of October make-up exams, and indeed, in the first, second, and third years of *ginnasio*, had been honored "for good studies and conduct" with the sought-after title of "Guard of Honor at the Monument to the Fallen and the Memorial Park," *I*, flunked, reduced to mediocrity, confused with the masses! And what about Papà? If, hypothetically speaking, la Fabiani had given me a temporary failure till October (she taught math also at the *liceo*, Signora Fabiani: for this reason she had questioned me, it was her right!), where would I find the courage, in a few hours' time, to go home, to sit at the table opposite Papà, and start eating? He, Papà, would perhaps beat me: and it would have been better, after all. Any punishment would have been preferable to the reproach that would come to me from his silent, terrible blue eyes . . .

I entered the hall of the Guarini. A group of youngsters, among whom I immediately noticed various friends, was calmly standing in front of the results of the middle grades. I propped my bicycle against the wall, beside the front door, and I approached, trembling. Nobody seemed to notice my arrival.

I looked from behind a hedge of stubbornly turned backs. My eyesight blurred. I looked again: and the red five, the only number in red ink in a long row of black numbers, was impressed on my spirit with the violence and burning pain of a brand.

"Well, what's wrong with you?" Sergio Pavani asked me, giving me a friendly tap on the back. "You're not going to make a tragedy out of a five in math, I hope! Look at me," he laughed. "Latin and Greek."

"Cheer up," Otello Forti added. "I failed a subject too: English."

I stared at him, in a daze. We had been classmates, deskmates in the first grade, accustomed since then to studying together, one day at his house, the next at mine, and both of us convinced of my superiority. No year passed without my being promoted in June, while he, Otello, always had to make up some subject: English one time, Latin another, or math, or Italian.

An now, suddenly, to hear myself compared to *an* Otello Forti: and by Otello himself, what's more! To find myself hurled suddenly down to his level!

It is not worth narrating at length what I did, what I thought, during the next four or five hours, beginning with the effect, as I was coming out of the Guarini, of my meeting Professor Meldolesi (smiling, he was, without hat and tie, the collar of his striped shirt turned up, à la Robespierre, and quick to confirm, as if there had been any need, la Fabiani's "doggedness" in my case, her categorical refusal to "close an eye one more time"), and then to continue with the description of the long, desperate, aimless wandering to which I abandoned myself once I had received, from the same Professor Meldolesi, a friendly pat on the cheek of dismissal and encouragement. Suffice it to say that around two in the afternoon I was still roaming, on my bicycle, along the Mura degli Angeli, in the vicinity of Corso Ercole I d'Este. I hadn't even telephoned home. My face streaked with tears, my heart brimming with an immense self-pity, I rode along almost not knowing where I was, meditating vague suicide plans.

I stopped under a tree: one of those ancient trees — lindens, elms, planes, chestnuts — that a dozen years later, in the icy winter of Stalingrad, would be sacrificed to make firewood, but which in '29 still held high, over the city bastions, their great umbrellas of leaves.

Around me, absolute emptiness. The packed-dirt path that, like a sleep-walker, I had covered from Porta San Giovanni to here, went on winding among the age-old trunks towards Porta San Benedetto and the railway station. I stretched out in the grass, prone beside the bicycle, my face, which was burning, hidden in the crook of my elbow. Warm, breezy air around the outstretched body, desire only to lie like this, eyes closed. In the hypnotic chorus of the cicadas, only an occasional isolated sound stood out: a cock's crowing from the nearby gardens, a slamming of clothes perhaps made by a washerwoman lingering to do her laundry in the greenish water of the Panfilio Canal, and finally, very close, inches from my ear, the clicking, slower and slower, of the bicycle's rear wheel, still seeking the point of immobility.

By now, surely — I thought — at home they had already heard the news: from Otello Forti, no doubt. Had they sat down to dinner? Yes, probably, acting as if nothing had happened: even if then, unable to continue, they had been forced to interrupt the meal. Perhaps they were looking for me. Perhaps they had unleashed Otello himself, the good friend, the inseparable friend, giving him the task of searching on his bicycle the entire city, Montagnone and walls included, so it was possible that I might see him turn up at any moment, Otello, with a saddened face assumed for the occasion, but overjoyed, as I would clearly realize, at having flunked only English. But no: perhaps, seized with anxiety, my parents had not been satisfied only with Otello, they had even set the police in motion. My father had gone there, to the Castle, to speak to the chief. I could see him stammering, distraught, frightfully aged, the shadow of himself. He was crying. Ah, but if he had been able to see me, two hours ago, at Pontelagoscuro, while I stared at the current of the Po from the height of the iron bridge (I had stayed there quite a while, looking down! How long? At the very least, twenty minutes . . .), then he would really have been frightened . . . then he would really have understood . . . then he really . . .

"Psst."

I woke with a start, but I didn't open my eyes at once.

"Psst!" I heard again.

I slowly raised my head, turning it to the left, against the sun, Who was calling me? It couldn't be Otello. Who then?

I was about halfway along that stretch of the city walls which runs for a mile or so, from the end of Corso Ercole I to Porta San Benedetto, opposite the station. The place has always been particularly solitary. It was thirty years ago, and it still is today, despite the fact that, to the right especially towards the Industrial Zone, that is, since '45, dozens and dozens of vari-colored little workers' houses have sprung up, against which, and against the smokestacks and warehouses that are their background, the dark, bushy, wild, half-ruined spur of the fifteenth-century bastion seems every day more absurd.

I looked, I sought, half closing my eyes against the glare. At my feet (I realized only now), the crowns of its noble trees swollen with the noon light like those of a tropical forest, there stretched the Barchetto del Duca: immense, really endless, with the little towers and pinnacles of the *magna domus* in the center, half-hidden in the green, and bounded, for its whole perimeter, by a wall interrupted only about fifty yards farther on, to allow the Panfilio Canal to empty.

"Hey, you're really blind!" a girl's merry voice said.

From the blond hair, that special blond, streaked with Nordic locks, which was hers alone, like a *fille aux cheveux de lin*, I immediately recognized Micòl Finzi-Contini. She was leaning over the park wall, thrusting her shoulders forward, her folded arms resting on the top. She must have been no more than twenty meters away. She was looking up at me, observing me: close enough for me to be able to see her eyes, which were pale, big (too big, perhaps, then, in her thin little-girl's face).

"What are you doing up there? I've been watching you for ten minutes. If you were sleeping and I've waked you up, I'm sorry. And . . . sincere condolences!"

"Condolences? What? Why?" I stammered, feeling my face covered with blushes.

I had pulled myself up.

"What time is it?" I asked, raising my voice.

She glanced at her wristwatch.

"I have three o'clock," she said, with a pretty grimace. And then: "I imagine you must be hungry."

I had lost my bearings. So they also knew! I even thought, for a moment, that the news of my disappearance had reached them directly from my father or my mother: by telephone, as, surely, it had reached countless other people. But it was Micòl who immediately set me straight.

"This morning I went to the Guarini with Alberto. We went to look at the grades. It hit you hard, eh?"

"And you? Were you promoted?"

"We don't know yet. Maybe they're waiting, to post our grades, until the other private students have also finished. But why don't you come down? Come closer, so I won't have to yell."

It was the first time she had spoken to me. Moreover: it was the first time, practically, that I had heard her speak. And at once I noticed how her speech resembled Alberto's. They both spoke in the same way: slowly, as a rule, underlining certain trivial words, whose true meaning , true weight, only they seemed to know, and skipping, in a bizarre way, over other words that one would have thought far more important. They considered this their *real* language: their special, inimitable, completely private distortion of Italian. They even gave it a name: Finzi-Continian.

Letting myself slide down the grassy bank, I approached the bottom of the wall. Despite the shade — a shade that smelled sharply of nettles and of dung — it was hotter, there. And now she was looking at me from above, her blond head in the sun, calm, as if our meeting had not been a casual encounter, entirely accidental, but as if, since the days perhaps when we were little children, the time we had made appointments to meet in the place were beyond counting.

"You're exaggerating, all the same," she said. "What does a make-up exam in October in one subject count?"

But she was teasing me, that was clear, and she also felt a slight contempt for me. It was fairly normal, after all, that such a thing should have happened to a character like me, son of people so common, so "assimilated": a quasi-*goy*, in short. What right did I have to make such a fuss?

"I think you have some rather strange notions," I answered.

"Do I?" she grinned. "Then explain to me, please, the reason why you didn't go home to dinner today?"

"How do you know?" The question escaped from me.

"We know, we know. We also have our informers."

It had been Meldolesi — I thought — it could only have been he (in fact, I was not mistaken). But what did it matter? Suddenly I realized that the question of being flunked had become secondary, a childish matter that would work itself out.

"How can you manage," I asked, "to stay up there? You look as if you were at a window."

"My feet are on my faithful ladder," she answered, separating the syllables of "my faithful," in her usual, proud way.

From beyond the wall, at this point, a deep barking rose. Micòl looked around, giving a rapid glance behind her, filled at once with annoyance and affection. She pouted at the dog, then looked my way again.

"Uff!" she sighed calmly. "It's Jor."

"What breed is he?"

"A Great Dane. He's only a year old, but he weighs about two hundred pounds. He's always following me. Lots of times I try to cover my tracks, but after a while, he's sure to find me. He's *terrible*."

Then, almost without a pause:

"Want me to let you in?" she asked. "If you want, I'll show you right away what you must do."

6

How many years have gone by since that far-off afternoon in June? More than thirty. Nevertheless, if I close my eyes, Micòl Finzi-Contini is still there, leaning over the wall of her garden, looking at me, and speaking to me. She was hardly more than a child, in 1929, a thirteen-year-old, thin and blond, with great, pale, magnetic eyes. I, a little boy in short pants, very bourgeois and very vain, whom a minor scholastic mishap was enough to plunge into the most childish desperation. We stared at each other. Above her, the sky was a uniform blue, a warm sky, already of summer, without the slightest cloud. Nothing could change it, and nothing has changed it, in fact, in my memory.

"Well, do you want to or not?" Micòl insisted.

"Um . . . I don't know . . ." I began saying, with a nod at the wall. "It seems very high to me."

"That's because you haven't taken a good look," she replied impatiently. "See there . . . and there . . . and there," and she pointed her finger, for me to observe. "There are lots of notches, and even a spike, up here. I drove it in myself."

"Yes, there would be footholds, for that matter," I murmured, hesitant, "but . . ."

"Footholds!" she interrupted me, at once, bursting out laughing. "I call them notches myself."

"You're wrong. They're called footholds," I insisted, stubborn and sharp. "Obviously you've never been in the mountains."

I have always suffered from vertigo, since childhood, and, slight as it was, the climb made me stop and think. As a child, when my mother, with Ernesto in her arms (Fanny was not yet born), took me up on the Montagnone, and she sat in the grass of the broad lawn facing Via Scandiana, from which you could just glimpse the roof of our house, barely discernible in the sea of roofs around the great bulk of the church of Santa Maria in Vado, it was with some fear, I remember, that I eluded Mamma's vigilance and went to lean over the parapet that bounded the lawn towards the country, where I would look down, into the abyss a hundred feet deep. Almost always, along the sheer wall, someone was climbing up or down: young masons, peasants, laborers, each with a bicycle over his shoulder, and old men, too, mustachioed fishermen of frogs and catfish, loaded with rods and creels: all people from Quacchio, from Ponte della Gradella, from Coccomaro, from Coccomarino, from Focomorto, who were in a hurry, and rather than come around by Porta San Giorgio or Porta San Giovanni (because at that period the bastions were intact on that side, with no breaches for a length of almost three miles), they preferred to take, as they said, the "wall road." Some were leaving the city: in this case, having crossed the lawn, they passed by, without looking at me, climbing over the parapet and slipping down until the tip of their foot touched the first outcrop or niche in the decrepit wall, until they reached, in a few minutes, the meadow below. Or they were arriving from the country: and then they came up with widened eyes that seemed to me fixed in mine, as those eyes timidly peered over the edge of the parapet. But on the contrary, I was mistaken; obviously they were alert only to select the best foothold. In any case, while they were there like that, suspended over the abyss — in pairs, as a rule: one behind the other — I could hear them chatting calmly, in dialect, exactly as if they were walking along a path among the fields. How calm they were, strong, and brave — I said to myself. After they had come to within inches of my face, so that often, besides mirroring me in their own flushed faces, they struck me with the wine-stink of their breath; their thick, callused fingers grasping the inner edge of the parapet, they emerged from the void with their whole body, and, *allez-oop*, they were home safe. I would never have been capable of doing such a thing — I repeated to myself each time, watching them go off: full of admiration, but also of revulsion.

Well, I was feeling something similar again, before the wall to whose summit Micòl Finzi-Contini was inviting me to climb. The wall certainly did not appear as high as that of the Montagnone bastions. Still it was smoother, far less eroded by the years and the weather; and the indentations that Micòl pointed out to me were bare scratches. What if — I thought — after climbing up there, I were to feel dizzy and fall? I might be killed all the same.

And yet, it was not so much for this reason that I still hesitated. I was held back by a repugnance different from the purely physical one of vertigo: similar, but different, and stronger. For a moment I even regretted my desperation of a moment before, my foolish, puerile tears of a flunked schoolboy.

"And besides, I don't see any reason," I continued, "why I should start mountain climbing here, of all places. If I am to come into *your family's* house, thank you very much, I'm delighted: however, frankly, it seems far more comfortable to come in that way" — and with this, I raised my arm in the direction of Corso Ercole I — "by the front door. It would only take a minute. With my bicycle, I can cover the distance in no time."

I realized at once that she didn't welcome my suggestion.

"Oh no, no . . . " she said, distorting her face in an expression of intense annoyance, "if you come that way, Perotti is bound to see you, and then it's all over, there's no fun then."

"Perotti. Who's he?"

"The gatekeeper. You know. You may have noticed him; he's our coachman and chauffeur, too. . . . If he sees you — and he can't help but see you, because, except for when he goes out with the carriage or the car, he's always there on guard, the beast — afterwards, then I'd absolutely have to take you into the house . . . and I ask you if . . . You see?"

She looked me straight in the eyes: grave, now, though quite calm.

"All right," I answered, turning my head, and pointing with my chin towards the embankment, "but what about my bicycle? Where can I put it? I can't leave it there, after all, by itself! It's new, a Wolsit: with an electric headlight, a tool kit, pump. . . .Imagine! . . . I'm not going to let them steal my bicycle *too* . . ."

And I said nothing more, suddenly gripped again by the anguish of the inevitable meeting with my father. That very evening, at the latest, I would have to go home. I had no other choice.

I turned my eyes again towards Micòl. Without saying anything, while I talked, she sat on the wall, her back to me; and now she sharply raised one leg, to sit astride.

"What are you up to?" I said, surprised.

"I've had an idea, for the bicycle. And, at the same time, I can show you the best places to put your feet. Now watch where I put mine. Look!"

She spun around, up there on the top, with great nonchalance, then, her right hand grasping the big rusty spike she had pointed out to me a little earlier, she began to climb down. She descended slowly, but sure of herself, seeking the footholds with the tips of her little tennis shoes, first one, then the other, and always finding them without much effort. She climbed down well. Still before touching the ground, she missed a hold and slipped. She landed on her feet. But she had hurt her fingers; and, scraping against the wall, her little pink cotton dress, a beach-dress, had torn slightly beneath one arm.

"Stupid me," she grumbled, putting her hand to her mouth and blowing on it. "This is the first time that's happened to me."

She had also skinned her knee. She pulled up the hem of her dress, baring her thigh, strangely white and strong, already a woman's, and she bent to examine the bruise. Two long blond locks, the paler ones, escaping the little ring which held her hair in place, fell down, hiding her forehead and her eyes.

"How stupid," she repeated.

"You should put alcohol on it," I said mechanically, without approaching her, in the slightly whining tone that all of us, in my family, assumed in such situations."

"Alcohol, my foot."

She rapidly licked the wound: a kind of affectionate little kiss; and promptly she straightened up.

"Come on," she said, all flushed and disheveled.

She turned and began to climb up obliquely along the sunny slope of the embankment. She helped herself with her right hand, grabbing the clumps of grass; meanwhile, the left, at her head, was removing and replacing the little band that held her hair. She repeated the maneuver several times, as rapidly as if she were using a comb.

"You see that hole, there?" she said to me then, as soon as we had reached the top. "You can hide your bicycle inside there. It's perfect."

She was pointing out, perhaps fifty yards away, one of those little grassy conical mounds, no more than five feet high, the entrance almost always sunk in the ground, that you come upon fairly frequently as you make the circle of the walls of Ferrara. At first sight, they resemble somewhat the Etruscan *montarozzi* of the Roman Campagna, on a much smaller scale, of course. But the subterranean room, often vast, to which some of them still allow access, never served as the home for any dead person. The ancient defenders of the walls kept their weapons there: culverins, harquebuses, gunpowder, and so on. And perhaps also those strange cannon balls, of precious marble, that in the fifteenth and sixteenth centuries made the Ferrara artillery so feared in Europe, and of which you can still see some examples in the Castle, placed as ornaments in the central courtyard and on the terraces.

"Who would ever guess there's a brand-new Wolsit down there? They would have to know in advance. Have you ever been down?

I shook my head.

"No? I have. Lots of times. It's *magnificent*."

She moved with decision, and picking up the Wolsit from the ground, I followed her in silence.

I overtook her on the threshold of the opening. It was a kind of vertical fissure, cut sharply in the blanket of grass that, compact, covered the mound: so narrow that only one person could pass through it at a time. Just beyond the threshold the descent began, and you could see eight or ten yards ahead, no more. Farther, there were only shadows. As if the passage ended against a black curtain.

She leaned forward to look, then turned.

"You go down," she whispered, and she smiled faintly, embarrassed. "I'd rather wait for you up here."

She stood aside, clasping her hands behind her back, and leaning against the grass wall, beside the entrance.

"You're not scared, are you?" she asked, still in a low voice.

"No, no," I lied; and I bent to raise the bicycle and hoist it to my shoulder.

Without another word, I stepped past her, entering the passage.

I had to proceed slowly, also because of the bicycle, whose right pedal kept banging against the wall; and at first, for five or six feet at least, I was virtually blind; I could see nothing, absolutely nothing. At about ten yards from the entrance opening, however ("Be careful," the already distant voice of Micòl, behind my back, shouted at this point: "watch out for the steps!") I began to discern something. The passage ended a little farther on: there were only a few more yards of descent. And it was there, in fact, starting from a kind of landing, around which, even before arriving there, I guessed a completely different space existed, it was there that the steps announced by Micòl began.

When I had reached the landing, I paused briefly.

The childish fear of the dark and the unknown, which I had felt the moment I left Micòl, had gradually been replaced, in me, as I advanced in the underground passage, by a feeling, no less childish, of relief: as if, having saved myself in time from Micòl's company, I had escaped a great danger, the greatest danger a boy of my age ("a boy of your age" was one of my father's favorite expressions) could encounter. Ah, yes — I was thinking now — tonight, when I go home, Papà may even beat me. But now I can face his blows with serenity. One subject to make up by October: she was right, Micòl, to laugh at it. What was one examination in October compared to the rest (and I trembled) that there, in the darkness, might have happened to us? Perhaps I would have found the courage to give Micòl a kiss: a kiss on the lips. And then? What would have happened, then? In the movies I had seen, and in novels, it was all very well for kisses to be long and impassioned! In reality, compared to the *rest*, they represented only a brief instant, a moment actually negligible, if after the lips had met and the mouths almost penetrated each other, the thread of the story could most of the time be picked up only the next morning, or even several days later. Yes, but if Micòl and I had reached the point of kissing like that — and the darkness would surely have fostered it — after the kiss time would have continued to flow calmly, with no outside, providential intervention to help us suddenly reach the harbor of the following morning. What would I have had to do, then, to fill the minutes and the hours? Ah, but this hadn't happened. Thank goodness I had saved myself.

I began to go down the steps. Into the passage a few weak rays of light penetrated: now I was aware of them. And a bit by sight, a bit with my hearing (a trifle sufficed: for the bicycle to bump against the wall, or a heel to skid down from the step, and immediately the echo enlarged and multiplied the sound, measuring spaces and distances), I soon realized how vast the place was. It must have been a chamber about a hundred feet in diameter — I calculated — round, with a high domed ceiling at least the same height: a kind of upside-down funnel. Who knows, perhaps, through a system of secret corridors, it communicated with other underground rooms of the same sort, nesting by the dozens in the body of the bastions. Nothing could be more likely.

The floor was of packed earth, smooth, hard, and damp. I stumbled over a brick, then, groping my way along the curve of the wall,

I trampled on some straw. Propping the bicycle against the wall, I sat down, remaining with one hand gripping the wheel of the Wolsit, and an arm around my knees. The silence was broken only by some rustling, an occasional squeak: rats, perhaps, or bats. . .

And if, on the other hand, it had happened — I thought — would it have been so terrible, if it had happened?

Almost certainly I would not have gone home, and my parents, and Otello Forti, and Sergio Pavani, and all the others, police included, would have hunted for me in vain! The first few days they would have breathlessly searched everywhere. The papers would have talked about it too, dragging out the usual hypotheses: kidnapping, accident, suicide, illegal expatriation. Little by little, things would have calmed down, all the same. My parents would have consoled themselves (after all, they still had Ernesto and Fanny), the search would have stopped. And the one who would really pay, in the end, would have been that stupid humbug, la Fabiani, who, in punishment, would have been transferred to "another educational institution," as Professor Meldolesi would put it. Where? Sicily or Sardinia, no doubt. And it would serve her right! She would learn, at her own expense, to be less mean and treacherous.

As for me, seeing that the others consoled themselves, I would do the same. I would count on Micòl, outside: she would take care of supplying me with food and anything I might need. And she would come to me every day, climbing over the wall of her garden, summer and winter. And every day we would kiss each other, in the darkness: because I was her man, and she, my woman.

And anyway this didn't mean I could never come out into the open again! During the day I would sleep, obviously, breaking off only when I felt Micòl's lips graze mine, and, later, dozing off again with her in my arms. At night, however, at night I could very well make long sorties, especially if I chose the hours after one or two in the morning, when everyone is in bed, and nobody, practically speaking, is in the streets of the city. Strange and terrible, but actually so amusing, to pass along Via Scandiana; to see our house again, the window of my bedroom, by now turned into a sitting room; to hide in the shadows and from afar glimpse my father, coming home, just at this hour, from the Merchants Club, and it never crosses his mind that I am alive and am watching him. In fact, he takes the key from his pocket, opens the door, enters, and then, calmly, just as if I, his older son, had never existed, shuts the door again with a single thud.

And Mamma? One day or another couldn't I try to inform her (through Micòl, perhaps) at least that I wasn't dead? And see her, too, before, weary of my subterranean life, I left Ferrara and disappeared definitely? Why not? Of course I could!

I don't know how long I stayed there. Ten minutes, perhaps; perhaps less. I recall precisely, in any case, that as I was climbing up the steps and entering once more the passage (relieved of the burden of the bicycle, I moved quickly now), I continued to think, to let my imagination range. And Mamma — I asked myself — would she also forget me, like all the others?

In the end I found myself outside again; and Micòl was no longer there waiting for me where I had left her a little while before; instead, as I saw almost immediately, shielding my eyes with my hand against the sunlight, she was up there again, seated astride the garden wall of the Barchetto del Duca.

She was arguing and parleying with someone waiting for her at the foot of the ladder, on the other side of the wall: the coachman Perotti, probably, or even Professor Ermanno himself. It was clear: having noticed the ladder against the wall, they had immediately become aware of her brief escape. Now they were telling her to come down. And she couldn't make up her mind to obey.

Suddenly she turned, and saw me at the top of the embankment. Then she puffed out her cheeks, as if to say:

"Uff! Finally!"

And her last look, before she vanished behind the wall (a look accompanied by a smiling wink: just as when, in temple, she peeped at me from beneath her father's *talèd*), had been for me.

CARLO LEVI

FROM *The Watch*

Carlo Levi and Alberto Moravia.

Courtesy of Fototeca Servizio Informazioni.

I MUST START OFF WITHOUT losing time; but it wasn't so easy. First of all, there was the newspaper, and I couldn't leave it in these days of crisis without giving careful instructions. And then, how could I get to Naples at this hour? There were practically no trains and they took a whole day to get there and were stopped at many points by the damage from the war — broken switches, ruined bridges and uprooted rails. An incredible crowd of men and women jammed into a few cattle cars. They had sacks, suitcases, bundles, automobile tires, various kinds of boxes, packs, demijohns, tin cans for oil, and all kinds of containers. They climbed up and down at every station and at stops in the open countryside as well, actively trading goods. These were voyages in search of food and business. There was no place among them for a traveler in haste. Busses and little broken-down trucks made better time, but they left early in the morning and there was no use thinking of them.

Casorin told me that the only possibility was to take one of those private automobiles or taxis that carried passengers and left when all the seats were taken. Piazza San Giovanni was the place where they arrived and departed. I could go there. It was easier to find them in the morning up till noon, but if I didn't wait too long I could still find something.

I decided to do that. I succeeded in getting Roselli on the telephone after many vain attempts and loss of time. He promised to take care of things at the paper, to supply the news and watch the editorials. But he urged me to come back as soon as I could, if possible to return the next day. Canio too came to the telephone and gave me his rustic and affectionate good wishes. He said:

"Don't worry about leaving. If you take an automobile it'll cost you too much. Remember to haggle over the price. . . . Of course I do realize you're in haste. . . . You don't need to worry. I'm here."

Now I had to arrange with Moneta and Casorin about the work. I entrusted Moneta with supervising the paper and making up the pages. I made a bet with him that our bearded editor, who worked by day in a shoe shop and for many months had been writing daily editorials on the profound philosophy of history that I'd then daily thrown into the wastebasket, would profit by my absence and Moneta's distraction to print at least one of these incomprehensible masterpieces of his on the front page. I advised them both not to abuse my absence too shamelessly, packed my bag, and was ready to leave.

The dead man's body was still on the staircase where I'd left it the night before, with his head hanging down the steps. They hadn't touched him, but were still waiting for the police permit. They'd covered him with a sheet, and hidden thus he looked like a white package, smaller and thinner than a human being. At his sides they had placed two candlesticks with lighted candles in them. The candles were half consumed and burned lazy and yellow in the shadows. On top of the sheet the dog was stretched out prostrate over his body, his head between his paws, exhausted by fatigue and by terror. He had no voice left. As I passed he scarcely lifted his muzzle or opened his eyes. Perhaps he tried to bark but from his throat came only a hoarse growl. Then, tired by even this effort, he lowered his head and was silent. I hurried across the landing below the corpse where a woman and a little girl, their heads covered by black veils, were saying prayers, and two men, leaning against the wall with a bored air, silently watched the bundle illuminated by the candles.

Why does one conceal the dead, closing their eyes, wrapping them in shrouds, in sheets, in covers, covering them before they are hidden forever under the soil with an anguish that is called pity? Is it perhaps from a magic terror of their spent looks, of their power? This was the latest of the dead, but how many we had seen in those years stretched on the ground of both the city and the countryside!

At Ponte del Pino in the smoke and the dust of the rubble I had counted eighteen of the corpses lined up on the pavement. There had certainly been more, because here and there on the street lay pieces of other men. The first people to run up had covered them immediately. They had hidden whole bodies under fallen window shutters. Over the largest fragments they had put sackcloth or coats, whatever came first to hand; over the smallest they had put handkerchiefs. It looked like laundry put out on the ground to dry. Except that among the stones of the street and the rails of the trolleys shreds had been forgotten: clots of blood or of brains, a toe, an eye, a piece of skin with long blond hair on it, the hand of a child.

Frightened people running toward their houses turned around and looked at the remains and without stopping made the sign of the cross with pitying disgust. How many other dead, everywhere in incalculable numbers, had been left on the earth of Europe, uncovered and naked, in the sun and the frost, looking at the sky, until they were reduced to putrefied flesh, the prey of stray dogs and of the rain. Everyone had seen them, or it was as if they had seen them. People now hurried to forget in order to live, even though the air was still crowded with the presence of the dead.

We went down the stairs with faster pace than the solemn princely staircase allowed. In the vestibule between the pillars, Teo, like a prehistoric stone, saw us hurrying by and hardly greeted us, nodding his frowning marbled head almost imperceptibly, like the statue of the Commendatore at the passage of a Don Giovanni in flight, followed by two Leporellos.

We ran to the corner of the Piazza Venezia. I didn't want to lose any more time. I was lucky. A little truck went by, and a boy sitting on the side leaned out and shouted: "San Giovanni!"

I said goodbye quickly to Casorin and Moneta, ran after the machine, grabbed the side and, helped by the occupants who pulled me up almost bodily, I jumped in.

This was an old discarded truck like all the others that after years and years of service had run to hide itself during the German epoch in some ambush, under some shed or some stack of straw where it had ended up by rusting and disintegrating. Later it had been adapted in a few hours for carrying people, equipped with wooden sides, iron frames that carried a canvas top for rainy days, two rough benches for passengers, tires that had been found at a bargain or stolen from the Allies. Bandaged and cured as well as possible, it had started to race the streets right after the liberation, to move people, to fill the road with noise and the stench of gasoline, cheerful, shoddy and clamorous. Streetcars and busses were lacking; the trucks had taken their places; tattered, irregular and disorderly, an army of sans-culottes in rags that held the traditional armies in check. They were ugly and uncomfortable but still they were a free popular invention of bad times, full of courage and initiative, and it was as if they knew this and demonstrated it in their sprightly, impulsive and even enthusiastic gait. They were usually packed. Since they had no time schedule they stayed at their terminals until at last they were unbelievably jammed with passengers who waited patiently or cursed, with their knees fitted into their neighbors' like Nantes sardines in a tin can.

My truck, however, wasn't full. There were no empty seats but by bending under the low iron framework I could stand up back of the driver's box and from up there watch the street rushing along under the wheels. The wind blew in my face and through my hair. I felt as light as a bird. I didn't know yet whether I'd find a way to go to Naples but I was already on my way, detached from things; from the town, from the people, filled with a delightful sudden sense of solitude. The world holds us with a thousand ties of habit, work, inertia, affections. It's difficult and painful to separate from them. But as soon as a foot rests on a train, airplane or automobile that will carry us away, everything disappears, the past becomes remote and is buried, a new time crowded to the brim with unknown promises envelops us and, entirely free and anonymous, we look around searching for new companions.

I held the light weight of my briefcase under my arm. It was my only piece of luggage. That pleased me too. It had taken the war to teach us this readiness, a happy scorn of the most necessary things. How far away those days seemed, actually so near, when at every departure I'd youthfully weigh down my valise with unnecessary stuff from which I thought I couldn't possibly be separated. How could one leave one's letters at home, or manuscripts, or notes on work in progress, or the dearest of one's books or all the other objects to which one was bound by affection? Things suffer when they're left alone, and when we leave them anything can happen: fire, earthquake, an invasion of rats or of the police. One had to take everything along to be prepared for everything. Only then could one feel safe. That's why a boy when he leaves home puts his knife in his pocket like a talisman, that jackknife with many blades, that can be used for anything, adapted to any circumstance, to cut bread or the branch of a tree, and especially as a defense against the enemy. I remember I'd seen at Martino's house an inventory, written by his grandfather at the beginning of the century, that listed all the indispensables to carry on a journey; objects the old man actually took along every time he happened to stir. It was an interminable list that covered eight written pages. It started with his linen, his suits, his shoes, and ended up with various kinds of nails, screws, clamps, hooks, hammers, pincers, wire, candles and every kind of rope, cord and string. We tried in those days to carry our lives along with our heavy baggage, but now we've learned to throw everything away without too much regret, and to start fresh every day.

From my lofty observatory I watched the asphalt run beneath the wheels. The houses fled, and the palaces, churches, ancient ruins, people on the sidewalk.

Farewell to Rome, to the time that is not time, and the place that is no place.

The Colosseum was already behind my back, and the poor little houses of a steep street, and the hospital, and the obelisk, and the Holy Stair that one ascends on one's knees. We had already come down into the square in front of the Basilica of San Giovanni, the place that is sacred to snails, to whistlers, to cloves of garlic brandished like bludgeons, to fireworks on the warm evenings of summer carnivals. Now a gray mist hung over it, from the open space in front of the façade of the Basilica to the most distant houses. It was checkered by trees, sheds, stands, and by people posturing as if they were actors in a play. And the squalls of cold wind seemed to make the draped saints in the cornices shiver, and the street vendors blocked the way, crowding against the walls with their knickknacks on trays like shells encrusting a cliff. I made my way among them, going under the narrow arch of the bastion with its blackened tiles, and I looked out over the expanse beyond the walls where the Basilica and the solemn ancient structures disappeared and a suburban part of town spread out, closed in by the geometric lines of tenement houses, squalid in their recent oldness, with their motion picture houses and suburban taverns. And radiating out as far as one could see was a stretch of desolate streets.

Here, as I'd expected, a few automobiles were beside the elevated sidewalks, and others were cruising slowly, waiting for passengers. They had signs with their place of destination written on them, or else the drivers would call out now and then: "Anzio, Viterbo, Civitavecchia!"

They were all going to nearby towns. Those for longer runs had left before noon. But I was lucky this time too. I saw an old black machine with its top covered by a shapeless mountain of valises and packages. The driver was tying it together with a rope as I approached. He was really going to Naples.

"Come along, come along," the man said to me. "It's the last that'll leave today. We usually leave earlier but we've had to wait to get a load. . . . Step in, we're leaving right away. There's just room for you . . . very comfortable . . . the tariff's one thousand lira. . . . Just look at this machine . . . in less than four hours we'll be there. . . . It takes off like a train. . . . The motor's like new . . . it's just been overhauled. . . . Rest easy . . . and the tires — all American. . . . We'll be in Naples before night. We leave right away."

As he said all this he opened the door of that broken-down wash tub of his, and I got in.

There was one folding seat free and I sat on it, with my briefcase on my knees. On the other folding seat sat a young man wrapped in a military overcoat. Three people were crowding the back seat, two women and a priest. They had already prepared themselves for the trip, swathed up to their necks in a thick blanket. The space between the seats was filled with sacks, packets, bags, handbags and baskets. Next to the driver in the front sat another man. They were all silent. And I too kept still without turning around to stare at my companions. The man outside the car had finished his work on the roof, but we didn't leave.

A young man in mechanic's overalls arrived, carrying more bundles that were somehow shoved into that already jammed and crowded space. Then others came, with mysterious faces, and started to confabulate in low voices with the driver. Then an old man with a big mustache and a piece of paper and a pencil started going over endless calculations with him. Presently the chauffeur went away with the old man. They walked under the archway, gesticulating wildly, and disappeared. It was getting late and they didn't come back. The priest and the women behind were mumbling to one another under their blanket. I was beginning to think we'd never leave when the driver appeared at the end of the square rolling along a big truck tire as if it were a boy's hoop. He tied it to the back of the machine on top of the head of valises that already jutted out behind like an irregular tail.

A young man with a little bag in his hand arrived on the run. They put him at my left on a box between the two folding seats.

And I could no longer move or even turn around. I knew it would be very tiring squeezed in like this for so many hours of the trip, but I'd acquired the necessary patience. While we were waiting with resignation it began to rain, a thin slow rain that in a few moments made the asphalt shining and dark. We had difficulty extricating our arms to crank up the windows with their broken handles. The fellow in the mechanic's clothes came back, talked to the driver and gave him a small bundle of 1000-lira notes. The driver counted them carefully and put them in his big portfolio. When I'd lost all hope that these ceremonies and preparations would ever end, the chauffeur said suddenly: "We're ready." Then he sat down, started the motor and we were off.

The folding seats had no backs. I adjusted myself to sitting rigidly, holding myself up straight. I couldn't move my feet because they were shoved into all that baggage on the floor. I made up my mind to endure this physical strain and that state of lethargy and voluntary torpor that brings with it a sort of laziness and artificial ennui. If one lets oneself go, it wins over the discomfort and almost changes it into a sort of slothful pleasure.

We had all become accustomed to exercise of this kind, to hard benches, to violent bumps, interminable stops, hours spent standing up and the forced immobility that numbs the limbs. The whole of Italy rushed from one end of the country to the other in cattle cars and little trucks, in a continuous voyage that was a discovery, an adventure, a revelation to everyone. People who had never moved in their whole lives were traveling, and a completely new land, a different Italy, opened before their eyes. Some were escaping from the ruins of their old homes, some were searching for relatives and lost friends, some were returning after having been driven here and there by unexpected events, some came and went without any real necessity except a mania to be on the move, an exuberance of vitality, a vague hope of work and gain. The mainspring of all this was trading of one sort or another, the black market, large and small, the bargaining and the exchanging. Men went to the cities looking for jobs, young girls hurried from all directions like moths, to Leghorn and other places where they could still find foreign troops. But most people were buying, selling, dragging bundles, exchanging merchandise. Everyone on his own and in a tacit agreement with everyone else was ready to circumvent the regulations, to overcome the obstacles and to endure the fatigue. Italy's body, pounded by bombs and by armies, bloodless from war, was breathing once again. New and unforeseen blood was circulating in millions of corpuscles, carried everywhere in the most dubious and illicit ways, supplying the necessary oxygen.

People had never traveled as much when everything had been at peace and in order, rails intact, trains running and carrying people to their holidays and to political rallies, and when a strange miracle for so long had filled millions of hearts with a sweet feeling of glory, consoling them for graver evils — the miracle that the trains arrived on time. The new race of travelers, sprung by enchantment from all villages and all markets, had no timetables. They went like migrating birds, trusting themselves to wind and chance.

We had left the city behind after long stretches of suburbs, filled with holes and with scribblings on the walls, while none of the passengers had said a word. Everyone pursued his own thoughts accompanied by the roaring of the old noisy motor. It was the first time since the war that I'd gone to the South. I was eager to see the landscape again that I'd almost forgotten after so many years. The rain striped the window panes. Through the veil of the glass the landscape looked gray, suddenly desolate and solitary at the gates of the city. The first ruins appeared, the hangars of an airfield twisted by the bombs. We continued to ride for a few miles in silence, without exchanging a glance in that monotonous expanse of naked fields. Puffing and sputtering, the machine started to climb a long steep hill. Just as we reached the top and the road widened and turned into a curve, a sudden and violent explosion shook us. We stopped. One of the front tires had blown out.

"It's starting early," exclaimed one of the women from the corner behind me, who must have been used to trips of this kind and such adventures. "God knows when we'll get there."

In those days the tires were old and rotten and often of the wrong size and kind. The roads were bad and sown with nails. Blowouts were very frequent. Therefore it sometimes took days to cover a few hours' journey. One might even think that the tires were malignantly ready to delay those who were in a hurry. I remember two blowouts in rapid succession in the heat of a highway on a summer noon when I was driving many years before, in a taxicab with a young friend. We were accompanying a veteran political refugee, who was wanted by the police, to an appointment with smugglers who were going to take him across the border. We were late. The man was being forced to become an expatriate and was emotional about it and turned pale when he heard those explosions (that seemed to him like gunshots) and the machine swerved. Our gay jokes, tinged perhaps with thoughtless youthful savageness, didn't comfort him, and he kept repeating, "We won't get there in time," as he sat waiting on the edge of the road for the car to be repaired, in the sun and the noise of the cicadas.

We got out of the automobile while the driver, helped by the man who'd been sitting beside him, fixed the jack to change the tire. The rain was light and didn't annoy us. In the distance at the bottom of the hill one could still see Rome and its vague domes. For a while we walked up and down to stretch our legs. I could get a better look now at my companions and exchange a few words with them, although they all seemed ill-humored and taciturn. The driver, who must have been the owner, was a dark-haired young man. He was short, had a little black mustache and long sideburns on a pointed little face. He wore a visored cap and high boots. While he was loosening the bolts he told me he'd brought some rubber cement that was very hard to find, and some tire patches, and also another spare tire. We could rest easy even if we had another blowout. He only hoped we wouldn't have another so we wouldn't have to drive too far in the dark. I looked at the vaunted American tires. Except for one front tire they were all ancient Pirellis full of patches that could hardly stand up. The other travelers were also eyeing the pneumatics with doubt. The two women stood beside the machine. The younger one, wearing a lot of rings, was about forty, with big swelling breasts covered by a dark silk dress. She had a short neck wrapped around by many loops of a necklace, and a red fox thrown over her wide shoulders. From this shining and hairy base emerged a huge face with painted lips, where two small black eyes were sunk in the fat under the shadow of a tuft of curly peroxide hair and the edge of a little felt hat trimmed with a very long vertical feather. The other woman looked somewhat older, perhaps over fifty, with white hair, a long thin pale face and bags under her eyes. Her manner was frightened and she looked demure in her simple black coat. She stood beside her companion in feminine solidarity, but it was evident they did not know one another.

The younger woman looked at a tiny watch, and one could see that they were thinking only of time passing and the perils of the road at night. The priest was ruminating on the same problems but in this casual gathering of strangers he didn't speak a word. He was advanced in years, big and fat, with gray hair, round bulging eyes, flabby cheeks and a highly colored face — the typical country priest. Everything about him, the worn and faded cassock, his corpulence, his thick shoes, his slow, kindly, ingratiating gestures, was tied by habit to a kind of professional manner, an expression at the same time inquisitive, humble and greedy. All this corresponded so precisely to the traditional picture that it seemed almost an imitation. He'd lighted a cigarette and was smoking it in great clouds, holding it straight in the middle of his lips, pursing them at every puff like a suckling. As he smoked away like that he kept throwing preoccupied glances at his big fiber suitcase on top of all the others at the back of the automobile. From the anxiety and fire of his looks, one might have supposed there was a treasure in it.

"It's well tied, your Reverence," the driver's companion shouted as though he were answering those looks. This was the man who had been sitting next to the driver when we left, and who had now finished winding up the baggage again in its complicated circles of rope after he had taken off the spare tire. I couldn't make out whether he was a second driver, an associate or a friend of our chauffeur, or a passenger like the rest of us. Perhaps he was a steady customer who went back and forth every day to Naples in this machine to take care of business he probably shared with the owner. He was a strong-limbed fellow. His face was more animal than human; a low forehead, short wiry hair under a visored oilcloth cap worn backward. His nose was fleshy, his features big and heavy, his jaw square and he was ill-shaven, his skin was dark and burned by the sun in thousands of small wrinkles like old leather. He'd taken off his jacket in spite of the cold and now ran to busy himself around the wheels. He wasn't wearing a shirt but a thick American sweater, dyed dark blue. His sleeves were rolled up. His right arm was entirely covered with tattooing. He must have been a sailor or an ex-sailor. I was looking at the tattoos upside down. Right above his wrist was a kind of complicated and confused coat of arms. Higher up started out a huge design that covered the rest of his arm and lost itself under the sweater toward his shoulder. It was a man and woman embracing and dancing with their legs entwined. She was almost naked with a short skirt like a chambermaid's white apron. Their heads were hidden by the sleeve and I couldn't make out the design immediately. Seen this way only partially, it looked like an undecipherable arabesque but I could finally distinguish the two bodies, the four long legs of the dancers, male and female. Under their feet was a big inscription in blue block lettering, a little irregular because of the curve of the arm and the movement of the skin over the muscles. It looked like one of those inscriptions lovers on the Riviera cut in the leaves of aloes and that are deformed as the plant grows. I went over toward him and while he was testing the strength of the rope around the baggage, I managed to read it without his noticing. Was it an innocent title for the naïve engraving on this skin, or was it a brazen declaration? It said: *Malavita Napolitana.*

The other two companions of the voyage, the young man with the military topcoat and the boy who'd been sitting on the box at my left, had gone farther off to the side of the road and were looking at the landscape. They hadn't yet found a way to talk to one another and stood silent and embarrassed. I walked toward them. The boy saw me smoking my cigar and asked me to let him light his American cigarette from it. He clumsily snapped open his big cigarette case and offered one to the other young man. And so we all started to talk together. The boy told me he was a Neapolitan student and had come to Rome to look for some relatives but he had to get back home before evening. He was certainly no more than eighteen, perhaps younger. He was small, thin and pale, with fuzz on his lip. He wore a black suit, simple and in style, the trousers a little too short, and he had a white silk scarf carefully wrapped around his neck. In spite of a certain affected nonchalance and the fact that his nasal voice was already deepening, one could see he was shy; the son of a petty bourgeois family who was well brought up, full of conventionality, ultra refinement, acquired opinions, courteous in his speech and totally insignificant.

The other was a Calabrian peasant. There was a withdrawn and wary effect from his round obstinate forehead, his little, deepset black eyes and his face with its stubbly beard. Under his overcoat he was wearing worn military clothes and he had on scuffed-out boots. He reluctantly spoke a few clipped sentences in dialect. he'd been a prisoner of war in Germany and Poland, in those deserts of snow. He'd escaped and crossed Europe on foot. He'd arrived in Italy and was finally going to his own countryside in the mountains of Calabria, where his people perhaps thought him dead.

The repairs were finished, the wheel in place, and we rushed back into the automobile. Now it seemed even narrower than before. Crowded together and soggy, we drove off. We were in the *Castelli*, and one village followed another. Everywhere were ruins, disemboweled houses, perilous walls, in those lands whose names are famous for gaiety, feasting and wine. In the midst of these ruins, a few inhabitants wandered about in an aimless manner. They took to the side of the road that was full of holes as the machine passed by splashing water from the puddles. Dogs came out suddenly from under the sheds and doorways where they'd been sheltered and sleeping, and flung themselves barking behind our wheels.

We were on a hill. Under us stretched a flat plain where the war had stagnated for endless months around a canal, a little ditch and a farm. Beyond, the sea appeared gray and smooth under the clouds. Presently we took a side road. We had to make a long detour of many miles because the great bridge at Ariccia had been blown up. They had started to work on it, but it would take a few years to rebuild. The country was bare at this late autumn season. A few twisted olive trees rose in the abandoned fields, sown with cardboard signs warning in English against the presence of mines. Every now and then, like wreckage from ships drawn to shore by the waves, appeared gutted German tanks, overturned there where a bomb or cannon fire had hit them, carcasses of monstrous animals left to rot, exposed to the rigors of all weathers. It was the usual spectacle of all roads and all battlefields. Some of the tanks seemed intact, with swastikas and skulls painted on the sides, their identification number, their mysterious initials, and all the long guns of their turrets pointed toward the sky. Others were ripped and lacerated by lipless wounds in their multicolored iron carcasses.

There they stood, temporary monuments of war, in the gesture with which death had captured them, like the figures at Pompeii transfixed in ashes. But the peasants from the neighborhood came, and bit by bit, day after day, they dismantled those heroic machines. They carried off everything they could use to mend their tools: pieces of iron, motors, wheels, bolts, screws; reducing the tanks to naked skeletons, as termites undermine and devour the royal hut of some black king and the home of the pious missionary.

These cemeteries of armor were thinning out month by month and would be swallowed up by the grain. On the slopes at Radicofani, where I'd gone at various times, I'd watched the many dozens of vehicles that were posed there in the most dramatic attitudes when I'd first seen them shortly after the liberation. They were getting less and growing smaller, reduced to a few heaps of iron. One of them had remained intact and was perhaps still there. It brandished a long cannon that had been hit at the middle of the barrel and torn from side to side, opening an unnatural mouth like a wild beast with its throat slashed by the bite of another wild beast stronger than itself.

"We shouldn't spend the night here," the student whispered to me. "They tell me there have been three holdups already this week."

"Jesus, Mary and God preserve us, what are you saying? . . . Three holdups!" cried the woman with the jewels. I looked at her out of the corner of my eye and I saw her hiding her face as if to protect herself under the blanket.

Finally we were back on the main road below Velletri. There we saw in front of the ruins of the railroad station the last of the tanks, pushed against an old crooked billboard, with an arrow pointing the way through that desolate and muddy desert to the "Tavern of the Mathematician."

It was now warm in the automobile, behind the glass that divided us from the driver and the tattooed sailor. After a few more curves we entered the interminable straight length of the "Fettuccia" highway that runs directly across the Pontine Marshes. The rain had stopped. It was a hogback road, sticky and slippery, and stretched out of sight between monotonous fields.

The priest must have opened his little basket, as he offered bread and cheese to the women. I heard them slowly chewing for awhile like animals in a stable. Then, when they had finished their snack, I realized from the regular sound of their slow snuffled breathing that they had fallen to sleep one by one.

The student also seemed to be drowsing. The Calabrian peasant sat upright watching the countryside with wide-open eyes and a blank rigid face, as if he were absorbed in obscure, painful, hostile, unsociable thoughts. Beyond the glass the driver and the sailor smoked one cigarette after another, exchanging words I couldn't hear. The motor made a monotonous and deafening sound, although we were driving slowly to avoid skidding on the smooth macadam that was slippery from the rain.

On the right ran a canal swollen with greenish water. The fields around us all looked alike, vast expanses covered with water and reflecting the livid color of the sky. The breakdown of the power plants and suction pumps had brought back the old condition of the marshes; aquatic birds and malaria mosquitoes flew over them in swarms.

On the left rose bare steely mountains, covered here and there on their crests by desolate villages, cyclopean walls and shreds of gray fog driven before the wind. Nobody was visible at the thresholds of the broken-down huts in the midst of the flooded fields. Now and then on the road we met a frightened flock of sheep, the motionless shepherd looking at us and the dogs busy.

At the sides of the road were a great many automobiles, trucks and *camions* that had crashed against tree trunks or against fragments of curbstones, or had turned over in the ditches or plunged headfirst into the canal.

This straight and slippery road was fatal for the convulsive traffic of these months because of defective machines, rusty steering gear and rotted tires. How many times I had seen this same spectacle of broken and abandoned machines on the roads of Europe, that haste, anguish and terror had overrun? I had seen the roads of France literally paved with the most undreamed of means of transportation; worn out, shattered, as if the machines themselves had sensitive nerves and could not bear the tension of those uncertain days of flight. I had crossed the whole country in a taxi, as I was now crossing the marshes, and I had found everywhere the same mechanical hecatomb. My first experience had been on the roads of gentle and orderly Touraine, with hills populated by miniature castles with graceful turrets and pointed slate roofs, the color of the soft and uncertain sky and of the cool waters of the Loire. It was the first of September, the eve of the war, and the announcement was expected from hour to hour with varying courage and contradictory emotions. The machinery was in motion. Men and gestures no longer counted, except for custom and appearance, nor heroic deeds that hadn't been accomplished, nor the feeble bellowings of the premier, "The Bull of Vaucluse," nor the official pronouncements, nor the radio appeals. Fate had turned on its heavy hinges and everyone was alone in front of the dark mystery of that iron gate that was swinging open.

A wave of fear invaded France, like a tide that cannot be arrested. It was the "September Fear," the preventive fear, the first of those waves that later for years and years were to run here and there like insane bolts of lightning. Autumn had descended over Tours, over the cafés on the squares, over the ancient pavements and the little peaceful streets around the cathedral. A light cold rain fell at intervals, with the first shivers of the wind (as it did now in the marshes), when one knew that the Germans had entered Poland, and voices spread the news that Paris would be evacuated and that in the next days the government and the Supreme Command would take refuge at Tours. These voices were more or less false like all the other thousands that were born at every moment, like lost fantasies of fear and hope. But the panic was real. One could see it like a factual presence on people's faces, in their movements and the sound of their voices.

The soldiers reported to the mobilization centers with faces like the dead, and with the disgusted mien of men who, contrary to all reason and with supreme boredom, are preparing to die, to die for nothing, to "die for Danzig."

At the monstrous and formless idea of war, everyone seemed to have been seized by a visceral nausea, like a man who is still on shore and already feels the seasickness of the future tempestuous voyage at sea. In Paris, crowds assaulted the stations to flee who knows where, to find refuge and above all hide themselves from an obsession. Invalids, the dying on stretchers, young people, women, old people and children, entire families crowded for hours and hours under the roofs of the platforms. They trampled each other in the crush. The most agile got into the cars through the windows or climbed on the roofs, fighting savagely for a place in the lifeboats of that insensate flight. In this way terrified fantasy created for the first time, needlessly, what would become the forced reality of the coming months. The aged joints of society creaked. Everyone closed themselves up like hedgehogs, saddened and offended at the inevitable injustice. Only the functionaries resisted this pressure without fear, apparently insensible to collective terror. They were sustained and rewarded by the natural increase in authority, comforted by bureaucratic sadism and the roseate thoughts of its future triumph. The Luigini of France didn't let the opportunity escape them, they wouldn't miss one stamp, one signature, one paper, one residence permit. Posters appeared on the walls of the city with little crossed red, white and blue flags and nicely printed letters that still had the smell of the Revolution about them. All strangers were ordered to leave the Department within twenty-four hours. All requests for delay and all protests were defeated by Military Necessity and Reasons of State. One could go wherever one wished in other zones. But there was no means of transportation, as the trains and busses were requisitioned for mobilization and forbidden to civilians. I met women with little children who had been thrown out of their houses by zealous landlords, who didn't know where to go and wandered sadly around in the rain.

Then I found a taxi, a big old shaky car like the one that was carrying me to the South today, and with women and babies we started for Brittany. This was one of the many journeys I made by chance means with unknown people on unknown roads. The countryside opened before us, green, feminine and deserted, wrapped in the vague morning mist, not yet touched by the reveille of war, asleep in its soft curves in a warm bed in a dream of peace.

But in the sulky villages, lines of peasants in their blue shirts waited sadly in front of the municipal offices to get their kepis and guns, and even then at the sides of the wet roads we came on the first automobiles overturned in the ditches.

And I saw many more some months later when I fled in another car with other chance companions from Paris when the Germans arrived. It was an uninterrupted forest of scrap iron, as though we were in a river and were forced to follow its course, its rapids and its eddies, prisoners of its waters. In front of us and behind us through the night, lost in the distance, a whole people was in flight on the road to Bordeaux by all possible means of transport: automobiles, bicycles, tandems, tricycles, wagons, carts, motor carts, vans, old cabs out of abandoned sheds, anything that would serve to leave home and the invader behind. Every breakdown, every stop arrested the column for miles. We proceeded slowly, in jerks, with frequent pauses. People on foot or on bicycles, bent under their packs, got along faster slipping by obstacles or walking on the edge of the fields. The automobiles advanced overloaded, their roofs covered with thick layers of mattresses and of every kind of valises, pieces of furniture, bird cages, pots and pans, toys and dogs.

For a while, in the midst of the forest, there was a funeral hearse in front of us. It was painted black, with torches, wreaths and golden angels, and on the top a cross shaking with the pace of the horses. It came from Belgium and had traveled days and days. It had gone through Normandy among troops in flight, had crossed Paris and was now on its way to Spain. A family of Flemish burghers were in it, pink and fat men, huge, blond and full-blown women, and children holding balls, dolls, hoops and rocking horses in their arms.

Perhaps this hearse with its angels, cross, and rocking horses would end up in a ditch at the side of some unknown crossroad. I left my chance companions at Bordeaux during a bombardment and never saw them again.

A few days later I looked out of the window at Arcachon where the gulf was planted with stakes like an underwater vineyard. Strange migrating birds were crossing the sky, airplanes of every kind in their flight toward the west, small tourist airplanes, big antiquated machines, and the last one with its stubby wings painted red, like a fish lost in the sky.

A friend called out to me from the street. "Come down at once," he said, "the Germans are entering the city. . . . We must leave. I've found a taxi and I've come to get you . . . there's no time to waste —"

In that confusion the only thing that stayed on its feet and triumphed was the police. We couldn't move without a permit. We'd have been stopped at the first roadblock. Fortunately this time the commissioner was a friend, and what counted even more, a man of good sense. He gave us a pass for the center of France, for Lot-et-Garonne, where we wanted to go to a friend's castle, as though we were two honest farmers "on farm business." It was summer. Cool brooks ran under the blaze of the sun, the thatched roofs shone and the fields stretched out easeful and indifferent in their great peaceful noonday siesta. And from afar came the crowing of cocks, solitary and pathetic in the heat. The war seemed remote, non-existent, a word in another world. But at the side of the road between the grass and the hedges there were from time to time the overturned cars. And soon after, in this illusory Arcadia of sun, meadows and shady woods, men dressed in black shot out like arrows on their black motorcycles across the road in front of us. They wore black helmets, black leggings, black gloves, and their skull-like faces were half concealed behind black masks; dreadful apparitions, the first heroic and monstrous heralds of the distant advancing armies.

Those were the first journeys. But how many more had followed later on, in how many countries and with what unknown companions.

The monotonous "Fettuccia" highway tied all these images together in a vague accumulation of names, countrysides, lands and men: the vineyards of Carcassonne under the towers of the castle; the mirrors in the enormous cafés of Beziers, where one talked of bullfights; the lady who hid her jewels; the mustachioed mechanic who wanted to cross the demarcation line with false papers; a dawn among the baleful ruins of Leghorn; a storm after the carnage in the hills of Casentino; a kitchen fireside in a farmhouse near Arezzo where they had just slaughtered a hog; an automobile radiator smashed against the soft earth of a bank; a night at bombarded Foligno in the room of two sisters, simple peasant prostitutes, with the stove burning, their knitting, and the little oil lamp lit under the Madonna over the head of the iron bedstead. And the faces of all countries changed by destruction, disorder and war, that appeared more foreign and newer because they had once been familiar; and the inside of gutted houses open to the indiscreet sun; and chance meetings, and the natural friendliness of strangers; and the people who walked in the midst of ruins on paths in the wood, with valises, handbags and laundry baskets, pails of water, bottles of milk, leading a child by the hand; and a man who stops to look with a questioning face: infinite glimpses of infinite destinies outside us and within us, without known limitations, except for a fragile image that escapes in the wind of the journey's course.

Driving on, we had reached the end of the highway under a high gray mountain. Already we found ourselves on a wide straight street, with houses on either side that were most of them bombed, running now and then into squares with crumbling fountains and the fragments of statues of men without hands and arms. We passed in front of a great building, perhaps a temple or a theater, with a solemn portico of peeling columns and badly chipped steps. At the end of the street we saw the sea. We were in Terracina. On the single long street there was nothing but ruins. And yet in the midst of them moved a busy crowd. Men and boys approached us at the entrance to the town, coming out from every home and doorway, inverting their thumbs to make the sign that showed they had gasoline to sell. At every door under the beams broken off by the bombardment there were little repair shops. Everywhere on the streets one saw mechanics straightening twisted iron or stretched on the ground working under motors or inflating tires with a foot pump. The street was filled with parked cars getting new supplies, heavy trucks with their high, closed cabs, and drivers who rested, smoked cigarettes, and superintended the loading. Crowds of people were standing in front of rooms that had cracked walls and propped-up ceilings. They were cafés with improvised counters piled with mountains of ham sandwiches, machines for *espresso* coffee, and on wooden shelves nailed to the wall, bottles of beer, liqueurs, whisky, gin, rum, all the precious merchandise of the war years.

We stopped in front of one of these cafés and got out. Our driver carried in a package and spoke to the bartender. Then he came back and went off with the machine, saying he was going to fill it up and he'd be back in a few minutes. And the sailor with his bundles hurried on some business of his own. I entered the café that was full of people and noise. One wall was half covered by a big fragment of broken mirror. The others were full of cracks. On the floor, in the corner and against the walls, were stacked valises, sacks, tire covers and empty bottles. A numerous public jammed in front of the counter. The men were wearing boots, windbreakers and berets. There were truck drivers in overalls, middlemen, youngsters in rags, old women wrapped in black shawls and painted young girls with provocative smiles.

This was the place to stop and change halfway from Rome to Naples, the posting station of the great artery that had replaced the railroad, had grown behind the armies and, all by itself, still tied the North to the South. Everybody had something to sell or to barter, to transport; some deal to arrange, some affair to conclude. All was merchandise, the means of life, in an excited, active, mysterious and dubious atmosphere like that of some secret society with incomprehensible rites. Time passed rapidly and these opportunities might not last. The town was almost destroyed but the automobiles went through it like a river that deposits fertile mud on its banks.

The townspeople set themselves up as improvised mechanics and merchants, as if they were on a new frontier at the edge of the prairies. A few months before there had been nothing but rubble, ruins and desolation. But there were the Emporiums of the Pioneers, where one could find all the essentials, those elementary things whose value had been rediscovered: eating, drinking, women, money and merchandise. In the cafés these ephemeral pioneers understood one another very well. One did not know where they came from. They arrived, left again. They labored at carrying their loads, with their minds full of calculations, obstinately pursuing their fortunes and their lives.

A bare-footed fisherman came in with a basket and offered me some freshly caught fish, but they were already sounding the klaxon outside and I was in a hurry. We jammed ourselves back into the machine and left the town. Then I noticed night was beginning to fall. In the gray twilight we drove along beside the almost invisible sea. The black outlines of the mountains were lost in the blackness of the sky. The road twisted in curves and bends as we approached the coast or went farther inland in that ancient borderland of the Kingdom of Naples. Every now and then some old houses appeared, abandoned outposts of customs guards and soldiers of the Pope. Our headlights were on and the mountains disappeared in the shadows and our eyes followed the holes in the road and the stones at the edges.

After the stop, my companions were wider awake. I heard the priest and the women murmuring something about where they would find lodgings in Naples. The student lit a cigarette and started asking me a few questions, the most futile and insignificant ones, like an inquisitive, ignorant and bored boy who didn't know how to pass the time and didn't even realize the shame of his own foolishness. And I answered patiently.

He wanted to know how much my shoes cost and where I'd bought them, whether I preferred English or American tobacco, what kind of house I had, whether I found it more convenient to eat outside or at home. I saw him little by little getting near the point where he'd be asking the question that the small village bourgeoisie ask each other by habit when they meet on the square, as I'd heard it so many times every day at Gagliano:

"What have you eaten today, Don Luigino?"

The boy was made from that same dough, from that same blood. And already the process of coagulation and dessication had started in his young brain, in which every idea is reduced to the conventional, to a cliché, an arid habit in a desolate desert of boredom and arrogant self-sufficiency. I therefore waited for the question about my supper, and I was already looking forward to enjoying it, like winning a bet, like the last brush stroke that would complete the portrait I was making of him, like the white lead highlight a genre painter puts on the shining nose of his beggar or his bibulous priest. Instead of that question he asked another that was nevertheless in a way its equivalent.

"You're a journalist," (I'd had to tell him that before), "directing a democratic newspaper, a newspaper of the Left," (a shadow of angry fear and obsequious disgust colored the words "democratic" and "Left"). "I wonder what you think of Guglielmo Giannini. I'm sure you hate and despise him and that you won't even want to talk about him, or who knows how many bad things you'll tell me about this enemy of yours. Do you know him? Have you ever seen him?"

I answered, naturally, that my ideas were very different from those of that sympathetic demagogue whose ephemeral star seemed to have risen to the crest of the firmament in these days. But that, although he was an adversary, I considered him a most deserving person; that I thought in spite of appearances and his obvious mistakes, he was performing a useful function in extracting the poison and virulence from his fascist followers by means of his primitive liberalism and his good-natured and clownish anarchism; that I only knew him by sight and I therefore liked to believe that in private life he was most honorable and respectable.

My answer had an extraordinary and unexpected effect on the student, as though a bomb had suddenly exploded. He turned and looked at me stupefied. I saw that my moderate words had thrown all his preconceived ideas into the air, and also the rules to which he was accustomed. It had displaced something of his rigidity and crystallization and especially it had contradicted his need or mania or miserable delight in persecution that supported at the roots those rules and crystallizations. The student was still so young, so ingenuous and shy that he didn't try to hide his stupor, but rather let himself be invaded by it and expressed it openly.

"But . . . I didn't believe . . . I thought you were enemies and that you couldn't possibly talk of one another so kindly. . . . I thought the democrats, those on the left, were more fanatical, so to speak, that they didn't respect the others. . . . It's the first time I've ever heard anybody talk this way —"

Yes, a new idea, a gleam of truth had entered his mind. From that moment he looked at me with respect and regard as if I were a strange and somewhat mysterious being, and he stopped asking me questions.

It was now deep night. The landscape had become wild and solitary among the desolate black mountains with their irregular and disorderly outlines. The road wound upward in many curves in a rough and obscure gorge, bordered by uncultivated land with only a few twisted trees and naked rocks on it. We drove slowly; something in the motor wasn't functioning, and the sound was sputtering and irregular. On top of the hill, at the dark entrance of what seemed to be an abandoned village, a tire collapsed with a whistling lament. We were at Itri.

We had to wait here for a long while. There was no light in the village. An icy wind cut down from the ravine. The houses crowded near one another as though they were defending themselves against an invisible enemy. They looked like the inhospitable ruins of a fallen castle, or the nests of wild birds on a rock.

This wild and bombed-out hamlet was also, like Terracina, a posting station, a ring in the improvised chain that led to the South. But it was evening now and the day's traffic had ended. Only a few latecomers adventured on the street. The houses were almost all in ruins and their windows were barred. The driver and the sailor, knowing this place well, went to find a mechanic friend of theirs, and then came back with him and a lantern to begin working. I started to take a walk among the houses and climbed the slippery pavement of a steep alley between walls with loose and perilous stones. A reddish light from oil lamps filtered through some of the doors that were half open to let out the sharp smoke. Old women wrapped up in black rags were stirring kettles of thin soup. Black figures with black hair were huddled around the fires like gypsies around a camp. As I went by and stopped to look around out of curiosity, someone would come to the threshold and, without answering my greeting, eye me with a mistrustful and dark air. The empty sockets of the windows and the jagged profile of the ruins against the sky had the same hostile air. A bristling atmosphere seemed to hang over the village like a baleful spell. A dog barked angrily and others answered him from near and far in the shadows. Then, when silence had returned, a screech owl cried out in the sky. People say mistakenly that the chant of his bird, and of his elder brother, the marvelous gray owl, herald angels of the Last Judgment, is a prophecy of death. It has become familiar to me, and I had waited every evening for it to start over the jail of Mantellate. I looked for the birds from the window of the cell until I could see them, small and black, cloaked in the cold whiteness of the moon, perched in a row, three, four, five, on the dark wall of the roof, watching the prisoners from up there and launching in freedom their nocturnal call into the silent air.

For a long while, half an hour or longer, I walked through the ruins, until I heard the sound of the horn and hurried down to the automobile. The motor was working better. They had taken it apart, cleaned the carburetor and changed the spark plugs. One of the travelers must have complained of the slowness of the trip because the driver opened the glass that separated his cab from us and made a lengthy defense of his machine as he drove. It was the best on that route. Yes, we were late, but we'd left late, the road was wet, and it was better to drive carefully than to slide into a ditch. Two excellent tires had gone flat, but that was nothing on a highway full of stone, pieces of glass, holes, nails and scrap. And besides, the worst was over and we were almost there. It was eight o'clock and we'd be in Naples by ten at the latest.

This speech calmed everyone and they started to doze off again. But now I became impatient. I imagined the fine wise face of Uncle Luca on his pillow, and his old yellow dressing gown. I wanted him to be alive and to speak to me. And perhaps that was what he was wishing at this moment, while I was being delayed with these strangers on these slow anguished four wheels. Still we were getting nearer, one yard after the other, climbing and descending on the road that never seemed to end, between bare fields and black solitary villages.

I didn't want to think it was too late, that my voyage was useless. I imagined what Uncle Luca and I would talk about. Perhaps for the first time I might remind him of those childish pastels that he had certainly forgotten.

While I was building up these fantasies, I was absently watching the light rain falling on the dark disorder of the countryside.

Wrapped in my overcoat, closed in by my thoughts, indifferent to the world outside, I let myself be carried on like a branch by the current of a river. I had scarcely noticed that at a point just before the fork at Sparanise there was a barrier closing the road. A bridge farther on had either not yet been repaired or had been carried away by the rain. We had to descend to our right by one of those rough bumpy detours that had been hurriedly dug by the monstrous Caterpillar tractors behind the first advancing troops.

We went down slowly into a narrow glen with a grove of oaks on either side. We were moving almost at walking speed, shaken by the uneven ground, when something appeared in the beam of the headlights between the grass and the bushes. I don't know whether I saw him first or first heard the sound, but it was a man and he was shooting.

Everything happened in a second. He stood facing us behind a low bush. From there he had started firing at us, aiming directly at the people. Then he stepped forward out of the bushes and was now on my side of the car not more than two yards away.

The sound of the successive shots was very familiar to me. They were like a sudden dry slap. I could see him clearly through the glass in the door. He was short, thickset and powerful, with the round head of a peasant, a long black unkempt beard on his cheeks. He wore an ugly old black hat with the brim pulled over his eyes, a black jacket and short trousers. From the knees down his legs were wound with white cloth tied with a braided cord. He was a brigand, a true classical brigand, with the body, the face, the costume and hat of a fairy-tale brigand, but nonetheless real, ferocious, present, with his weapon in his hand. That was the only thing I didn't have time to distinguish precisely. It was a long dark object that he held to one shoulder and that spouted red flashes at every shot.

The image of peril, the strangeness of the adventure woke me suddenly from the fantasies to which I had abandoned myself. And immediately I felt myself invaded by that clear sense of coldness and lucidity, the absolute lack of emotion that fortunately for me comes over me whenever I find myself in a difficult moment.

It may be a paradox, a reversed form of fear, or a simple and physical nervous reaction. And actually, what credit is it to me that the heart continues to beat calmly, the hands don't tremble, the eyesight becomes more acute, the senses tuned, the memory entirely present and open, the thoughts clear as serene winter mornings, and everything becomes easy, instinctive and calm, with so unnatural a calm that I myself feel it with both hilarity and disgust?

I saw the brigand shoot at two paces, as clearly as an apparition in a dream, and in some sort of stagnant compartment of my mind, I was astonished and laughed because he was in every way the identical, childish and popular picture of the brigand, with the pointed hat, the black costume, the blunderbuss . . . but was it a blunderbuss that he was shooting, or a machine gun, or a big pistol? Who knows? I caught myself thinking in spite of myself that this similarity had something miraculous about it, that the art of the people is the repetition of a plot in which what seems to be real coincides magically with what is real, that the brigand is a brigand if he looks like one, and that you only have to know it to be safe from him. But these absurd thoughts (that I confess here with pretended shame) did not prevent me, on another level, from feeling that my companions were all the prey of surprise and fear, and that naturally, whether I wanted to or not, it was up to me to act for them. I saw that the driver, terrified and uncertain, was abandoning the wheel. I grabbed his shoulder through the opening and shouted:

"Go on! Go on! Don't stop. Quick!"

At my order he pushed down the accelerator mechanically, the machine jerked over the uneven ground and speeded ahead. The brigand, left behind, continued to shoot, and was lost in the darkness.

Now the road went up the other side of the narrow glen. I noticed that the glass of the door I was leaning against had been pierced at the height of my shoulder and pieces of it were scattered over my sleeve. We climbed the hill for two or three hundred yards and came out onto the big highway. We were safe. If there weren't any other bandits posted farther on, we had escaped the ambush. My companions were already shouting with relief (we hadn't gone more than some twenty yards up the road) when a flame leaped up from the motor. We stopped immediately and the headlights went out. The driver got down in a hurry, burning his fingers as he opened the hood, pulled off his raincoat and jacket and threw them over the motor to smother the flames and prevent an explosion. The red and blue light that was shooting up around him vanished, and we were in absolute darkness. The bullets had perforated the gasoline tank and the motor in many places. The tires were intact because the bandit had been aiming at the level of a man's head. What could we do? We opened the doors and got down on the road.

Then I noticed it was snowing. Small stinging flakes whirled in eddies in the wind and melted when they touched the ground. There was the smell of snow, gasoline and scorched wool. My companions were all crowding in a dark group beside the machine. Nobody was hurt. It was so dark that one couldn't see two steps ahead. None of us were armed. If the brigands had reached us, we couldn't have defended ourselves. We had seen only one, only one had shot, but probably there were others with him in the underbrush. If they noticed the silence of the motor and found that we had stopped, they wouldn't hesitate to come and attack us. And whether they were many or few, or even only one who was well armed and, as we had seen, without scruple or regard, we couldn't escape. I told the others I thought we ought to get away from the machine without wasting time, taking along the baggage that didn't have to be untied and, hiding in the fields, wait there protected by the darkness, then return to the automobile if the brigands didn't follow.

This was the most reasonable thing to do. But I gave it as advice, not as an order, and realized that they couldn't follow it easily. They were all still paralyzed by fear and, along with fear, by the terror of darkness and an irrational attachment to their possessions. The driver looked despairingly at his motor. He and the sailor were already figuring the cost of the damage. The priest had been fingering his valise that was tied behind the car, feeling with his hands in the darkness for the holes from the bullets that must have hit it.

"Your suitcase saved us from the last shots, Father," I said, but he wasn't consoled. The woman with the jewels complained like a child. At the idea of having to move she seemed about to faint into the arms of the priest. The other woman wept, the student kept walking around me in a daze. The only one who seemed calm was the Calabrian peasant. He was quiet, and it wasn't clear what he intended to do.

Since nobody moved, and I couldn't leave them there like that in confusion, I stayed with them. I sat on a curbstone at the side of the road and waited. Who could tell when we would arrive in Naples? We were now in the hands of fortune. I asked myself how late it was and realized with pleasure that I had no watch, and that the old paternal machine would not fall into the hands of brigands.

The minutes passed very slowly as we waited for something unpleasant and disgusting to happen that we couldn't avoid any longer, when, from the direction of Naples, we saw headlights. We strung ourselves in a chain across the highway. A huge white automobile with a round radiator and no running boards approached at high speed and stopped in front of us. The driver, a young man with a red mustache, leaned out questioningly. We all circled around him, pointed at the burned machine and shouted: "The brigands! The brigands!"

It was as though he had heard the devil mentioned. As swift as lightning, and without answering, he threw his car into reverse and turned around, leaving us on the road, and retraced his route in flight, disappearing into the dark. We were left disconsolate, listening to the sound of his motor growing fainter as he went farther like a fading hope, until complete silence returned.

More minutes that seemed extremely long passed. It was cold. The snowfall was thicker and started to settle, white on the ground, when, as gay as the light of dawn, we saw far away in the sky beyond the brigand's glen from the direction of Rome the glow of a line of headlights approaching. There must be many cars driving together for protection, as one often did in those days. Perhaps the bandits hadn't dared attack them. Here was the first one emerging safely from the road through the woods. But it didn't stop for our signals, and escaped at high speed. Then came the second, third and fourth, almost together. They too grazed us without taking heed of us and went on. Behind them, slow and heavy, came an enormous red truck pulling a trailer. It sparkled with splendid round and triangular red lights. The truck stopped. Our driver took courage and showed his cunning. Winking his eyes and twisting his foxlike face, he asked us to keep quiet by moving his finger over his mustache, and whispered:

"Leave it to me! Don't you mention the brigands or he'll run off too. . . . Quiet now," and he stepped forward.

From the driver's cab of the truck appeared the wide good-natured face of a mechanic, one of those calm faces, sure of themselves, that you have confidence in the minute you see them. Then the door opened, he got out and stood in front of us. He was a giant, one of those enormous truck drivers you find in American films and on the highways of the North, a kind of solid cliff to which one can hold on. He came toward us, big and athletic in his overalls, and asked us briefly what had gone wrong. He was a Roman with an Olympian face and a lock of black hair over his forehead. The owner of our car was hanging around him with a thousand cajoleries like a little dog around a great Saint Bernard. I heard him explaining that our motor had caught fire, that we couldn't move, asking him at least to tow us to the next village. The truck driver gave one look at the machine and grumbled his assent.

"I'll take you right to Naples if you like. It's all the same to me. This is no place for you to stay. The roads aren't very safe."

Our foxy little driver winked at us to keep still, while the other one, calm and slow, was getting a rope and a hook out of his truck. The two of them attached the grapple to our bumper and I noticed the feverish movements of our driver's hands, who couldn't wait to leave, since the brigands might still arrive even now when we felt we were safe. He couldn't reveal his reasons to the other who was working deliberately to make the rope hold fast.

"That's all right, that's very good. We can leave now," insisted the little one while the big one was not convinced but would have liked to fasten the rope even more securely. At last, with God's blessing, the truck driver climbed up to his seat and we dashed to ours faster than soldiers called by an alarm. The truck roared, a cloud of smoke came out from under the wheels, the rope tightened and, dragged like a derelict, gently and happily we were off.

We were hardly in motion when the passengers, as though suddenly freed from an oppressive weight, relaxed with sighs of relief, in exclamations, shouts and bursts of laughter. Their faces smoothed, they waved their hands around, they took deep breaths and, excited and hilarious, they all talked at the same time. The journey now became as gay as it was dreary before, and the company as sociable and loquacious as they had been somber and taciturn. They were happy and proud of themselves.

There had been an adventure, a great adventure, one of those stories one could often retell, rare, almost incredible. Since it had ended well they felt they were heroes, and congratulated themselves and their destiny. Then too they considered themselves subtle, tied together by a pleasant conspiracy in deceit, because they'd kept still to the truck driver about the existence of brigands. They decided they wouldn't say anything until they got to Naples; and that it might be better to keep quiet even there. Perhaps they felt particularly virtuous since they were manifestly protected by fortune.

"A miracle! A miracle! It was certainly a miracle, a miracle from heaven!" they said, wondering in loud voices how it could have happened. There surely had been a multitude of bandits and very ferocious ones. How was it possible they hadn't jumped on us and stolen everything we had? Nobody had even been wounded and the wheels were whole! If they'd punctured our tires we'd still be exposed to assault there on the road. Indeed we would have been stranded in the bottom of the glen and never have come out alive. Could they have believed we'd succeeded in escaping? They must have noticed that we stopped. Perhaps they thought we were armed? Or perhaps they saw the headlights of the approaching machines before we did, and were disturbed in their terrible plans? The passengers went on discussing and analyzing until they lost their breath. The owner showed us a piece of iron from the motor pierced in two places, and we passed it around from hand to hand examining it as though it were a holy relic. What excited them even more was the hole in the glass beside my shoulder. It was as round and regular as a coin.

Moving around, turning, twisting in that narrow crowded dark space, lighting matches and clicking cigarette lighters, they searched under the seats and among the packages on the floor for the bullet. Judging from the hole, it should have drilled me from side to side. But to the general disappointment it was impossible to find it. Perhaps it had ricocheted out, or dodged into some inaccessible hiding place. The hole, the undiscovered and innocuous bullet, the crumbs of glass on my arm struck everyone as the most miraculous fact of all. This now gave them a pleasant shudder of fear and heroism. I confess that I, for one, would have liked to find the bullet. And I kept thinking about the strange fact that in all those past years of blood and civil war, death had never come so near to me, physically, and that I had never looked so closely into its face as now. Perhaps this time, in deference to fate and the absurd, death had chosen the shape of anarchistic revolt, like the magic mask of a savage warrior, the dark and serious face of a poor peasant brigand.

"It's been a miracle, a miracle of the Madonna," said the owner, turning his head around from the driver's seat. "I had the car blessed this morning, this very morning, with holy water, just a few hours before we left. This is the first trip after the blessing. And this morning I put a picture of the *Madonna del Divino Amore* up there too," and he pointed to the figure pinned over the windshield. "It's She who saved us."

Nobody doubted there had been a miracle, but opinions differed as to who had performed it, or at least as to who had interceded for it. The presence of the holy image should perhaps have put an end to all doubts, and it certainly made a big impression on all. But the woman with the jewels, fingering her necklaces and bracelets to reassure herself of their presence, shouted in a strident throaty voice:

"It was Teresa who performed this miracle . . . I saw her myself . . . St. Teresa of the Holy Child, my own little saint, the saint of roses. . . . It's certain . . . when that black face jumped up, I saw I was lost . . . I said, "*Mamma Mia*, this is the last moment of my life' . . . I closed my eyes and the saint appeared to me, smiling in the midst of roses. . . . She's always protected me . . . she's my saint. . . ." and here she set her big painted lips in lines of ecstasy.

"She's granted me favors ever since I was a girl, before I married my first husband, and she didn't allow me to be a widow for long —" and here she started in to tell the story of her first husband who's been a *commendatore* and a holy man. She told us how he'd died and how she'd married again, and now she was separated from her second, but that she was very well off because, thank heaven, she had money of her own and was handling her own affairs. She knew how to live . . . the man was yet to be born who could cheat on her or put her in a sack . . . and many other things that possibly concerned her private life rather than the little saint of the roses. But where Teresa had intervened in the most explicit and indubitable fashion was during an illness of hers a few years before, and she recounted at length its symptoms and course.

She'd had salpingitis. She'd had many attacks with fever, pains in her belly, and complaints of all kinds. She'd had every sort of cure: douches, injections, diathermy. She'd even gone to the waters of San Pellegrino. Finally she'd gotten into such a bad state, only skin and bones, in danger of peritonitis, that everybody had given her up. Then one night when she couldn't sleep and felt like dying she remembered her patron saint, implored her protection, and by the next day the pains had stopped, the fever had gone down, and a few days later she was so plump and rosy that, she shouldn't say so, but that actually men turned around as they passed her on the street. This time, too, there was no doubt at all, it had been her saint.

"Perhaps in your case, Signora," said the owner. "I won't deny that . . . but for the machine and for the rest of us, let's not waste another word, it was the Madonna. What more could you want than having been blessed shortly before and having her image along with us. I can't wait till I get back to Rome to commission a fine picture or a solid silver statuette, and carry it as a votive offering to the *Madonna del Divino Amore.*"

The sailor agreed with his associate. He too believed the Madonna had saved us. As to the saints? They were all good. And he had nothing against Teresa who was certainly most powerful and who had perhaps protected the signora from the final shots that had been aimed at them from behind and had perhaps lodged in the reverend's valise or in the other baggage. But without any question the most powerful of all was St. Nicholas. He had tested him in a thousand storms at sea where all seemed lost. Even that time when his oil tanker had been torpedoed and the naphtha caught fire on the water, and a great many of his companions had been burned or drowned, while he himself clung to a board for twelve hours between Tunis and Sicily before they came to rescue him. St. Nicholas, there was a saint for you!

The sailor faced us and lifting up his sweater from his chest he showed us, in the light of a match held by the student, a picture of the saint on the dark hairy expanse between his stomach and his navel, tattooed in blue and bestowing a blessing. On both sides of the saint were boats with big unfurled flags, and the inscription "Royal Navy." Farther up, halfway between the nipples, almost hidden in the shady forest of black hair, the Madonna sat upon a cloud, and over her crown and halo was a band with the inscription, "Ave Maris Stella."

"Fine piece of work. It was done by an artist. This is the Virgin of the Sea," said the sailor, touching her with a finger. "And this is St. Nicholas, the first of all saints. . . . Don't you agree, Father?"

The priest, questioned thus, got out of the theological dispute with diplomacy. He didn't mention miracles, avoided comparing the power of saints, and said that Divine Providence had surely wanted to protect us after having first put us through such a hard test. What seemed to be more deeply on his mind were the bullets in his valise. He asked us if we really thought the valise had protected us and whether or not it had been hit. It was a pity he couldn't get out and have a look. He feared a disaster might have occurred since it contained a little flour . . . just a little bit . . . and then there were some little cans of oil in it . . . if the oil has leaked into the flour, you know what that would mean! Well, there was nothing to be done, one could only have patience and trust, and he hoped that since we'd all been so providentially saved, his poor valise wouldn't be the only thing to suffer from our terrible adventure.

While we went on talking and arguing during this slow ride, undisturbed by the sound of the motor, the truck that was towing us slowed down and stopped. It was a road block at the entrance to a village. We were surrounded by *carabinieri* who came from all sides out of the black depths of the night, with their white belts and shoulder straps, guns over their shoulders and flashlights in their hands. I've never been able to find out what these road blocks were good for, whether to hinder smuggling that was after all indispensable and necessary, or to make it more profitable to smuggle, by adding a touch of danger to it. These were the days when the bandit Giuliano, an unknown peasant, carried a sack of wheat on a bicycle into an isolated village in Sicily, and killed among the prickly pear trees the first guard who tried to confiscate it. At the same time immense mountains of all kinds of merchandise were being calmly transported hither and yon on the big highways in spite of laws and controls.

This new encounter provoked in my companions, if not the mad terror of the other one, a minor but plainly visible discomfort and agitation. Evidently the machine carried not only the priest's flour and oil. The travelers became dumb, with preoccupied faces. They made themselves seem small, to avoid attracting attention, so as not to be scrutinized and searched. I thought that the Calabrian and I were the only ones who weren't carrying anything illicit and could sit there with a peaceful conscience, were it possible not to feel somehow guilty faced by those representatives of the state, by their warlike disguise, their firearms, their divinely inexpressive faces and their ritual of blame.

The guards were examining the truck driver's papers. A few snow flakes fell in the icy air. I signaled one of the *carabinieri* to come closer and told him about the attack, so that they might save other travelers from the same experience. He wasn't astonished by my story and said there had been various attacks in the preceding days, and he called the sergeant who came up and asked me to repeat the details and describe the scene. Then he said with a preoccupied air that he'd report it and do all he could but that they had too much work and couldn't be everywhere, and he went off into the dark calling his soldiers and ordering us to be on our way. In this fashion, thanks to the brigand, we avoided opening the valises, and once more Divine Providence had protected us, and this second ugly encounter had also resolved in the best of ways. But what anxieties are necessary to save life and possessions, and that little bit of hard-earned wealth!

As we drove slowly down the road, our spirits were relieved and gay, freed at last from worry and fear. After my companions in various ways and with various exclamations had congratulated one another on escaping from danger, the conversation turned back to saints and their miraculous power and to the private lives of each traveler. After what had happened they all now felt united. They had no more secrets and they were fired with the desire to tell the most intimate things. The sailor, who came from Apulia, told of his voyages to distant lands; the woman with the jewels informed us that she was born in Forli, but had lived in Rome ever since her first marriage to the *commendatore*, and that she was obliged to make frequent trips for business reasons. She had a house in Rome and one in Naples, but the nature and purpose of these houses remained obscure; the fate of her second husband also remained a mystery although she talked of it for a long time. He had disappeared suddenly, but it wasn't quite clear to us whether he had fled for love, for business, or for some small reckoning with justice. Over these mysteries fluttered her protectress, the saint to whom she never ceased proclaiming her devotion as she kept adjusting her red fox around her neck. It was she who presently started to question the woman who shared her seat, calling on her as a witness to the virtues of Teresa.

I then heard, for the first time since we had left, the voice of the other woman and I was amazed because its violent and youthful tone did not at all correspond to her sad and old appearance. It was the voice, inflection and pronunciation of a *vasciarola,* of a washerwoman of the slums of Naples, used to standing on her threshold and shouting constantly to the neighbors and children in the tumult of the street. It was one of those voices that starts out from the first syllable at top pitch and full power, and maintains itself on the same level of inflection, dropping only at the very end, as though every word were a shout calling out to someone very far away, from one end of a deserted valley to the other.

"St. Teresa of the Child Jesus," shouted the woman, "if she would only help me too. I've made a vow to St. Rita, St. Rita, so that she'd help me find my son again, that poor boy. I've covered Italy and I can't find him. I've been to Leghorn, Florence, Bologna and Milan, I've been everywhere. Now I'm going to Padula, to the internment camp. They say I may find him there. It would have been better if I'd never borne him."

She had been so silent before, so mute, wrapped in her own secret, jealous of it and hiding it, that she now unburdened herself with greater freedom, abandoned herself more completely in this speech that was like a shrill, monotonous lament for the dead, a desperate and visceral cry.

"I'm telling you the truth," she said. "I've never spoken about these things to anybody but you're like brothers to me. I talk to you as though I were talking to my brothers. This son of mine, Antonio, is my eldest. I made him when I was just fifteen years old. He's a fisherman and a sailor, as lovely as a flower. When the Germans came he was in the submarines. The bad kind got hold of him, they took him along to the North with the Tenth M.A.S. torpedo boats, with those bad people and Commander Borghese. Everybody said the commander was like the devil, he was worse than the devil, he killed the poor things, gouged out their eyes, and didn't even respect the priests.

"But not Antonio. He wouldn't have hurt anyone, he's a good boy, he's his mother's son, the son of my bowels. . . . And he can't be found any more. Look here, just look how lovely he is, my poor son —" And she took out a photograph of a young sailor in uniform from the canvas bag she held on her lap, and also another picture where that same Antonio was dressed like a fisherman standing in the middle of six other boys and girls from five to fifteen years old. They were all brothers, her seven children, she said, as I looked at the picture in the light of a match. She also wanted me to see her identity card and her marriage book where the names of her seven children and the dates of their births were entered.

"Look here, won't you have a look?" she went on, holding the book open as though it were a precious text. "Everything's in order — legitimate. . . . What difference does it make if I'm the daughter of 'Unknown,' that I haven't an education, that they didn't even teach me how to sign my own name? . . . I brought them up myself, those seven children. . . . I took the bread out of my own mouth . . . and he, the first one, so lovely and big, was already helping me, and those bad people have taken him away."

I saw from the book, to my astonishment, that the woman, Grazia Jannilli, born Butrito, wasn't yet forty years old. She was of Sicilian origin, she told me. She'd been born in a village of the interior, in the region of the sulphur mines. She didn't know who her father was. She'd been brought up by an aunt at Torre del Greco, and had become Neapolitan that way.

"When I was twelve I was already a woman. At fourteen everybody wanted me. But I was childish and only wanted to play and to laugh. I said no to everyone, even a sergeant of the *carabinieri* who wanted to marry me, and another one too, a gentleman, who had wanted me absolutely and who went away because of his disappointment. I didn't want to get married because I still wanted to play. Then the one came along who was later my husband and I said yes right away. To my misfortune I said yes without thinking for a moment, who knows why? I was convinced, my head was full of him, and a lover's spell is worse than a witch's.

"He was the best-looking boy in Torre del Greco. When we got engaged, the girls and the old gossips were so angry that they made the sign of the cross upside down. Then he started to make me babies, one a year. . . . Look, the little book says so . . . Seven are alive and two died when they were small. He shipped off to sea, traveled, came back home, and I made another baby, then after awhile he started to get tired of it, and was furious and said I was making too many, and he beat me and stopped sending me money. And yet he was earning a lot, he was a waiter on board. Finally he didn't come back to Torre del Greco, he had set himself up with another woman but I didn't know. I went to look for him in Genoa and he took me to her house where he was living, saying he lived there because it was cheaper. And she received me in her house and started to give me a song, but she had it all mixed up. She said love changes but you've got to let him fly away. Then I understood the whole business and I told her in Naples we say it different. And I gave it to her right, that song: that if love changes, the one who's unfaithful's got to die. . . . And I should've done it, but I didn't. My husband gave me a thousand oaths and kept me from it, and so I went back to Torre del Greco by myself. Later, during the war, he died at sea, and I had to keep my seven children from going hungry all by myself. I can make nets and help the fishermen. We live all in one room, but nevertheless there's never been a day without its piece of bread. And now, if he's alive, I must find Antonio, and the saints ought to help me."

"My name's Antonio too," said the Calabrian, as though Grazia's story had touched his heart with the sound of something recognized and familiar, and had walked him from that sort of hostile, painful and diffident daze in which he's been plunged before. "I also am called Antonio and I've returned. Also your son will return. Also I can't write, the same as you. I'm young, but I don't know whether Regina, my fiancée, has waited for me . . . I don't know a thing. . . . They think I'm dead . . . I don't know whether there's any work at my village or whether I'll find my sheep. I'm a shepherd and I've had a hard life but never like in these years. There's things you can't tell. I've been in accursed places where the Lord never passed. Your son couldn't have been in worse places, nor with worse people than those who commanded me. It was really bad . . . they made the blood come out of our eyes . . . they made us eat the garbage like pigs and do labor like mules and tortured us like Christ on the Cross. The people died like mad dogs, they had no bodies left, only skin and bones, not even a voice to complain with. You can't say those things . . . your son can't have seen worse ones. . . . And yet, as you see, I'm here and I'm on my way home. You can see that my saint, my St. Antuono, held his hand over me while I was in the middle of those devils. . . . Also your son, if he hasn't harmed himself by offending the Christians, St. Antuono will bring him back.

So it was that, undefended and unprovided for, armed only with the name and the very certain but supernatural power of the saints, men and women went about on the streets of the world, driven into a time which was not their own.

Besides, At. Antuono, the St. Anthony of the peasants, is more than a saint. He is an ancient divinity of the earth, full of a powerful and ambiguous mystery. He is the tiller and herdsman of Christ. It was St. Antuono who first cultivated the earth and domesticated the animals, and taught for the first time those unchanging arts. He was also the inventor of fire, a saintly Prometheus that no eagle can wound on the rock. One day there was no fire for Christ's supper and Jesus told him to look for some. Antuono went down into hell and stole a firebrand from the devil, brought it to earth and the supper was cooked. From that time forward fires were lit each day under the kettles in the houses, and in memory of this thing that happened at the beginning of the world, on his saint's day big bonfires rise on all the peaks of the mountains and in the village squares.

He also invented the packsaddle for the asses. One day he went into the forest to bring wood to his Master, Jesus. But how could he carry it home when there was so much of it? He had with him an ass, who until then could do nothing but bray and kick out. Antuono slipped two green branches of a tree under the skin of his sides and they were immediately transformed into a packsaddle, the first that had ever been seen. In this way he carried the wood to Jesus.

He domesticated, protected and healed the animals. He himself, one can say, was half man and half cow. He remained for a time in the shape of a cow so that his fiercest enemies, the devils, would not recognize him. Once he was carrying images of Christ and the Madonna, and the devils with a thousand cunning wiles wanted to steal them from him. Antuono, disguised as a cow, went out into the countryside carrying the images with him. He went into a cave and hid them at the bottom. As soon as he came out, his friend, the spider, wove a gate with his thread and closed the mouth of the cavern. The devils who were looking everywhere passed by and saw the gate that was shining with the silver of the dew and thought that nobody had gone within. Only a cow, and one could see the tracks, had stopped there shortly before to browse in the grass. Thus they did not enter the grotto, they were fooled, and the images were saved and are still there.

Every year, on his feast day that falls on the seventeenth of January, the peasants too, as the shepherd told us, disguise themselves as cows. They put on white undershirts and long white drawers, cover their faces with white veils, hang a tail on behind, and ribbons of all colors. Only one is dressed in black and he is the bull. They all gather in the square, mooing. Each of them carries around the neck or in his hand a huge bronze bell. Ringing their bells and mooing, the flock of peasant-cows, followed by children, the sucking calves, climb to the chapel of the saint on the mountain and make the round of the sanctuary three times to be blessed. Then they descend into the village and for a whole day one hears the mooing and the sound of bells and firecrackers, until night comes, and the flames on the mountains, and fireworks in the winter sky. So true a saint does not abandon his peasant flock.

One cannot count the wearied mules and lame horses that Antuono heals every year. One cannot count his miracles.

"A neighbor of mine, a boy who was called Nicola," said the shepherd, "had gone to gather wood. The weather was bad. A big rain came and thunders and lightnings. To be quick and get home Nicola didn't go in the big woods. He made his faggots in a little woods around the chapel in a hurry, and down he comes with his load on his right shoulder. He got home, wet everywhere, threw the faggots on the floor by the fire. And right then he couldn't move his neck any more. It stayed twisted like his bundle of faggots was still against it. His mother was frightened. She asked him: 'Nicola, what's the matter? Where did you get that wood?' Nicola said he'd taken it, because of bad weather, from the little woods of the chapel. 'That's the saint's,' said the mother. 'Take it back right now.' She picked up the wood, put it back on his neck, and pushed him outside and it was the time when even the wolves are so cold they come out of their holes and nobody trusted himself on the roads. It was luck that did this, that Nicola climbed to the sanctuary, left the wood on the ground in front of the chapel, and hadn't even put it down when his neck turned straight and well. And if he hadn't done it, he'd have been twisted all his life."

While we were talking we drove quietly over the road at the slow even pace of the truck. We'd already passed Formia and its lugubrious ruins, and the distant lights of Gaeta, crossed a temporary wooden bridge over the flat banks of the Garigliano, that had been so fiercely contended, and climbed up and down through a vague stretch of country among grape vines and olive trees toward the Volturno. It had stopped snowing and the north wind was blowing and drying the road. One could see a star through a rift in the sky, and of a sudden, between the clouds, veiled by shifting brightness, the timid moon.

Perhaps at this same hour the poor brigand of Sparanise was hiding from the pale light that sifted through the branches like a human glance as he squatted in the shadow of a bush in some thicket, or some cave in the rocks, all one with the trees and the animals, strained to listen for rustlings and the voices of wild animals, breathing the smell of wet earth and grass. He must be concealing in some lonely convolution of his mind the desperate rage and anguish of a life that was decadent in our time but that perhaps in another time and among other men would have been a powerful and yet equivocal nature. Was it the same nature as that of the earth spirits, of the peasant saints and devils, the same as that of St. Antuono? In such a nature, is there any distinction between man and animal, between man and plant; where the sun, the rain, the forest, conception and death, the entire world that surrounds us are one with the man who lives like a tree, plants his roots in the soil, flowers, bears fruit, and, in his own time, withers away? Good and evil abrogate one another and mingle alternating in the vicissitudes of day and night, in endless seasons and ineffable presences.

One day at Matera many years ago I met an old man at the threshold of one of those cave dwellings dug in the clay of the Sasso Carveosa. He was a visionary, tall and upright for his eighty years, with a big white mustache and a long black cloak. He rose at dawn and looked fixedly at the sun, and in that sphere of fire he saw the future.

"The Deluge will come," he told me. "It will come very soon, for everyone, for the whole earth . . . Within me, it has already commenced." He added that not everyone would die, some would save themselves, and that after the Deluge many things would return that now seemed lost, and that outlandish people, evildoers and brigands, would appear in the heavens, like angels.

"Because," he said, "everything is double. All the saints are demons."

We crossed the Volturno in the light of a moon that appeared and disappeared behind the clouds, and we drove through a ghostly countryside full of high trees and shadows. The plants and the leaves looked as though they were coming toward us, like slender human beings twisted and bent forward, hoping to reach the level plain. Naples was nearing us and we already felt its presence, and the thoughts of my companions turned to their arrival, to what they would find when they got there, the business deals, the miseries, the necessities, the weariness. They started to talk of life in the city, of the thousands of ways the poor devise in order to exist; of the thievery, the black market and the daily cunning.

The student, the woman with jewels, the sailor, started to tell anecdotes that everyone had heard before, but were nonetheless true. The stories of drunken colored soldiers whose bodies the Neapolitan street boys passed from hand to hand, selling them like any other kind of merchandise; the tales of ships that had been unloaded right in the bay without anyone's knowing how, or that had actually disappeared; or about the life that went on after the war in the deep caverns that had been used as shelters; of the pimps, the prostitutes, the resourcefulness of pickpockets and the markets for the most unbelievable objects. The woman with the jewels mentioned thefts and warned me to be careful because I wasn't familiar with Naples. They stole everything right under your eyes. They leaped on moving automobiles and made their getaways, carrying off baggage and spare tires. It was enough just to set a package or a valise on the ground for a second, and it had already disappeared, heaven knows how. It seemed, she said, that they used containers with double bottoms. They knew all kinds of ingenious tricks. They'd come by with a little bag of fleas and throw them on your jacket. Then they'd tell you that you've got bugs on your neck, and while you turned around to catch the bugs they'd make off with your watch or your wallet. They even succeeded in stealing the hats from people's heads without getting nabbed. A young man comes by with a basket on his head. Inside it a little boy is hidden who quickly snatches the hats.

"They even know how to steal the shoes from your feet," said the student. "One of them says, 'Would you like to have a fine pair of American boots? Just exactly like the ones that soldier is wearing? . . . Two thousand only . . . it's a deal . . . want them? . . . Wait here and I'll let you have them right away. . . .' If you say yes, the boy will approach the soldier and offer him, *sotto voce,* a young girl, a dark-haired fourteen-year-old girl as lovely as a flower. 'Come with me and I'll bring you to her.' They go into a house, and when they're on the stairs the boy points to a door and says, 'She's in there. Her name's Concetta. But you mustn't make any noise because her father and mother are there too. Take off your shoes and walk on the tips of your toes. Then knock at the door. Concetta expects you and will open it. Go on, I'll wait here for you.' And he's off, taking the boots to his customer."

They told these stories and many others of the same kind, with gratification and a trace of pride. They were part of the now classic and established legend of the ingenious and quick-witted poor of Naples, the penny epic of a subterranean world that was daring, fanciful, without illusions, miserable and yet full of resources in the daily fight against hunger. This shifting rabble was cautious, active and shabby. These people in rags, these good-for-nothings, street urchins and picaresque beggars had not only a legend of their own but a king, a true king, the King of Poggioreale. It was the sailor, who knew him and perhaps had done some business with him, who told us his story.

The King of Poggioreale was not a mythological figure. He really existed. I'd heard about him and seen pictures of him in the newspapers. He was a rather stout pale man with yellowish flabby cheeks, lively fanatical eyes, filled by a black fire of cunning and a strong will. He was above all a king. His house at Poggioreale was a palace with a throne room and a real gold throne, where he sat when he gave audiences to his subjects and the dignitaries of his realm. The walls of the salon were decorated with great portraits of Victor Emmanuel II, of Umberto I, of Victor Emmanuel III, and of his son Umberto, now a mere Lieutenant of the Realm, and of himself, Giuseppe I, the real king. His wife was the queen, and his sons the princes. He had a court and his ministers, which he, as a monarch by divine right, named according to his own indisputable caprice, and revoked at will. When he was receiving he always wore a crown on his head. And always, morning and evening and perhaps even at night, he wore a kind of vest with the cross of Savoy in a royal coat of arms embroidered on it.

He was as rich as the sea. In a few months he had earned billions. He had bought land with this money and rented it at a low price to laborers who were out of work. He also bought palaces in town where he let the families of his poorest subjects live for a modest rent. He had also acquired splendid automobiles with gold handles. He ordered his royal doctor to attend the beggars who were sick, and the old, the ailing, the feeble. Then he made them get into his open automobiles with their golden doors and drove them to the Via Caracciolo, to the Riviera di Chiaia, and Posillipo, so that they could benefit from the pure sea air, away from the usual stuffiness of their alleys and basements.

Giuseppe had become king by his wits and not by birth. He'd been a very poor junkman and had a rag shop in an alley behind Toledo where he lived miserably. His name was Giuseppe Biscaglia, the same as the owner of the great Biscaglia department store that everyone in Naples knew, but he wasn't a close or distant relative of theirs. He was the son of poor folk and lived alone, hardly earning a living. One day, many years ago, he met a lovely dark-haired girl at the market. She was buying linen at the counter, and as soon as he saw her he fell in love with her. He took off his hat and asked her why she was buying tablecloths and sheets.

"I'm the right age," said the girl, "and I'm preparing my trousseau."

"And have you found a husband yet?"

"No, but I'll find one," she replied.

"You have already. Tomorrow I'll come and wait on your father."

The girl's parents were rich merchants of Bagnoli. Giuseppe borrowed a black suit and a carriage and presented himself to his future in-laws as the son of his namesake Biscaglia, the department store owner. Of course he was received with open arms and the two old people agreed that they would go the next day to settle everything with his father. They came to Naples and while they were hesitating in front of the big department store, an elegant young man came up to them and asked them what they wanted. When he heard they were going to visit Signor Biscaglia, the young man obligingly pointed at the windows of the apartment over the store, and added in a confidential manner that he wasn't sure they'd be received, since the signor was beside himself with fury, having had a frightful scene with his son all night long because the boy seemed to have fallen in love with a middle-class Bagnoli girl, while his father wanted him to marry a very rich princess. The husband and wife looked at one another, thanked the young man for his courtesy, and decided it was wise to put off their visit to another day. In the meantime, Giuseppe, with his black suit and his equipage, was back in Bagnoli while his in-laws were still standing in front of the store. And he abducted the girl on the pretext that he was taking her to his angry father, but when he had climbed into the carriage he carried her to his basement full of rags. Then he said:

"I'm not the son of Biscaglia. Everything I have is these rags. But if you'll stay with me I promise you that you will become a queen." The woman stayed, and Giuseppe kept his promise.

The war came. Don Giuseppe started in to trade, first in a small way, then larger and larger. He found work for everyone: the poor, beggars, gangsters, fences, pimps, prostitutes, stevedores, pickpockets, people without skill or profession, those who'd been bombed out of their homes, the resourceful and the miserable, all those human beings who needed a living and had no one to help them. They worked honorably with soldiers, merchants and speculators. They worked in the squares, the markets, the streets and the port, by night and by day. The town was half destroyed, the factories closed, but they got on.

Don Giuseppe became king and his wife queen. He was beloved by his people and had an immense power. In Naples nothing was done against his will. It was he who arranged the election of the mayor, his own creature, and of the other functionaries as well.

"Of course," said the sailor, "that's the official city government. As for his own, he puts it together the way he wants it. He has a Minister of the Navy, who is charged with reporting the ships that come into port and what's good about their cargo, you understand what I mean. The Minister of the Interior keeps up his relations with the police, and aids the subjects who have gotten into trouble. The Minister of Industry and Commerce keeps track of the market for tobacco, canned goods, watches, and all such, including the women and everything else too.

"Sometimes he's quixotic about his nominations. He's capable of making ministers, or at least undersecretaries, out of poor devils who don't know a thing, that are perhaps even a little bit touched in the head. There's one, they tell me, who's really a fool. But the king says he's a good boy and a devoted subject and protects him. He's also got him a special privilege such as you couldn't imagine, because Don Giuseppe's human and kind-hearted and knows you have to take care of the helpless. Two months ago they changed the Commissioner of Police in Poggioreale. The old one was wise to the situation but the new one was a stranger and nobody knew what was in his head. The commissioner arrived at his house the first day with a wife and a beautiful new automobile. He left it outside and the five tires vanished, the four on the car and the spare. The commissioner gets in a fury, goes to the king and says:

"'Your Majesty, hand over those tires, and quick!" The king started to laugh. 'What do I know about your tires? Aren't you the commissioner? . . . Go find them yourself. It's a big world . . . you'll have to go a long way to find them.'

"The commissioner realized he'd used the wrong approach, and changed his tone, asked for the king's help in getting them back and that he'd show his gratitude.

"'Favor for favor,' said the king. 'I don't know a thing about your tires. But if you're to find them home again, you must consent to something. It's a just thing and will cost you nothing.'

"'I'm at your service,' said the commissioner, and shook hands on the bargain.

"'Look at that subject of mine,' said the king, pointing out his feeble-minded protégé. 'He's a good boy, but he's not too bright. I even tried naming him Undersecretary of War, but he isn't even good at that. He's really out of luck. He tries, but what can you expect? He's not fast enough . . . he hasn't any agility. He tries a few jobs, but they catch him, and he spends more time inside than outside. Now he's got to live, don't you think? Now Your Honor must consent to let him work on a trolley or on the street twice a month, only twice, not more. Two small jobs, of course, watches or wallets, things of little value, enough to live and to keep his hand in. . . . Do you agree to it?' The commissioner gave him his word, went home and found the five tires waiting for him at his door."

But the greatest undertaking of the monarch of Poggioreale, the sailor went on to tell us, had touched the heart of the whole city a few months before, and could only have been accomplished by him. It was his by right. Wasn't he perhaps the most commoner-king, the foremost worshiper of the most commoner-saint, the one whose saintly blood boils twice a year as a sign of good luck, the one whom the old women address with the affectionate *tu*, and curse out of love?

The treasure of San Gennaro, an incalculable amount of gold, was taken to Rome during the war to save it from bombing or plundering. And it had remained there. Nobody would bring it back. The government wouldn't undertake it. The roads were much too unsafe and full of brigands. There weren't enough soldiers to escort such a precious load. But what brigands would dare to touch or interfere with Giuseppe Biscaglia, that human and transient king of the beggars? Supplied with the necessary formal papers, the sovereign left for Rome in his automobile of the golden doors, covered by flowers. The treasure was consigned to him and, secure and fearless, he crossed the countryside sown with bandits, bringing the gold untouched to his people, to Naples in triumph. "I was there to witness it," concluded the tattooed sailor. "Feats like that won't be seen again."

In the legendary shadow of kings, saints, brigands and beggars, the last stretch of the road before we entered the city flew past. We drove down a long, straight, tree-lined road and crossed the streetcar tracks, then coasting along the big wall of the royal palace of Capodimonte, we plunged into the descent between high houses into streets that at this late hour were almost empty. The woman with the jewels looked about anxiously, turning around to the rear window as though she feared some winged street urchins would descend in the night from the sky to steal her valises tied on the roof. We turned into long half-dark streets and came into a wide shadowy square surrounded by ruined houses. Here the truck stopped in front of a garage that was closed by an iron lift gate. We had arrived.

The truck driver got out and, as he leaned against the side of the automobile, he noticed the hole in the glass of the window. The owner then told him about the brigand of Sparanise and the attack. The truck driver put his finger through the hole, examined the door with the look of an expert, shook his head and said one word:

"Miracle."

While the garage was being opened, the student left us in a hurry in search of a late streetcar to take him home, and the Calabrian shepherd went with him. The others stayed in the machine to wait at ease while their valises and packages were being assembled inside the garage. I remained alone on the sidewalk, my briefcase in my hand. The stone slabs were loose and shining, full of puddles from the recent rain. The sky was overcast, and a wind with a hint of snow in it was blowing. I didn't know in what part of town I'd landed. In a side street I saw the lights of a restaurant, its shutters half closed. I walked toward it and was received by the bow of an obliging and tired waiter who was piling the chairs on the tables. And I went into the deserted place.

ABOUT THE AUTHORS

PREPARED BY KRISTINA OLSON

GIORGIO BASSANI

(1916–)

GIORGIO BASSANI WAS BORN IN Bologna on April 4, 1916, into a Jewish family from Ferrara. Although it was not his city of birth, Bassani considered Ferrara his native city. He spent his childhood and adolescence there, only to leave when he decided to specialize in literature at the University of Bologna, where he studied with Robert Longhi (future teacher of Pier Paolo Pasolini). Outside of the University, Bassani was the disciple of two other masters: Giorgio Morandi and Benedetto Croce.

After obtaining his degree, Bassani returned to Ferrara, where he joined the fight against Fascism. Involvement with the anti-fascist movement coupled with his Jewish origins led to Bassani's arrest in May 1944. He was released in July, within a few days of the fall of the regime.

In the same year he moved to Rome, where he applied himself to many different projects. He worked for several literary journals and newspapers, including *Botteghe Oscure*, a plurilingual literary review sponsored by Princess Marguerite Caetani, which Bassani edited from its conception in 1948 until 1960. Bassani also worked for *Paragone*, the literary journal founded by Roberto Longhi and his wife, the writer Anna Banti. At the same time Bassani collaborated on several film productions, writing screenplays. He also taught at the Accademia di arte drammatica.

Despite his many obligations, Bassani was a prolific writer. At the beginning of his career he wrote both prose and verse. His first publications include the novel *Una città di pianura*, published under the pseudonym Giacomo Marchi, 1940, and the collections of poetry *Storie dei poveri amanti e altri versi*, 1946, *Te lucis ante*, 1947, *Un'altra libertà*, 1951, and *L'alba ai vetri: Poesie 1942-1950*, 1963. His collection of short stories, *Cinque storie di Ferrara* ("Five Stories of Ferrara"), appeared in 1956. One of the stories, *Gli ultimi anni di Clelia Trotti* ("The Last Years of Clelia Trotti") won the Charles Veillon prize in Italian literature, and the volume itself was awarded the Premio Strega in 1956.

In these first works one can see the difficulty in classifying Bassani a neo-realist writer. Even though his works depict Ferrarese society from the rise of Fascism until the period after World War II, giving his writing an immediate historical concern, the intimate introspection of characters and closed environments place Bassani near the movement of hermeticism.

Sometimes Bassani's enclosed, private worlds are invaded by history, as in Bassani's most popular book, *Il giardino dei Finzi-Contini* ("The Garden of the Finzi-Continis"), 1962 (of which the opening chapter is included in this volume). Awarded the Premio Viareggio in 1962, this novel received worldwide acclaim. Director Vittorio de Sica adapted the novel for a film released in 1970. *Gli occhiali d'oro* ("The Gold-Rimmed Spectacles"), 1958, also tells the story of a victim of society, in this case the alienation of a Jew and a homosexual. Also situated in Ferrara, this novel was awarded the Campiello prize in 1969.

The following decade saw the publication of *Dietro la porta* ("Behind the Door"), 1964, an autobiographical work, *L'airone*

("The Heron"), 1969, which recounts the destructive powers of solitude, and *L'odore del fieno* ("The Smell of Hay"), 1972, a collection of short pieces. *Le parole preparate e altri scritti di letteratura*, 1967, is a compendium of literary essays. Bassani's later publications are two volumes of poetry, *Epitaffo*, 1974, and *In rima e senza* , 1982, bringing his arc of production back to his first collections of poetry.

From 1958 until 1963 Bassani was an influential editor at Feltrinelli publishing house, during which time he discovered Tomasi di Lampedusa's *Il gattopardo* ("The Leopard"). In 1969, Bassani received the Nelly Sachs award for the body of his works. He served as President of Italia Nostra, an association for the protection of the nation's cultural and architectural heritage.

CARLO EMILIO GADDA

(1893–1973)

CARLO EMILIO GADDA WAS BORN on November 14, 1893, in Milan, where his father, Francesco Ippolito Gadda, from Como, worked for the textile firm "Ronchetti & Co." Of Austro-Hungarian origin, Carlo's mother Adele had earned a degree in literature and taught history and geography in Grosseto and Milan; in the later part of her career she was a headmistress in several different towns. After the death of Francesco Ippolito, who left his family without sufficient finances, Adele worked to support and educate their children, Carlo Emilio, Clara and Enrico.

The young Carlo Emilio excelled in school. To please his mother he enrolled in the Istituto Tecnico Superiore (Milan Polytechnic Institute). Gadda later lamented a painful childhood and adolescence, strained by poverty and deprived of the inspirational experiences of travel. At an early age he criticized the faults of society, and found allies in Ariosto, Dante and Shakespeare. He composed a few poems, one an homage to Walt Whitman, which was then published in *Menabò*. But his first committed efforts at writing came with his war diaries of 1918, published later under the title *Giornale di guerra e di prigionia.*

In 1915 Carlo Emilio had been assigned to the Brigata Cuneo, stationed in the Italian Alps. He claimed that his years passed in the war were some of the happiest in his life. As a soldier Gadda was not inspired by nationalism, but rather appreciative of military discipline. When Gadda was taken prisoner, held first at Rastatt and then Celle Lagar, Germany, he resented the "inane morality" of captivity, but succeeded in writing his first short story, *La passeggiata autumnale* (published in *Letteratura*, 1963). Released in 1919, Gadda returned to Milan, only to learn of his brother Enrico's death in combat a few months before the armistice. The death of his brother submerged Gadda in deep sadness; he is quoted as saying that he lost the best part of himself.

In 1920 Gadda matriculated into the philosophy department at the University of Milan but decided to specialize in electrical engineering. After obtaining his degree, he was offered work in Sardinia and Argentina, where he was employed by the Compania General de Fósforos. Gadda wrote a few poems which were published later in life (as was most of his early work) in the journal *Strumenti critici*, 1967. In 1924 Gadda returned to Italy and resumed studying philosophy at the "Accademia scientifico-letteraria" while supporting himself by teaching math and physics in the "Parini" school in Milan. At this time he wrote the essay *Apologia manzoniana* on his favorite author, Alessandro Manzoni, whom was always regarded as superior to the other two authors he admired, Carducci and d'Annunzio.

Gadda would slowly enter the "literary life," and the period beginning with 1925 signaled the start of this new phase. He moved to Rome in order to work for the "L'Ammonia Casale." In Rome and then in Florence he made the acquaintance of intellectuals, artists and writers, including Eugenio Montale. These friendships would lead to publication in the Florentine journal *Solaria*, founded in 1926 by Alberto Carocci. Gianfranco Contini, Giacomo Debenedetti, Giuseppe Ungaretti and Elio Vittorini edited and contributed to *Solaria* until Fascist censors prohibited further issues. *Solaria* published a few of Gadda's first books, such as *La Madonna dei filosofi*, 1931, a collection of short stories, and *Il castello di Udine*, 1934, which won the Premio Bagutta.

After a period of travel and work abroad in Belgium, France and Germany, Gadda obtained his degree in philosophy (although he never presented his thesis written about the "theory of consciousness" by Leibniz). The late 1920's were a time of fruitful independent study for Gadda, focusing on the writings of Spinoza, Kant and Einstein, and the product of these efforts were *Meditazione milanese*, 1928, a philosophical essay, and the story *La meccanica*, a fragment of which was published as *Papà e mamma* in 1970. Gadda left "L'Ammonia Casale" to work for the Vatican's "Servizi Tecnici," which he would consequently leave in 1934 for health reasons.

Adele Lehr, his mother, died in 1936, and Gadda began the novel *La cognizione del dolore* ("Acquainted with Grief"). The book was awarded the Prix Formentor in 1967 and the Premio International de Littérature in Corfu in 1963. *Letteratura* had published the novel in episodes from 1938 until 1941, and Einaudi issued the title in 1963. *La cognizione* is set in an imaginary country in South America, which critics believe to be a metaphor for Brianza, Gadda's native region between Milan and the Alps in Lombardy. In fact, many read *La cognizione* as the "most agonizingly personal of Gadda's books."

Gadda moved to Florence in 1940 to remain there for ten years. At this time Gadda was enjoying a very productive season. While working for the *Gazzetta del popolo*, he wrote the travel articles and short stories that would form *Meraviglie d'Italia* ("The Wonders of Italy"), 1938. The most important accomplishments of these years are the completion of the volume *Adalgisa*, 1944, and *Quer pasticciaccio brutto de via Merulana* ("That Awful Mess on Via Merulana"), 1957. *Adalgisa*, a collection of portraits of bourgeoisie family life in Milan, delights in the novelty of linguistic experimentation and uplifting power of satire. *Pasticciaccio*, his *summa*, finally established Gadda's position in the literary world. It was printed in five episodes in *Letteratura* during 1946, and Garzanti printed the complete volume eleven years later. It has been translated into many languages, including English, French, German and Dutch. *Pasticciaccio* displays Gadda at his best as a writer of "hyperbolic digressions" and "verbal acrobatics" disguised as the author of a detective novel. The language truly is a "pastiche," combining obscure scholarly allusions and equally obscure terms from the Roman, Molisano and Venetian dialects, and because of this innovative nature it has often been compared to *Ulysses*. Unfortunately, many did not realize the importance of this novel at the time of its publication, and, as Gianfranco Contini noted, Gadda's work has been best appreciated by later generations of literary scholars.

The excerpt included here is the eighth chapter of the book, in which the protagonist Francesco Ingravallo, detective, is called by duty to venture outside of Rome. Ironically (in the spirit of Gadda) the chapter is full of reflections on Rome, and the Eternal City never leaves the narrator's thoughts, even during the urgent chase for information and evidence towards the end of the book. It is also, in this passage, that one can understand Moravia's statement that Gadda was a great "comic writer."

Contemporaneous with the writing of *Pasticciaccio* was the composition of *Eros e Priapo*, essays viewing Fascism through the lens of sexuality. Also Gadda at this time began his collaboration with Alessandro Bonsanti for *Il mondo*, lasting from 1945-1947. Gadda returned to Rome in 1950, working for the RAI, the Italian state radio. A series of his RAI programs were published under the title *I Luigi di Francia* in 1964. *Il primo libro delle favole* was issued in 1952 by Neri Pozza in Venice, and *Novelle dal Ducato in fiamme*, winner of the Viareggio Prize, was printed by Vallecchi in 1953. Critical essays concerned with the literature of his contemporaries as well as his predecessors were issued as *I viaggi la morte*, 1958.

Carlo Emilio Gadda died in Rome on May 21, 1973.

NATALIA GINZBURG

(1916–1991)

ONE OF ITALY'S MOST FAMOUS WOMEN writers, Natalia Ginzburg, née Natalia Levi, was born in Palermo in 1916, the youngest of five siblings, children of Giuseppe Levi, professor of anatomy at the University of Palermo, and Lidia Tanzi, daughter of the socialist lawyer Carlo Tanzi. Natalia grew up in Turin. The Levi family boasted many illustrious members: musicologist Silvio Tanzi and Cesare Levi, theater scholar and critic. Natalia attended the Liceo Vittorio Alferi but did not formally complete her education, and instead was tutored by her parents (Giuseppe was afraid that Natalia would catch diseases at school). Natalia did, however, pursue higher education at the University of Turin, matriculating into the Department of Literature; she never obtained her degree.

She made her writing debut very early with the story *I bambini* ("The Children"), published in *Solaria* in 1933. In 1938 she married Leone Ginzburg, a writer of Russian origin, co-founder of the underground anti-fascist group *Giustizia e Libertà*. Natalia, also an anti-fascist, together with her husband and other Turin intellectuals (including Cesare Pavese) formed the Einaudi group, centered around the publishing house. Einaudi published her first novel, *La strada che va in città* ("The Road to the City") under her pseudonym, Alessandra Tornimparte, in 1942. Natalia followed her husband while he was in political confinement in the region of Abruzzo, accompanied by their children. Leone tried to flee but was recaptured. Transferred to Regina Coeli in Rome, Leone died, a Nazi prisoner, on February 5, 1944. Natalia returned to her family's house in Turin after the war, worked with Einaudi, and revealed her true identity in the byline for a poem published in the journal *Mercurio*.

Ginzburg worked as a journalist and a translator of French texts, including Proust. She later wrote for the Turin newspaper *La stampa* and the Milan daily *Corriere della sera*. In 1947 she published *È stato così* for which she was awarded the Premio Tempo. In 1950 she married Gabriele Baldini, Professor of English Literature at the Universities of Trieste and Rome, and later Director of the Italian Institute in London. After they moved to Rome, Ginzburg left Einaudi and became a full-time writer. Within ten years she published *Tutti i nostri ieri* ("All Our Yesterdays"), 1952, for which she won the Prix Veillon, *Le piccole virtù* ("The Small Virtues"), 1961, a collection of essays, and *Le voci della sera* ("Voices in the Evening"), 1962.

Ginzburg's oeuvre includes many non-fiction works, plays and criticism as well as fiction. In the Roman years she wrote the acclaimed *Lessico famigliare* ("Family Sayings"), 1963, an autobiographical work which won the Premio Strega, *Mai devi domandarmi*, 1970, a collection of essays, and *La famiglia Manzoni*("The Manzoni family"), 1983. The play *L'inserzione* ("The Advertisement") won the Marzotto Prize for European Drama in 1968, and *Ti ho sposato per allegria* ("I Married You for the Fun of It"), 1965, was performed to great acclaim.

Valentino, the novella printed in this anthology, was awarded the Premio Viareggio in the year of its publication, 1951. The narrator is typically Ginzburg: a passive, frustrated being who lives only insofar as she must live for others.

Ginzburg's style has often been criticized as "overly simplistic." Other critics believe that her apparent simplicity, her tendencies to use common, "bland" words and straightforward dialogue are methods of creating an unexpectedly greater impact. She has been compared to Anton Chekov, and in more recent times her work has been regarded as a great accomplishment. William Weaver wrote in *The New York Times*, "Her simplicity is an achievement, hard-won and remarkable, and the more welcome in a literary world where the cloak of omniscience is all too readily donned." Her topics primarily deal with quotidian affairs, family issues and a profound sense of the "hard life" in a modern capitalist society. A vein of perseverance sometimes enhanced by humor runs throughout her works, rendering the reader a peaceful survivor of everyday tragedy as lived by her characters.

Ginzburg acted as a member of the Italian Parliament for the Left from 1983 until the last years of her life.

Natalia Ginzburg died on October 7, 1991.

CARLO LEVI

(1902–1975)

CARLO LEVI WAS BORN ON November 29, 1902, the son of the merchant and painter Ercole Levi and Annetta Treves. Levi graduated from the University of Turin in 1924, specializing in medicine, but did not then practice. Unexpectedly, Levi turned to painting, a career that began in the last years of medical school with an exhibition at the "Quadriennale dell'arte moderna" at Turin in 1923 and was later confirmed with the group show "Sei pittori di Torino" in 1929.

Levi had early exposure to political activism. His uncle, Claudio Treves, was a famous and active socialist of the time. During his years at the University, Levi also made the acquaintance of Piero Gobetti, who founded the political review *Energie Nuove* in 1918. Staff meetings functioned as social gatherings, attracting intellectuals from Turin as the local Einaudi group did. The friendship with Gobetti led Levi also to write for other publications, including *Rivoluzione liberale* and *Il Baretti*. In 1926 Levi, by now an activist himself, helped fellow socialists escape Italy to

France and Switzerland. After the death of Gobetti in the same year, Levi moved to Paris to work with Carlo and Nello Rosselli, both leaders in the anti-fascist movement. Together they founded the group *Giustizia e libertà* in 1929, with Levi and Leone Ginzburg as directors of the Italian center.

Involvement with G&L led to Levi's being arrested three times, the first in 1934, when he was jailed in Turin. Levi was arrested a second time in 1935 and sent into confinement in the southern region of Lucania. His portrait of the people there was written nine years later in *Cristo si è fermato a Eboli* ("Christ Stopped at Eboli"), 1945. In the *New Yorker* Hamilton Basso stated the Levi "looks at their [the people of Gagliano] customs with the curiosity of a scientist and the delicacy of a poet." Most notable about Levi's style is the sympathy that infuses his observations of peasant life, completely different from his own affluent background.

Levi was released during a period of amnesty after the Ethiopian War. Before the outbreak of World War II he returned to France. He intended to save G&L after the murder of the Rosselli brothers in 1936. His efforts were not successful, and because of the constant threat of the Fascist police Levi took refuge in Brittany, where he wrote his first book, *Paura della libertà* ("Fear of Freedom"), 1946. Levi wrote this work for himself, in order to clarify certain political beliefs; he did not intend it for publication.

Between 1940 and 1941 he briefly took refuge in southern France, which he soon left for his native Turin and then Florence. In Florence Levi was arrested a third time and incarcerated in the Murate prison, only to be released after the arrest of Mussolini. During the time of the German occupation, Levi found safety in the Palazzo Pitti in Florence and could devote six months to writing *Cristo si è fermato a Eboli*. The work was awarded the Corriere Lombardo Prize in the year of its publication.

Levi stayed in Florence during the Liberation. He joined the Comitato Nazionale per la Liberazione della Toscana and directed the newspaper of the Comitato. After the armistice Levi moved to Rome, pursuing a job as editor-in-chief of *Italia libera*, the voice of the Partito d'Azione. His work with *Italia libera* supply the material of *L'orologio* ("The Watch"), 1950. Seen as a continuation of *Cristo si è fermato a Eboli*, which portrayed the nation during the war, *L'orologio* describes Italy in the wake of destruction. The excerpt here is a collection of passages from the book, intended to give an idea of the wealth of characters, events and reflections to be found in the narrative.

Most of Levi's works do not fall easily into any specific genre, but *L'orologio* has been called Levi's only *novel*. This definition is due to the book's unconventional time structure: the protagonist is without a watch for three days, during which time the story occurs. The narrative defies chronological progression, jumping from the past to the present, from reflection to simultaneous observation.

The rest of Levi's life was lived with the same energy and fervor. His painting career flourished, and many of his works were included in exhibits in Europe and the United States. His experiences in Sicily are described in the book, *Le parole sono pietre* ("Words Are Stones"), 1955, which won the Viareggio Prize in 1956. He traveled to Germany and Russia, recording his journeys in the books *La doppia notte dei tigli* ("The Two-fold Night"), 1959 and *Il futuro ha un cuore antico* ("The Future Has an Ancient Heart"), 1956. In 1963 he was elected a senator on the Communist Party ticket, and served in that capacity until 1972.

Carlo Levi died of pneumonia on January 4, 1975.

ELSA MORANTE

(1912–1985)

ELSA MORANTE WAS BORN ON August 18, 1912. Irma Poggibonsi and Francesco Lo Monaco, the biological parents of Elsa and her siblings, were not married. The children — Elsa, Aldo, Marcello and Maria — were raised by Irma and her husband, Augusto Morante, who worked as a disciplinarian at the reformatory school Aristide Gabelli. Irma, from Modena, taught in various elementary schools.

A few months after Morante's birth the family moved to the Roman district of Testaccio, the proletarian neighborhood later depicted in the novels of Pier Paolo Pasolini. In 1922 they moved a second time, to the Monteverde quarter. For a part of her childhood Morante lived in the Nomentano district with her wealthy godmother Maria Guerrieri Gonzaga. Exposure to the lives of the working class and the bourgeoisie laid the foundation for the class tensions depicted in Morante's work. Her appreciation of folklore and the culture of the poor (which she also shared with Pasolini) can be seen in her collection of songs and poems in *Il mondo salvato dai ragazzini* ("The World Saved by Little Children"), 1968.

Morante read voraciously from an early age. Following in the footsteps of her mother, who composed song lyrics and poems, Elsa wrote verse as well as short stories. The then important journalist Guelfo Civinini of the *Corriere della sera* sponsored her first newspaper publication: *Storia dei bimbi e delle stelle* ("A Story of Children and Stars"), which was divided into episodes and printed in *Corriere dei piccoli.* Her first book, *Le avventure di Caterina* ("The Adventures of Caterina") was later published by Einaudi in 1941. After this first phase of her literary production, Morante only occasionally returned to writing poetry or to the conventional format of children's stories.

She did not attend elementary school but studied at home and received a high school diploma. When she was eighteen years old, Morante had the choice between accepting a teaching position and a secure income or devoting her time and energies to writing. She chose the second option and left her family to begin a new life. Morante supported herself by giving private lessons in Italian and Latin, and by ghost writing school assignments. Another source of income was the publication of short stories and poetry in various magazines.

The period that follows, including the years of World War II, was crucial in Morante's career. It saw the publication of her first books, *Le avventure di Caterina, Lo scialle andaluso* ("The Andalusian Shawl," a novella) and *Il gioco segreto* ("The Secret Game"), reviewed favorably by the writer and critic Giacomo Debenedetti. She wrote for the weekly magazine *Oggi* and translated works by Katherine Mansfield. Also at this time she met Alberto Moravia, who became her husband in 1941. Moravia's growing reputation as an anti-fascist during the time of the German occupation caused the endangered couple to flee their Roman apartment, seeking refuge in a town near Fondi, between Naples and Rome. They remained in hiding for nine months, until after the Liberation.

During this time Morante had begun to write *Vita di mia nonna* ("My Grandmother's Life"), which later became *Menzogna e sortilegio* ("House of Liars"), her first novel. The narrator, Elisa, recreates the history of her Sicilian family in the privacy of her bedroom. Betrayal and deceit, unbounded narcissism and manipulation imbue this novel with a dark, Gothic sensibility. The extreme personalities which populate the novel seem too horrible to be true, and, characteristic of her style, boundaries between reality and fantasy are vague. Lukács claimed that *Menzogna e sortilegio* is one of the most successful twentieth-century novels in accurately depicting the alienation of the bourgeois world. Natalia Ginzburg, editor at Einaudi, was instrumental in the acceptance of the manuscript. *Menzogna e sortilegio* shared the Viareggio Prize with Aldo Palazzeschi in the year of its publication, 1948.

During the rest of her career, Morante completed three more major works and some articles, including "Pro e contra la bomba atomica" (*Europa letteraria*, 1965), in which Morante defines the atomic bomb as the "natural expression of contemporary society." Her second novel *L'isola d'Arturo* ("Arthur's Island") tells about a young native of Procida, focusing on the father-son relationship and the ambiguous line between childhood imagination and true experience. Morante was awarded the Premio Strega in 1957, the year of its publication. Unlike the rest of her writings, *La storia* ("History"), her third novel, possesses a unique realism, asserting the failure of politics to assist humanity. Her final novel, *Aracoeli*, was awarded the Prix Médicis Etranger in 1985.

The tragedies suffered by the family make this novel particularly bleak, and the coincidence between the deaths of Morante and of her protagonist Aracoeli, both suffering from a brain disease, haunts her readers. Morante died, after a heart attack, on November 25, 1985.

ALBERTO MORAVIA

(1907–1990)

Born on November 28, 1907, in a house designed by his father in the Roman quarter of Parioli, Alberto Pincherle resided for almost his entire life in his native city. His father, Carlo Pincherle-Moravia, was the brother of the playwright Amelia Rosselli and the uncle of Carlo and Nello Rosselli, two brothers assassinated in France for their anti-fascist activities. His mother, Gina (Teresa) de Marsanich, raised in Ancona, came from a family of Slavic origin. He had two older sisters, Adriana and Elena, as well as a younger brother, Gastone, who died in Tobruk in 1941. Their French governess read stories to them at night, and the young Moravia quickly became fluent in French. In his late teens, he mastered English. Alberto chose to use his father's last name as a pseudonym.

Moravia claimed that his childhood was "normal, although lonely." He showed an early gift for narration, and improvised a book-length story which he recited to himself "by episode." At nine he contracted bone tuberculosis. He underwent a seven-year cure at home and then five years in the Codivilla sanatorium in Cortina d'Ampezzo, filling the days by reading Dostoyevsky, Rimbaud, Manzoni, Shakespeare, Goldoni, Molière, Ariosto, Dante and many more authors. He suffered from extreme loneliness, and recalled writing on his window "solo col sole" (*alone with the sun*). Unable to go to school, Moravia studied at home, having attended Liceo "Tasso" for only one year. Substantially he was an autodidact. As Moravia wrote, "Our character is formed by those things we are constrained to do, not by those things we do of our own accord."

His first attempts at writing were poems, in French and Italian. At the age of twenty, during his convalescence in the Italian Alps, he completely abandoned writing verse to embark upon his career of writing prose. A friendship with the older novelist Corrado Alvaro led to the publication of the short story, *Cortigiana stanca* in the magazine 900, edited by Massimo Bontempelli. Soon after he began to compose *Gli indifferenti* ("The Time of Indifference") in the same way that he recounted stories as a child, that is, aloud. This style of composition was perhaps due to an appreciation of theatre and the desire to write "a play disguised as a novel," a technique he sensed in the work of Dostoyevsky.

With his father's support, *Gli indifferenti* was published in 1929, and received mixed, yet intense, reviews. It was the subject of great controversy for many reasons. First, with virtually this one novel, he had established himself as Italy's leading writer of fiction. Instead of composing the traditional flattering portrait of Italian aristocracy, Moravia exposed the moral decay of the upper-middle class.

Many critics assert that this novel contains all of the themes that would be repeated throughout his oeuvre. Moravia justified the single-minded nature of his novels as an effort of concentration upon his own professional affairs. "Good writers are monotonous, like good composers. Their truth is self-repeating. They keep rewriting the same book. That is to say, they keep trying to perfect their expression of the one problem they were born to understand."

Moravia's novels encountered repeated hostility. In 1935 *Le ambizioni sbagliate* was published and the Ministero della Cultura Popolare prohibited any reviews of it. At this time Moravia also lost his job with the *Gazzetta del Popolo*. His novels were attacked because of their almost obsessive investigation into sexuality. Eventually, in April 1952, all of his works were placed on the *Index librorum prohibitorum* by the Holy Office for their presumed charges of obscenity (the same year André Gide's *opera omnia* were also placed on the *Index*). The author defended his work stating that sexuality exposed the "less ineffable sides of the human soul," and functioned as a necessary tool for examining the mysterious faces of humanity. On the other hand, two months later Moravia was named the Chevalier de la Legion d'Honneur and won the Premio Strega, the latter for a collection of short stories, which included one of his most acclaimed short fictions, *Inverno di malato* ("A Sick Boy's Winter").

Inspired by a restless curiosity as well as the need to escape from the oppression of Fascism, Moravia traveled all over the world. Commissions for travel articles and teaching positions made these adventures possible. During his time as a correspondent for *La Stampa* of Turin, he went to England and visited illustrious literary salons, meeting eminent writers such as T.S. Eliot, W.B. Yeats and E.M. Forster. In Paris he attended the private gatherings of Valéry and the members of "Art 1926." He escaped to America after the failure of *Ambizioni*, and was able to find work at the Casa Italiana at Columbia University as a lecturer.

On the wanted list of the Fascist police after the occupation of Rome, with Elsa Morante he embarked on a hazardous journey to Naples, but ended up near Fondi, where they lived in a state of starvation and anxiety for nine months. His observations of the destruction of rural life appeared in *La ciociara* ("Two Women"), 1958. According to Moravia, along with his childhood illness, the years of fascism determined his life.

When he returned to Rome, he wrote for the *Corriere della Sera* under the pseudonym "Pseudo." These writings, often short stories, would be collected under the title of *Racconti romani* (Roman Tales) to be published in several volumes. His novel, *La romana* (The Woman of Rome), printed in 1947, launched

Moravia's fame in America with the publication of its English edition in 1949.

He traveled to Mexico, Greece, China, Japan and to Africa, often with the writer Dacia Maraini, his second wife and his close friend Pier Paolo Pasolini. These journeys would inevitably be used as material for books such as *Passeggiate africane*, 1988, *Un'idea dell'India*, 1962, and *Un mese in* URSS, 1958.

Moravia's oeuvre totals over fifty published works, the most popular of which have been translated into at least one dozen languages. He attributed this productiveness to a regular work routine, which demanded only a few hours of writing every morning. Besides being a prolific fiction writer and journalist, Moravia also collaborated on screenplays and distinguished himself as a film critic, most notably as a columnist for *L'Espresso* as well as *La Nuova Europa*. A selection of his literary, social and political essays came out under the title of *L'uomo come fine* (Man as an End), published in 1964. Along with Alberto Carocci he cofounded *Nuovi Argomenti*, a literary journal that had Pier Paolo Pasolini as one of its editors. Moravia also wrote for the theatre, notably the plays *Beatrice Cenci* and *Il Dio Kurt*. Many of his novels were adapted into films, including: *La noia* ("The Empty Canvas"), directed by Vittorio de Sica, 1965; *Il disprezzo* ("Le mepris"), directed by Jean Luc Godard, 1965; *Il conformista* ("The Conformist"), directed by Bernardo Bertolucci, 1970.

Agostino (like *La Romana*) marked the return of Moravia's popularity after the oppressive silence of the war. Moravia composed *Agostino* in 1942 at about the same time that Morante began to work on *Menzogna e sortilegio*. *Agostino* was first printed in 1942 by *Documento*, the publishing house of Moravia's friend Federico Valli. Five hundred copies of the book were issued with an illustration by Renato Guttuso, but the Fascist censors halted its printing. In 1945 Bompiani re-published *Agostino* to great acclaim; that same year it was awarded the *Corriere Lombardo* prize (the first literary award in Italy after the war).

Critics view Agostino as a younger version of Michele, the twenty-one year-old protagonist of *Gli indifferenti*, who also dreamed of an innocent world that was in the face of a much harsher reality. Agostino, however, must deal with his troubled awakening into adolescence. Moravia himself saw *Agostino* as the bridging work between *Gli indifferenti* and the rest of his work, reviving the themes of sexuality and class distinction that were present in his first book.

On September 26, 1990, Moravia died of heart failure while shaving. His editor Mario Andreose had come to bring him the first copy of *Vita di Moravia*, an autobiography in the form of an interview between Moravia and Alain Elkann. The eighty-four year-old author had the completed manuscript of his latest book, *The Leopard Woman*, on his desk.

IGNAZIO SILONE

(1900–1978)

IGNAZIO SILONE, PSEUDONYM OF Secondo Tranquilli, was born on May 1, 1900. His father, Paolo, was a small holder, and his mother Annamaria was a weaver in their native town, Pescina dei Marsi, in the region of Abruzzi. Silone attended a Catholic grammar school in Pescina, and then left home to go to boarding school at the Istituto Pio X, in Rome, but was then expelled for leaving the grounds without permission. After a brief stay at the Collegio di San Romolo with the priest Don Orione (the experience would be recorded in *Incontro con uno strano prete* "Encounter with a Strange Priest"), he entered high school in Reggio Calabria.

Two natural disasters had led to the destruction of the Tranquilli family. First, a disease infested vines on Paolo's property and consequently he fled to Brazil to seek work, only to die on his return to Italy in 1911. In 1915 an earthquake struck Pescina, causing the death of thirty thousand people in thirty seconds. Among the victims was Silone's mother. These calamities made his financial situation even more precarious than before: fortunately his maternal grandmother took him and his brother Romolo into her care. Scholarships allowed him to complete his high school education.

The dismaying aftermath of the earthquake stimulated Silone's social concern, and he embarked on his long career of political activism. He wrote articles for the socialist newspaper *Avanti!* regarding the misappropriation of land in the region of the Marsi after the earthquake. Silone joined the local union of farmworkers and was elected secretary of the regional league of peasants at the age of seventeen. In 1918, just after World War I, he moved to Rome and became the secretary of the Socialist Youth League of Italy. He edited the Roman weekly for socialist youth, *Avanguardia*, as well as the Trieste newspaper, *Il lavoratore*, often burned by the *squadristi* (the violent Fascist squads).

In 1921, Silone was one of the founders of the Italian Communist Party, participating in the crucial Congress of Leghorn. Not only a member, Silone served as an international representative for the P.C.I., often traveling to the Soviet Union. He collaborated with Gramsci, involving himself in the underground political movement and assisting in the production of Party newspapers and pamphlets. Various party missions sent Silone to France, Germany and Spain, where he was incarcerated. During his imprisonment in Barcelona, Silone first adopted the pen name that became his permanent identity. The name derives from Quintus Poppedius Silo, a Roman leader born in Marruvium, near Silone's Pescina. Silo's claim to fame lies in his leadership in the Marsi resistance during a civil war against Rome in 90 BC. Silone saw his own ideals mirrored in the life of Poppedius Silo, a man who craved justice, in accord with the writer's other influence, the teachings of Jesus.

Silone remained with the party, declared illegal by the Fascists, for approximately ten years. Called twice before the notorious Tribunal, Silone escaped accusations of illegal political activity. In 1929 his friends smuggled him into Switzerland where he would remain in exile for about thirteen years, and where he met his future wife, Darina Laracy, correspondent for *The New York Herald Tribune*. Two years later he chose to break with the party, for reasons explained in the essays *Uscita di sicurezza* ("Emergency Exit"). The 1927 summoning of the Central Executive of the Comitern in Moscow was decisive in the process of his leaving the party. It was then that he detected a large breach in ideals between the party and himself (especially when faced with the principles of Stalinism), and declared that he was a "socialist without a party, a Christian without a church." Another factor that decided the break was the fate of his brother Romolo, falsely accused of collaborating with the Party and tortured by the police in a prison in Procida, where he died in 1932. Silone's departure to Switzerland was in part an attempt to exculpate Romolo of any dangerous associations; unfortunately, this effort was in vain.

Silone's first place of residence in Switzerland was Locarno, and then Davos, where he was hospitalized for tuberculosis. After a brief period, he arrived in Zurich where exiled writers, including Brecht, Mann, and Musil, had found refuge. "During my years in exile in Switzerland I became a writer." Indeed, Silone produced four of his most important works during that time: *Fontamara*, 1933, which was published in German in Zurich, *Pane e vino* ("Bread and Wine"), 1936, *La scuola dei dittatori*, ("The School for Dictators"), 1939, and *Il seme sotto la neve*, ("The Seed beneath the Snow"). The publication of *Fontamara* led to Silone's international literary fame, as the book was translated into more than twenty languages. It was regarded as one of the best examples of non-conformist European literature. Portraying the *cafoni*, the farmers and peasants from the Abruzzi region, *Fontamara* narrates the trials of the people from his native Pescina, specifically their strugglers with landowners. This portrait of sympathy and hope for the people of "Bitter Fountain" has associated Silone with Camus and Orwell. Many of his later books repeat these themes of socialist struggle and spiritual transcendence.

Even in exile Silone would not remain idle on political fronts. Between 1932 and 1934 he founded and edited the monthly journal *Information*, a Zurich-based publication in German. He created *Le Nuove Edizioni del Capolago*, a journal of ex-communists, which included his articles on fascism. In 1939 he founded the Centro Estero of the PSI in Zurich, and was arrested for illegal activity. Silone spent the years between 1939 and 1944 as a prisoner in Davos and Baden.

He returned to Italy after the Liberation, resuming a career in politics as an "independent socialist" while devoting more time to his literary production. Silone joined the editorial staff of *Avanti!* and created the periodical *Europa socialista*. He participated in the conference of the "Congress for Cultural Freedom" in West Berlin, 1950, which gave birth to a new journal, *Tempo presente*, edited by Silone and Nicola Chiaramonte. Disappointed with all political organizations, Silone eventually decided to remain outside political parties. *Una manciata di more* ("A Handful of Blackberries"), 1952, *Il segreto di Luca* ("Luke's Secret"), and the play *L'avventura di un povero cristiano* ("The Story of a Humble Christian") would be published over the course of the next twenty years, often to critical acclaim.

Pane e vino, first published in a Swiss edition as *Brot und Wein* in 1936, was completely revised by Silone in 1955 and then published in Italy as *Vino e pane*. The excerpt is taken from the later version, in which Silone stripped away what he considered non-essential elements and further developed the inner lives of the characters. Similar to Silone's own life, the protagonist Pietro Spina suffers great disappointment with the Left and its slogans and dogmas. He returns to Italy after fifteen years of exile, and to escape suspicion disguises himself as the priest Don Paolo Spada. Pietro wants to incite the peasants of the Abruzzi to revolt, and finds instead that his desperate country has lost its will to act. The Ethiopian War encounters no political opposition, to Pietro's disappointment. Pietro faces the challenge of retaining his identity as a human (which Silone translates into the basic teachings of Christianity) while being threatened by the all-consuming power of the state. We meet Pietro Spada as he visits his old teacher, Don Benedetto, who first encouraged Pietro to speak his own truth even if it does not correspond to the principles of popular movements. The character Luigi Mursica re-enacts the tragic destiny of the writer's brother, Romolo.

Ignazio Silone died on August 22, 1978 in Geneva Switzerland. His wife Darina has movingly described his last days in her edition of his posthumous novel *Severina*.

ABOUT THE BOOK

The text for this book was composed by Steerforth Press using a digital version of Electra, a typeface designed in 1935 by William Addison Dwiggins. Electra has been a standard book typeface since its release because of its evenness of design and high legibility. All Steerforth books are printed on acid free papers and this book was bound by BookCrafters of Chelsea, Michigan.